The CITY in FLAMES

Also by Michael Russell

The City of Shadows
The City of Strangers
The City in Darkness
The City of Lies

The CITY *in* FLAMES

A Stefan Gillespie Novel

MICHAEL RUSSELL

CONSTABLE

CONSTABLE

First published in Great Britain in 2019 by Constable

Copyright © Michael Russell, 2019

13 5 7 9 10 8 6 4 2

The moral right of the author has been asserted.

A CIP catalogue record for this book
is available from the British Library.

ISBN: 978-1-47213-036-5 (hardback)
ISBN: 978-1-47213-035-8 (paperback)

Typeset in Dante by SX Composing DTP, Rayleigh, Essex
Printed and bound in Great Britain by Clays Ltd, Elcograf S.p.A.

Papers used by Constable are from well-managed forests and
other responsible sources.

Constable
An imprint of
Little, Brown Book Group
Carmelite House
50 Victoria Embankment
London EC4Y 0DZ

An Hachette UK Company
www.hachette.co.uk

www.littlebrown.co.uk

For my uncle,
Edward Constantine Miall,
Newry, Armagh, 1929

You have asked me why I stay in this small country
Where nothing happens while perhaps the last chapter,
Europe's swan song, is being written in the chancelleries.
You picture me tramping the Wicklow Hills and among trees . . .
Without the stagnating waiting for air-raids and war nerves

'Letter from Ireland'

Ewart Milne

Foreword

In the autumn of 1940, Nazi Germany occupied almost all of
Europe and seemed invincible. Britain was the only country
still resisting. But Hitler had suffered his first defeat, in the air
war of the Battle of Britain. Though British cities, London
especially, were bombed nightly, the imminent German invasion had been called off. Across the Irish Sea, Ireland had
chosen to stay out of the war. Its Prime Minister, Éamon de
Valera, maintained an intransigent neutrality. The reasons
were many, but one was his certainty that if Ireland joined
Britain the inevitable presence of British troops, barely twenty
years after the War of Independence, would provoke civil war
and revitalise the then weak Irish Republican Army, which
still claimed to be Ireland's legitimate government and considered de Valera a traitor. But Ireland's neutrality was always
odd. De Valera's belligerent even-handedness masked increas-
ing trade with Britain and, secretly, high levels of cooperation
between British and Irish Intelligence services. The Irish government expressed disapproval of its citizens joining the
British armed forces but did nothing to stop them. By 1945 at
least 50,000 Irish would leave to join up. Travel between the
two countries was surprisingly easy, and as many as 250,000

Irish would emigrate to Britain between 1939 and 1945. They became indispensable to Britain's war industry as more and more workers were called up.

In Germany and Britain Irish neutrality was viewed in different ways. In Berlin it was seen as a huge blow to the British. When Britain was invaded, it was thought, Ireland would not only become a base for rearguard attacks, the Irish government would reveal its true support for Germany and join in. The Germans seemed blind to the fact that de Valera's hostility to England did not translate into any kind of enthusiasm for Nazi Germany. There were Germans who wanted to use Ireland more effectively, however. By supplying arms to the IRA, they aimed at mounting sabotage operations against the British and even starting an uprising in Northern Ireland that might drag de Valera into the war on Germany's side. The IRA, believing that England's difficulty was Ireland's opportunity, as always, awaited German help and German victory. Britain regarded Ireland's neutrality with a grudging acceptance, but some felt it was a betrayal that could not be tolerated. In 1940 Winston Churchill came close to agreeing to the invasion of Ireland. The Irish government had very good reason to believe that both the British and the Germans were preparing plans to invade the country. And there were people who wanted to put those plans into operation . . . one way or another.

PART ONE

DEATH BY WATER

I am directed by the Minister for External Affairs to refer to your minutes of the 19 and 30 September, relating to the measures which would have to be taken by the Government in the event of either belligerent making an attack on this country. The first task of this Department, on the occurrence of such an emergency, would be to make a protest to the Government of the country concerned and to inform the Governments of neutral countries, especially that of the United States, that Irish neutrality had been violated. The Government of the other belligerent Power would also be informed, and if our Government so decides, would be requested for aid against the invader.

Letter from Joseph Walshe,
Secretary Department of External Affairs, October 1940

1

The Fever Hospital

Wicklow, 1921

David Gillespie felt the hard stone of the floor first, and it was all he felt. The stone flag was cold, and for a moment that coldness was a kind of comfort against his cheek. He didn't know why it seemed a place to stay in, but it was somehow soothing; it held the weight of his head, as if it was fixed. He couldn't move and he didn't want to. For some seconds that was all he was aware of: a dark, enfolding dream he was struggling not to wake from. Then the pain shot through his jaw, sharp, hot, and he pushed himself up. He opened his eyes and saw only a blur of yellow light. He tasted vomit in his mouth and the iron tang of blood. He had been unconscious for barely a minute. Now, as he sat up on the stone floor, he knew where he was again. The blow had come from a rifle butt. It followed a series of punches to his stomach and face. They had got heavier as the tempers of his interrogators had turned from amusement to anger.

'Davie, am I getting through to you yet, you fucker?'

In David's eyes the blurred light sharpened then diminished. It was an oil lamp, sitting on a table above him. Over it was the face of the man who had just spoken, round and red, sweating. David stared up, unmoving, trying to focus. He saw the sweat more clearly than he saw the face. It was glinting in the light.

'Get him up.' The voice was Scottish, maybe Glasgow. It was an odd thought, but David had tried to identify where the interrogator came from since the start, where they all came from. He had Scotland; London for another; then Leeds, Yorkshire anyway. It was a way to harden his mind, to distance himself from what was happening. He had to ride this out until they got fed up with it.

The man turned to the table. He picked up a bottle and drank.

Hands clutched David on either side and pulled him up, dragging him backwards and pushing him down on a chair. The pain pierced him again, from his jaw upwards, into his head, stabbing, sawing. There were two uniformed men standing on either side of him. A fourth sat on a chair close by, smoking a cigarette, the rifle that had smashed into David's face lying across his lap. Four Black and Tans. There had been more at the start. They all wore, in various combinations, the black and brown tunics and trousers that gave them their name. There was silence in the room now. The man who had spoken bent to take bottles of beer from a crate on the floor. He walked a slow circle, handing them to the other Black and Tans. It was a lull anyway; the anger was on hold. None of them looked at him. They didn't speak to each other; they just drank. Only minutes ago the room was full of their fury, full of blows, full of shouting.

David Gillespie reoriented himself to the room. Several oil lamps lit it, but it was big and high. There was darkness above; the light around him and his interrogators disappeared into black corners. It smelled of dust and stone and stale urine. It was empty apart from a scattering of old and new debris: broken, wood-wormed benches and pieces of rusting iron that had once belonged to bedsteads; bottles and tin cans made up the midden of the present occupants. Although he had never been in this place before, he did know it. The Black and Tans had brought him from the square in Baltinglass, out of the town, to the derelict Workhouse where they were barracked. And at the back of the Workhouse was the Fever Hospital, set apart from the other buildings so that the weak and emaciated inmates of the Workhouse could be taken away to die, not so long ago, when cholera and typhus beat their way into the overcrowding and the filth. Then it had been evidence that even amidst the most carefully structured degradation and misery, things could still get worse. But if that brutality had gone, another now replaced it: the brutality of war. David Gillespie had not anticipated what would happen that night. He knew he should have done. He had fled that brutality before; he had believed it was all he needed to do. He had ignored how arbitrary it was, how capricious. He sat in the Fever Hospital now, watching the Black and Tans drink. He knew it wasn't over. The man who had spoken turned back to him, still sweating, smiling.

'Why are you Irish such cunts, even when you're on our fucking side?'

At the end of the main street in Baltinglass, where the road broadens and the buildings spread out on either side and a triangle is formed by a terraced row of houses and the white courthouse behind them, there is a statue of a man with a musket at his side. He is Sam McAllister. When the 1798 rebellion against the British collapsed and the last whispers of the struggle were being fought out in the mountains above Baltinglass, McAllister died to save his commander, Michael Dwyer, and allow him to live and fight a little longer. The statue had been erected in 1904 to commemorate 1798, in the name of the people of Wicklow, though by no means everyone who gazed on Sam McAllister and his musket shared that sentiment. The people of Wicklow had killed each other in considerable numbers in 1798, and when the statue went up it surprised many that it was not Michael Dwyer, the hero, who stood at the centre of the Triangle, but his lieutenant, who had the advantage of coming from the other end of Ireland. He was remembered for his bravery and self-sacrifice, not for killing anybody's ancestors, and he carried no list of his own relatives, executed and murdered by their neighbours. He became, within a few years, part of Baltinglass. Even for those who, had they referred to Sam McAllister at all, might have called him just another Fenian bastard, he had somehow become their own Fenian bastard. And when, in 1921, a group of drunken Black and Tans decided to destroy the statue, the response was not what they expected.

The Black and Tans were stationed in Baltinglass, as every-where else, to deliver the kind of reprisals in the war for Ireland that it was unreasonable, even tasteless, to ask of regular troops, let alone the Royal Irish Constabulary, who suffered, despite everything, from the disability of being uncomfortably Irish. The Tans had no such problems. They were ill-disciplined irregulars who had been given clear assurances that they would not be held accountable for their actions. Even in Wicklow, with its high proportion of Protestants and loyalists, everyone knew they were another mistake in a long list of British mistakes.

The Tans weren't about to kill anyone that night in the Triangle, as a dozen or so stumbled across Main Street from Sheridan's Bar. Two of them used the iron railing round the plinth of the statue to clamber up to the top. Others hacked at Sam McAllister with their rifle butts. They were shouting, singing, laughing, clapping. People were coming out from the pubs and houses now. They said nothing; they simply watched. Whether they took a side in the war or tried not to, all they wanted was for this to stop. They wanted these men to leave them alone. And as David Gillespie wheeled his bicycle along the street, that was what he heard in the silence. The Tans heard nothing. It was an audience, no matter who was there to applaud, who was there to be taught a lesson. They were enjoying themselves. One Tan pushed his way through the ring of his comrades, bringing a sledgehammer from the armoured car outside Sheridan's. He was roared on as he smashed it down on McAllister's right leg.

It wasn't David Gillespie's business to tell the Black and Tans to stop. He had been at the market earlier, looking for a new bull and finding nothing he liked for the money he had. It wasn't often that he drank, but he stayed in the bar of the Bridge Hotel later than was good for him. It wasn't long since he had left Dublin, and the life of a farmer that he returned to, for the first time since his teenage years, didn't sit as easily on him as he claimed. He had been a policeman too long. It had been taken away from him, and he still resented that. And now, as he walked towards the Triangle, heading home, there was more of it. More of what had forced him out of the Dublin Metropolitan Police. Whether it was one side or the other, there was always more of it. But none of it was his business. If people wanted it to stop, any of it to stop, it was up to them. The business of his life, since resigning from the Dublin Metropolitan Police and bringing his family back to the farm below Kilranelagh, had been to stand outside it all. He asked only that. He had no reason not to walk past it now.

'They haven't paid for half what they drank. They never do.' It was Johnny Sheridan who spoke, quietly, sourly, standing in the entrance to his bar. 'Now they may break up the town. And will we ever see a policeman? They'll be shut away in the barracks right now, waiting for it all to pass them by.'

'Aren't we all waiting for that?' Another quiet voice.

'Wouldn't they listen to you, David?' Johnny was looking straight at David Gillespie, whose progress had been blocked by the press of people.

'Why would they do that, Johnny?'

There was a great crack as the sledgehammer hit the statue again and the leg splintered. At the same time a shot rang out, to another roar of applause, and the tip of Sam McAllister's musket flew into the street below. The murmuring in the crowd was louder now. People were pressing forward. Someone shouted.

'Would you piss off back where you came from!'

The Black and Tans round the statue took no notice. The sledgehammer rose and fell again. But outside Sheridan's the two men in the armoured car looked uneasy. They had expected acclaim, from some at least, but they could feel the anger that was growing. There were more people now. Men and women; children, too. David looked across at the armoured car as one of the Tans climbed from the front seat into the back. He had just picked up a rifle.

David pushed his bicycle forward. He only wanted to go home.

'Someone has to tell them to stop.' It was Johnny Sheridan again.

The people David was trying to push past were looking at him. There was no real reason why they should be. It was a response to Johnny's words. David was a policeman, a sergeant. At least he had been. And there had been a time, not that long ago, when he was highly regarded. Word was that he was so well thought of in the DMP, that they might even have made an inspector of him.

'Go home and leave them to it. What's the point?' David Gillespie addressed the words to no one in particular.

'You'd know what to say to them, Mr Gillespie!'

It was a woman's voice, and as she spoke he saw Johnny

6

Sheridan's wife ushering her children back through the pub door. The roaring and laughing of the Tans continued. One of them, at least, had realised the mood in the street, looking down from Sam McAllister's shoulders, waving his rifle over his head.

'We'll destroy the cunt! Do you like that, you fuckers, do you?'

'Let them alone,' David said. 'They don't care what they do.'

'You're the one they'll listen to.' It was still Johnny's persistent, quiet voice, but it was joined and echoed by the crowd that was now pulling closer.

'Sure, weren't you one of them yourself?'

The words were thrown at him from further down the street. They were met with harsh murmurs of disapproval, but not from everyone. He could feel the expectation. He would do something. He could do something. If he walked away it was no longer about minding his own business, it would turn into a kind of acquiescence. And his instincts were still, despite everything, those of a policeman. If there was trouble, if it went that way, the Black and Tans would do as they pleased. They wouldn't hold back. Maybe he could calm things.

'For fuck's sake.' David shoved his bicycle at Jimmy. 'You may hold it.'

He walked towards the armoured car and looked at the driver.

'Is there an officer here?'

The driver grinned and pointed towards the statue.

'He's the one on top, mate.'

David continued across the street. Several of the Black and Tans, growing tired of what they were doing, watched him. He stood in front of them, saying nothing, looking at the man who was climbing down from Sam McAllister's shoulders. The sledgehammer struck once more. As it did, the man

7

wielding it lost his grip. It hit the cobbles and flew across them towards David. There was more laughter as three Tans scrambled to pick it up, fighting over who would use it next. One of them stood up with his prize, looking at David Gillespie.

'What the fuck do you want, then?'

'To speak to your officer.'

The man looked at him, frowning, puzzled by the quiet tone.

'Are you an officer today, Ernie? There's a feller wants to talk to you.'

The solitary figure in the Triangle had their attention. The attack on the statue paused. There was some sniggering and laughing. It could be new sport.

The man who had climbed down from Sam McAllister's shoulders stepped towards David, grinning broadly, with a wink to the man holding the sledgehammer. They were all young, but he was younger, in his early twenties. He was English, blond haired, fresh faced. His accent said well educated.

'And how can we help you, sir?'

There was more laughter from the young Englishman's men.

'People would like you to stop. That's all.'

'I see. And you speak for them, do you?'

'You've had your fun.'

'Do you think we're here for fun?' The Englishman's tone changed.

'Whatever you're here for, this won't help.'

'So, who the fuck are you? Whose side are you on?'

'It doesn't matter where people stand. They don't want this.'

'I asked you a question. Who are you?'

'Does it matter? I live here.'

A short, dark Tan walked forward, cradling a rifle.

8

'His name's Gillespie. He was a DMP man. One of the RIC fellers said.'

'Dublin Metropolitan Police, eh!' The officer spoke. 'Bit off your beat?'

'Story is he walked out on them,' said the short Tan. 'Couldn't take it.'

There was silence in the Black and Tan ranks now.

'I see,' continued the young Englishman. 'The middle of a fucking war, and he says, "That's not for me, lads, good luck to you!" A very poor show.' He turned back to David. 'Wouldn't you say that was a poor show, Mr Gillespie?'

David said nothing. Nothing would help until this was finished.

'But you'll be well informed, I'm sure. Are you well informed?'

David had to answer. 'I don't know what you mean.'

'What I mean is, we have in you a capital asset, an ex-policeman with all the local knowledge we lack. You'll know who everyone is. You'll know where they sit, loyal and not loyal. You'll know the Fenians who like to keep it quiet. You'll know what side everyone is on. So what side are you on, Mr Gillespie?'

'I'm not on any side.'

'A neutral, by all that's holy! A neutral! You know what I think of that?'

He walked closer. His face was inches from David's face. He spat.

'No neutrals, you cunt. No room for them, old man.'

The officer turned to his men.

'Bring him back. He's a spokesman! Let's hear what he's got to say.'

The Englishman walked towards the armoured car. His men followed him, forgetting the statue as easily and as idly as they had attacked it. Two of them grabbed David Gillespie's

9

arms; another covered him with a rifle. As he was marched away, he made no attempt to resist. Outside Sheridan's the crowd watched and Johnny Sheridan still held the bicycle that David had left behind.

The beating didn't start straight away. There were a few kicks as David Gillespie was dragged from the armoured car into the Fever Hospital, but only questions followed. Questions about why he had left the Dublin Metropolitan Police; about what he was doing now; about his wife and his son; about who he knew, who he drank with, who was Protestant and who was Catholic. There were empty, meaningless questions he answered simply enough. There were questions about the DMP he didn't even begin to answer. He said he had left because he didn't want to do it any more, because the farm at Kilranelagh was a better place for his family. He was happy to be called a coward, a traitor. The weaker he seemed the less he would matter. But the questions they came back to were about what he knew now, the politics of his friends and his neighbours.

Everywhere they went, the Black and Tans quickly ran out of targets, at least among those who didn't shoot back. They knew the Irish nationalists who were fighting with the Volunteers. They knew the anti-British politicians, hard and soft, in plain sight or on the run. But when it came to the network of secret support that was everywhere, they knew barely anything. Yet that was where terror and intimidation had to be directed; not at the real Republicans, but at the half-convinced, half-afraid, half-baked, fair-weather nationalists who made up most of the population. Without them the hard core were nothing. The rest needed to know their bodies could as easily end up in a ditch as the Volunteers they pandered to. But about all that David Gillespie claimed profound ignorance.

It seemed he never talked politics with anybody. For a man who grew up in the Church of Ireland in Baltinglass, he barely knew a Protestant from a Catholic, let alone the degrees of Republicanism, nationalism or loyalism his neighbours practised. He had nothing to say, except that he had been away too long to know. The young Black and Tan officer became bored very quickly. He took a bottle of whiskey back to the Workhouse and left it to his men to beat something out of the ex-policeman. By that stage he had no interest in whether it was anything useful, but there was a point to be made. Too many Irish people thought they didn't have to take a side, and that amounted to taking the wrong side. If David Gillespie's beating provided no information, it would at least be a lesson.

In the darkness of the Fever Hospital ward, the Scottish Black and Tan sat on the edge of the table, looking down at David. He was drinking whiskey. He had lost any notion of what questions he should be asking now. He had asked them too many times. The questions didn't matter anyway. He didn't make much distinction between one kind of Irishman and another. None of them could be trusted. They might all hate each other, one tribe and another, but they hated everyone else more. Why anyone thought the fucking shitehole was worth fighting over at all was a mystery. The only Irishmen he respected were the ones who had the guts to fire a rifle. He had killed a few of them and most had died well, even when they were dragged out of bed and stuck against a wall.

The Scotsman stood and walked to the chair propping up David.

'I'm sorry to say I think you've broken your jaw.'

David stared at him. The man's tone was almost gentle for a moment.

'That can be a nasty business, painful, eh?'

He leant forward and clasped David's jaw. He jerked it sideways. It was impossible for David not to let out a scream of pain. The two men who stood on either side held him pushed him down on to the chair. He screamed again as his jaw was wrenched back the other way. The Scot let go and stepped away.

'Aye, broken; I'd definitely say that's the problem.'

He took out a cigarette and lit it.

'You'll want to be careful you don't break anything else, Davie.'

David held his head as stiffly as he could. Any movement was agony.

'You fucked off my boss, you know that? Myself, I'm not unimpressed. Nothing to say about anybody. Why do you think it matters? You could have given us any old shite, you know that. Any old shite about anyone. We don't care. And you know what? We'll let everyone know you're an informer anyway. When we've finished, you may expect a call from the Volunteers one dark night. You know what they say, Davie. Once a peeler, always a peeler.'

The Scotsman was angrier than he wanted to show his men. There was a look on David Gillespie's face, behind the blood and the bruises. It was contempt. The other Tans couldn't see it, but the Scot did. The young Englishman had seen it too and had felt the same anger. The look was still there.

'Why waste bullets? When your Republican boyos will shoot you for us?'

The Scot kicked the chair from under David, and again David's face hit the floor. Again, he screamed as shards of bones ground together and pain stabbed into him. Again, he wanted to sink into the cold stone. He lay for a long moment, unmoving. They were talking quietly now. There was laughter, but that was quieter too. There was movement around him. A chair scraped the floor. The lights were moving. As his mind swam into some kind of focus he thought they were leaving. Suddenly it was very dark. A heavy door slammed. He could feel the tears on his face, through the pain. He was crying, silently.

2

Tirpitzuferstrasse

Berlin, 1940

A thin, pale man gazed out of the upper window of a building on the edge of the great park that was Berlin's Tiergarten. He looked down at the tree-lined banks of the Landwehr Canal from a room full of people. He was there because it was expected of him. The deafness that had been growing slowly in his head for a long time made such gatherings difficult. The buzz of conversation was a blur of sound, awkward and uncomfortable, but his distance from what was happening went deeper. Wherever he was in Berlin, isolation enfolded him.

Marked by no more than a brass plate that stated its address, 76/78 Tirpitzuferstrasse formed the unassuming boundary of a complex of buildings that stretched back towards the Tiergarten, making up the High Command of the German Armed Forces, the OKW. The offices on Tirpitzuferstrasse looked out on the city's inner suburbs and breathed the calm air that was the Landwehr Canal's corridor of trees and moving water. It was one of the most visible of the OKW buildings, and one of the least visited. It consisted of little more than a few floors of narrow corridors and cramped offices. The buildings that contained the machinery of military command spread into the Tiergarten, but 76/78 Tirpitzuferstrasse was almost shut off from them; unless asked, few people from Army Command entered the domain of the Abwehr, Germany's Military Intelligence arm, jealously commanded by Admiral Wilhelm Canaris.

The man looking out of the window on a bright autumn afternoon in 1940 was an occasional visitor to Tirpitzuferstrasse. He was an Irishman who lectured Abwehr agents, about to be sent to Ireland, on the overlapping, contradictory visions of Irish history, rebellion and unity that the Irish government and its declared enemy, the IRA, shared and fought over. Frank Ryan had left Ireland to fight fascism in the Spanish Civil War, to fight an army financed and supplied by Adolf Hitler. Captured in 1938, he spent two years of torture, mock-execution and sickness in one of Franco's gaols. He was released into the hands of the Abwehr and taken to Germany. No one else wanted him, including his own country. To survive, he had to turn to a regime he despised. The Abwehr had been persuaded, by Ryan's German friends, that he was a valuable asset, an ex-IRA man who could bring the warring factions of Irish Republicanism together to support Germany against Britain. He had believed the Germans would let him return to Ireland. Instead, he lived under an assumed name in Berlin, protected by Admiral Canaris's men but watched by the Gestapo, which had a more accurate understanding of what went on inside the head of this ex-anti-fascist than his Abwehr minders. If Frank Ryan, or Frank Richards as he was known in Berlin, ceased to be useful enough to warrant the protection the Abwehr afforded him, the Gestapo was always there, waiting.

'You just need to send them on their way with a smile, Frank.'

The German who now stood at the window with Ryan wore the uniform of the Brandenburgers, the Abwehr's Special Forces battalion. Helmut Clissman was an old friend. The two men had known one another in Ireland before the war. It was Clissman's plan that rescued Ryan from death in a Spanish prison.

They spoke in English.

'If I could go with them, I'd smile a bit more, Helmut.'

'Me too,' said Clissman. He poured Sekt from a bottle into the empty glass Frank Ryan was holding. 'Let's drink to that – to Ireland – someday soon.'

The Irishman raised his glass. 'Sláinte. Let's leave it at that. I've stopped counting chickens. I've seen too many throttled. But you're going back to Copenhagen tomorrow. Isn't that easy enough? Good beer and no bombing.'

'It could be worse.' Clissman spoke slowly; it could be better too. 'The bombing's not so bad in Berlin, is it? Nothing compared to London, they say. We're too far away.'

'I'm sure it's grand. Every day the tobacconist tells me the British are beaten. I don't know how many days that is. How many days in six months?'

Clissman shot a warning glance at his friend. Ryan hunched his shoulders. He stubbed out his cigarette and embarked on the process of making another with a paper and tobacco. Making the cigarettes meant as much as smoking them. It occupied him when he didn't want to speak, which was often.

The two men turned back into the room. A dozen people talked in small groups. They were all men, apart from a solitary woman. Only one man besides Clissman was in uniform: a tall, elegantly featured army major who was talking more loudly than anyone else and sounded as if the Sekt had already flowed too abundantly. However, most of the other men were officers of one kind or another. In a city where uniforms were not only a sign of patriotism and service in time of war but also of political orthodoxy, their absence was a mark of how the Abwehr distinguished itself from the military beehive of the OKW and, more especially, from the Nazi Party and its competing Intelligence arm in the Reich Main Security Office, the SD, the Sicherheitdienst. The Wehrmacht major was distinguished from the others by something other than a uniform: he was a member of the SD; he didn't advertise it now, but he carried an SS rank.

'You're here to mingle,' said Clissman. 'It's why I made you come.'

'It's all bollocks!' Ryan laughed. 'What do they care?'

'Mà thugann siad aire duit go bhfuil tú sábháitte.' Clissman spoke quietly but urgently in Irish. If they care about you you're safe. It was the Irish language that had brought the two men together, years before in Ireland, when Clissman was a student of Irish as well as a German spy. He continued speaking in English. 'You understand.'

Frank Ryan nodded. 'I understand too well.' He drained his glass and held it out to be refilled. Clissman poured the drink. The woman approached.

'Last goodbyes, Herr Richards!'

She had fair, fine hair, and a face that was fine too, almost sharp. Her eyes were blue, but very dark. It was a face that was easy to remember. She was an Abwehr agent. Shortly she would be going to Britain, and then on to Ireland. There were no hard details at this gathering. No one spoke too much about what everyone was aware of. But these were unacknowledged farewells. Frank Ryan liked the woman, but he looked at her with a sense of unease. He recognised the bright purposefulness in her face. He saw it in other young Germans. It was a commitment to something dark that filled them with light. He knew her intensity. What she was doing was serious; she felt its seriousness. It was for Germany and for Germany's leader. Yet it was an adventure too. There was passion and expectation in her face as well as determination. She spoke English with barely any accent; there was enough Irish in it to hide what little was there.

'And thank you for all your help,' she said, briefly touching his arm.

'A safe journey, Fraulein Eriksen. I don't think my potted history was very much use to you. You've lived in Ireland. You know yourself, as we say.'

'Well, I thought I did. You managed to confuse me at times.'

'You should know you won't get far in Ireland without some confusion.'

She laughed. 'For an IRA leader, you don't have much faith in the IRA.'

'Ah, well, those are words of warning for your colleagues rather than someone with a foot in Ireland and a foot in Germany. Just a way of warning them not to expect the degree of – what should we say? – efficiency I suppose.' It was hard to catch the tone of Ryan's words, but Clissman caught it and scowled. 'The degree of efficiency we are all so used to in the machinery of the Reich.'

Clissman gave another warning glare. Frank Ryan grinned.

'There are idle feckers, you mean.' The woman laughed, showing off her ease with the English of Ireland, but perhaps testing Ryan too. He puzzled her.

'Ah, it's in us all, Vera, me too.'

'Well, one thing you did teach me, Herr Richards, that I'm told is useful in any agent anywhere: to talk with ease and facility yet say nothing at all.'

'An Irish art,' replied Ryan, raising his glass. 'To all the Irish arts.'

They were interrupted by the man who wore the uniform of a Wehrmacht major. He was still loud, not unpleasantly, still smiling a smile that spoke of too much Sekt. He stumbled as he stretched out his hand towards Frank Ryan.

Vera Eriksen reached out to steady him. He looked at her and winked cheerfully. He clasped Ryan's hand in both of his enthusiastically.

'Thank you, my friend! To the Emerald Isle and all who sail in her!'

'Safe home, Major Kramer,' said the Irishman quietly.

'And before long, you will follow us. The time is coming, yes?'

Kramer's English bore his German accent softly, but clearly. He spoke confidentially now, knowingly, saying more than Abwehr etiquette demanded.

Frank Ryan smiled politely and extracted his hand.

'Ah, well, who knows what the times have in store, Major?'

Helmut Clissman put his arm through Ryan's. It was the gesture of an old and easy friendship, but the message in his eyes was not only that they had done enough. His friend's taste for ambiguous statement needed no more wine either.

'The time that definitely has come is the time to leave, Frank. I have to be up at the crack of dawn for the train to Copenhagen. You'll want that lift home.'

As they walked away, they stopped for a moment to shake hands with a man in a carefully cut lounge suit, the third German agent who was about to leave Berlin for Britain and Ireland. Major Kramer watched them. There was a half smile still on his face, but the distaste in his eyes was clear to Vera Eriksen.

'Herr Richards is not a man to be trusted,' said Kramer, shaking his head.

'Don't be silly,' laughed Vera. 'You've had enough, Erik! A lot of what he says about Ireland is worth listening to. I know that. You should listen. You won't ever understand the Irish if you don't take things with a pinch of salt.'

'Perhaps I know more about Herr Richards than you do, Vera.'

'Come on, he was an IRA leader. That's what matters. He's trusted here.'

'That doesn't say much. Never mind the Irishman; I

wouldn't trust most of the people in this room. From Helmut Clissman up.' Erik Kramer lowered his voice again. He seemed more sober. 'All the way up. We both know it, don't we?'

He touched her hand. As he did, her eyes shone. What was between them was unknown to anyone else. They had had to keep it that way. She nodded.

'Don't drink any more, Erik,' she said. 'Don't say any more.'

He laughed, draining his glass and stepping forward to take another from a waiter holding out a tray. He clapped his arm round one man after another, beaming enthusiasm and camaraderie. He worked too hard at it, Vera thought. She loved his confidence, as she loved his commitment and his furious passion, but she knew his weakness. It was not a weakness in Germany, yet she worried how well it fitted him for England or Ireland. The English and the Irish were different from each other in ways it was easy to understand; they were the same in ways that were harder to fathom and far more dangerous. She knew that. He couldn't comprehend it. He underestimated anybody who did not share his faith.

The next morning, when Frank Ryan came out of his bedroom in the apartment in Katzbachstrasse that he shared with Helmut Clissman, the German was sitting at the kitchen table looking down at an untouched cup of coffee. It was early and Clissman was due to catch the train for Copenhagen, where he was stationed with his regiment. He was ready to leave, his suitcase by the chair.

'I thought you'd be gone, Helmut.'

'Yes, I'm heading off now.' He stood up, evidently thoughtful, even preoccupied. He spoke slowly. 'I've just had Tirpitzuferstrasse on the phone.'

'That's what woke me up.' Ryan grinned. 'It's one sound I still hear. I can't make out what the fuck anyone says when I pick it up, but when it rings—'

'It seems they won't be landing Major Kramer in Britain after all.'

The Irishman took a cup and poured coffee from the pot on the stove.

'Why is that? I thought he was raring to go. A bit of a gob-shite, in my humble opinion, but a quare enthusiastic gobshite, if that counts for anything.'

'It won't count for much now.'

Frank Ryan heard the finality in the throwaway words.

'His car went into the Spey last night on his way home. He's dead.'

'Jesus, I knew he'd had a bit to drink . . .'

'Perhaps he had more.' Clissman's words felt oddly abrupt. He gave a shrug and then bent to pick up the suitcase. He moved towards the door.

'You don't sound very convinced, Helmut?'

'He died in a car accident. How much more convincing can it be?'

'You don't anticipate deep mourning in Tirpitzuferstrasse?'

'He wasn't everyone's choice, was he? As I understand it, the SD rather forced him on us. I'm not sure Admiral Canaris is keen on joint operations with Nazi Intelligence. I wouldn't dis-cuss this with anyone, Frank. I only mention it so you can put it on that ever-growing list of things you know nothing about.'

3

The Moat Field

Wicklow

The last of the ewes splashed her hooves through the foot-bath, out through the wooden hurdles that made up the pens at the corner of the Moat Field at Kilranelagh. Stefan Gillespie watched her scuttle indignantly across the field to join the rest of the flock, eating the grass that had been saved for this time. It was the last good grass of a hot, dry summer that had produced less and less grazing as the season wore on. The ewe was limping, as too many of them were limping. The sour, sickening scent of foot rot was everywhere: on Stefan's hands and on his clothes; wafting from the hoof parings in the pens, where the knife had trimmed the hooves and scraped out the green, diseased puss. It was deep in his nostrils, too, and even a hot bath would not quite get rid of it.

It had been a long day getting the ewes ready for the rams; Stefan and his father, drenching them with wormer, cutting away the dags that held the summer's filth from their tails, trimming and cleaning the hooves. Now they would be flushed on the best of the grass that was left, which wasn't much. It was late for this, with barely a month to go till the rams were put out. Stefan watched David Gillespie walk across the field, heading back to the house. There had been little conversation between father and son that day. Stefan had arrived home from Dublin unexpectedly and with no explanation. And when gossip found its way from the Garda Barracks in Baltinglass, to the effect that he was back because he had been suspended from Garda Special Branch in Dublin Castle, he only told his father and mother there had been a problem and that time would sort it out.

That was the end of the discussion; it was Special Branch business. If it was clear to Stefan's parents that he was uneasy and preoccupied, despite attempts to brush everything off as a misunderstanding, it was equally certain he wasn't going to speak about it. And if there were things Stefan didn't want to talk about, he quickly realised his father had his own reasons to be distant. There was work to do at Kilranelagh, and a lot of it. At first Stefan was glad of that. But things were not right. There were too many ewes with foot rot this year. What should have been done weeks before to ready them for tupping was barely begun. A calf had been lost for no apparent reason from their easiest calving cow. There was mastitis, too, unnoticed when it must have been there weeks.

After a hard day working together, like the day just gone, father and son would normally share a sense of achievement along with their weariness. For David, there would be all the more to share because Stefan was so rarely there. He would never have walked away without contemplating what they had done and taking pride in it. He would never have ended this job without talking about his ewes. Now he had simply left Stefan to clear the pens and drain the footbath, to pile up the hurdles, to disinfect and burn what needed burning. He muttered something about a grand job and some beer at the house, then he was gone. He wanted to get away and Stefan knew it. Too much was wrong. Stefan Gillespie saw his father cross the Moat Field to the gate. His head was bowed. He was older in ways he hadn't been even a few months before. Stefan had registered something last time he was home, but he hadn't taken it in. He had seen, for a moment, and forgotten. Now he knew his father had been struggling, struggling with the farm and struggling to hide that. And there was little he could do about it. If there was time to see the sheep right for the coming spring, and to do a little to put the farm in better shape for the winter, it would have to do. He didn't know how long he would be home. Not long, he thought. He would be there until he was told where they wanted him to go. Those had been Detective Superintendent Gregory's words. It was no clearer than that.

When Stefan Gillespie was forced into the Garda Special Branch, at the start of the war, Terry Gregory had told him he thought he would be useful, though he did say he hadn't worked out how. It seemed that now he had. It would involve Stefan disappearing somewhere. He didn't have to add that somewhere would be unwelcome, uncertain, uncomfortable and also unsafe.

'A little bit of serendipity, Stevie, you know what that is, I'm sure.'

Inspector Stefan Gillespie looked at Superintendent Gregory's smiling face and said nothing. He wasn't expected to reply. He knew the smile. It had the qualities of the Cheshire Cat. It wasn't that the heavy, red-faced figure was in the habit of becoming invisible, apart from his grin, but for all you could tell about what was going on behind that smile, he might as well have been. Like Carroll's cat, the broader the smile, the more jovial the banter, the more reason to be uneasy. And Stefan had been uneasy even before he was summoned through the glass partition that shut the superintendent's office off from the detectives' room at Dublin Castle. All morning, Gregory had been pacing his office, stopping, pacing again, looking out. Stefan knew his boss well enough to gauge his mood. Though their eyes never met, he knew he was looking at him.

'Well, it's a coming together of things at least, and happy in its own way. It will mean you're suspended, awaiting an investigation. I don't know how far that has to go. Not far, I hope, if it's any reassurance. As long as the paperwork's there, I doubt it even needs to start. The paperwork's everything as far as the Department of External Affairs is concerned. Beginning and end. And on paper you're compromised enough. That couldn't have come out better. For a while we may talk about kicking you out of the Gardaí, at least around the office.'

Gregory pondered the last words and gestured vaguely in the direction of the room beyond the glass partition. 'It will all need to convince the lads, so.'

'I have no idea what you're talking about, sir. You know that.'

'Call it thinking aloud. Or maybe making it up as I go along. You'll catch up when I catch up. You'll know what happened on Friday, in Templeogue?'

'The German agent who got away?'

'It was a close thing. But your man knew we were coming. This place still leaks. You stop up one hole and you find another. You know yourself.'

The words were thrown away. Stefan Gillespie had been with Terry Gregory the last time he stopped up one of those holes. There was no question that the man the superintendent shot and killed in a dark room behind a shop in Smithfield had been an IRA informer. He had also been Terry Gregory's friend for twenty years. The report Stefan had written stated that Chief Inspector Danny Skehan fired first. That was, strictly speaking, true. It was also true that the gun he'd used had no bullets in it. Superintendent Gregory had removed them. Whatever reasons Gregory had for choosing murder rather than a prison sentence, he kept to himself. But every so often it was useful to remind the IRA that it had no monopoly on killing to make a point. Terry Gregory had his own points to make, though they were rarely anything other than opaque. It seemed he did not want Skehan in a courtroom. There may have been too many questions about his own relationship with the IRA. Perhaps it had been more personal. Maybe the fact that Terry Gregory and Danny Skehan were close meant the price of betrayal was high. Whatever the truth, the superintendent made Stefan part of it. With elegant economy he had just reminded him of that.

'We've picked up several German agents in the last two months. Not because of our efficiency, but because they seem to be remarkably incompetent. Short of walking up to a Guard and asking where they can find the nearest IRA man, it's hard to think of much more they could do to get themselves noticed. No one knows what they're here for. They don't seem to know themselves.'

Stefan waited as the superintendent paced the room, lighting a cigarette.

'They've done better with a man who was parachuted in a month or so ago. A man called Goertz. We know something about him. He's made his way through various safe houses around the country. And he has made contact with the IRA. They got him to Dublin, and he's been here a fortnight. He's been wandering around fairly freely, posing as a refugee. Gerry de Paor got Military Intelligence involved. They thought the best thing was to keep him loose, on the basis that he couldn't do much damage and we'd find out who he was meeting. He hasn't been under close surveillance, but we've kept an eye on him. Last week the powers that be decided it was time to pick him up. He was in a house in Templeogue owned by a man called Stephen Held. A bit like you, Stevie, only the other way round. A German parent somewhere. Not so much Irish with a bit of German, more German with a bit of the Irish. Not enough Irish to stop him having a radio transmitter in his attic to keep in touch with friends in Berlin.'

'And you knew that?' asked Stefan.

'Gerry de Paor's fellers in G2 picked up some shortwave broadcasts from Held's transmitter, but it was just IRA propaganda. He let them use it. The usual banter. Germany's winning. Rise up against the English and their lackeys in Leinster House. The Jews are behind it all. You'd wonder who's tweaking the cat's whisker in the middle of the night to listen to that bollocks. Except us and British Intelligence. It doesn't matter whether these fellers have anything serious to transmit or not, it's the embarrassment. A stick for Churchill to beat us with. De Valera's a divil for having Ireland's holy neutrality compromised.'

There was nothing in Ireland that mattered more than neutrality. It was an article of faith that the Prime Minister, Éamon de Valera, held with a fervour that made it seem as if the survival of the country depended on it. In many ways it did. But fervour was essential to the show. Neither Germany nor Britain could be offended by anything that happened in Ireland. Yet as the curtain went up, and Ireland made sure no newspaper printed a bad word about Hitler or said anything too enthusiastic about Winston Churchill, tens of thousands of Irishmen fought and died for Britain; tens of thousands worked to maintain its war economy. Germany pretended Ireland was a secret ally. Britain pretended Ireland was stabbing it in the back. In private everyone, German and British alike, knew de Valera's neutrality was so one-sided that it was more sleight of hand than diplomatic policy. But Ireland believed, and de Valera presented himself to the world as the truest of believers, in uncompromising neutrality.

'You got Mr Held and his transmitter. But Herr Goertz got away.'

'They knew we were on our way, Stevie. Not by much. Held had started burning papers. Goertz only just got over the back wall. That doesn't make me look good. Complacency, Stevie, that's the word. From time to time I make the mistake of trusting my own men. That's not the way of it, eh? What a world!'

'Do I ask if there's a point to this, sir? You started by telling me I was going to be suspended and then investigated for something. Or was that a joke?'

'Only after a fashion. Let me tell you one thing about our friend Goertz's perambulations around Ireland. He has managed to get in a bit of sightseeing. Well, you wouldn't want anyone to come all this way and miss the glories of ancient Ireland. And at least he got as far as County Wicklow and the Vale of Glendalough. Now, as a Wicklow man wouldn't you feel pleased he did?'

Stefan waited as Terry Gregory lit a cigarette. Whatever the diversions, they were nearer to it now. He knew from experience that the more idle the superintendent's words became, the closer he was to saying what he meant.

'You'll know that Mrs Stuart lives in Laragh.'

'At Laragh House, yes.' Stefan laughed. 'Not a place I'd be calling into.'

'Ah, but a place Herr Goertz did call into. In fact, he stayed there until the IRA took him off to meet the Chief of Staff and plan whatever bollocks they're planning. He found his way to Laragh House not long after he landed. That was his starting point. Iseult Stuart's home and the home of her husband, of course. A mutual friend. I mean a mutual friend of you and Goertz. Mr Francis Stuart, now in Berlin, working for the German government. And as chance would have it, didn't you find time on your jaunt to Berlin as a courier to catch up with the man himself? You even brought us back a report about it.'

Terry Gregory stood over his desk and opened a file.

'Hardly catching up. I never saw the man before Berlin.'

'And you also caught up with two other people of interest to the government and to G2 and the Military Intelligence lads. Charles Bewley, our disgraced ambassador, sacked for his over-enthusiastic frolicking with the Nazis, and Frank Ryan, an old IRA man who spends his time advising German agents on Irish politics or something similar, at least so I'm told. Now, add that to Francis Stuart writing propaganda for Lord Haw-Haw to broadcast to England – doubtless very well-written propaganda, maybe a credit to us all—'

'What?'

'You see, when you put it altogether like that—'

'Come on, sir!' Stefan laughed. 'There was an innocent Irishwoman on a murder charge in Berlin. The ambassador asked me to help her. You know all that. I trailed round Berlin with a German detective who was interviewing Irish people who knew the man she supposedly killed. It was his list. What is this?'

'Someone tipped off Held and Goertz. However that tip-off reached them, it came from here, Special Branch, directly or indirectly. And what do I have? I have a spy whose first point of contact in Ireland is Mrs Iseult Stuart. I also have a detective – a detective of German ancestry – who was sent on a mission to the Irish legation in Berlin that included a bit of a chat with Herr Goertz's friend and Mrs Stuart's husband. I only have your word for what was said in Berlin.'

'You're not serious, are you?'

'Not in the way you imagine, Inspector.'

'It's called coincidence.'

'I've never been very happy with coincidences. I always feel, if that's the answer, perhaps I haven't asked the right questions yet. But never mind the coincidences; I'll go back to where I started. Let us stick with serendipity.'

'And that means?'

'That means that it suits me – and by me I mean it suits other people too, higher up the greasy pole – it suits me to have your loyalties questioned by a trail of circumstantial evidence that needs serious investigation. I'm sure we'll find there's nothing in it, Stevie. In the meantime, it's my business to let the word circulate that there is something in it, even that I have proof of that. I will, of course, be very circumspect, but over a drink in Farrelly's I will express my disappointment to your colleagues. It is going to upset me, Stevie. You're a man I liked and trusted, don't you know that? I am still struggling to believe it. Sure, but it'll be easier for others. Not just German on his Mammy's side, they'll say, a Protestant German!'

Stefan Gillespie was trying to bring some coherent meaning to what he was hearing. He had been left, struggling, halfway through the last few minutes of the conversation; he was still trying to catch up. Terry Gregory smiled the wry, slightly sour smile that said he was enjoying himself. It amused him to see people floundering, even when they were people he liked and, in his own ambivalent way, cared about. He enjoyed games as he enjoyed power, quietly.

Abruptly, the superintendent's voice became harder. It became louder. It wasn't loud enough for the detectives in the outer room to hear what he was saying, but it was loud enough for them to know that something was wrong.

'You will leave Dublin Castle immediately, Inspector Gillespie. You will not go near your desk. You will take nothing away. You will say nothing to anybody, and that includes your sergeant, Dessie MacMahon. You are to have no further communication with Special Branch or anybody in it, except me. You will be escorted to your flat by uniformed Guards. The flat will be searched by Intelligence officers from G2. Sad to relate, I can't trust my own men to do it.'

*

It was little more than a week since Stefan Gillespie stood in Superintendent Gregory's office and received the startling news that he was now either an IRA informer or a German agent, or both. He had been taken straight from Special Branch by a uniformed Garda sergeant and a Guard. Neither man had been from Dublin Castle. He had exchanged no words with anyone in the detectives' room. The best he could offer Dessie MacMahon, his sergeant and his only close friend in the Branch, was a shrug. He was driven along the Liffey to Wellington Quay and the flat above Paddy Geary's tobacconist's. Paddy was, as always, hovering in the shop doorway. Usually he was interested only in gossiping with whoever was passing or exchanging views on whatever news he had gleaned from that day's newspapers. Now he was waiting anxiously for his tenant. As the black Ford stopped and Stefan emerged, flanked by Guards, Paddy pushed forward.

'There's two fellers upstairs in your flat. They walked in and they went straight up there. They'd even a key, I'd say. I went up, Mr Gillespie. I asked them what they were doing. They just told me to fuck off. In my own house!'

'It's what you need to do, Paddy.' It was the Garda sergeant who spoke. 'Do I know you?' said the tobacconist.

'Fuck off and you won't need to, will you?'

There were two men in the flat when Stefan reached it with his police escort. They both wore civilian clothes, but he knew they were officers in G2, Military Intelligence. He recognised one of them immediately, Geróid de Paor.

'Commandant de Paor. I should be flattered.'

'Well, someone has to do it. It's a sorry day, Inspector.'

'Have you found anything?'

'Is there something to find?'

'Your guess is as good as mine. I'd say it's probably a lot better.'

'That's not impossible, Stefan.'

De Paor stood looking at him for a moment, as the other G2 man searched methodically through a chest of drawers, carefully replacing everything as he moved from drawer to drawer. Stefan assumed de Paor knew what was happening, what was really happening. Out of the confusion that had filled his head at Dublin Castle, what was now forming was simply anger.

'Are you part of all this shite, Gerry?' The words were ambiguous enough, but he had no doubt Commandant de Paor would understand them.

'I didn't ask for it, if that's what you mean.'

'Nor did I,' said Stefan more quietly. 'I didn't get a choice.'

'No, well, that's the way of these things.'

'Is it? You're some bastards, all of you. Mad bastards, too.'

'That's entirely likely, Inspector. There is a war on, after all.'

The last words were knowing enough. There was no question that de Paor knew. It didn't help. It made Stefan angrier. He didn't know how many people were pulling the strings, but it was their game. He had no idea even what it was.

In the corner of the Moat Field, where he had raked the daggings and the dirty wool he had clipped from the ewes and the sour trimmings from their hooves, Stefan Gillespie watched the smoke rise from the fire he had lit. It was a still evening. The smoke trickled up in a thin, grey streak until it disappeared into the air. Nothing had happened since his return to Kilranelagh. He had heard nothing from Superintendent Gregory. Dessie MacMahon had telephoned, demanding to know what was going on. He had threatened to appear at the farm. Stefan said what he had been told to say. Nothing. He was allowed to say nothing. He felt what was happening at the other end of the line: hurt, confusion, anger. The word was out, whatever it was that Terry Gregory had let catch fire in Special Branch. Dessie would be defending him, Stefan knew that. It would be bollocks to Dessie, all of it; it would remain bollocks. But there would be those who thought differently. He had been an ill-fit ever since Gregory pulled him into Special Branch. If he had gained the trust of some, there were still those who were suspicious of him. He wasn't one of them. It was less about the fact that his family was German than that it was Protestant. It was a prejudice that didn't sit easily with the news that he was suspected of passing information to the IRA, but when a man couldn't be trusted in one way, well, it wasn't much of a stretch to find that he couldn't be trusted in another.

And then there was the death of Danny Skehan. Essential to the world Detective Superintendent Gregory created for his Special Branch officers was the control of information; whether that information was significant or insignificant, trivial or profound, didn't matter. His men, along with their informers, were there to give, often without knowing what they were giving; preferably without knowing what they were giving. Nothing came back unless there was a reason for it to do so. No one knew for sure that Chief Inspector Skehan had worked for the IRA inside the Branch, at least no one who wasn't doing the same thing. The circumstances of his death were obscure and Terry Gregory left it that way. The truth was known only by Ned Broy, the Garda Commissioner, and a few others. But everyone knew Stefan was there when the body was found. Now, with his trustworthiness suspect in ways that Gregory made sure were never quite specified, there were those who wondered what Stefan's involvement in Danny Skehan's death had been. There were those who didn't believe he had told the truth. And they were right, of course. He hadn't.

The telephone conversation with Dessie MacMahon ended in anger, and Stefan let it happen. Anger and hurt on Dessie's part offered the only way to shut him up. He let Dessie tell him that if he couldn't be trusted after all these years, well, Stefan could fuck himself. And that was that. David Gillespie hadn't used the same words to his son, but what he did say was close enough. He wanted an explanation too. Stefan would give him nothing but sour silence.

These were all thoughts in Stefan Gillespie's head, as his eyes ranged up and down the wisp of rising smoke in the Moat Field. They had been the repeated thoughts of his idle hours since returning home. He had thrown himself into work on the farm because it stopped the endless ordering and reordering of questions that led nowhere. Even the time he had with his son, Tom, wasn't as easy as he longed for it to be. Tom was nine now, and he could feel the coolness between his father and his grandfather. He could see, without comprehending, how hard his grandmother worked to stop that showing. He recognised, without quite realising it, that they were all pretending nothing was wrong. He pushed most of that aside, and most of what was left the business of being nine years old disposed of in its own way. His father was home, as he so rarely was now. That was something to hold on to and enjoy. And mostly, when Stefan and Tom were alone, making the moment matter was enough. But it couldn't work all the time. However hard Stefan tried to push aside the confusion and uncertainty, the fact was that he was waiting for something unknown to happen that he didn't want.

Stefan Gillespie looked up abruptly, conscious that someone was there. As he turned, he saw a man with dark hair and a carefully clipped moustache. The man was a few years older than him, but not many. He carried a rucksack. He leant on the wooden gate that led from the Moat Field into the narrow, wooded valley that marked the western edge of the townland and the Gillespies' farm.

'You look like a man with a lot to think about.'

'I am. A lot to think and not much sense to make of what I'm thinking.'

'Ah, now, didn't I always say philosophy would suit you, Stefan?'

Stefan laughed. 'Did you? I don't remember.'

'Probably I didn't then. Still, I do know that feeling.'

'Not heaven and earth I'm dreaming of, just fucking Dublin Castle.'

The man pushed open the gate and walked into the field.

'It's a long time, Stefan.'

They shook hands for a little longer than either was quite comfortable with. There was old affection and old friendship there that a handshake wasn't really enough to show. It was all that was available. They were pleased to see each other, but when they had absorbed that, there was a moment of silence.

'You should have let me know you were in Ireland, Peter.'

'It was a last-minute thing. I wanted a break from England. It's easy enough to get over here now. You can never be sure how long that will last.'

Another beat of silence. The war was there. It had to be.

'Where have you come from?'

The man gestured vaguely in the direction of the hills behind him.

'I've been walking.'

'You'd be hungry then.'

'I would be so, you're right. And thirsty.'

'Well, I'm sure we can do something about that.'

They began to walk across the field, back towards the farmhouse.

'The moustache is new.'

'Not so new. It was probably a mistake, but it doesn't rank very high on my list of mistakes. I live with the rest. I decided to live with that one. I wasn't sure I'd find you here. I thought you might be in Dublin. Spur of the moment—'

He stopped, smiling, slightly embarrassed by too many words.

'Well, I'm here, as you see.' Stefan spoke the words simply enough. They implied no more than they said, but there was a hesitation. He knew his friend felt it. 'So, when were you last home?' continued Stefan. 'Or is it still home?'

'A good five years. More, in fact, when I think about it.'

'Come on,' said Stefan, 'let's do something about that thirst.'

4

The New Line

In the kitchen at Kilranelagh, there was a smell that mixed sweetness and sourness and carried a kind of soft perfume. The room was hot; pans boiled on the stove. They had been boiling all afternoon, as Helena Gillespie made jelly from the fruit of the quince tree that grew behind the house. Where other fruit trees, the apples and pears and plums, had a small orchard below the farmhouse, the quince stood on its own, at the centre of a patch of rough grass. Helena had planted it almost twenty years earlier, when David left the Dublin Metropolitan Police and they moved to the farm outside Baltinglass. A quince tree had always been her mother's dream. It was a dream that came from the stories of a house in southern Germany, looking out at distant mountains that her mother barely remembered, perhaps only thought she remembered. The life that brought the family to Ireland, and to the streets around St Patrick's and the Liberties, offered no space for quinces, but when David Gillespie abandoned his career as a policeman, the first thing Helena wanted to do at Kilranelagh was plant a quince tree. Her mother had seen the quince growing, though she had not lived to see it bear fruit. It was an unpredictable tree. It didn't much like Irish summers. Some years it gave nothing; other years it might produce a dozen small, yellow fruits. The spring would see it weighed down with white blossom, but the wind and rain of May would usually strip it away before the fruit set. Yet every so often, when May was kind and the summer was dry, the great yellow pears would shine in their hundreds and pull the branches almost to the ground. This year had seen just that kind of summer. Helena couldn't keep up with the fruit, as it dropped and bruised and started to rot. She had spent a week at the stove, filling so many jars she had to collect more from her neighbours.

It was that sweet, perfumed scent that Stefan Gillespie and the new arrival, Peter Tully, walked into. The fluster that surrounded the surprise of the visit from this old friend of Stefan's was short-lived. Helena took charge and shooed them out into the yard to enjoy the last sun of the evening. David Gillespie followed with bottles of beer, and Tom gratefully abandoned his copybook; no one now cared whether he was doing his homework. David disappeared to dispose of a chicken that would soon be roasting in the Rayburn's oven, while Helena behaved as if a roast chicken was a very ordinary thing at Kilranelagh. And as Stefan and Peter talked, Tom demonstrated how well Jumble, the sheepdog puppy, could round up ducks. The ducks had other ideas and soon scattered into the orchard and the fields beyond. Jumble was shut in the barn and Tom set off to retrieve the birds. Helena looked out from the kitchen. Already the smell of the roast was mixing with the scent of the quinces.

'It will be a little while,' said Helena. 'I've this jam to finish. If I don't it will be set in the pan. Will you go and fetch me five big quinces for baking?'

Stefan and Peter collected the biggest, yellowest quinces and when they came back in, Peter, prompted by Stefan, made the right noises about the quince tree. He said he had never seen one with so much fruit, and since he didn't remember ever seeing one at all, that was true enough. David brought out more beer, and as the chicken cooked, Stefan and his friend went back out to the yard, where they sat under the great horse chestnut, heavy with its autumn colours.

A lot of years had passed since Peter Tully had visited Kilranelagh. Stefan knew him in the short time he spent at Trinity College. Peter was older, already teaching, and Stefan stayed only briefly before losing patience with a place in which he felt he didn't belong. He left to join the Irish Free State's new police force. But the friendship remained, fading only when Peter moved to England.

Kilranelagh was very different when Peter last visited the farm. Stefan was not long married; there was a baby. Maeve, Stefan's wife, was alive, and it seemed the conversation was always bright and always about the future. But now, as they all sat over the meal, it was natural that the past should feature prominently in the conversation of two friends who had not seen each other for a long time. It was a past fondly remembered. The future was something no one had much to say about, and even the present seemed hedged about by uncertainty and awkwardness. Partly, it was just the time that was in it. Peter Tully lived in Oxford, teaching at the university, and the war and England was a topic that arose inevitably. The news was not good. The invasion everyone expected had not happened, but the threat remained. Europe was in darkness. The bombing of British cities, especially London, was constant. Peter made light of it. He was on holiday; he was in Ireland to leave that behind. The adults felt his reluctance and read what it said. The details of ordinary life were easier to speak about. Only Tom was disappointed that the business of fighters and bombers should be so readily abandoned for the blackout and evacuated children and rationing.

At first Peter didn't notice how often the talk came back to the war and England whenever there was a lull, or how quickly his questions about the farm and about Stefan's work came to a dead end. And when he returned once more to the Gardaí and Stefan's life in Dublin, he finally registered his friend's unwillingness to answer and David Gillespie's barely suppressed irritation.

'You know how it is, Peter,' said Stefan, 'it's a job like any other job. You just get on with it, so, and most of the time that's all there is to say.'

'Except when there's nothing to say,' snapped David. 'Bugger all!' He picked up his glass and walked to the door. 'There's beer in the cupboard, if you want it.' He walked out to the yard, dragging the kitchen door shut behind him.

Helena got up. 'I'll see to the quinces. You'll have some, Peter?'

'I've no room, but I will anyway. They smell wonderful.'

Stefan went to the cupboard and came back with more beer.

'I take it that's a subject to avoid,' Peter said softly. 'You and the Gardaí. I'm sorry, I should have twigged earlier. Stupid. I just kept hammering away.'

Helena worked noisily at the stove. Stefan filled the glasses.

'There's a war on. Isn't that what they say over there?'

'It is,' Peter Tully laughed, 'about everything.'

'Same here.' Stefan raised his glass. 'Even as we pretend it's not there.'

The night was very clear as Stefan Gillespie and Peter Tully walked back to Kilranelagh from the pub at Talbotstown. It was Stefan who needed to escape from the farm kitchen; his friend was happy enough to stay. But the night air and some easier conversation had made them freer in what they said. The past still occupied them, but it was light and funny for the most part, and it became more comfortable and more personal. Even so, both men were aware that the present was being side-stepped. Peter Tully had not forgotten how awkward a subject Stefan's job as a detective in Dublin was. Stefan could not help but feel there was more to his friend's walk through old haunts in the Wicklow Mountains than air unchoked by war. And as they headed back under a bright moon, following the road that ran from Talbotstown to Woodfield Glen, the New Line, the effects of a little too much beer made them both probe harder.

'Wasn't there a woman?' said Stefan. They had been walking in silence. 'I remember one summer you disappeared, off into the hills. Walking again, of course. Always walking. It was meant to be about stone circles and hill forts and Irish legends, and making one fit the other. That was your big thing. You came to stay for a bit. I'd say the free accommodation was the attractive thing so.'

'Do you think I'd have put up with you if it cost money?'

'You were always the mean bastard, Peter.'

'And I'm still looking for a free meal and a bed for the night.'

'You didn't answer the question. Wasn't there a woman?'

Peter walked on, gazing the length of the road. 'There was.'

'And?'

'And there was a summer in the mountains when I didn't look at many hill forts and I forgot all the legends I was writing about.' He smiled. 'That's all. A pair of blue eyes from Aughrim, a summer of sunlight. Brenda was her name. At one time we thought . . . the kind of things you think at that age. It didn't work. Perhaps I didn't want it enough. The wrong time, wrong place.'

'It didn't last.'

'That's how these things are, isn't it?'

'I don't know. A lot of things don't last. Some of the best things . . .'

'Yes, some things should, Stefan. You and Maeve—'

'Come on!' Stefan cut Peter off. 'You haven't said anything about now. All I know is you sit around in some Oxford college. You're not married, so?'

'A couple of near misses.'

'Is that good or bad?'

'What?'

'Are you sorry about the misses?'

'Sometimes, I suppose. It's like I said, there is a list of mistakes and not all of them are as reversible as a moustache. Not all of them as insignificant.'

'Well, if something can be reversed, reverse it. I'd lose the moustache. Who knows, you might do better.' Stefan laughed. 'Could it be the problem?'

'I'm not so sure I'd be good at marriage.'

'Do you have to be?'

'I would. But what about you, Stefan? You never remarried?'

'That makes it sound deliberate. It hasn't happened, no.'

'A lot of years, but I imagine Maeve will still be a hard act to follow.'

'I don't think about it like that. I kind of assume it'll happen, eventually.'

'Eventually can be a long time.'

'I'd say the same to you, Peter. Things don't happen unless you let them happen. I know. Or did those blue eyes make more impact than you realised?'

Peter Tully didn't answer. Stefan's words were only a joke, but as they turned into the road to the farm, he knew his friend would not say any more.

They ambled on in silence. There was a light from the farmhouse at Woodfield Glen. There was the sound of cows, breathing and belching in the field beyond the ditch. Other noises echoed in the darkness. The scream of a vixen; the shriek of an owl; crashing bushes as they disturbed a deer drinking in the stream that ran through Kilranelagh and Woodfield Glen to the Slaney.

'So, are you on leave or what, Stefan?'

'Or what is close enough.'

'Sounds mysterious.'

'It's meant to be, officially that is. I'm here because of the job, but I am actually suspended. I don't know why and I'm not allowed to explain anything, not even to my father. I can't tell anybody about it. But you'll be back in England. You're close enough to nobody. Isn't it almost like a confessional?'

'Do you need forgiveness then?' Peter laughed.

'I don't know. If I could have it in advance, it might be useful.'

'Continue, my son. And don't worry, I'll go easy on the penance.'

They walked on in the darkness. Stefan tried to find the words that might explain what it was he was struggling with. He didn't even know what he was trying to say or why he needed to say it. The desire to tell someone what he wasn't supposed to tell anyone – it wasn't much more than that. But he couldn't find many words. It was either nothing or it was meaningless. He was doing a job that involved someone, any-one, somewhere, anywhere, believing he might be a German spy or an IRA informer or just a policeman with a big mouth, while the head of Special Branch paced Dublin Castle pretend-ing he was being investigated for something unspecified that he hadn't done, that would be forgotten whenever it suited. Stefan gave up. He found himself laughing.

'It doesn't matter. We have our own ways of seeing the war, and in Special Branch it's through the looking glass. What else would you expect?'

'Special Branch, I see,' said Peter Tully, more thoughtfully. Stefan had not mentioned where he worked. What he said explained little, but his friend seemed to understand that those words were explanation enough in themselves.

After a few moments, coming up the hill, Peter spoke. '"You are old, Father William, the young man said, And your hair is exceedingly white, And yet you incessantly stand on your head, Do you think, at your age, it is right?"'

Stefan laughed. 'There you are, I think you have it exactly.'

When Peter Tully had gone to bed, Stefan was settling down with a blanket on the sofa in the best room. He had given Peter his bed. He heard footsteps on the stairs and he recognised his father's tread. The door opened. David came in.

'I thought I'd better wait till he'd gone to bed.'

'What is it, Pa?'

'There was a telephone call from your man Gregory.'

David Gillespie spoke Superintendent Gregory's name as if he didn't much want it in his mouth. Stefan grinned. There were times he felt the same.

'Was there a message?'

'He said you may call him. He's there late.'

It hardly needed saying; Gregory was always there late.

'I'll call him now. Thanks, Pa.'

David looked at Stefan. He wanted to say more but there was no more to say. Despite everything, he knew it. He had known the same world once. He turned and climbed upstairs. As Stefan listened, he could feel the weariness in the older man's steps. Whatever else was wrong with his father, he wasn't helping. He walked into the hall. The Baltinglass operator put him through to Dublin Castle.

'Ah, Stevie, out on the piss? All right for some.'

'That's right, sir. It's all grand down here. The barracks in the town has the message I'm about to be kicked out of the Gardaí, so it's all going to plan.'

'That's the state of us, eh? A bunch of old women couldn't do worse.'

'Or better?'

'Ah, Stevie, I miss that sense of humour. Needs must, though.'

'So, is this your natural concern for me or is something happening?'

'You have a week, maybe less.' Terry Gregory's voice was sharper.

'And then?'

'London.'

'I see.'

'Once the arrangements are made, I'll be down to see you then.'

The sharper tone irritated Stefan even more than the lazy sarcasm.

'I appreciate you sorting out the arrangements personally, sir.'

'Not my arrangements, Inspector, the IRA's. Just be ready to go.'

5

Waverley

Edinburgh

When the train pulled in to Edinburgh Waverley Street, among the passengers getting off were a man and a woman who had spent a long morning and part of the afternoon travelling from Port Gordon in Banffshire, via Aberdeen. She was tall, in her mid-twenties. Her fair, fine hair was cut close now, shaped into her neck. Against her strong, sharp features, his were softer. He had hair of a nondescript brown colour, and although he was not much older than she was, it was receding at the temples and thinning on the crown of his head. It was neatly cut. He put a lot of time into getting it cut to hide what was now going missing. But the subterfuge was no longer successful. The two had travelled further than anyone else on the trains that had carried them down the greater part of eastern Scotland, from the Moray Firth, through Banffshire and Aberdeenshire, Kincardine, Angus and Fife, and across the Forth Bridge. The woman took in so much of the countryside on the way, that for a time she almost forgot why they were there. Mostly, the man slept, or tried to.

★

Vera Eriksen and Karl Drücke had started three days earlier, in Berlin. They left the Abwehr offices in Tirpitzuferstrasse and travelled by train to Copenhagen, then to Aalborg in Jutland by car. From Aalborg they flew to the east coast of Scotland in a Blohm & Voss BV 138. In the early hours of the morning the seaplane set them down in the Moray Firth, along the coast from Spey Bay, close to Port Gordon, a small fishing town with a railway line. The landing was well chosen: a deserted stretch of the coast with a low, shallow beach. The two Germans rowed a rubber dinghy into a quiet bay and came ashore. They pulled the boat into a spinney, where the man slashed it and rolled it into a ball. They buried it among trees and set off across fields towards the road to Port Gordon. There they would catch the early-morning train to Aberdeen, connecting to a mainline train to Edinburgh. From Edinburgh they would travel to London.

They were vulnerable on the road, however dark it was. It was an unusual journey to be making on foot at three o'clock in the morning. But at three in the morning they were unlikely to meet anyone. They had studied the Ordnance Survey maps endlessly. They knew the road and its twists and turns. They knew where there were trees and ditches to hide in. There would be time to hide too. The lights of any approaching vehicle would be visible long before they saw it.

The station at Port Gordon was a little way out of the town, and they had only two miles to walk. The woman would now call herself Vera Kennedy; that was the name on her identity card. Although she was German she had spent part of her childhood in Ireland, where her father worked as an engineer. She spoke English naturally and fluently; the hint of an Irish accent would serve her well. The man would call himself Karl Dirkse; he would be a Dutch refugee when required. His English carried a thick accent, but as a German growing up on the border with Holland, he spoke Dutch well enough to explain it. He had paid a visit to England in 1938, as an agricultural feed salesman, attempting to collect information about RAF airfields. He'd achieved nothing, but he had not been caught. It was enough. He had proved himself. Where Vera was cautious, Karl was confident. She was uncomfortable with his confidence. There were other things she was uncomfortable with. The man who had been the unquestioned leader of the mission had died only a week before, in a car accident. Now everything was rushed, incomplete, uncertain. Vera felt the loss of more than a leader. Erik Kramer had been her lover, too. He had not trusted Karl Drücke.

They had walked the route from the Scottish coast to the railway station at Port Gordon a dozen times in their heads, following the Ordnance map. Though the precise distance would depend on how close the seaplane got to the intended landing place, they had identified a building they could hide in till it was nearly time for the train. In fact, the plane hit the coast almost where they were aiming. They covered the distance in little more than two hours. They saw a rotting field gate and Karl untied the baling twine that held it shut. In the field, behind a hedge, was a low stone barn. He pointed at it with a theatrical flourish.

'Sanctuary, to the letter! A home from home!'

Vera walked through the gate. The barn she saw was strangely familiar. She recognised it had been a house once; single-storeyed, rough, un-mortared stone, a cabin as it would have been called in Ireland. It had the echo of family holidays in Kerry when she was in her teens. What had once been a thatched roof was corrugated iron. Now it was a cowshed. As they walked towards it, several heavy shapes appeared out of the darkness, lumbering forward. The cows stopped and peered lazily. It was as much interest as they could produce. They turned back into the gloom, mouths tugging idly at the grass. Vera pushed open the door. Karl followed her in. He looked as if he wanted congratulations.

'So, not bad at all.' In the absence of her words, he congratulated himself. 'We're exactly where we should be. Three hours to go before the train.' He put his case down and sat on the strawy floor, leaning back against the wall. He took out a cigarette. He spoke in German, seeing no reason not to. 'We shouldn't arrive at the station too early.' He grinned at her as he lit the cigarette. 'Don't worry, they're not German. Woodbines. They managed to get me some.'

'Speak no more German,' she said quietly. 'Get that in your head.'

The smile he gave was almost a sneer, but he continued in English.

'Do you think the cows might hear?'

'I think you need to ensure you don't make stupid mistakes.'

'You know what, it's a pleasure to work with you too, Vera.'

She ignored him. She didn't like him any more than she trusted him. She wasn't sure why she didn't trust him, but it was more than a mere echo of Erik Kramer. Partly it was an awareness that he wasn't good enough. He laughed too much. He didn't think enough. Those were reasons to be wary. She thought of the man whose grave she had stood beside only a week before, in Berlin. His death had foisted Karl Drücke on her at the last minute as an equal. He was a sorry substitute in every way; as an agent and in ways no one else knew about. He thought she liked him. He was too stupid even to see that she despised him.

She opened the small suitcase she carried and took out a dark wig, a torch, a small mirror. She propped the mirror on the ledge of a boarded-up window. She would have propped the torch up too; she tried. It wouldn't work.

'Hold this,' she said, annoyed that she had to ask Karl anything.

'I would say, "Jawohl", but you'd prefer, "Certainly, madam", yes?'

'Just point it at the mirror, Karl.'

He shrugged and did as she asked. She pushed her fair hair into a tight net and pulled on the wig. She adjusted it in the dim light until she was satisfied.

'I don't think they've got a picture of you, sweetie.'

'You can save the endearments until required. It could be some time.'

He laughed. 'Just making sure I don't make any stupid mistakes.'

It was almost light when they set off for the station, carrying their suitcases and wearing their raincoats buttoned and tied. Their clothes were still damp in places. Before they left the cowshed, Vera went through the contents of her suitcase, checking again for errors. The suitcase was her own; it had been bought in Clerys in Dublin. She took out a revolver and a box of cartridges.

'I'm burying these. You may do the same.'

'What?'

'If we'd been intercepted coming ashore, there might have been a point. We're here. There's no one to shoot. They won't do anything but identify us.'

'You don't think they'll mind my radio transmitter, then?'

She breathed in deeply, tightening her lips; no one had told her.

'Get rid of it.'

'You're joking.'

'I'm not joking at all. Dig a hole and bury it. It's about information, not making deliveries. Why the hell did they send it? It's not what we're here for.' She stopped. There was no need to say more. They would go their own way sooner or later. He would have nothing to do with her. He would not go to Ireland with her, as she and Erik Kramer would have gone, together. She would go alone. 'There are radios here. You should have nothing that identifies you.'

'If we don't make contact in London, we will need a transmitter.'

'Get rid of it, Karl.'

'You don't give me orders, sweetie. Fuck off. Good English, eh?'

At the station, they were lucky, though only Vera knew it. They were working from a pre-war timetable that was over a year old. There was no guarantee that trains would be running to those times now. But the train came, and despite the size of the town, there were enough people on the platform to make them less conspicuous than she had feared. She had told Karl to keep his mouth shut as far as possible throughout the journey. Their story, if questioned, was thin enough. They were a couple taking a few days holiday, and they would play at being too absorbed in one another to engage in speaking to others. The fact that Karl made a point of enjoying that, nuzzling into her neck as they sat at the station, only added determination to the decision she was beginning to make. The sooner she was rid of him the better. Even his accent asked questions and in this out-of-the-way corner they had no convincing explanation of where they had been, where they had come from. The most cursory check would draw a blank. The first necessity was to reach somewhere it was easier to become invisible.

However, the tickets were bought without difficulties, though as the station master looked at them through the ticket-office window, Vera was aware they were oddly dressed for a country railway station at six o'clock in the morning. They would fit in in Aberdeen and Edinburgh, but here they looked too much as if they were about to go to the office or out for the evening. Odder were the turn-ups of Karl Drücke's trousers, still wet from pulling the dinghy ashore. His coat couldn't cover that. They would dry soon enough, but the less anyone looked at them both the better. She had brushed away the cloying sand that he had not even noticed, but he carried no change of trousers. Instead, his case was almost entirely taken up with the unwanted transmitter. He was amused by her caution. He mistook it for fear. And he thought it was exactly what might be expected from a woman. In reality the only fear she had was him. On the platform at Port Gordon, she decided their ways would part sooner not later.

Karl slept on and off most of the way to Aberdeen, his head on Vera's shoulder. He had a useful facility for sleep if nothing else. She gazed out of the window, taking in the unfamiliar landscape, trying to avoid any eye contact that might lead to talking. The train became more crowded as it made its way south, and the busier it was the less ready people seemed to start conversations with strangers. But although Vera was never asleep herself, when anyone caught her attention and smiled, even in passing, she would pretend for a time that she was.

At Aberdeen the two Germans had an hour to wait for the train to Edinburgh. For that journey too they would remain together, playing the same parts — two tired and self-absorbed lovers, probably not married – for anyone who cared to look. It was a profile that went with war. Vera Eriksen understood that. War had changed the way people thought about such things very fast. She had observed it in Germany; it would be no different in Britain. Without thinking people registered demonstrations of intimacy and affection, snatched in the face of the new turmoil of life, with an understanding that offered immediate privacy.

In Edinburgh they would separate. Vera's unease with Karl was growing along with her dislike. He had none of the right instincts, and the right instincts meant survival. Erik Kramer had said that over and over again. You couldn't be taught those instincts. But you could exercise the proper caution. Something was already wrong. There had never been any question of bringing in a transmitter. The journey had been planned meticulously. Erik, who planned it with her, made initial survival the essence of the mission. Without surviving the first days, the most dangerous days, everything was futile. Once they found their way to a safe house, once they entered a network that could hide them, move them around, communicate with Germany, change their cover, it would be easier. He ensured they would bring nothing that identified them. Their clothes would be English or Irish; anything they carried would be English; their documents would withstand all but the closest scrutiny. They had to be able to get through the irregular checks and searches that could happen at any time. Once they reached London, they could disappear. Now there was not only a radio, Karl also refused to dump his revolver. Even the papers unsettled her. She took out the British identity card again. She had only been given it on the plane, and it was poor work. Most Germans would not have noticed, but she had grown up in Ireland. Each time the number one appeared, it was written with a slanted upstroke unknown in Britain. It could only have been written by a continental. It drew attention to itself. Even a very ordinary British policeman might look at it twice, if only to puzzle whether it was a one or a badly written seven. A seven on the card was not crossed, yet still, the more she looked the odder it seemed, as if it was waiting for just such a continental cross. On such things hung survival. Put them together with Karl Drücke's accent and it was enough reason to open his bag. And opening it would be all that was necessary.

Karl had insisted on walking round the station. She told him they should sit and wait for the train. When he returned she could smell alcohol on his breath. He was pleased with himself, too, as he flopped down beside her.

'Lot of soldiers about,' he said, as if stating the obvious meant something.

'Don't talk about it. No one else would, you know that.'

'Is there anything I can do right, sweetie?'

'You could do better than drinking at this time of the morning.'

'Don't fret, I didn't talk to anyone. Just listened.'

Vera ignored him, hearing an announcement. She got up.

'Come on, the train's in. As before, corner seat, by the window.'

They walked towards the train.

'In Edinburgh we separate and take different trains to London.'

'Oh, baby, just when I was starting to enjoy it.'

'We've travelled as a couple. If anyone has a reason to ask questions, that's how we'll be described. Being alone, we won't meet that description.'

'All right, who goes first?' he asked.

'I'll take the first train, Karl. You take one a few hours later.'

He accepted the decision with a shrug of sour indifference.

'You have the telephone number I gave you, to call in London.' Her voice was a whisper. 'You have memorised it? You did destroy the paper?'

'Yes and yes. Did anyone ever tell you, you're a pain in the bottom?'

'Arse!' She laughed. It was the first time he had made her laugh.

'What?'

'Backside will do, but bottom will not. And arse, for preference.'

54

Arriving at Edinburgh, they waited until the compartment was clear. Vera Eriksen nodded. Karl Drücke got up and moved to the door to the corridor.

'I shall see you in London, Vera.'

'Maybe, maybe not. It depends what they do with us.'

He hesitated, less confident than he wanted to appear.

'Yes,' was all he said, knowing that she could see the doubt.

He stepped into the corridor and out through the door to the platform. She turned to the window, looking out as he walked past, pulling on his hat. She unclipped her handbag and took out a compact. She opened it and dabbed some powder on her face. She stood up and took her suitcase down from the rack. Then she left the train and joined the trail of passengers. She walked slowly, easily, more comfortable now, keeping Karl Drücke's bobbing hat well ahead.

There was only half an hour until the next train to King's Cross. Vera Eriksen bought her ticket and walked through the station concourse. She got a newspaper at the Menzies kiosk and sat on a bench reading it, at least looking at it. Avoiding catching anyone's eye remained important, even in the busiest places. It was eye contact that made people remember faces, even faces they only saw briefly. Especially if it was a face you liked. It was something else Erik Kramer had told her. She remembered him saying it once when they were lying in bed, as he gazed down at her face. It wasn't long ago that she and Erik had lain in his bed for the last time. It was two days later that he died, after the party in Tirpitzuferstrasse that was meant to celebrate their departure for Britain. Driving home, he lost control of his car. He went into the River Spey. He was drunk, there was no doubt about that; she had told him not to drink so much herself. No one knew if he was unconscious as the car sank into the canal. But conscious or unconscious, he drowned. The fact that they were lovers had been their secret. It still was. If there had been even a hint of it, if Colonel

Lahousen or Colonel Ritter or Dr Veesenmayer had known, let alone Admiral Canaris, they would never have been allowed to work together. Two people in love, whatever the depths of their loyalty to the Führer and the Fatherland, could never be relied on to sacrifice one another if that became necessary. But they had no doubts about their work. They were strong enough.

As Vera looked up again, through the crowds in the station concourse, she picked out Karl's hat. Even the way he walked irritated her; a kind of self-satisfied jauntiness. She half smiled; she would have no problem sacrificing him. The smile faded as she continued to watch. It went deeper than irritation. There were things she had to do – things the men from the Abwehr had not asked her to do. She had other instructions; Erik Kramer had left them to her, it was her inheritance. Those instructions didn't come from Lahousen or Ritter or Veesenmayer. They came from the Nazi Party's own Intelligence Service, the SD. Her work was in Ireland, but only part of it was what the Abwehr had sent her there to do. There would come a time she might have to leave the Abwehr behind to fulfil what Erik Kramer didn't live to fulfil. He had made her part of it; now she was all of it. She didn't know if she could do it. She had only what he told her, only the aim not the means. But she had to try. And she had to shake off anything that would put it at risk. Karl Drücke could do that. If he didn't get them caught, she might end up tied to him. He seemed to be stupid, but how stupid was he really? He was an Abwehr man through and through. Beneath the simpering grin and bad jokes, she had felt he was watching her.

Karl's hat was still bobbing across the station. Then he was in the open, on his own. He stopped at a doorway and pushed it open. Vera strained her eyes. She could just read the sign: *Left Luggage*. She stood up, folding the newspaper, slowly and carefully. She couldn't believe what he was doing. He had several hours to wait for his train and he was leaving his case in the left luggage office. It contained a radio transmitter and a revolver. It was far more reckless than she expected, even of him. The only thing to do with a bag that announced exactly who and what you were was to keep it with you at all times.

She maintained her gaze across the concourse, unmoving, for a full five minutes, waiting for Karl to come out, until she realised she was in danger of doing what she should never do, drawing attention to herself. There was a slightly irritable, 'Excuse me.' She was blocking people trying to walk past. She moved on quickly, looking up at the platform indicator, but keeping an eye on the door Karl Drücke had entered till he emerged minus his suitcase. He began to wander back the way he had come, his hands in his pockets. It looked like he was whistling. She lost him for a moment in a group of people coming off a train, but when she picked him out again, the next door he reached was the station buffet. He went inside. For a drink, of course. For several, she thought.

Vera Eriksen had twenty minutes before her train left. She walked slowly across the station, making her decision. She reached a telephone box. She went into the kiosk and picked up the receiver. She asked for a number in London, and then put the coins into the box. She had made sure she had coins in Berlin. She needed a quick connection. She was lucky; the call went through in only a few minutes. She pushed the button and the coins clattered down noisily.

'Hello, I'm calling you about some tickets. For the opera.'

'And which opera would that be, madam?'

'*The Magic Flute.*'

'And did you have a date in mind?'

'Any day in October, but not a Friday and not the fifteenth.'

'Mrs Wright isn't here, but if you want to leave a message, do.'

'Yes. Would you tell her I will be calling her on another number? I have had problems with this one and I shall not be using it again. I hope that's clear.'

'Very clear.'

The telephone went dead. She hung up. The message that had been delivered was that the number was no longer safe. She had another. Karl didn't. It wouldn't matter. She picked up the phone and dialled 999. The operator asked what service she needed, she said police. She spoke in her most English accent.

'I know this is very silly, but they tell us if we are at all suspicious of anyone, to say something. I don't want to cause trouble. I know it will be nothing. But there was a man in the left luggage office at Waverley Station, and he had a German accent. I'm sure it was German. He seemed very nervous. I didn't really think anything, even then, but I have just seen him again, in the station buffet, buying drinks for soldiers, and asking all sorts of questions—'

Vera put the receiver back and left the box. When she got on the train to London, she had been into the Ladies and had shut herself in a cubicle. She removed her wig and stuffed it into her pocket. She emerged fair-haired. She would find a time, in the WC on the train, to lose the wig through the window.

When Karl Drücke returned to the left luggage office he was even jauntier than before. He had drunk several whiskies, feeling it was something he should do to fit in. He was, however briefly, in Scotland. Two police officers awaited him. They had not opened his case, though they had it in front of them. They had done him the courtesy of waiting. They asked him, politely, if he would mind opening the suitcase. He took a deep breath and did so. As he lifted the lid he reached for the revolver under a clean shirt and a pair of underpants. But he left it where it was. One of the policemen held a gun now. Vera was right about that anyway. A revolver was no use here. They had him; that was the end of it.

6

The Mass Rock

Wicklow

It was still early as Stefan Gillespie and his father cycled eastwards, up towards the mountains, with the high, square length of Keadeen keeping them company most of the way. It was a bright day, but cold for October, and there was still a whisper of mist burning off as they came out of Rathdangan on the Military Road to reach the sheep sale at Rathcoyle. It wasn't a long ride, but it suited them that the cycling was uphill some of the way; they didn't need to speak.

Preparations for putting the rams out with the ewes had continued for several days after Peter Tully left the farm to continue his walk and to return to England. It was when Stefan came to the rams that he saw how bad things had become. The sheep at Kilranelagh made no claims to purity. They were mostly the offspring of Wicklow Cheviots, some bred on the farm and some bought in from time to time from the mountain sheepmen. There was a Cheviot ram for breeding ewes and two Suffolk rams for the lambs that produced whatever income was to be had from meat. The Suffolks were the problem, and it was the same problem again: foot rot. Only when Stefan came to look at them did he realise how bad they were. One, with careful trimming and

60

attention, would be all right in a few weeks. But it would be longer, too long, even with money spent on veterinary help, before the best ram could put enough weight on his back legs to do his job. He was the heaviest sheep on the farm and difficult at the best of times, but the more painful his hoofs became, the harder he was to control. David drove him through the footbaths but the rot had gone too deep. It wasn't easy for Stefan to grasp that his father had let this happen. The loss of the sheepdog, Tess, at the end of the summer had made the situation worse, but David could have bought an older dog as well as the new puppy. Somehow he didn't act, that was all. But it was done. The ram would not work that year. There was no point arguing about it, though father and son did. David defended himself against failures he would never have tolerated in anyone else. He defended himself too often, even when Stefan said nothing. But wherever he directed his anger, it was inside that David felt it. Each time an argument flared he would, eventually, walk away, disappearing into the fields and woods and returning with nothing to say. Stefan blamed himself for ignoring what he had already seen. His mother blamed herself for silence. Neither had wanted to see that David was growing old.

'It's my fault for not saying anything,' said Helena.

'How can it be your fault, Ma?'

'Because I didn't want to know it. But I'm here. I see it every day.'

'I've got eyes myself,' said Stefan. 'I've done the same, haven't I?'

'He doesn't have the strength, Stefan. He gets tired. But it's not only that. It's more . . .' She stopped. 'He doesn't see things, not the way he did. When he does, he forgets. He forgets a lot now. I think he knows that's happening, and he finds ways to hide it. I see lists in his pockets, lists of everything, just everyday ordinary things to do. Sometimes I have to remind him to go and milk the cows. I make a joke of it. But there are days he has forgotten. And it's getting worse.'

For now, Stefan and David did what they could for the ram. He would recover, but not till too late. To meet spring lambing there had to be a new ram.

It was a journey, as well as an expense, that should not have been necessary, but the sheep sale seemed to bring David Gillespie out of himself, and for that morning, with his own concerns ticking in his head, Stefan felt it was doing the same for him too. The noise of the ewes, crowded into the makeshift hurdles and gates that made up the pens, was something old and comfortable. The sounds and smells were memories of his teenage years. He saw people he had not spoken to in a long time, farmers he had known when they were boys, men from the mountains he had long forgotten but who remembered him. He moved along from pen to pen with the crowd, as the sheep were sold, hearing the auctioneer's rattle of prices, barely comprehensible and utterly familiar. And they found the ram they wanted. Stefan let his father make the decision, but it was the decision he would have made himself. He watched David in the pen, examining the ram's teeth, holding him against the side of the pen as he looked at his hooves. There was laughter and there was energy again, even strength. There was sharpness too, in the deal David Gillespie made for the ram, and the banter that went back and forth between him and dozens of old friends.

It was as his father was making arrangements for the haulier to bring the new ram to Kilranelagh that Stefan Gillespie saw a skinny, pale youth, seventeen or eighteen, staring at him with a fixed, anxious expression. With him was another man, older certainly, but how much older it was difficult to say. The older man had a round, white face and a crooked, open mouth, open in a way that meant it somehow never closed. It was a strange, moonlike face. Stefan remembered him well. As a child he had, along with everyone else, mocked and ridiculed the man, and then, just as often, run from him in terror.

It was the youth who spoke.

'Mr Gillespie, will you come, so?'

Stefan could feel the anxiety. It wasn't distress, it was colder.

'Is something wrong?'

The older man stuttered, incoherently at first.

'D-d-d-down, d-d-d-down, by – ri-ri-ri—'

'The river.' The younger man finished the sentence. 'You need to come.'

The man with the twisted face tugged at Stefan's arm, pulling him away.

'You know me, y-y-you know me. D-d-dog found him, so.'

He pointed at a mud-spattered Jack Russell on a length of string.

'I know you, Jimmy Page,' said Stefan gently. 'What is all this?'

'And q-q-quiet, so. Need the Guards.' Jimmy screwed up his face and tried to speak. For some seconds there was a strangled, tight groan. 'D-d-dead!'

'Not so loud!' The youth nudged him and turned to Stefan. 'He's dead.'

'F-f-f-fucking dead!'

'What?'

'You're a Guard, aren't you?' hissed the youth. 'You may come, now!'

The moonfaced man struggled to speak again. His voice was a strange combination of a whisper and a roar. Stefan could see that he was crying now.

'All right, I'm coming. Tell me what's happened.'

They set off across the field. The young man walking ahead and Jimmy Page limping, his body leaning to one side, intermittently tugging at Stefan.

'B-b-blood, Mr G-G-Gillespie. His f-f-fucking face.'

'Where are you going?' The voice was David Gillespie's.

'I don't know,' shouted Stefan, turning back and shrugging.

'You in a hurry?' laughed his father.

Stefan stopped, waiting for David. Jimmy limped on, following as fast as he could after the younger man. He paused, beckoning back furiously to Stefan.

'There's something wrong, Pa.'

'What do you mean?'

Stefan pointed. 'Jimmy Page. I don't know who the other one is.'

'What do they want?'

'They want a Guard. I don't know why, but Jimmy's afraid.'

Across the field from where the sale was still in progress, a gate led into a narrow, grassy lane, bordered by the tumbled stones of long-broken walls. It fell steeply downhill and twisted through a scrubby wood of beech and alder. It turned sharply at the bottom. There was a thin glimmer of light, snaking through the trees. Jimmy and the youth, still walking ahead, had reached the River Derreen, little more than a stream here, still fresh from the mountain slopes of Lugnaquilla. The two men disappeared among the trees. The Jack Russell was barking excitedly, angrily. Stefan and his father walked to the river, following the noise. They had not gone far when the trees opened up into a small clearing. At the centre of it, a short way from the stream, was a great boulder, almost square, covered in lichen. Stefan knew it, though he not seen it since a summer day in his childhood, when he had followed the Derreen from Rathdangan, up towards Lugnaquilla. It was a Mass Rock. There were several in the area, some remembered, some forgotten. In the days when the Catholic Church was proscribed, when there were no churches and supposedly no priests, the Mass Rocks, hidden away in secret places, were the only churches of the people.

The youth and the moonfaced man stood between the Mass Rock and the stream. Something lay in a grey heap, half in the water and half out of it. Jimmy held the dog by the tight string. It was barking, snarling, struggling towards the grey heap of clothing. The young man turned to Stefan as he gazed down.

'It's my father.'

The anxiety in his face had gone. The words felt distant, almost matter-of-fact. They did not seem to be addressed to Stefan. The youth's eyes showed only puzzlement now. The dead man was big and heavy-set. His face was turned up to the canopy of trees, still wet where he had been dragged from the pool. The features of his face were hard to see. It was a pulp of black and red. Next to the body, close by the pool's edge, there was a twelve-bore shotgun.

'It's Joe Coogan.' The voice, behind Stefan, was David Gillespie's.

Stefan Gillespie crouched, looking at the body intently. He had a name: Joe Coogan. He now knew the youth was the man's son, Paul. The name may have meant something once, but what it meant was no more than a vague familiarity. A farmer, beyond Rathdangan. It was a memory of sorts. He had probably seen him before. He might have spoken to him; in a pub, at the mart, at the barracks when he was stationed in Baltinglass. But he didn't know the man. He had no picture in his head to set beside the mess that was Coogan's face. He turned to his father.

'You knew him then, Pa?'

David said nothing. He was also staring down at the bloodied face.

'Did you know him?'

David nodded, as if he only half heard.

'He farmed here?'

David Gillespie turned, slowly, as if pulling himself back from something, somewhere, that was deep in his head. He

65

looked a long way off. It was an odd reaction, thought Stefan. His father was not a squeamish man, even if he had been away from the police for a long time. David nodded again. Stefan registered that his father seemed more shocked than he might have expected.

'You all right, Pa?'

'I knew him, yes. Not very well. Hardly at all . . .'

He spoke the last words as if there was something unfinished about them.

Stefan looked back at the other two men.

'Is this your land, Paul?'

'Across the river is.' The youth pointed. 'Daddy's fields come down to here.'

'So how did you find him?'

'The dog did. I was walking with Jimmy.'

'The d-d-dog,' echoed Jimmy. 'The d-d-d-'

The dog had been silent for several minutes. It began to bark again.

'Can you shut him up, Jimmy?' said Stefan.

Jimmy's mouth opened wider. He looked surprised and shook his head.

'Take him away then. Tie him up in the trees. Do something with him!'

'He's o-o-only b-b-barking, Mr G-G-G... He d-d-doesn't like it!'

'I'd say he likes it too much. For fuck's sake, Jimmy. Just do it!'

Jimmy Page glared at Stefan then pulled the Jack Russell away.

'When did you see your father this morning, Paul?'

'I didn't.'

'He was out?'

'I'm not living at home. We don't have much to do with each other.'

The words were spoken with little emotion. It was simply a fact.

Stefan got up slowly, looking at the ground, the body, the shotgun. He made a detour to the side of the Mass Rock, treading very carefully. He had not gone right up to the body. He stopped now, taking in the bare patch of earth and grass between the rock and the Derreen. He gazed at the mud around the river's edge, where the body had been dragged back from the water, towards the rock.

'How far was he in the river?'

'Just his head and his shoulders.'

Stefan was still staring down at the ground.

'Would you step back, Paul, beyond the rock. Don't go in front.'

The youth shrugged and did as he was asked. Jimmy Page was returning, disgruntled. The Jack Russell was still barking in the trees, but at some distance.

'Jimmy, just stay there! I don't want anyone else walking here.'

Stefan looked at his father. David nodded, understanding.

'You two have been all over this, I suppose?' Stefan looked from Jimmy Page to Paul Coogan, gesturing at the muddy ground between river and rock.

'We'd to get the d-d-dog off him. He f-f-found Joe.'

'We had to pull him out,' said Coogan's son.

'How was he lying when you found him?'

'Upside down.'

'His face was in the water?'

'Yes.'

'And the gun?'

'Where it is now, I'd say.' Paul Coogan looked at Jimmy.

'No, b-b-by him. I p-p-pulled it out the water, Mr G-G-Gillespie.'

Stefan crouched down again, looking at the body, at the

river's edge, the Mass Rock, the gun. It was a mess. It was already very hard to read it.

'Pa, will you cycle into Rathdangan and phone the Guards in Kiltegan? I'd better stay here. This has all been disturbed enough already. We'd better try and make sure it doesn't get any worse. Have you told anyone else, you two?'

Jimmy Page and Paul Coogan glanced at each other awkwardly and then shook their heads decisively. Stefan was not convinced, especially by Jimmy.

'I'm on my way,' said David, heading back the way they had come.

Stefan took out a cigarette and followed his own footsteps carefully back to where Jimmy and Paul were standing. The Jack Russell still barked angrily.

'You'll have to stay. The Guards will need to talk to you.'

Jimmy Page looked uncomfortable, but he always did. Stefan smiled, lighting the cigarette. Joe Coogan's son leant against the other side of the Mass Rock. He seemed calm now. Any signs of anxiety had long gone from his face. Yet even calm wasn't the right word, Stefan thought. Untroubled was closer.

'So tell me again, what happened? Were you looking for him?'

'Jimmy was, after a fashion. He thought Daddy would be at the sale.'

'I do be w-w-working for J J Joe. He w-w wasn't at the farm, I was w-w-walking up to Rathcoyle, over the r-r-river – the d-d-dog ran – it was the d-d-d-'

'The dog,' said Paul Coogan, 'it was the dog! He's got it, Jimmy.'

Stefan was surprised to see that Coogan's son was holding back a smile.

'So where did you come from, Paul?'

'I was putting up pens at the sale. Jimmy was in a state about

68

the fucking dog. I came down to help him find the bugger. He's always losing it, aren't you, Jimmy? Even your dog doesn't like you! We found the dog, so. And we found . . .'

Jimmy was sniggering at the joke about his dog.

Stefan added another word to Paul Coogan's reactions: indifference.

'I n-n-never thought Joe . . .' Jimmy crossed himself. 'G-God save him.'

'You never thought what, Jimmy?'

'It was bad, w-w-worse and w-w-worse. M-m-money. It was the b-b-bank, the feckers. Wanted the farm. M-m-money. They had him. The f-feckers!'

'What do you mean?'

'No way out. He s-s-said that. He said only one w-w-way out.'

Jimmy pointed at the shotgun.

'He'd been saying that for fecking years.' Paul Coogan's words could have meant he was agreeing with Jimmy or simply that he couldn't care less.

'So when did you see him last, Jimmy?' asked Stefan.

'Yesterday. I went home at f-f-four – t-t-teatime.'

'Dad was in the shite,' said Paul Coogan. 'That's no secret.'

'Out of the sh-sh-shite now, J-J-Joe.' Jimmy Page looked back at the body and again he crossed himself. 'And m-m-maybe for the best, so.'

Stefan Gillespie looked at the twisted face, the dribbling mouth. There were tears in Jimmy's eyes. He was mouthing a Hail Mary. Stefan could pick out the words. Pray for us sinners, now and at the hour of our death. He could not read the expression. There was sorrow, yes, but there was something else. He felt as if he wouldn't have been surprised, when the mumbled prayer ended, to see the man spit with contempt. As for Joe Coogan's son, he was smoking a cigarette now. Stefan had the impression there would be no Hail Marys from him.

69

There was something like conflict in Jimmy's face, or fear. In Paul Coogan's there was nothing. There was no reason why any of this should mean anything. These were small things. It was a habit of Stefan's to remember small things. Sometimes, when all the big things had been noted, investigated, explained and filed away, the small things that didn't mean much were still left.

By the time his father returned from Rathdangan, Stefan Gillespie's doubts about what Paul Coogan and especially Jimmy Page might have blurted out on their way through the crowd at the sheep sale proved more than justified. A dozen people had already appeared along the path through the trees and the word would spread now. Stefan had pushed them back as far as he could, detailing Paul and Jimmy to keep them at bay, until David arrived to do a better job of it. The talk was low and half-whispered. The Jack Russell, still tied to a tree, had lost interest and was asleep. There was the stillness that went with the observation of death, like murmuring at Mass. And the number of onlookers was growing. They came in twos and threes; mostly men from the sheep sale, with a scattering of women and children. It was easy to keep them back once they had come close enough to get a glimpse of the body, but it was impossible to stop the disruption to the approaches to the Mass Rock, either through the woods or across the Derreen from Joe Coogan's fields on the other side. With time to think, Stefan assumed that was the way the farmer had reached the Mass Rock, through his own land, over the little river to the place where he died.

The low hum of rumour and conjecture among the trees was all about the state of Joe Coogan's life and his financial troubles. It seemed it was a state he had chosen to extract himself from. That story was told quickly. If people were shocked by the conclusion that he had taken his own life, in a way that was not unfamiliar to farmers in the hills of Wicklow, they did not linger over their surprise. It made sense of what they knew, and what was in front of them all.

Standing watch over the body, Stefan felt how subdued it all was. There was little feeling of distress for a neighbour and friend. And while the onlookers offered Paul Coogan nods of condolence as they caught his eye, no one engaged him in conversation. He sat on a fallen tree, looking away from his father's body, smoking one cigarette after another. But it was the body that disturbed Stefan; the body, the gun and the muddy ground, on both sides of the river. There were questions to ask, and where there were questions everything was important. The ground was as important as the gun, maybe more so. It had been badly churned up, but he kept looking, unsure why. Something troubled him.

As David Gillespie marshalled the onlookers, Stefan turned round. He had hardly spoken to his father since his return, but several times, glancing across the clearing, he saw the same, slightly distant look on David's face that had been there when they first reached Joe Coogan's body. He assumed that in some way his father knew Coogan better than he said, or knew something about him.

Half an hour had passed before the Guards arrived from Kiltegan. Stefan recognised the brash voice before he saw Garda Sergeant Basil Donegan.

'What the feck is this circus all about? Have you got no homes!'

The stout figure and the thick, moustached face came into view.

'Will you get the fuck out of here? Have you no decency at all!'

No one even attempted to move. It was more interesting now.

Trailing behind Sergeant Donegan came the slight figure of a younger Guard. Stefan didn't recognise him, but he was probably not long out of training in the Phoenix Park. He looked self-important and uncertain, all at once. As the sergeant stopped, gazing coldly and calmly at the body, the young Guard crossed himself and bowed his head. The sergeant sniffed his disapproval.

'You may save the prayers for the priest. Every man to his job.'

Sergeant Donegan gave a curt nod as he passed David Gillespie.

'You'll know him well enough, Basil,' was David's only reply.

Donegan nodded. He walked past Stefan without a word.

'He's been dead a while,' said Stefan. 'I don't just mean the rigor mortis. First glance says longer than that. He was in the river, face down, when they found him. They pulled him out and they've trampled about a good bit. The gun's been moved. It was in the water. No one's touched anything since then.'

The sergeant turned back, saying nothing, but looking hard at Stefan.

'I think the ground around the rock needs a good look at, Basil, and the other side of the river. The farm's that side, so it's probably how he came down here.'

'You think so, do you, Inspector? Well, thank you for that.'

The tone was cold, even hostile, but Stefan didn't hear it immediately. He heard enough to speak more carefully.

'There's already an assumption, Sergeant . . . that he shot himself.' Stefan shrugged. 'That's probably got to Baltinglass by now. I'm not saying it's wrong. But a few things don't look right – well, I do know it's early days—'

'If I need a detective, I'll get one. You're a witness, that's all.'

'Well, as a witness you might want to know what I've seen,

72

Sergeant. I'd wonder how some of the shot managed to take off a bit of the back of his head.' Stefan was puzzled by Basil Donegan's tone. He wasn't interfering. He knew the man. But the words weren't well chosen. Sergeant Donegan's lips tightened.

'If we need you, Inspector Gillespie, we know where you are. You'll be handy enough after all. We certainly won't have to go to Dublin Castle to find you, eh? I don't think your current situation allows you to interfere in Garda business. Well, that's what we've all heard. Or would I be wrong about that?'

'I'm hardly interfering, Sergeant. There's a dead man here.'

'Thank you for reporting it. You can go. You're not wanted.'

'And what the fuck is that supposed to mean?'

'The word is you'll be out on your ear pretty soon, Gillespie, that's if they don't lock you up. We're not so grand down here as to be told what you've been up to, but the little birdies say you'd a habit of talking to people you shouldn't. The kind of people who might take a lot of pleasure in shooting a Guard or two. I won't say it didn't come as a surprise. I'd never have thought it of you, but then you always were a bit too good for the rest of us, so. Not now, though, eh?'

Donegan walked on, across the area Stefan had tried to preserve. He stood over Joe Coogan's body and bent to pick up the shotgun. He opened the breach and sniffed at it, then pulled out a spent cartridge. He turned to the young Guard who looked profoundly impressed by his sergeant's authority.

'Horan, go up to the road and see if that fecking doctor's here yet!'

As the Garda scurried away, Donegan looked back at Stefan.

'If you didn't get the message, Gillespie, I told you to fuck off.'

Stefan Gillespie turned round and walked away, his eyes fixed ahead. He was watched intently by the onlookers in the woods, now finding even more in the day's events than a dead body might have led them to expect. Stefan said nothing to his father as he passed him. David looked at Basil Donegan for a long moment, saying nothing either, then he followed his son through the trees.

7

The Haggart

The haggart was a small field beside the road, just below the farmyard at Kilranelagh. It had been planted as an orchard when Stefan was a child and his grandparents were still alive. He had watched it grow as he had grown, but now it had become something else at the farm that a lack of care was taking its toll on, something else he had not noticed until recently. There was disease in some of the apple trees that should have been cut out long ago. The plums and the pears had not been pruned in three seasons; now they were all wood and leaf; there had been barely any fruit this year. None of it was urgent in the way the problems with the sheep were, but as the leaves were falling now, Stefan decided to spend a day in the haggart, bringing in the crop there was, cutting out diseased wood and pruning back the bushy growth so that there would be more fruit next year. He tackled it with determination, but his real reason for being there was to escape the house and his father's now open anger and frustration. It had not worked. David had followed him down into the orchard.

'I've put up with this long enough. You may tell me what's going on?'

Stefan worked steadily, his eyes on the tree he was pruning.

'I don't know what's going on.'

'That's bollocks, isn't it?'

'You're probably right, Pa. Bollocks is altogether the word.'

'You're suspended. They know all about it in the barracks in town, in Kiltegan too, and you say nothing. For what? They didn't give you a reason?'

'The reason is an investigation. It won't come to anything.'

'What won't come to anything?'

'It's nothing,' said Stefan quietly.

'That's not what Basil Donegan thinks. He's saying you're some kind of informer. What else did he mean but the IRA? And what sort of shite is that?'

Stefan pushed a stepladder closer into a pear tree. He climbed up it.

'He never liked me much when I was stationed in Baltinglass. You always said he was an arsehole. Why would he waste the chance to prove it?'

'In the arsehole stakes, he's got nothing on you, Stefan.'

Stefan laughed, but he still looked up into the pear tree, sawing a branch. There was silence between father and son. Stefan tried to turn the conversation.

'Did you hear any more about Joe Coogan?'

'Not much. They all say he shot himself. That's the story.'

'Yes,' said Stefan. He looked down. 'You knew him. I mean, you knew him better than you said, isn't that right? You didn't look very easy up there.'

'I didn't know him. I hardly knew him at all. But once . . . well, a long time ago . . . he helped me. I don't know why. We never spoke about it again. If I ever saw him, we'd do no more than talk about the weather or the price of cattle. And that wasn't often. I owed him a lot. I don't even know how much.'

Stefan waited for his father to say more, but he didn't.

'He's dead,' said David abruptly. 'For the rest, it was in another time.'

'Do you know if Donegan had any detectives up there?'

'I haven't heard. Why would he? Doesn't it seem simple enough?'

'I don't know, Pa.'

'Why not?'

'I'm not sure he shot himself. I'm not sure he was there on his own.'

'Then you need to say so.'

'Who to? Basil Donegan?'

'I don't know. I'm not sure I care much. I'm more interested in what Basil Donegan had to say about you. You think I'm supposed to forget that?'

Stefan laughed. 'It was worth a try, Pa.' He began sawing another branch.

'He's not making it up, Stefan. There's word out about why you've been suspended, why you're here. If none of it's true, why don't you say so? These things don't stay in Dublin Castle for long, you know that, and they're always going to find their way home. So answer it! The IRA my arse! I know better than that. So should the lot of them. Any fool knows better, for God's sake.'

'Basil Donegan's not just any fool, Pa.' Stefan smiled.

'Is that it? After all this, you're still going to make a joke about it?'

As a branch fell to the ground, Stefan climbed down the ladder.

'All right, it's not a joke, but the investigation is, in a way.'

'They've got you in the right place, haven't they, Stefan, whatever you say. You're a real Special Branch man now. You speak but nothing comes out. Round and round, saying the words and telling me nothing. Is that the answer?'

Stefan stopped working. He had to say something now.

'The suspension is about nothing because there is nothing, nothing real. You know that. It's a reason for me to be investigated.

That's the beginning and the end. Whatever the reason, when it suits them I'll find out. Does that help?'

'Do you think it should?'

'No, Pa.' Stefan shrugged. 'But it's the best I can give you.'

'So, you're an IRA man, is that it? Is that the game?'

'Terry Gregory didn't give me a title, Pa.'

'I suppose you have to talk to me as if it doesn't matter. But that's not it at all, is it? You don't think it's funny either, I do know that. Why? Why you?'

'I'm too German for my own good, that's the problem.'

'What?'

'You see, I know Germany's going to win the war. All my sympathies are with the Reich. That's my line, then. I'm not so much on the side of the IRA as on the side of my old ancestral home. A bit of information found its way out of Special Branch that helped a German agent or two avoid arrest. Nothing big. I'm not planting bombs. But if you have a man like me in the Branch – with a Nazi family across the North Sea – where else would you look for an informer?'

'And that's it?'

'That's it.'

'And what does it mean? Why is it happening?'

Stefan picked up the stepladder and moved it to a plum tree by the ditch that bordered the road. An unseen car passed along the road on the other side.

David Gillespie was silent. He knew there was more. None of this expressed the full extent of his son's knowledge; Stefan had simply reached the limit of what he was prepared to say. It took David back twenty years, to the cellars of the Dublin Metropolitan Police HQ and the office he had sat in, surrounded by the archives and files that were a British weapon in the War of Independence being fought in the streets of Dublin and across the whole country. He remembered the detectives who came and went and the British Intelligence officers from Dublin Castle who came and went with them. He remembered men who came to give information or sell it. He remembered the faces of some of the men who were beaten in the cells along the corridor from his office. Some of those men talked and some didn't. When they didn't they went to Dublin Castle, where the beatings were harder and not every man came out alive. That was the place he had walked away from in 1921, but he heard now, in his son's words, an echo of it, an echo of conversations between the detectives he worked with, as he collated their interrogations, cross-referenced the details of informers and filled in the forms that recorded their successes and failures. Behind everything, always, was their deep faith in lies and deception.

Stefan Gillespie and his father looked round at the same time. The shrill, urgent yapping of Jumble was followed by the sound of a car. Looking towards the house, they saw a black Ford pulling up. It was the car that had passed along the road, on the other side of the ditch, only moments before. Stefan knew who it was before the door opened and Superintendent Terry Gregory got out.

Terry Gregory and Stefan Gillespie walked away from the house, across the road and into the fields that led towards Kilranelagh Hill. Gregory was not a man with much appetite for the countryside. It was no more than somewhere to say what he had to say. He had made what small talk he needed to with Helena Gillespie, over a cup of tea, but he abandoned the attempt to do the same with Stefan's father when the greeting he brought from the Garda Commissioner, who had once worked alongside David in the Dublin Metropolitan Police, was met with the observation that Ned Broy had come a very long way for a gobshite. The superintendent laughed and said it was true of most senior officers, himself included. David Gillespie didn't disagree. When Gregory told him, as a kind of confidential aside, that any problems Stefan might have at the moment shouldn't be taken too seriously, and they would be resolved in time, he was well aware that the old DMP man felt the word gobshite was well chosen. But as Stefan Gillespie and his boss walked from the house, the niceties were over.

'You go in two days.'

'And where exactly?'

'When you get to London, you go to Camden. There'll be somewhere for you to stay and a job for you to do. That's it, apart from keeping your eyes and ears open. You know how to do that. Nothing specific. Except sniffing the air.'

'That sounds very specific to me. What am I looking for?'

'You know Camden?'

'Not really, apart from where it is. I know bits of London, but not that.'

'Ah, Stevie, you're altogether the wrong sort of Irishman, that's always been your problem. You won't be able to move for your fellow countrymen, but you won't bump into too many Protestants. And thank God for that, says I. Still, I'm confident the Bedford Arms will be a home from home for you altogether.'

'A pub.'

'The landlord's name is Willie Mullins. A London Irishman. I say an Irishman, because he would say it himself, but born in England. He runs a bar that will make you feel you never left the ould sod. It makes a lot of people feel like that. Mr Mullins is welcoming to all and sundry, but he has a special fondness for the Boys of the Old Brigade, if you take my meaning. It's not much of a safe house these days, since there's probably rarely an evening there's not a Scotland Yard Special Branch man popping into the snug for a barley wine. There's a war on after all. But the IRA men funnel through the place, in the shape of builders and barmen and drunks, and your man Willie usually finds them somewhere to stay. It's a bit of a post office too, for homesick Irish fellers longing for a message from home, especially in code. In fact, the Bedford Arms offers a range of consular services that would make our High Commissioner in London altogether green, naturally enough, with envy.'

'And I'll be working there?'

'Have you never worked in a bar?'

'I've worked in a bar. Is that all you want?'

'It'll help.'

'So what will Mr Mullins know about me?'

'Bugger all. Don't fret about Willie. He's pissed most of the time.'

'And why would he give me a job?'

'Because someone will tell him to.'

'You?'

'No, not at all. I only know the man by reputation. You'll come highly recommended. All he'll be told is that you're in a bit of trouble over here. The Guards are on to you for something and you need to get out and lie low.'

'He won't know I'm a Guard?'

'He won't know anything about you. He won't want to. You're not the first to pass through the Bedford Arms. And if anything came out, well, aren't you a rare sort of Guard after all. Didn't you give the nod to a German spy?'

'Down here they think I've been giving it to the IRA.'

'Ah, Stevie, don't you just fit in everywhere you go?'

'What does that mean?'

'As far as Willie's concerned, you've been recommended to him from a very reliable source. And one that scares the bollocks off him when he's sober.'

'I take it that means someone inside the IRA?'

'One thing about playing the detective, you need to know when to stop.'

Stefan walked on. He knew what he was doing, but he also

knew he wasn't going to find out much more. He wondered if Gregory knew much more himself.

'So how long am I there?'

'I don't know.'

'You don't know how long and you don't know what I'm looking for.'

'Commandant de Paor will give you a better idea.'

'I see, this is for G2 now?'

'It's for Ireland, Stevie.' Gregory gave a wry grin.

'Your reliable friend who's not an IRA man knows that, does he?'

'There's nothing to trip you up. That's why even a culchie sergeant in Wicklow can tell the world you're an untrustworthy gobshite. If anyone looks, you are who you are. And you are lying low. You've a streak of the German in you, and you've been lending the Jerries a hand. What could be more natural? There is a letter from me on the Commissioner's desk at this very moment, recommending you're sacked. There's even the evidence to put you away. I had it typed in the Castle typing pool and I left it lying around for an afternoon before it went to Ned Broy. I wouldn't give it a day before the Boys had sight.'

'If you didn't make it sound so easy, I might believe it was.'

'You're too clever for me, Stevie. I didn't say don't watch yourself.'

For the first time, Superintendent Gregory looked more serious.

'But I am on my own?' said Stefan.

'There'll be someone to go to if you're in trouble.'

'No one watching my back, though.'

'Mullins is a fierce eejit, from what I'm told. But he won't be looking for trouble. He's enough of his own. He's worked for G2 as well as for the Boys.'

'Jesus, and that's meant to reassure me, is it?'

'You've got nothing to hide. He's got too much. Gerry de Paor thinks Willie's forgotten his friends in G2. He wants to know why. That's your job.'

'And he'll tell me, will he, if I run his bar well enough?'

'I wouldn't send you if I didn't know you're up to it.'

'What if I told you to fuck off?'

'I think you realised some time ago, you're here for the duration.'

Stefan did not reply. If he didn't want that to be true, it still was.

Superintendent Gregory reached out and touched his arm. The look was one Stefan did not often see on his boss's face: concern. Without another word the two men turned away from Kilranelagh Hill, heading back towards the farm. Stefan heard a voice, high and shrill, calling below. He saw Tom waving, standing in the road as it passed the haggart ditch. He was home from school.

'You've a good nose,' said Gregory. 'If it smells, get out. Don't wait.'

8

King Street

London

Vera Eriksen sat in a small attic room, looking out through the gable window at the evening below, as she had done for several days. The journey from Edinburgh to London had been uneventful. She breathed in the atmosphere of war and found it somehow reassuring and exhilarating at the same time. In her own way she was fighting now; even by sitting on a train, unknown and unobserved, she was defying her country's enemy. But the atmosphere was not quite what she expected. It felt very different from the Germany she had left behind. In Berlin there was a mood of triumph. The easy victories of the summer had made the inevitability of triumph as real in fact as in faith. If the bombs that had fallen on Berlin had come as a surprise, they had not shaken anybody's faith. They were few in number, after all; little more than the last, desperate thrashings of a defeated British nation. Germany, for all the intermittent fury of war, was barely touched by it. Everyone knew that what was now being visited on Britain was a level of destruction that would erase any British spirit to resist. Everyone knew that all the British people wanted was an end to a war they had somehow been tricked into. There was, of course, no similar triumph to be felt in the air Vera

Eriksen was breathing now, but she found the mood she picked up on her journey from Scotland puzzling. She wasn't looking for the signs of fear or despair or defeat she had been told would be everywhere. That was propaganda. She knew it wouldn't be like that. And it wasn't, certainly not at first impressions. She might have looked for something else, resolution or determination, but she felt none of that either. Mostly what she encountered was the ordinariness of everything, as if the remarkable was to be treated as wholly unremarkable. There was no shortage of conversation about the war and about bombing in the cities especially, but people seemed to slip in and out of those conversations with a peculiar disregard for the weight they ought to carry. If there was a great deal of talk in Berlin about victory and imminent peace, so far Vera had heard no corresponding talk of defeat here, let alone any feeling that the war was nearing an end. There was an odd laziness about the way people spoke, as if war was only deserving of so much attention.

At King's Cross Vera telephoned her alternative number, the one she had not given to Karl Drücke. She spoke to a woman who directed her to an address in King Street. She took the Piccadilly Line to Covent Garden, diving immediately into the anonymity of the city. In the course of her brief walk through Covent Garden, she saw sandbagged entrances and the white criss-cross of taped windows, but nothing else. No bomb had yet hit the streets she walked.

The smell of rotting fruit and vegetables was there before she reached King Street, as was the noise of the market. The long, low market hall stretched in front of her, with the pillared booths almost invisible behind the piles of boxes on the pavement and the vans and lorries and horses and carts that filled the cobbled street. Before the war it would have been late for Covent Garden, which was at its busiest through the night and early hours of the morning, dispatching London's fruit and vegetables across the city. Now, while some work started before the blackout ended, the timetable had shifted. It was a scene of noise and bustle that Vera found herself enjoying. For a moment it pushed her out of herself into the life around her. It irritated her. But a clearer route to what she had to do, a clearer way to carry it forward, would come.

At the house in King Street the woman who opened the door said almost nothing. She led Vera up several flights of stairs. There was a small room with a chair and a table, overlooking Covent Garden; another door led to a room with a bed and no window; there was a toilet and a wash basin. In the first room there was a gas ring and a kettle; there was tea and milk. The woman brought food that evening. She said very little and the only instructions were about blackout regulations. Irrespective of bombing, Vera was to stay where she was. The two attic rooms were her only domain until further notice.

'And how long will I be here?' Vera asked.

'There'll be someone. They'll come when they come.'

When it was dark the street below began to empty itself of vehicles and market workers, leaving only the men who came in to clean the stalls and the streets of debris. Vera left the light off in the front room and still spent most of her time looking down at Covent Garden. The night was not dark, and she occupied herself watching what came and went below until, suddenly, the sirens started; the harsh, wailing sound from every direction. Then the first explosions. Looking out from the high gable, she saw the flashes, one after another. She was aware she was looking south and though she could not see it, she knew the River Thames was only a few streets away. She took the A–Z from her case and counted them across the rooftops. Henrietta Street, Maiden Lane, the Strand, Victoria Embankment. The bridges too: Waterloo, Hungerford, and then Westminster. She had visited London only once when she lived in Ireland. She had walked along the river there. She remembered Cleopatra's Needle, the Houses of Parliament and, for some reason, the Embankment Underground station. There was silence for a moment. She could hear the low, heavy buzz of the Luftwaffe bombers. Great beams of light shot up into the sky from searchlights. As they moved they caught the grey barrage balloons that floated over the city. Then there were more explosions and more flashes of light. There was the rhythmic pounding of the ack-ack batteries, softer than the bombs, bursting into the air. Below, in King Street and the market, people were hurrying but not running, and soon the street was empty. The explosions increased in frequency, blending into one another with a growing intensity.

It was harder to hear the drone of the bombers over the noise now, but although the gable windows rattled and shuddered, and the building shook as several bombs exploded along the river, between the bridges, nothing came closer. It was difficult to know how close even those bombs were. They could have been on the south bank. Vera imagined that as you became used to it, you got better at judging such things. She watched intently, fixated, feeling no real fear, knowing only that she had to stay where she was. It was like nothing she had seen in Berlin, where the bombs had always been somewhere else. She had for a moment, as the sky started to light up and the shock waves were strong enough for her to sense them physically, a feeling of something almost like joy.

Before long, over the dark horizon of roofs, there was a different light. She knew it must be the fires the bombs had started. They were not close either. They were to the south and east, along the river, and in the momentary gaps that came between the explosions, she could hear the fires, a kind of low roar interspersed with great cracks of sharp sound, utterly different from the bombs.

She was unsure how long it lasted. Certainly hours had passed by the time the bombs stopped and the drone of the planes had gone. She heard the sirens again, that said Raiders Passed and All Clear. The fires in the distance were still burning. She pushed open the window; she could feel heat. She closed it and pulled the blackout curtains across. The room was in darkness. As she walked towards the bedroom she rubbed her eyes. She was surprised to find she was wiping away tears, unsure where they came from. There was nothing ordinary about what she had just seen. Maybe that was it. She had seen invincibility.

The next day, very early, the woman brought a cup of coffee and some toast. When Vera remarked on the intensity of the night's bombing, the woman nodded and said it had been bad south of the river. She knew that the response had nothing to do with the fact that the woman was well aware she was a German agent. Vera had not made her remarks with any pleasure; she could not avoid the feeling of being a part of what she had experienced. The woman's response was another example of the unsettling acceptance of things, by someone, anyone, who lived in the middle of London. Vera opened the black felt curtains and looked down at Covent Garden again. The lorries and vans and horses and carts were arriving; fruit and vegetables were loading and unloading. The costermongers threaded through the clutter with baskets on their heads. There was shouting; there was arguing; prices were called out; there was laughter. Beyond the rooftops, to the south, there was a grey haze of smoke. Somewhere buildings were still burning. She could hear a steady tinkling sound; someone was sweeping broken glass. Vera realised that what she had witnessed the previous night was not what she thought. It was not extraordinary at all.

The door opened again and the woman stuck her head in.

'He's here now,' she said abruptly, 'and he'll see you downstairs.'

The man who sat opposite Vera Eriksen was small and dark. He had introduced himself, in German, as London Kontrolle and said she should call him Adam. That name would be used in any further communication. He was in his forties, but almost bald. He had a quiet intensity that made her feel he was watching her, reading her, measuring her, even in the most idle words about the journey from Berlin. At first he barely listened to the answers she gave; he was looking for what was behind them. She saw that. He was distant, though his words came easily enough. The thick-lensed glasses increased the sense that he was peering into her. He spoke German for a time and then moved, without explanation, to English. It didn't matter what she said to him, he was judging how she sounded now, her accent. He nodded as she spoke; she assumed it was approval. When he moved to more serious matters, his tone did not change. The words seemed to come as idly as before. Vera recognised a shift to more dangerous ground.

'You know that Drücke, your colleague, has been captured?'

'No, I didn't.'

She showed concern, but no surprise. She felt surprise would be naïve.

'They picked him up at the station in Edinburgh.'

'I see.'

'That's all you have to say?'

'What else should I say? I'm sorry.'

'Yes, we all are. You left him at Edinburgh. To travel separately.'

'It seemed a sensible precaution.'

'Events rather prove that to be the case, don't they?'

'Yes.'

'Do I gather that you're not surprised?'

89

'I didn't say that.'

'No, you didn't say it. Perhaps you didn't need to.'

Vera didn't reply.

'Drücke didn't impress you, I'd say. Is that why you dumped him?'

For the first time Vera felt that how she answered mattered. Adam was watching her more closely. She had something to hide. Maybe he was looking for that. She knew it was always best to keep as close to the truth as possible.

'There was no dumping. We'd pushed travelling together far enough. We had been lucky, maybe luckier than we deserved. To be frank, I think the landing arrangements were poor. Arriving at such a small station in Scotland, and so early, was a bad choice. We were lucky not to draw more attention to ourselves there. But I won't pretend I wasn't uncomfortable with Karl.'

'In what way?'

'The agent who was supposed to be working with me was killed in an accident. Karl Drücke was meant to travel with us, but there was never any intention he would stay with us. He was always meant to remain in England.'

'And your mission, Fraulein?'

'Ireland.'

'Yes.' Adam nodded.

The man knew the answers to the questions he was asking her, but Vera couldn't know how much more he knew. He was suspicious about Karl. He sat opposite her, smiling slightly, waiting for her to say more. She said nothing; expanding on what she had said needed more care. Minimum information, even among the people you worked with most closely, was always the right option.

'Drücke still wasn't meant to go to Ireland with you, though?'

'I assumed not, but there had been changes. Things weren't

as clear. I'm not entirely sure what his mission was, to be honest. And the changes had disturbed me. We were meant to carry nothing to identify us as German. What was important was that we got through and found cover. We all understood there had been arrests, in England and Ireland, very easy, very quick arrests.'

'But Drücke was doing things differently?'

'He must have received instructions no one had told me about. It was not my understanding that we would bring in a radio transmitter. The original aim was for me to go to Ireland from England, with an Irish passport, with Erik – Major Kramer. Those were still my instructions. If you want to send equipment, it's foolish to give it to agents who have more important jobs to do. It was another unnecessary error. I felt safer without any additional baggage.'

Adam smiled. She regretted the reference to additional baggage.

'I see. And what other errors have been made, Fraulein?'

'What do you mean?'

'Another, you said.'

'I think the station at Port Gordon was a mistake. So is this.' Vera opened her bag and took out the identity card. She handed it to him. 'Look at the numbers. The ones, the seven. No one in England would write them like that. I don't imagine it's easy to get these things perfect, but this wouldn't make it past a constable on the street. If anyone at the station had asked . . . I wasn't given this till I was on the plane. If I'd still been in Berlin I would not have accepted it.'

The man who called himself London Kontrolle examined the card.

'You have a point.'

'Looking at that,' said Vera, 'it's no surprise people get picked up.'

'The reputation of the Abwehr is excellent.' He paused for a moment, assessing her. 'But some might say its efficiency can be overstated. It isn't always the case that what comes out of Tirpitzuferstrasse serves the Party as well as it should. Indeed, there are those who say the Abwehr pursues its own ends sometimes, with less regard for the Party than is appropriate. I wouldn't say that myself, of course. We are all working towards the Führer in our different ways. I'm sure you are, Fraulein. But not all ways can be right.'

It was Vera's turn to examine the man who was talking to her. He was doing more than judging her. He was probing. He was an Abwehr agent, like her, but his words were carefully chosen. He was asking her to question the Abwehr. Or was he pointing out that she already had been? Was it a code to seek out where her true loyalties lay or a trap that was asking the same thing? He sounded like Erik Kramer. She felt he knew something about what she was hiding. But he left his words hanging over her. He did not wait for her answer.

'It's an odd route to Ireland, I have to say, Vera.'

She noted that he used her name for the first time.

'I didn't choose it, Adam.'

'Why do you think it was chosen?'

'I assume it's what I said before. People have been picked up. From U-boat landings and parachute drops. It's the same problem. You appear in the middle of nowhere and someone asks you why. It's easier to disappear in London. After that an Irishwoman taking the boat home from Holyhead is unremarkable. My Irish passport is a lot better than the English identity card.'

'And when you get to Ireland?'

'I will be dependent on my contacts there.'

'Ah, I see. Not my business then, is that right?'

'Isn't your business to get me there?'

'My dear Vera, you're very good. Just the right tone to point out that I am not here to give you orders. But I think you're more than capable of getting there yourself. My only advice, whatever the precise details of your mission, would be to avoid whatever you come across in the way of fellow conspirators.'

'I don't know what you mean by that.'

'We're all a little too much in each other's pockets. There are certainly agents who have been turned by British Intelligence. We have identified some and disposed of them, but by no means all. There are double agents we don't know about and there is no doubt that the British have some access to our radio traffic. They may even control some of it. There's no shortage of unreliable players in the game in Ireland either. One answer is not to join in the game.'

'I think I know what I'm doing, at least as far as getting to Ireland goes.'

'It's only a pity about Major Kramer. I had heard already. A great loss. And you're right. From what I know, Karl Drücke was no replacement. Any loss is serious, of course, but perhaps his may be less serious than some others.'

London Kontrolle waited to see if she replied. Vera said nothing.

'You don't agree?'

'I have no opinion on that.'

'I wonder if he did have new instructions – to keep an eye on you, Vera.'

'Is there some cause to think I am unreliable?'

'Major Kramer was a Party man,' said Adam, 'in every way.'

'I have no reason to doubt that.' She spoke slowly, cautiously. He had not forgotten the questions he had asked minutes before. He was asking them again.

'He was an SD man, isn't that right? The Abwehr weren't keen on him.'

'We all worked together. We all worked for the same thing.'

'Of course, Vera. We are all on the same side. Still, my information comes from Berlin, but not all of it comes from the

Abwehr. I hope you understand why I say that to you. My instructions have other sources too. I think you understand what I mean. I'm sure Major Kramer would have understood perfectly. The Abwehr approach to Ireland is a very timid one. Let's say no more than that. The results are inevitably ineffectual. Do nothing, nothing happens. Unsurprising. Timidity isn't a characteristic of the Reich Main Security Office, however, or the Sicherheitdienst. There are results to be achieved in Ireland. Don't you think? And they are results that could hit the English very hard. We know softly, softly doesn't really catch many monkeys. Major Kramer must have said something similar to you. You were very close to him.'

Whether it was a trap or not, the man who designated himself London Kontrolle was telling her that he owed his allegiance not to the Abwehr, but to the Nazi Party's Intelligence arm, the SD. He knew that Erik Kramer had been working to SD instructions, irrespective of his Abwehr mission. Vera Eriksen wanted to trust this man. It felt as if she was no longer alone. There would be clarity, purpose. She felt, more deeply, that Erik Kramer was there again; he had not left her after all. But she said nothing. Now she would see what happened.

'For now, Vera, what's best is that you disappear into London. You have an Irish passport and you now have a perfectly good identity card.' He opened a folder and pushed a card across the desk. 'It's the real thing. No stupid errors.'

Vera examined the new identity card. She nodded.

'Where do I go?'

'You pass as Irish. I don't know why they send us people who speak English as if they never left Bavaria. What do they think will happen? You don't have that problem. You can merge with the Irish in London. Do nothing. Get some casual work, the kind everyone Irish does. Work in a shop, do some cleaning. Be as Irish as you like, but don't play the anti-English

Republican. You don't have to like the English but steer an easy course. If you have a real background of work in London, however briefly, you're convincingly normal. When you cross to Ireland, you're just like everyone else. Leave it to the Abwehr to send us spies who might as well have it written on their hatbands.'

London Kontrolle stood up. He took his hat from the table.

'Stay here a couple more days. After that, you're entirely free. Any arrangements you make will be better if they're your own. We will inform Berlin you are safe. No more than that. Too many double agents, as I've said. You'll have a number to keep in touch with me and only me. I can't even truly guarantee my own radio operator at the moment. But no one will know where you are. Just hope the Luftwaffe avoids Covent Garden for the time being.'

He smiled more broadly than he had before. He reached out and shook her hand. Vera smiled in return. She felt reassured. She was in safe hands.

'What made you call to change the telephone number, Vera? You know it meant closing down a safe house. Quite a palaver that. Right, as it turned out.'

'Perhaps I have good instincts, Adam.' She spoke with more confidence.

'Yes, poor old Drücke wasn't so good on the instinct front, was he? I'll send in a few newspapers while you're here. So you'll know what people are talking about out there. By the way, they'll hang Drücke in the next few days. They like to make a splash about such things. So you will see it in the papers.'

He smiled again and pulled the door shut.

Vera Eriksen took out a cigarette. Her hand was shaking slightly. She put the cigarette to her lips and flicked her lighter. It was a silver Ronson that Erik Kramer had given her, bought it in London before the war. That was how thorough he was.

He had less time for bare instinct than for getting things right. Detail mattered; it meant survival. Now it meant her doing the job Germany had asked him to do. And she had support. Adam understood detail too. He was an Abwehr man, but he recognised that there were deeper loyalties. He had revealed that to her. She had to trust him, but not too much. Those were Erik's words too. The man knew a lot about her. He knew where her own loyalties lay. He knew more too. He knew something about Erik Kramer's real mission. It was unspoken, but it was there. And there was a reason why her hands had been shaking at the end. Adam knew she had betrayed Karl Drücke. He didn't say so, but he knew. He must believe she was right. She had not doubted that at the time. She could not doubt it now. There had been a price. The price was not important.

9

Tom's House

Wicklow

David Gillespie had not slept easily for several nights. Past and the present were creating a level of activity in his head that he wasn't used to. He didn't altogether dislike it. It seemed to clear a way through the clutter of his mind. What was happening now and what happened long ago. They had the same smell. And as for where his son was in all that, he could not understand why Stefan wouldn't take the simple way out. Just as he had walked away from the Dublin Metropolitan Police, Stefan should walk away from Detective Superintendent Gregory and his Special Branch. David did know it wasn't the same. There were not the same demands for betrayal. There were not the same threats of reprisal. The dangers were different. He didn't even know what they were. But they were there, however much his son shrugged them off. The death of Joe Coogan took him back to what some of those dangers could be, or to the darkness that bred them at least. In his head it was a darkness that didn't feel so very different. He had to remember that walking away had not protected him from everything. Danger had come. And that was the other thing in his head that he couldn't let go of. The night in the Fever Hospital was back in his head. And it was the body of Joe Coogan that had opened the door. Now it was the dead farmer in Rathdangan who had brought him into Superintendent Mulvaney's office in the Garda Barracks in Baltinglass. There was nothing he could do about Stefan now. He knew that. Stefan would soon be gone. Yet he still had Stefan's questions about the body by the Mass Rock in his head. He wanted answers to those questions. It was an obligation, almost forgotten. There was a bloody-mindedness about David Gillespie's visit to the barracks in Edward Street. It was a bloody-mindedness he had not felt for a long time.

'Is this a complaint about Sergeant Donegan, David?' Superintendent Mulvaney was smiling. He didn't see any reason to take this seriously yet.

'It's not a complaint; it's a question, Ger.'

'So it wouldn't have anything to do with what Donegan had to say about your son. I guess it wasn't too complimentary. Still, not good to hear, I know.'

'I'm not interested in that.'

'It's an odd business, though, David. But you can't blame the men for what they think. There's been three Guards killed by the IRA in the last year.'

'You know Stefan, Ger. Do you believe all that shite?'

'You'd never be sure what shite comes out of the Special Branch.'

'So you do believe it?'

'No, I don't fecking believe it. Of course I don't, David.'

'Then we'll leave all that, shall we? I'm not here because Basil Donegan has a big mouth. I'm here because his brain isn't close to matching it in size.'

Mulvaney laughed. 'I'll pass that one on to him.'

'So, the thing is . . . Joe Coogan.'

'And what's Joe Coogan to you?'

'A dead man.'

'Yes, and that's about it.'

'I'm not sure it is, Ger.'

'Look, David, I've had the report from Kiltegan, and I have taken it over. I've asked for a post-mortem so. I've sent a detective up to Rathdangan. I've looked at the statements, and so far I don't see anything to make a fuss about.'

'That's the job now, is it? Not making a fuss.'

'I know what this is about. I was told. Stefan saw some things he didn't like. I did get the message. But the short version is it has feck all to do with him. At the last count Inspector Gillespie had been suspended from duty. I don't know whether he's got some point to make about what a bunch of eejits we all are down here, but I wouldn't care very much . . . even if he wasn't suspended.'

'So what he saw doesn't matter, is that the story?'

'I'm looking at what's in front of me. If something comes up, we'll look again. In the meantime, what I see is that the man shot himself. And you know what, some might say that if someone did kill Joe Coogan, would anyone care?'

'Maybe someone should.'

'And that's you, is it, David?'

'Well, it doesn't look like it's you, Superintendent.'

David spoke Mulvaney's rank as a kind of weapon. It didn't work.

'If there's something to investigate, it'll be done. I have better things to do than make the stuff up. I don't have to care; I just have to do my job. You remember what happened sixteen years ago when Paddy O'Halloran was shot. Across the road, outside the bank. Two IRA men tried to rob it. And when they fucked it up altogether, it was Paddy's bad luck to be coming over the bridge. He was between them and the car. So one of the bastards shot him. I found him a few minutes later. If I'd been quicker, they'd have shot me. But they'd gone.'

David Gillespie heard the story he knew well enough. He

had no idea why the superintendent was telling it or why there was quiet anger in his face.

'They drove out through the town towards Kiltegan. They were well away before we could get after them. All I could do was hold Paddy's hand while he died. Not something you forget, is it? Some maybe have. Not me.'

'I don't think many have forgotten, Ger.'

'Ah, you know better than that. Aren't some things best forgotten?'

David Gillespie frowned, trying to remember the events of those days.

'They hanged one for it. Didn't they get him the next day, in Tallaght?'

'For what it's worth. I'd have hanged more if I'd had my way. They didn't go straight to Tallaght. The two of them disappeared, along with the car. They drove through Kiltegan, towards the Military Road. That's the way they found their road back, eventually. But not straightaway. They hid themselves.'

'I don't remember any of that.'

'We had a good idea where they hid. At Joseph Coogan's farm.'

'I see,' said David quietly. 'I didn't know.'

'Never proved. And they never said a word at the trial. Your man McMullen did the shooting, and he was for the drop. The other one, Jordan, got ten years. But you know what? He was a cousin of Coogan's, and of course Coogan was an old IRA man. I don't know that he ever did much, but he'd not stop shouting about his glory days when he was pissed. And that was often enough. He never lost the taste for it either. Didn't they find guns hidden up beyond Rathcoyle after the Phoenix Park raid? If someone topped the bastard, you know what? I could be tempted to shake his hand more than lock him up.'

'If he was killed, I doubt it was because he was still fighting the Civil War.'

'Ah, that's what comes of being a Protestant, David. A man of hard and unbending principle so. I'm just an ignorant Papist. Retribution will do for me. Sufficient unto the day . . .'

'So that's it. If there's any doubt, suicide will still do.'

'Maybe you have it right. Or not. Either way I'd leave it alone, David.'

As David Gillespie cycled home to Kilranelagh, none of what he felt seemed like a matter of principle. It did feel like a debt. It was a debt he had almost forgotten, but it was not something he could dispose of by adding up the pluses and minuses of the life of a man he knew almost nothing about. There were few people unscarred by the years of war and civil war, but unless those years could be left behind, there was nothing to do except pick at the scars and open them up, endlessly. He knew that well enough and he heard it often enough; he saw it in all its complexity. But this was simple; it was personal. The events in the Fever Hospital all those years ago were closer now than they had been for a long time. Whatever he owed Joseph Coogan, it was more than accepting an invitation to ignore the circumstances of his death, when those circumstances might be murder. The doubts about the farmer's death were no longer only Stefan's; now they were David's. It would not have been in Stefan's nature to turn away if he had a choice. And that was part of it too. This was simpler than an old world of deceit and betrayal that he seemed to hear being echoed now, all over again, in his son's life. There was nothing of that world here. There was a dead man, a possible murder, no more. There was a simplicity about it that was almost comforting. David Gillespie had good reasons not to look away, and maybe not all of them were about an obligation to Joe Coogan. It was as if he needed a purpose, a simple purpose, to help him push his way out of all the things he spoke to no one about: his failing strength, his forgetfulness, the way he saw the running of the farm slipping away from him. It was age; he knew that was unavoidable now. It was only recently that he had truly felt its dull heaviness in his head as he woke each morning. It was clogging his mind as it slowed and weakened his body. He needed something to make him fight it.

That afternoon Stefan Gillespie walked through the trees behind the farm to a field where his father was mending a gate. He didn't find him by the gate. He was sitting on a pile of stones in a thicket of sloe and hazel that grew out of the low tumbled walls that marked the shape of a small house and some farm outbuildings that stood there a hundred years earlier. There was little to see, but this had been the farm at Kilranelagh before an earlier generation of Gillespies had built the bigger two-storey house lower down the hill, close to the road. The ruins had grown into the ground as the ground seemed to grow up around them, ever more invisible as what stone was left was used to repair the stone walls or drain some patch of boggy land. It was still an oddly quiet place, and generations of children, Stefan included, had played there. Tom Gillespie had been no exception, and though he came there less now, as he and his friends found other things to do, the ruins were still called Tom's House.

The pile of stones offered a place to sit. The gate David Gillespie was supposed to be mending was untouched. He was examining a twelve-bore shotgun he had brought with him, holding it out to the side, bringing it close to his face. He was unaware of his son, standing among the trees, watching him.

'I thought I'd give you a hand with the gate, Pa.'

'I haven't started.'

'I can see. I wondered if you'd got sidetracked shooting pigeons.'

'I didn't bring any cartridges.' David laughed.

'That's what I thought. I don't need to ask why you're doing this.'

'You're the one who said you couldn't see how he shot part of the back of his head off. I was trying to see if you were right. But I couldn't get rid of your mother, though. I wasn't entirely sure what she'd make of me doing this.'

'So what do you think?'

'I think you're right, son. It wouldn't be easy.'

'But would it be possible?'

'I don't know. But someone should be asking the question.'

'Why?'

'What do you mean, why? They're your questions. I told Ger Mulvaney.'

'I have another question, Pa. What's Joe Coogan to you?'

'He's a man who might have been murdered and nobody gives a shite.'

'You need to give me more. You hardly knew him, but there is more.'

'I don't think you've got time for more, have you? You'll be gone.'

Stefan Gillespie took the shotgun from his father and laid it down. He sat opposite him on another low pile of stones. He took out a cigarette and lit it.

'I'd still like to hear. It has to matter, doesn't it?'

'There's part of me that wants to say it doesn't, but, yes, it has to.'

Stefan waited. David frowned, not so much thinking about what he was going to say, as trying to find some order in it. It was a story he had never fully told.

'It wasn't long after we moved back here from Dublin, after I left the DMP. You know a bit about what happened, but I never told most of it. I don't know whether I only walked out because I was afraid. I was; no doubt about that. Maybe if I'd believed in what I was doing, I might have made a different choice. Some did. But if your life is on the line and if you've got a wife and a child, you'd need a lot of belief to stick with it. It was already a job I hated. We'd stopped being policemen.'

'I know. But they let you go.'

'They couldn't stop me. They couldn't stop you either.'

'It's not the same, Pa.'

'Isn't it?'

'When it is, I'll do something. It's your story I'm asking about.'

'I had lots of reasons for why I left, Stefan. I needed a lot.'

'You didn't want to take a side. That's simple enough, isn't it?'

'Ned Broy is the Garda Commissioner now. In 1920 he was a Dublin Metropolitan Police officer, like me, but he was Michael Collins' man. He was getting information out. Some of that information would be used to save lives and some of it would be used to kill the men he was working with. When Collins had the Intelligence men from London killed, it was on the back of inside information, from the DMP as well as Dublin Castle. I didn't know much about the Castle, but I was in the DMP archives. I knew where every file went. I knew when they went out, when they came back. None of them could leave the building. But some did, and it was Ned taking them out, for Collins to read.'

'And you knew that?'

'I watched him do it. And he knew it. He took me for a drink one day. He didn't ask me to join him, but he told me to keep my mouth shut. He told me I had two choices. I could turn a blind eye to what he was doing or I could leave the DMP. I say he didn't ask me to join him but that's really what the first choice was. He said there was a third choice. He didn't recommend it. I could shop him. They'd put him away. They might kill him if the Castle mob got hold of him. But whatever about that, I'd be dead in a week. A week if I was lucky.'

'And now he's the Garda Commissioner,' said Stefan, laughing.

'He earned it.'

'He did give you a choice. And you had no reason to stay then.'

'No one thanked you for not taking a side.'

'Did you expect them to?'

'No, but I did think that was the end of it.'

'And wasn't it?'

'I never told the whole story, about the Tans. Not even to your mother. I was on my own when it happened. You must have been at your grandmother's. The Black and Tans picked me up one night, in Baltinglass. They were . . . that doesn't matter . . . it's not the point. They were all pissed. I tried to calm them down. I must have thought I was still a policeman. Everyone knew you didn't argue with them. They took me back. They knew who I was. They said they wanted me for an informer. But it wasn't that. They had to punish me. I was a traitor. That's what I got for trying to stand to one side. There were no neutrals.'

David Gillespie paused. Stefan saw it wasn't an easy memory. It was harder because it had been shut in his father's head for nearly twenty years.

'They beat the shite out of me. They were experts at that.'

David said no more. The weight of the silence gave Stefan enough.

'I don't know if they were always going to let me go in the end. That's how it seems, looking back. It didn't at the time. I didn't think I'd get out of there. They did what they liked. They answered to no one. They'd shoot a man for telling them to feck off. I do know they'd have done me a lot more damage.'

'So what happened?'

'Joe Coogan happened.'

Stefan was searching his own memories now; this one didn't gel.

'Wasn't he an IRA man then? I don't know much, but I'd know that.'

'He was. He was also an informer.'

'Did anybody know?'

'Maybe. But sometimes you could never tell what was real and what wasn't. They brought him into the Fever Hospital. That's where they had me. I didn't even know who he was then. They'd just dragged me off the floor for another beating. The officer came in with Joe. He wanted to know if I'd be any use. Joe told them they were wasting their time. He looked down at me and laughed. He said there was nothing I knew they couldn't get for the price of a pint in Sheridan's. That was it. He was gone. I didn't see him properly then. But he'd taken the heat out. The Tans stopped. They dragged me out and dumped me at the Workhouse gate. I was crawling. I couldn't walk. A dogcart came up then. It was Coogan. He pulled me into it and he brought me back home.'

'So what did he say?'

'He said we didn't know each other, and it would be best to leave it that way. I found out who he was later, but I never told anyone. He said he had his reasons for talking to the Tans, but they weren't reasons they'd like. He thought, as a DMP man, I'd know what he meant. I didn't care what he meant. But I knew I was back in that pub with Ned Broy. I had a choice. I don't know if he was a real informer. I don't know if he was playing both sides. I don't know if he was codding the Tans, which took some balls you'd have to say. But he got me out. I won't say he saved my life. But I didn't know that. I'll never know.'

'You were never friends, though?'

'No, we'd pass the time of day. No more. I never knew much about him. I never thought much about him. The little I knew was just gossip. He was a big drinker. I think that got the better of him, so. No one much liked him. I recall something about his wife leaving him. I couldn't tell you when. I know it didn't surprise anyone. He wasn't much of a farmer, they say. And that was about it.'

'Maybe someone still didn't like him much,' said Stefan.

'The Guards say he shot himself. They're not looking further than that.'

'That's what Ger Mulvaney said?'

'He said a lot more.'

'About me?' asked Stefan; there was a knowing smile.

'Some of it. Not much. I think he's enough nous to know bollocks when he hears it. But no one's too bothered to ask questions about how Joe Coogan died. I don't think they liked you asking them. You won't be here anyway, will you?'

'No,' said Stefan.

His father nodded. He asked for no explanation.

'So I may do it myself. I didn't expect Joe to call in that debt. He has.'

10

The Mail Boat

Tom Gillespie lay in bed, listening to his father read. It was the last night. The next day Stefan would leave. For Tom it was simply the job his father did. He would be away a time. Those times were uncertain. He was used to it. It was a part of how time worked. Now he was listening hard, but his eyes were closing.

Stefan was reading about William Brown and the Outlaws. It was a vision of the blackout in Britain that provided an opportunity for the boys of Richmal Crompton's stories to run even wilder and freer than they ordinarily did. All the rules had been suspended; grown-up vigilance was otherwise occupied; and discipline had disappeared. The new darkness was full of possibilities, full of adventures, full of unexpected comedy. If it wasn't real, it was comforting.

'What does the blackout do?' asked Tom, yawning, waking himself up with a question, as his father read the William story to him, but now fading fast.

'It wouldn't be very different to you than looking out of the window. It just means everything's dark, especially in big cities, like London. You can have lights on inside, but the windows have to be covered so not even a glimmer gets out.

It means the bombers, up in the sky, can't see anything, just the darkness.'

'Do you wish we had more of that, a proper war?'

'We don't want any war,' said Stefan, smiling. 'I promise you.'

'I knew you'd say that,' replied Tom, looking slightly doubtful.

Stefan nodded. It wasn't time for a conversation, but he wished he had read something else, something that had been further away from the war. Tomorrow he would leave Kilranelagh. Within a few days, the blackout that was a children's story, with all its darkness, would be part of a daily routine.

'You've stopped, Daddy.'

'I'm sorry, I've lost where . . . here we are.' Stefan read on. While each of the Outlaws' parents thought their son was safely in the homes of other parents, the boys were roaming the countryside in its newly unlighted state. They were robber bands, tracking each other down. They shoved each other into ditches and jumped out to terrify passers-by. They were almost run over every night.

Tom's breathing had become deeper. He was asleep. Stefan stood up and closed the book. He put it down and bent to kiss Tom's forehead. He didn't want the war to come any closer to his son than it had in the exploits of William Brown and the Outlaws. Somewhere in what he was doing, he felt he was part of keeping it at bay. That's what he told himself, amidst all the doubt and deceit that surrounded the world he moved in. It was what he tried to believe. It didn't always work. His job involved risks. There was no way round that. It was what he did. It didn't help to have to think that besides him, Tom only had his grandparents. His mother, Maeve, had died when he was barely old enough to remember her. Maeve had been murdered, though Stefan had found that out only years after her death. No one else knew. It was something he carried alone. Now, for a moment, looking down at his son, Stefan felt Maeve was close. It didn't happen very often now, but he smiled. It still did happen. He turned out the lamp. The room was in darkness. He stood a moment longer, listening to Tom's slow, contented breathing. He walked out and went back downstairs.

Helena Gillespie looked up from the book she was reading.

'Has Pa gone up?' asked Stefan.

'Yes, he was tired.'

'He's tired me out too, Ma. I don't know what happened, but I think you'll have to listen to a lot more about your man Coogan. If you didn't get the message, Pa's decided he's going to investigate it all himself. Good luck!'

'I know what he owed him.'

'Yes, he told me. So you did know?'

'Some of it. I was in Dublin with you when it happened. He didn't tell me the truth for a long time. Even then it was only a version, a softer version. He made up some story about an accident, falling off the horse. I knew it wasn't true. But sometimes then, you felt it was easier if you didn't know what was happening. As long as he was all right. It was better to forget things or pretend they hadn't happened. You never made a fuss. You kept your head down.'

She got up and walked to the stove. There was a pan of quinces bubbling. She peered down at the fruit pulp, then pushed the pan off the heat and stirred it.

'Some things don't change. We're better still keeping our heads down.'

'I don't know what he'll find, Ma. Maybe nothing. No one cares much.'

'He's decided to do it. But it's only partly about Joe Coogan, isn't it?'

'I don't know what's in his head. I suppose so. I can't help that, Ma.'

'He's upset, he's angry. For all sorts of reasons. Because he's getting old. Because he can't do the things he used to be able to do. Because he can't talk about it. He can't even admit it. Because of you. He's afraid for you, Stefan.'

'He doesn't need to be.'

'He doesn't know that. I don't know that either. Do you?'

'It's the job. Pa knows it involves a lot of shite. It always has.'

'Perhaps that's the trouble, Stefan. He knows too much.'

'I know what's happened has stirred up the past for him. Perhaps it would be better if it hadn't, Ma. But these are not the same times. We're not even in this war. I spend my time keeping an eye on people who'd like to drag us into it, one way or another. But there aren't many of them and most of them aren't even very clever. They just make a lot of noise. Sometimes they need watching and sometimes they need locking up. Sometimes they need to be told to pipe down.'

'You can't even tell us where you're going.'

'It's a game, Ma; most of the time that's all it is.'

'And when it isn't?'

'I'll be back before you know it. We can sort things out then.'

Stefan's mother looked at him uncertainly. Whether that uncertainty was about him, about David, about Tom, about what it was that really could be sorted out on the farm, she didn't say. Perhaps it was all the same thing in the end: a future that had seemed more comfortable, more sure not very long ago. But she said no more. She did not want Stefan to leave with any problems but the ones he already had. She would carry on as always. She turned to the range and picked up the pan of quinces. She walked to the table and poured the pulp into a muslin bag that was stretched out over an earthenware bowl. The smell of sweetness and sourness was there again, rising up from the still steaming fruit.

Stefan stepped closer. He put his arm round her. The words he wanted to say weren't there. And she wouldn't want them if they meant nothing. They both stood, looking down, breathing in the scent of the quinces. He kissed her cheek. Then he walked away, without a word, out to the hall and upstairs again.

Stefan Gillespie sat in the back bar of Dunphys in Dún Laoghaire, as he had been told to do earlier that day. It was evening and he had been there for some time. The order had been given to him by a barman in a pub in Dublin's Dorset Street where he spent the afternoon, also as instructed. He had been watched and followed intermittently for two days, since arriving in Dublin from Baltinglass by train. He spent much of that time in a dingy room at the top of Finn's Hotel in Nassau Street, doing nothing. When he went out the IRA men who followed him had been easy enough to spot, though he made a point of ensuring they believed they had not been. It was hard work to keep them with him; they seemed to lose him without him even trying. None of it was elaborate; it felt simply futile. He was being tested to see if he did as he was told, and he was being followed to make sure he had no contact with Garda Special Branch.

What further contact he needed he had before arriving in Dublin to offer himself up to his IRA handlers. He had seen Superintendent Gregory once more, with Commandant de Paor of Military Intelligence. G2 had nothing for him other than some five-pound notes and a contact in London that could not be used except in exceptional circumstances. Neither Terry Gregory nor Geróid de Paor envisaged any exceptional circumstances. G2 did not want to be compromised; the Intelligence budget only ran to one safe house in London.

There were no more instructions about what Stefan was to do at the Bedford Arms in Camden, other than work as a barman and keep an eye on the landlord, Willie Mullins. There was no suggestion Mullins' connections to the IRA were under scrutiny, only that the man himself was. Gerry de Paor said there was no need to follow up any Republican leads that came Stefan's way, quite the opposite. It was about Mullins; that was the information he was to bring back.

It was clear the operation was more G2's than Special Branch's and that could never be a recipe for clarity. Inevitably there was a lot that Commandant de Paor would not tell Superintendent Gregory about Intelligence work in London, and as much, if not more, that Gregory would not reveal about his ability to manipulate someone in the IRA to get Stefan into the Bedford Arms. Terry Gregory and Gerry de Paor watched each other as closely as they watched the people and organisations that were meant to be their official targets. Beneath the pleasantries they guarded their territory and trusted no one.

Stefan left thinking less about the difficulties of the job than its apparent pointlessness.

Now he had been at the bar in Dunphys for two hours. He had nursed several glasses of Guinness, but there was a limit to how long he could take to drink them, and he had drunk more earlier, during the long session in Dorset Street. It was closing time when a dark, nervous youth appeared, barely in his twenties, and sat on the stool next to him. The pub was almost empty. The barman put a whiskey in front of the newcomer and went to the other bar. The staff clearing glasses disappeared too. The youth reached in his pocket and pulled out an envelope. He handed it to Stefan, saying nothing. Stefan drained his glass, then opened the envelope and took out a British identity card.

'You're Eddie Griffin,' said the youth. 'Not that anyone cares.'

'A pleasure to meet you too, son,' replied Stefan. 'Is the card real?'

'How the fuck do I know?'

'And you are?' asked Stefan, smiling.

'Liam, for what it's worth.'

There was a sneer behind the nervousness. The youth was delivering something, that's all, but Stefan knew he knew. He knew this was a Guard with a reason to get out of the country. On the right side, but still a Guard. Stefan assumed there would be IRA men in London who might know too. He wasn't sure what that meant. They probably wouldn't know much, just as this one didn't. The story was that he had been giving Germans information. He'd pushed his luck and he was looking at a spell in Mountjoy. It didn't feel like very much.

'I hope it's worth something,' said Stefan. 'Where am I going?'

'London, isn't that it?' The sneer was still there.

Stefan still wasn't supposed to know his destination. He stood up.

'Why don't you deliver your message? Or will I shake it out of you?'

'Don't fuck with me,' said the youth. He wished he hadn't.

'I owe somebody a favour,' said Stefan pleasantly, 'but not you. I don't think the Boys are going to mind if I put one on you. Do you think they will?'

Liam stood up and took a few steps back.

'You go to Camden Town, the Bedford Arms. The landlord knows.'

'Is that it?'

'There's maps on the Underground. What do you want, a Cook's Tour?'

'That's not bad, Liam. When you grow up, don't be an arsehole.'

The IRA man scowled, but not any more than he thought entirely wise.

Stefan Gillespie walked down through Dún Laoghaire to the harbour. The streets were quiet until he got to Marine Parade and saw the mail boat, its funnel pumping smoke into the night air. The harbour was full of light and noise. People had been boarding for some time; he would be one of the last. He walked up the gangplank and turned to look back at the town. He thought for a moment of walking down again, finding Terry Gregory and telling him to fuck off. He was conscious he had drunk too much. But it didn't matter. It was the same as every other time he thought that, drunk or sober. Somewhere, in the shadows he had grown used to walking in, he trusted Gregory enough to believe there was a reason for what he was asked to do. He still didn't know why he believed it. He wasn't always convinced he was right. He wasn't convinced now. He was leaving Ireland with no understanding of what he was supposed to be doing. He stepped onto the boat and headed to the saloon, and one more drink.

PART TWO

THE FIRE SERMON

Canon W. Wood (my parish priest) has his presbytery between two of the kinds of target at which the German airmen have aimed in the London area – one a municipal power station and the other a commercial trading undertaking. He and his three curates spend their nights at casualty stations – where a few nights ago they had to deal with eighty-five dead, mostly Irish, taken from an underground shelter, the entrance to which had received a direct hit from a high-explosive bomb. But the distribution of the damage leads one to think that the Germans have been keener on the disorganisation of the ordinary daily life of the people than on a strategic plan of concentration on key military objectives.

Confidential report, John Dulanty,
Irish High Commissioner in London, October 1940

11

Tivoli

Copenhagen

The invitation to go to Copenhagen, to spend a weekend with Helmut Clissman, came as a surprise to Frank Ryan. He was officially a guest of the German government but keeping his presence in Berlin a secret made the city feel like an open prison. He had been in worse prisons, much worse, but an easier life and broader horizons did not mean there were no walls. A secret identity was as much about containment as protection. The Gestapo knew he wasn't Frank Richards. They were kept at bay only by his usefulness to the Abwehr. It was part of a game. The game wasn't his; he couldn't know the rules. He played it to his best ability. The Irish government knew where he was, of course. There was no shortage of sources. And he wanted them to know where he was. The only hope he had of getting out of Germany, getting home, was if the Irish government took him back, whatever the conditions. He was no real use to the Abwehr, and he was sure there were people who knew that all too well.

Although Helmut Clissman sometimes shared the apartment Frank Ryan lived in, he had been based in Copenhagen since the German occupation of Denmark. As an officer of the Abwehr's Brandenberg regiment he had been in the Danish capital, out of uniform, weeks beforehand. Now he had set up home there with his Irish wife, also an old friend of Ryan's. There had been talk of a trip to Copenhagen, but for Frank, aware of his uncertain position, it seemed little more than wishful thinking. But a phone call had come to Katzbachstrasse unexpectedly, from Denmark. The phone rarely rang in the apartment. Frank Ryan's deafness and his poor German meant he struggled with the phone anyway. He was allowed no connections outside the Berlin area and it was tapped by both the Abwehr and the Gestapo. Now, marvellous to relate, he was free to travel to Copenhagen to see the Clissmans. A railway warrant and all the necessary papers were at the Abwehr offices in Tirpitzuferstrasse. It was officially sanctioned, as the smallest elements of his life in Germany had to be.

The overnight journey from the Stettiner Bahnhof was a mixture of exhilaration and disappointment. Simply to leave Berlin was to breathe another air, even travelling through Germany. But it was not escape; he would be coming back. It was still a taste of what escape might feel like. He was given a first-class ticket. He travelled in a compartment with a mixture of civilians and army and navy officers. For a time he was a figure of good-humoured interest. His shaky German and a now-practised repertoire of self-deprecating explanations about his Irishness meant conversations he would rather have avoided altogether. Yet the atmosphere was relaxed. Copenhagen was no war zone; for most of the military it was either a soft posting or an even softer leave. The question he kept being asked was when England would surrender, or at least when the British would start negotiating a way out. The belief in German invincibility was stronger in the railway compartment than it felt even in the corridors of the Abwehr offices. The queries about peace between Britain and Germany were framed with a kind of puzzlement. No one could understand what the English were about. It must be clear they had lost. Everyone knew it. Ask the French and all the else! The British had their empire, after all, and Hitler was happy to leave them with what they had. Germany was only looking to Europe as its natural sphere of influence. Why would the English not accept the inevitable?

The passengers seemed all the more confused when Frank Ryan said he wasn't sure England was about to surrender at all. It wasn't the answer they wanted. Feeling he had said too much, he offered a variety of shrugs in response. Whatever he felt about the English, he didn't share the enthusiasm for their defeat that surrounded him. He wasn't always comfortable that he didn't share it. There were times when not sharing that enthusiasm felt like a betrayal of Irish friends who had died fighting Britain. But to share it at all meant betraying the men who died all round him on the battlefields of Spain's civil war and beside him in Franco's prison in Burgos. The conversation faded as night drew in around the train. The end was clear for the other passengers, whether the English took the hard road or the easy way Hitler was prepared to offer. If anyone else in the compartment wasn't convinced German bombing was reducing Britain to rubble, and that panic and terror were everywhere, no one said it. By the time the carriage rumbled on to the train ferry at Warnemunde, people were asleep. Interest in Frank Ryan had worn itself out.

If Copenhagen had no shortage of German soldiers, it was still not Germany. Even in the taxi from the Hovedbanegård to the apartment close to the Tivoli Gardens, where Helmut and Elisabeth Clissman lived, it felt further from Berlin than an overnight train journey. Frank Ryan was grateful for that. There was no destruction here. Denmark had been occupied without any fighting and its atmosphere reflected that. Most of the men wearing German uniforms were on holiday. If red and black swastikas flew from some public buildings, they flew in small numbers, and they flew beside the red and white of the Danish cross. This was the way Germany wanted it to be. Denmark surrendered as a friend; Germany was there to protect it. This was what happened if you didn't resist.

For Frank Ryan to be with friends in a city where there seemed to be no war was as much of a holiday as he needed. In the Clissmans' flat, for a time, even the uniforms and flags could be ignored. Their talk had little to do with battles and bombs. In most of Europe there was no fighting now. What was there to say? Before long the subject was Ireland. That was what united them. It was where Helmut Clissman had met Frank, as well as his wife, Elisabeth, who was called Budge by almost everyone. News from home found its way to the Clissmans in Copenhagen more easily than to Berlin, but they had little real awareness of Ireland, except as a place where nothing important happened and where things, somehow, simply stayed the same. When the talk was of fighting, it was of the fight for Ireland's independence. When it was of the war it was, for Budge above all, of German victory bringing a United Ireland. Frank Ryan did not argue, but he lived in a different place. He was a heretic. He had no dreams of German victory. Helmut Clissman knew that. And when the subject of Spain came up, he steered Budge away from it. For Frank the war in Spain had been as much a war against Adolf Hitler as Spain's dictator, Francisco Franco. But as the evening wore on Ryan felt there was more and more conversation that needed steering away from. More and more could not be said. Budge Clissman didn't see it, but Helmut recognised it acutely. Whatever his own feelings, he knew what was behind Frank Ryan's patient smile. Even with old friends everything was tainted by darkness. The air only seemed to be different.

The next day they walked through Copenhagen, and the city itself was their conversation. That was easier. It was late in the afternoon, as they returned home, when Helmut said Frank could not leave Copenhagen without seeing the Tivoli Gardens. He would take him, then and there. Budge was surprised. They had the next day. But Helmut was adamant. He knew a little bit of Tivoli went a long way with Budge anyway, so she could sit at home with her feet up. It was very rushed when there was no need for rush, especially as Frank had already said he was tired. But Helmut Clissman was determined. They went straight out.

The Tivoli was busy; the bars and restaurants were full. There were queues at the rides and the sideshows. There was music everywhere, from bandstands and bars, from the windows of the concert halls and theatres. There was the sound of busy voices, adults and children, noisy with laughter and excitement. Yet still, walking among the bright drifts of flowers along the lake, it could be quiet. Couples walked hand in hand, talking softly, or not talking at all. And where the groups of German soldiers walked among the crowds, the uniforms seemed no more threatening than the red tunics of the life-sized toy soldiers that lined the avenues. It was, again, a place where war was far away.

If the spirit of the Tivoli was something to enjoy, it was an enjoyment Frank Ryan wanted to experience quickly. Crowds were becoming difficult as his hearing deteriorated. Noise created a kind of incoherent hash of sound that was like radio static. He wasn't keen to stay, but Clissman seemed eager to explore the gardens thoroughly. They stopped for a drink by the lake, in a small bar that was an imitation of an Austrian inn. It was full of German soldiers. Helmut bought two bottles of beer and they walked out along the side of the water. They carried on to an area where flower beds stretched out around them. There were no sideshows here. The music was further away.

'Did you notice we were followed earlier?' said Clissman.

'No. I can't say it surprises me. They follow me sometimes in Berlin.'

'I'd say these ones have given up now, Frank.'

'I don't know what they all think I'm going to do,' said Ryan.

'It doesn't matter. Everyone's watched. I am from time to time.'

'I did think about escaping to Sweden this afternoon,' said Ryan, laughing, 'when we were at the mermaid. I thought, well, two things really. The mermaid's not as big as I expected, and how many miles to Sweden?'

'It is called the Little Mermaid.' Helmut Clissman grinned. 'And however many miles it is to Sweden, it's too many. There are people who wouldn't mind you trying to find a way to get there, though. Not only the SD and the Gestapo.'

'If people don't want me in Berlin, I don't want to be there either.'

'It doesn't work like that. You're either a friend or an enemy. That's how it has to be. You don't fit, Frank. In Spain, you were an enemy, that's what the Gestapo have on the file. They have only one answer to that. As far as the Abwehr is concerned, you're here to help Germany. It doesn't matter why. No one in Tirpitzuferstrasse cares about your politics if you're useful. Some people don't think you are very useful. What you've got to say about the IRA is—'

'Is true. Don't you think your agents are better off knowing the truth?'

'You're supposed to be an IRA man, Frank.'

'Ah, well, once one of the Boys, always one of the Boys.'

'You need to show some commitment.' Clissman's voice was harder.

'I'm meant to give your spies a picture of what's at the other end when they get off the U-boat. There's no point pretending the IRA's more competent than it is. Or that Ireland is on the verge of a pro-Nazi uprising. They decided they didn't trust me enough to land me in Ireland a couple of months ago; that's the truth, isn't it? So what am I supposed to do? I give history lessons. I tell your people what they're walking into. But I lay off the fact that the IRA's in the hands of a bunch of loudmouthed gobshites. Won't they find out soon enough?'

'The SD know you argued with Seán Russell in Berlin.'

'There was a lot we didn't agree about. There always was. If he was so keen to get back to Ireland as IRA Chief of Staff, maybe he shouldn't have left at all. He went to America because people were more likely to listen to him in New York than they were in Dublin. He came to Germany for the same reason. If he hadn't died on his way back to Ireland, he would have found out nothing had changed. Nobody would have listened to him, so. No one who mattered.'

'You know it was Seán's decision, though, to take you to Ireland with him.'

'I know that.'

'Even though he didn't trust you.'

'He was Irish, Helmut.' Frank Ryan smiled. 'We're like that.'

'I always wondered what you'd have done if he hadn't died on that submarine, if you'd both been landed in Ireland. What would have happened?'

'Not very much. I'd have found myself locked up again. In the Curragh, for a change. I didn't make any pretence about what I wanted. To go home. I didn't say I was going to spy for Germany, or bomb the North, or start a rebellion against de Valera. If there were people who wanted to believe that—'

'But you would have spoken to de Valera?'

'I couldn't say whether Dev would have spoken to me. From what I recall, our Prime Minister's not a great one for catching up on old times, unless there's something in it for him. I wouldn't think he has too many old friends.'

'And if you had talked to him, what then?'

'Is someone going to send me back on a U-boat to find out?'

Clissman didn't answer.

'No,' said Ryan, 'I think we're past that too.'

'You know what Seán wanted you to do, Frank. He thought you were the man to bring de Valera and the IRA back together, against the English. He thought it would be more than they could handle with Germany about to invade. We were ready for something here. Going in by plane and parachute. Whatever they've given me to do in Denmark, it didn't need a whole regiment of Brandenburgers. And that's what I had, sitting in Jutland all summer. Waiting. It's dead now, everyone knows it. But we were waiting for something. I think if something had happened in England – well, it's a straight line from here to Donegal, mostly over the sea. It wasn't so stupid. A few thousand of us, the Irish Army, the IRA . . . a hell of a lot for the British to take on with an invasion on the mainland. We would have been the very devil on their back doorstep.'

For a moment Helmut Clissman looked into the distance. There was a vision of something half-desired, but it disappeared. He looked back at Ryan. He wasn't sure he much liked the vision. It already belonged to another time.

Frank Ryan finished the beer he was drinking. He took out his tobacco and started to roll a thin cigarette, gazing out across the flowers to the lake. There was the sound of children's laughter again as two boats on the lake collided.

'I don't know why you want to tell me about all that, Helmut. I don't speculate about such things. You know that well enough. I give my history lessons in Tirpitzuferstrasse and I keep my head down. That was your advice.'

'Well, you can't keep your head so far down that you haven't heard there's not going to be an invasion of England. Not yet. They're holding off.'

'That's the rumour.' Ryan lit his cigarette.

'You never did believe in it too much, Frank.'

'The invasion? Why wouldn't I believe that?'

'No, Ireland. Would you ever have been a bridge from Dev to the IRA?'

'I know what you had to say to get me out of Spain, Helmut. I don't know what your bosses thought they had in Frank Ryan, but I'm not too sure I came as advertised.'

Helmut Clissman laughed.

'For the rest,' continued Ryan, 'it's the wrong game. I'm an Irishman; I know better than Abwehr experts like Lahousen and Veesenmayer. You know better too. You know how weak the IRA is. Do you believe Seán Russell thought Dev would cross that bridge just because someone asked him nicely? War against Britain my arse! But in Berlin, I keep my counsel. So do you.'

'So de Valera waits it out?'

'Of course he does. He wanted Irish neutrality. He got it, so. He won't give it up. Unless England invades, or Germany does, he'll sit on his arse. He'll let the storm break round Ireland and he won't move an inch. It's all he has. And whatever way he moves, he's got more to lose by moving than by standing still. And don't kid yourself, Helmut. Every other Irish expert in the Abwehr knows that Dev's a lot closer to the British than he claims to be. Behind all the blather and feck John Bull, Kathleen Ni Houlihan's neutrality goes one way.'

'And where do you really fit in to that, Frank?'

'Do I need to fit?'

'Seán Russell thought there was only one way forward. The old way.'

'Times change,' said the Irishman, 'Seán couldn't.'

'Do they? He intended to put the IRA back in control. If de Valera wasn't going to take the right way forward with Germany, he would have wanted him dead. Isn't that what he told you? Dev had to go, the way Michael Collins did?'

'It doesn't matter what he thought. They'd never get to Dev, Helmut.'

'Would anyone have been prepared to take that chance?'

'What do you mean?'

'It's not what the Abwehr wanted.'

'You still sent Seán to Ireland, though! You don't know what you fucking want.'

'Russell was sent to do two things. To organise sabotage in the North. One. To get the IRA ready for whatever was necessary when Germany invaded England. Two. The second meant working with de Valera, not replacing him.'

'So it wasn't all bollocks?'

'What?'

'The inquiry about how Seán died. Did someone in Tirpitzuferstrasse think twice about him?'

'He died of natural causes. That's what it said.'

'And did he, Helmut?'

'As far as I know. I have no reason to doubt that.'

'It's not impossible, is it? Someone decides to send Seán home, then someone else decides maybe he's not going to do what he's supposed to do. So maybe they get rid of him. Jesus, no wonder I've got people following me!'

'It's not about what did or didn't happen to Seán Russell. It's about an idea, Frank: the idea that trouble in Ireland can only be good if it makes England send troops in, if it means fighting there. It drains resources. It's one more thing to push them to give up, to find a way out. People still think that.'

'But not you, Helmut, not the Abwehr? Is that right?'

Clissman finished his beer. He looked round before continuing.

'There were three agents due to go to Britain, Frank. One for England, two for Ireland. We wanted to try a new way of getting people into Ireland and linking up over the Irish Sea. You know who they were. We were at the party.'

'And one of them died in a car accident. Major Kramer, wasn't it?'

'Yes. The other two went as planned.'

'Helmut, didn't you tell me the less I know—'

'Kramer was an SD man, as you know,' continued Clissman. 'They're trying to force their way into Abwehr operations. Heydrich wants to take it all for the Party. Admiral Canaris is too strong. Hitler won't have it, for now. He doesn't like too much power in the hands of his closest friends. But they got Kramer on that mission. Obviously he didn't go. And there were questions about his death.'

'All he had from me were history lessons on Ireland and the IRA.'

'Well, you know what Berlin's like for rumours.'

'No, I don't. I make damned sure I don't.'

'In Tirpitzuferstrasse the rumour is, in the form it got to me – and most things about Ireland get to me eventually – the rumour is that Kramer had instructions from the SD that did not tally with his Abwehr instructions.'

'Why would I want to know about that?' Ryan lit another cigarette.

'Because those instructions included a plan to dispose of the thing that some see as the real obstacle to Ireland and Germany uniting against England.'

'This is not my business, Helmut. Don't do this to me.'

'I mean Éamon De Valera.'

'Dispose? Just like that.'

'You're not going to tell me there aren't IRA men who are fed up to the back teeth with doing nothing while England's on its knees, Frank? Think about it. If the old way means German arms, German troops, real war with England . . .'

'No,' said Ryan, 'the IRA Army Council may be gougers and gobshites by the bucketful, but there's not so many of them want that. I've told you already.'

'Did all the anti-Treaty men want Collins dead? Did you?'

Frank Ryan shook his head.

'The Abwehr doesn't want it to happen either. We don't want it at all.'

'Isn't Major Kramer dead?'

'Yes. Erik Kramer's dead. British Intelligence have the other man – picked up within a day of landing – but Vera Eriksen has disappeared. She was meant to go to Ireland with Kramer. However, I think they were slow on the uptake at Tirpitzuferstrasse. The view now is that she had been turned, by Kramer. She was acting under his SD orders. She was too close to Kramer. They kept it a secret. Some letters were found, but only after she left Berlin.'

'If she hasn't been picked up, shouldn't you know where she is?'

'We don't.'

'Perhaps you should ask the Reich Main Security Office, then.'

'They don't know anything. They say they don't, anyway. We don't know how practical Kramer's plan was. We don't know anything, except it was about killing de Valera, somehow, somewhere, and creating enough chaos to force the British into Ireland. If there's an unholy mess, it's ours. If it achieves anything the Führer likes, the SD will discover it was down to them. That could be a nail in the coffin Heydrich and Himmler want the Abwehr in. We have to assume that the plan could work. And stop it.'

'There's no chance, Helmut,' said Ryan. 'It's a fantasy.'

'It would be useful, nevertheless, to let the Irish government know.'

'You could phone them,' Ryan laughed. 'Or an anonymous letter?'

'Maybe it does deserve a few jokes, Frank. But what do you think the consequences of civil war and an English invasion would be in Ireland? We have to ensure this particular fantasy doesn't turn into reality, but convincing Dublin of a problem will help. It might be better coming from a reliable source.'

'Me? I'm not sure I'm a reliable source as far as Dublin goes.'

'Oddly, I think information like that is more reliable if it comes from someone who seems to be on the German side. And I doubt they're unaware of, well . . . let's just say how uncomfortable you are with your present situation.'

'I'd like to think they know that at home,' said Ryan quietly.

'It might even help you. It's information about something that threatens Ireland. And if you're prepared to take the risk of getting that to Dublin . . .'

'And how much of a risk is it?'

'You know you're watched by the Gestapo. You're in their sights.'

'I know.'

'Then you know what the risk is, Frank. I can't make you take it.'

12

The Open Air Theatre

London

Vera Eriksen, now Vera Kennedy, sat on an uncomfortable fold-up chair on a slope of grass, looking towards a wall of trees and bushes that made up the backdrop to the stage of the Open Air Theatre in Regent's Park. The theatre sat almost at the centre of the park, behind a wall of wicker fencing that shut out the neat hedges and roadways of the Inner Circle. It was afternoon. All performances were matinees now; they had to be over before the blackout. The season was almost at an end. The trees that were the Open Air Theatre's living scaenae frons were still green, but the leaves were wilting, tinged with yellow. Autumn had arrived. Looking at the trees in front of her, and the audience all round, Vera was surprised that here, for this short time, there was barely anything to say they were in the middle of a city that was being bombed relentlessly every night. Even the barrage balloons were out of sight beyond the trees. There was, perhaps, just the hint of the acrid, burning scent that was everywhere in London's air, almost an accompaniment to the wisp of smoke that rose up in front of the trees. Around a small fire were three women in rags. The play was *Macbeth*. A kettle drum beat. The first witch looked up at the sky.

'When shall we three meet again, In thunder, lightning, or in rain?'

The second answered.

'When the hurlyburly's done, When the battle's lost and won.'

The third continued.

'That will be ere the set of sun.'

When Macbeth arrived, emerging from the trees with Banquo, he wore dark clothes: a black shirt, black trousers, black riding boots. There would be others dressed like him, more as the play progressed and Macbeth killed his king. The black clothes did not carry an insignia, but there was no doubt they were meant to echo the uniforms Vera saw all around her at home.

She didn't know the play, except by the name everyone was vaguely familiar with. It had something to do with a man who killed a king to take his place; it had something to do with good and evil. Her first reaction to the dark uniforms was to smile. It felt a rather sad gesture from a nation under siege by an irresistible enemy. It reminded her of the only other time she had been to London. It was shortly before her father finished his job in Ireland and the family returned to Germany. She was seventeen. It was soon after Hitler had come to power. They came just before Christmas to look at the museums and to shop.

They went to a pantomime one evening, for her younger siblings' sake. It was *Robin Hood*, and the Sheriff of Nottingham was played by an actor with a small, black, paint-on moustache and a fat cigar; Adolf Hitler as Groucho Marx might have played him. The younger children laughed every time he appeared. The Eriksens left at the interval. Vera had been furious, but what she remembered now, in the dark atmosphere of *Macbeth*, was not the anger she felt towards the English then, for their cheap insults towards her country and its

Führer, but the bitterness she felt afterwards towards her father. As they all left the theatre and walked back to their hotel in silence, she had assumed he shared her indignation. At the hotel, while her mother put the youngsters to bed, Vera's father sat in the bar on his own, drinking in a way he never did. When she came down to talk to him, he told her he had left the theatre because of the shame he felt, the shame he felt for Germany, the shame he felt about the man who was now his country's leader. Vera had cried herself to sleep that night. Father and daughter had never spoken about it again.

When the family returned to Germany, and Vera joined the Nazi Party, her father said nothing. Increasingly he said nothing about anything. To anyone. And now he was dead. It was only a year since his death. But Vera recalled that night after the pantomime now, for the first time in a long time. Something died between her and her father that night. They had always been close; through all her years growing up in Ireland they had shared their love for the country that had become their second home. After that night they were never close again.

Vera Eriksen was at the Open Air Theatre to meet the man she knew only as London Kontrolle, or Adam. In the days since leaving the safe house in Covent Garden she had established herself in London among the Irish community in Camden Town. It had been as easy as Adam said it would be. Her documents were good, though no one asked to see them. She had a room in a house and she had work. She was any young Irishwoman working in London, barely distinguishable from any Englishwoman doing the same thing. She had an odd consciousness of that. She was uncomfortable with how comfortable she felt in London after only a few days. She had grown up in Ireland with a passionate dislike for the English that was very different from the feelings she encountered when she returned to Germany. Most people she knew wanted to like the English. They had, after all, the same racial origins, hadn't they? They should be natural allies against the forces that threatened civilisation: the Jews, the Blacks, the mixed races, the Bolsheviks. Even now, her friends at home felt that war between Britain and Germany was a kind of mistake. It would be rectified when the English saw sense. Wasn't that what Hitler himself thought?

Vera had phoned Adam as instructed. Once he had changed the number. Now he had asked to meet her. The theatre, he said, offered the necessary combination of anonymity and open surroundings. He would find her there.

When the interval came, most of the thoughts that had been in Vera's head at the play's beginning had been swept aside: about what she was doing in London, about what she might get from Adam in the way of instructions, about going to Ireland, and then unexpectedly, uneasily, about her father. The play had pulled her in. Then, as she stood with a cup of tea, thinking about the words she had heard more than anything else, the man called Adam was in front of her, smiling. She registered the smile; lazy, she thought. She didn't much like it.

'You look like you've been enjoying it.'

'I suppose I have.'

'Do you know the play?'

Vera shook her head.

'I'm sorry to tear you away, then. But a walk would be the thing. Assume more deaths, naturally. And I'm sure you can guess all will not end well for Macbeth, or indeed Lady Macbeth. Obvious enough from the moment he appears in a black shirt and riding boots. Good triumphs, as does true kingship.'

As Vera and Adam walked away from the theatre, into Regent's Park, London Kontrolle kept up an easy, jokey conversation about the play and Shakespeare.

'Have you ever read Karl Kraus?'

'No. I've probably read more Shakespeare.'

'He was a satirist, in Vienna, during the last war.'

'I know who he was.'

Adam took out a cigarette. He offered one to Vera. She didn't take it.

'Banned in Germany now. A Jew, of course. But a very perceptive one.' London Kontrolle walked on. 'I always remember him writing about some German propaganda – the Great War, of course – that consisted of rolls of toilet paper with quotes from Shakespeare on every sheet. The idea being that you could literally wipe your arse with the words of England's greatest writer.' Adam laughed then stopped to light his cigarette. 'Kraus remarks on two things. The German thoroughness with which all those extracts from Shakespeare's plays had been assembled by someone who had studied them and must have admired them. Then, the fact that using Shakespeare's words to wipe your arse says a lot more about Germany than about England. You couldn't imagine the English doing the same thing with Goethe, could you?'

Vera didn't respond. London Kontrolle liked the sound of his own voice. There was no need for her to reply. But he also unsettled her. It felt as if he said things to shock. She lived in a world where what you said, even how you said it, mattered, where wrong answers were recorded and remembered. She couldn't work out whether his words were just reckless or whether he was testing her.

'You're settled anyway, Vera?'

'Yes. I found a room in a house in Mornington Crescent. Most of the people are Irish, some English. I took you at your word. I found some adverts for cleaners. I'm working for several people. There's a woman downstairs who cleans too and she put me in touch with the landlord of a pub. I clean there.'

'You fit in perfectly. You're already invisible.' Adam smiled. 'What else do the English expect of the Irish, other than that they should clean up after them?'

'I have made one mistake,' said Vera.

'And what was that?'

'I'm working for a doctor who has a surgery in Camden. He's Jewish.'

London Kontrolle laughed.

'I don't want to look as if I don't need the work . . . it was the landlord at the Bedford Arms who recommended me. I didn't know the man was Jewish.'

'The things we have to do for Germany, my dear!'

Vera was aware he was laughing at her. It wasn't funny.

'I would have avoided it if I could, that's all,' she said coldly.

'It's a war. You can safely leave the mumbo-jumbo in Germany.'

Adam's words were harder.

'I'm simply telling you, Adam. You wanted to know.'

'You're an Irishwoman, Vera. By all means hate the English, when and as appropriate, but not too much of anything else . . . it's, well, embarrassing.'

'Are we here for a reason?' asked Vera.

She took a cigarette of her own. Adam paused to offer her a light.

'Yes, we are. I think the game's afoot.'

'I don't know what you mean.' She found it hard not to show impatience.

'Assassination, I mean. Mr de Valera. When the hurlyburly's done . . .'

Vera took this in. It was unexpectedly blunt and it was real. She was aware, now, how unreal the same idea had felt when the man talking to her about it had been Erik Kramer. It hadn't felt unreal, yet it was, compared with these words in a London park. Erik's voice had been full of a different kind of reality, a combination of duty, passion, expectation, even excitement. That had felt very real, then, because he was real. But it was different. It was a reality that was about her country, about her Party, about her Führer. Erik felt that with every fibre of his being. He felt it as a pilot felt it, he had told her, as a soldier advancing into battle felt it. That was the only reality: fighting for the Führer. She wanted to believe that too. This was a much cruder reality somehow. But she nodded.

'And are those orders from Berlin?' she asked quietly.

'Yes. Orders from those in Berlin who instructed Major Kramer.'

'I only know the plan was a possibility,' said Vera. 'I never had the details. You must know that. I don't know who to go to, who to trust. Where to start.'

'You can leave the details to me, Vera. I don't think you can trust the IRA in the South at all. At least I don't know who we trust and who we don't. Not only that, there are other Abwehr agents in Ireland who should not get wind of this. They may well get instructions to stop it. I am in touch with a number of IRA men in Belfast who think the right way, men who are prepared to act. Men who will take on the British and, if necessary, an Irish government that won't. I expect you to be prepared to go to Ireland in ten days, a fortnight. When you get there, you will do nothing except meet the contacts the Abwehr told you to meet. You give nothing away. I will tell you when the thing is happening.'

'I see. And what is my role in it?'

'Your role will become clear when it needs to be.'

Vera drew on her cigarette and dropped it to the ground.

'You do have to remember one thing, Vera. It shouldn't need saying, but your relationship with Ireland, while helpful in so many ways, does carry . . . Well, let's just say the Irish are a notoriously sentimental race, aren't they?'

'I don't know what you mean by that,' said Vera.

'I mean that although the interests of Germany may serve Ireland in the long term, which is what we want the most reliable IRA leaders to believe, the reasons for disposing of de Valera are only the benefits that will bring to Germany.'

'I understand.'

'I know you do. You had the sense to get rid of Drücke, after all.'

Vera looked away. Drücke had died for this. She wasn't sure where her doubts about that had come from. They had not been there when she stood on the platform at Waverley Station. It felt, overwhelmingly then, that he was a risk to what she was doing. He was undisciplined and reckless. London Kontrolle had as good as told her she was right. It had felt right. But she wondered if she hadn't moved too quickly. Would it really have mattered if they had simply gone their own ways? Karl Drücke stuck in her head more than she wanted him to do. She needed reasons for what she had to do. It was something Erik Kramer always teased her about. It was a weakness she had; too much time spent away from Germany. His orders did not require reasons or explanations.

'You don't need to contact me again,' said Adam, 'unless something goes wrong. Keep on with the cleaning, my dear. I will be in touch when I'm ready.'

'You don't know where I am.'

London Kontrolle smiled his now familiar, irritating, lazy smile.

'I already know where you are. And remember, when things take off, they will take off fast. When 'tis done, then 'twere well it were done quickly.'

Adam watched Vera walk away across Regent's Park. They were quite close to Camden now, and it was beginning to get dark. He would walk back the other way, into town. She was a more thoughtful woman than he had judged her to be at their first meeting. He rather liked her, but it would not pay to let her have any more information than was necessary. With someone clever, it was best not to be too clever. The way she betrayed her Abwehr colleague had led him to believe she was more fanatical and therefore more malleable than seemed to be the case. Not that it mattered, in terms of the job she had to perform in Ireland. She wouldn't question what she had to do, but she might wonder how little it was. That wouldn't matter either. She would still fulfil her purpose admirably.

13

The Bedford Arms

An uneventful journey brought Stefan Gillespie from Dublin to London, and to Arlington Road, a street of flat-fronted terraced houses that ran parallel with Camden High Street. The street had seen better days; its houses, now part of urban London, had once been suburban villas. But the suburbs had moved ever outwards and Camden was pulled further into the heart of the city. The neat villas of Arlington Road had grown scruffier and increasingly they were bought up and let as flats and single rooms. But only yards from the noise of Camden, it was still a quieter place, where people knew each other. And a lot of those people were Irish; new Irish and old Irish. Once they came to build the canals and railways, and they still came; for some to build what needed building now; for some to escape what needed escaping, even if there was nothing very much to escape to. Now it was familiarity that drew the Irish. It was a place to start, a place you didn't need to feel a stranger. In Arlington Road there was not a county of Ireland unrepresented. There, and in the streets for miles around, wherever you came from, you'd find someone who knew it, and someone who knew someone, who knew someone, who almost knew who you were. For some it was a comfortable place to be; for others it was bleaker. At the top end of Arlington Road, by

Camden Lock, was a great red-brick building, rising like a fort over the terraced houses. Rowton House was a hostel for single men; more Irish men lived there than in any building outside Ireland. Like everyone else in Arlington Road, they found their way, at some point, to the Bedford Arms.

The pub was close to the bottom of Arlington Road, nearer to Mornington Crescent than Camden Town. Its flat brick front reflected the houses around it, but it was older. It had stood there when there were no rows of terraced houses on either side; barely a street at all. At the back there was a stone-flagged yard and a flowerless garden and a warren of broken-down outbuildings that had once been stables. The Bedford Arms had two big rooms downstairs, a saloon and a public bar, linked by a small snug. It was a busy, brash place, with the shelves of alcohol behind the bars set out like altars, and with big mirrors in the saloon that reflected the bar and its customers back on themselves.

Stefan was greeted with a mixture of irritation and indifference by the landlord, Willie Mullins. He was old Irish, London-Irish, and his voice was the voice of any other Londoner. He stood at one end of the saloon bar, reading the *Sporting Life* and smoking a Burma cheroot. The only questions he asked were whether Stefan could pull a pint and change a barrel. He then folded the paper, stuffed it into his pocket and turned to the door to the street. He paused.

'You been in an air raid?'

'No,' said Stefan. It was true that he hadn't experienced any bombing close up, but he had been in London recently and he had been in Berlin. His alias, Eddie Griffin, of course, had not been out of Ireland. He knew nothing.

'Up to you what you do when the sirens go. There's an Anderson shelter in the yard. Or you can take your chances. Sometimes you wonder if it's worth the bloody effort. I haven't heard they're aiming for the pub.' It was the closest he had got to a smile. 'And there's public shelters down the street if you want.'

As Willie Mullins left, the barman lifted the flap and came out.

'I'm Anto. I'll show you your room. Eddie, is it?'

Stefan nodded. They started up a dark staircase.

'If the bombing's bad, fuck the shelters. The Underground's deeper.'

'How bad is it?'

'Depends where they drop the fucking bombs.'

Stefan would soon discover that Anto was the man who really seemed to run the pub. He was small, wiry and of indeterminate age. He could have been forty, fifty, even sixty; his skin was dry and lined, tightly stretched over his face, as if he didn't have enough of it. His accent said he came from Dublin. He spoke little behind the bar, and when he did it was usually about the weather. On any other subject his words were short and non-committal. Mostly, standing at his post, serving drinks, he listened and chain-smoked. Even on the subject of the war he rarely had much to say that wasn't an echo of what someone else had said moments earlier. He asked Stefan no questions. He just left him in a room at the top of the pub, in a corridor of rooms, all of which were unused. No one lived in the Bedford Arms other than Eddie Mullins, who had a bedroom on the floor below. Whatever the noise and bustle of the pub below, the rest of the building was empty. The rooms were cold, damp and shut up. And there was almost no daylight upstairs. Most of the windows had been boarded up because of the blackout. And the boards were never taken down.

Stefan's room was tucked into the sloping roof that lay behind the parapet wall at the front of the pub. It was blacked-out when he came in. Anto left him in the darkness, with only a dim light from the corridor, even though it was day-light outside. Stefan pulled back the heavy curtains and let in the day. The room looked out at houses on the other side of Arlington Road. There was a bed, a table and chair, a ward-robe. It was clean, at least the bed linen was. There was scuffling in the ceiling. He screwed up his face. With luck, they'd be mice.

Stefan went back down to the pub. It had been empty when he arrived but there were a few customers now. Anto took him behind the bar and after a few peremptory words and gestures, left him to start serving. The pub wasn't busy and the bars, public and saloon, were better ordered than a first glance at Eddie Mullins might have suggested. Later he noticed Anto watching him.

'All right?' asked Stefan.

'You'll do,' said Anto. 'But you'll need to speed up evenings.'

Stefan turned away to pull a pint of bitter. Willie Mullins came in. He nodded at a number of customers. He looked from Stefan to Anto. Anto shrugged. Willie, satisfied, resumed his position at the end of the saloon bar.

'He won't want to pay you.' Anto spoke quietly.

'You what?' said Stefan.

'Willie. He never coughs up. You'll have to pester him, so.'

'Then I will.'

'You need to do it when there's money in the till. A Friday or Saturday night, when he's closed up and he's on the whiskey.' Anto grinned. 'You have to get it out of Willie while he's got it, and he doesn't have it for very long.'

Willie Mullins was the kind of man who was bathed in sweat from the moment he got out of bed in the morning until he fell back into bed at night. Usually he did fall back into it; as a matter of course, he drank through most of the day. Mostly what he drank was beer, which simultaneously replenished the liquid he was losing through his pores and added more to lose. He would drink spirits once the pub closed, not in huge quantities but enough to send him to sleep or, more often than not, into a state of unconsciousness which passed for sleep. He had run the Bedford Arms for fifteen years and what it was now was very much what it had been when he took it over. There had once been plans. There had been a Mrs Mullins, too, and the plans were hers. She saw a restaurant on the first floor and she saw a small, private hotel on the top floor and in the empty buildings at the back of the pub. At one point she had even commissioned an architect to realise her vision on paper. It was when Mrs Mullins began to spend money that her husband came to the conclusion that visions were expensive and unnecessary. He liked the Bedford Arms as it was. In the end, Mrs Mullins didn't like it the way it was. She came to the conclusion that she didn't much like her husband either. When she left, Willie Mullins joked that a wife could be replaced a lot more easily than a pub like the Bedford Arms, but he never did replace her. He kept the pub as it was. The rest of the building didn't matter.

Surprisingly the pub was well run. Willie himself did very little. He stood at one corner of the saloon bar, sometimes behind it, sometimes on the customer's side. The real work was done by Anto and an assortment of barmaids. From time to time, during opening hours, Willie gravitated through the archway that separated the saloon from the public bar and stood in more or less the same place in the other room. His conversation consisted of little more than greetings and how's-it-goings. Much of the time he simply watched what was going on around him with a kind of amiable contentment. He read several newspapers in the morning, the *Daily Mail*, the *Daily Herald*, and sometimes the *Irish Press*, though the paper that was almost always open on the bar in front of him was the *Sporting Life*. Through the course of the morning and the afternoon, much of which he spent studying the *Life*, he would walk out of the pub and along Arlington Road to the Southampton Arms, a pub that sat at the corner of Mornington Crescent and Camden High Street. He passed money and scribbled betting slips across the counter of the snug bar. Sometimes banknotes in considerable numbers would cross in the other direction, but never in numbers that compensated for what went out. Since off-course betting was illegal, only familiar faces were welcome in the snug of the Southampton Arms. The police turned a blind eye as long as there was no trouble, and there was usually a thug on the door to ensure there wasn't. Occasionally an over-zealous inspector, new to the area, would insist on a raid, but good community relations demanded that the proprietors of the Southampton Arms receive reasonable notice of police action. Over-zealous inspectors didn't stay long in Camden.

Behind Willie Mullins' amiable exterior he was often in a state of some financial anxiety. It wasn't so much the betting that brought this about, as his unshakable belief, despite a lifetime's evidence to the contrary, that he was a serious judge of form in horses. He wasn't. But somehow he survived. The Bedford Arms did make money, and in the shape of Anto, Willie was a better judge of bar staff than he was of horseflesh. It was a popular pub, especially with Camden Town's Irish population. But it never made quite enough to cover Willie's losses. He supplemented those losses as best he could. Not everything he did was legal, but then not much that was legal could offer any assistance.

Stefan Gillespie had been working at the Bedford Arms for three days. He knew the pub's routine and the conversation across the bar was undemanding. There might be the odd question about where he was from, but no one expected much of a reply. He watched Anto and took lessons in how to engage in a conversation and say nothing. In the saloon bar the general conversation was about bombing and rationing and when it wasn't, it was about the ordinary business of the lives that were contained in the streets of Camden; as often as it reflected on the war it was as insubstantial and as empty as if there was no war at all. In the public bar, where the customers were almost only ever men, the war had its share, but it was work that mattered most. The bar acted as a kind of informal labour exchange. It was somewhere to find someone who knew of a job. There was no shortage of building, but there was a shortage of men to do it. The Bedford Arms was a place to find Irish foremen looking for Irish workers.

Stefan had worked only one full evening session at the Bedford Arms. The bombers had come every night except one, when there was heavy rain. Sooner or later, as it got dark, the sirens would sound. Willie Mullins would complain, with the same words every time, about the money Hitler was costing him. The pub would empty, as people made their way to the shelters and the Underground. The first night Stefan followed them, up to Camden High Street and down into the Underground. He had gone unprepared, without even a coat, let alone a blanket and a pillow. He spent that night sitting against a wall at one end of the platform, breathing in the atmosphere that pushed away the cold, metallic smell of the Underground: dust, sweat, cigarettes, urine. He was surrounded by people who had bedding and food; there were even deckchairs and picnic tables. People filled the stone corridors; they spread along the platforms, even as the trains rumbled past; men, women, children. They sat through the night, talking and playing cards, reading, knitting; and they slept through the night too. The sound of bombs was there. Stefan heard it; even below ground it could be felt. But nothing was close. He was no judge of these things, yet, but people told him the Germans were hitting the docks again. It seemed to be a standing joke that there was nothing to bomb in Camden. He had not really slept, but people around him had. They were used to it. He nodded off, finally, as the night was ending and All Clear was sounding above ground.

He woke abruptly, to find the crowds around him packing up their bedding and piling it neatly against the walls. He left the station and came up into a bright, clear morning. He could smell the smoke. The conversations around him were about what had been hit. There were fires in the City, still burning. There were words about the dead, no more than fragments, muttered, accompanying a shake of the head. Somewhere children had been killed. Somewhere a shelter took a direct hit. All dead. The words were broken up with other fragments, even with laughter. Words about nothing very much. Stefan walked along Arlington Road to the Bedford Arms. Others were returning from the Underground and the shelters; some were heading to work. It felt, oddly, as if nothing much had happened. All there was was the smell of smoke in the air. When he walked into the pub, Willie Mullins was sitting at a table in the saloon bar, eating eggs and bacon. He said nothing about the night that had just gone.

'There's bacon in the pan, Eddie, in the kitchen. Help yourself.'

That day Stefan worked through the lunchtime session as usual. He didn't know if watching Willie Mullins was proving unproductive or not. But it was already uninteresting. He had no idea what it was anybody in Dublin wanted to know, but he already knew the landlord's habits. When he wasn't standing in the pub he was on his way to or from the Southampton Arms to place a bet and, almost without fail, lose more money. It put Mullins in the same position as thousands of other men from Camden to Kentish Town. It was about as unusual as an

Irishman in Rowton House. One afternoon Mullins disappeared, quite late, and didn't reappear for several hours. One morning he wasn't in the pub at all. He arrived back at about eleven. At a time when almost everyone was spending nights in the Underground and in air-raid shelters, it couldn't mean much. Life at the Bedford Arms, even after a few days, was predictable and repetitive. And whatever might have happened at the pub in the past, it was certainly no hotbed of Republicanism now. If there were IRA men in the public bar, they were only there for a drink. Stefan knew the smell of it from Dublin; there was nothing.

As the pub was about to close one lunchtime, two men came into the saloon bar. It was almost empty. Willie Mullins had his head buried in the *Sporting Life*, marking horses with a pencil. The two men stood at the bar.

'Mild and bitter and a White Shield.'

As Stefan picked up a pint glass, Mullins looked up.

The man who had ordered the drinks smiled. 'How's life, Willie?'

The landlord spoke slowly. 'Could be worse, Mr Simpson.'

'That's good to hear. Busy, are you?'

'Busy enough.'

As the man called Simpson walked across to Mullins and continued talking, quietly, the other man watched Stefan pulling the pint. He took out a packet of cigarettes and offered one over the bar. Stefan shook his head.

'Thanks, not just now.'

Stefan already knew they were policemen.

'You're new, then?'

'It's just a bit of work, sir,' said Stefan. He put the pint on the bar and opened a bottle of White Shield. The man smoked, watching him pour the beer.

'You worked for Willie before?'

'Not at all, sir. But I've a pal who did. Mr Mullins was kind enough to give me a job. I'm looking for something a bit more permanent. But it'll do.'

As Stefan put the White Shield down the other man, Simpson, walked back along the bar and picked it up. He drank it down in one, slowly. The man with the pint of mild and bitter sipped at it several times, screwing up his face.

'You pour a fucking ropey pint, Paddy.'

'Can I get you something else then, sir?'

'It'll do for now.'

Simpson gave Stefan a nod then both men walked out. Stefan knew that routine well enough. He made no attempt to ask for payment for the drinks.

'I assume you didn't want me to ask them to pay, Willie?'

'You have it right.' The landlord grinned. 'They're not the sort that pay.'

Stefan walked along the bar, wiping it as he went.

'Police?'

'Special Branch.'

Stefan nodded. He didn't know whether he should show some unease.

Mullins laughed. 'I can see they have you scared half to death, Eddie.'

'Do they come in here a lot?'

'You're safe enough with those boys. Bottom feeders the pair of them. It doesn't mean a thing. They come in to show me they can. But they don't come in on a Friday night when there might be a few who'd take exception to them.'

Stefan Gillespie thought no more about the English Special Branch men. He was not thinking about them that night as he walked along Arlington Road, back to the Bedford Arms. There was heavy rain again and a strong wind. It was not the weather for bombers. The sirens had sounded earlier but Raiders Passed wailed out shortly afterwards. A false alarm.

The pub had been quiet. Willie Mullins had gone out that afternoon. He hadn't come back. Anto had told Stefan to take the evening off. With nothing else to do, he walked up to Camden Lock and along the canal. He went into another pub and sat over several pints of beer before he made his way back to the Bedford Arms. It was quiet. The difference between the nights when the bombers came and the nights they didn't was a difference between two worlds. In the silent streets it was hard to believe what had happened the night before and what would happen again, almost certainly, the next clear night. He had seen little bomb damage. He had not left Camden since arriving in London; in those few days no bombs fell closer than the railway lines into King's Cross and St Pancras. He had seen the fires on the horizon that night, much closer than before, but still safely in the distance.

His thoughts had been more of the last time he was in London. It was little more than a month ago. He was on his way back to Ireland, on a journey that had brought him from Berlin and Stockholm, to Scotland and England. He had been there to see a woman, in Hammersmith. It was a relationship that had started the year before. Now the relationship was over. He didn't even know where she was living. Kate O'Donnell was still in England, but that was all Stefan knew. He had not wanted it to end. She hadn't either. But whatever they found in each other, it was not the overwhelming love that, somewhere, both of them were looking for. Stefan was unsure that kind of love came more than once. Perhaps it only came when you were young enough to let it. Perhaps they hadn't given each other much chance. Perhaps the distance the war opened up between them, when Kate went to work in London, was too much, on top of other distances. Some of that distance was in what he did, he knew that, the world he inhabited that he couldn't quite shake off when he walked out of Dublin Castle. Perhaps it simply wasn't the right time. It wasn't something he let himself think about very much. It had to be enough that it was finished now. That was how things were.

He had been too preoccupied to notice the black car that pulled past him slowly along Arlington Road. He noticed it only as he approached the Bedford Arms, and a small alleyway that ran down its side to Camden High Street. He recognised the man who was getting out of the passenger side. It was the Special Branch man, the one Willie Mullins had addressed as Mr Simpson.

As the policeman stood, blocking the way, the other man walked from the car to join him.

'Good evening,' said Stefan, attempting a smile.

'We were looking for you,' said Simpson. 'Eddie, isn't it?'

'It is Eddie, sir. How can I help you?'

'Now there's a question. How can he help us, Dan?'

'I don't know, Sarge,' said the other policeman.

'What have you got to offer, Eddie?'

'I don't know what you're talking about, sir.'

'He's good on the "sirs", I'll give him that, Sarge.'

'So who are you, Eddie?' asked Simpson.

'I'm just minding my own business. Would you let me go in, please?'

'A man who knows his rights, I'd say. So apart from being a cunt, what sort of Irishman are you, Paddy?"

Stefan said nothing. He took out his identity card.

'I don't care what your name is,' said Simpson. 'That's not the question.'

'I'm working at the Bedford Arms. You know that, sir.'

'Bit of a Republican, are you, Eddie?'

'I'm a barman.'

'A clever one too,' said Dan. 'There's no fooling him.'

'Do you know who I am?' asked Simpson insistently.

'You're a policeman.'

'I don't know what they're doing to these Irish bastards these days, but you know I'd almost say they're not as thick as shit any more, Dan. Hard to believe, I know. But you're right, Eddie, I'm a policeman. A detective. What I specialise in is giving the runaround to fucking Irish bastards like you. And one way you can avoid that is by making sure you keep on the right side of me.'

Stefan said nothing. He frowned. It was a look somewhere between incomprehension and fear. He comprehended readily enough; but he was not unafraid. He recognised the style. The slow, casual insults. These men were in a different league to Terry Gregory; where he hid his wit and his knowledge behind such language, Stefan knew that all these two had to hide was violence.

'It does no harm to keep your eyes open in Mullins' gaff.'

'I don't know what you're after at all,' said Stefan.

'You know what Special Branch is, Paddy? I'd say most Paddys do.'

'Yes, I know what it is.'

'You never know what you might come across in a pub full of drunken Irishmen. Might be in your interests to remember some of that, what about it?'

Stefan didn't answer.

'There could even be a few quid in it.'

'I don't know what you mean.'

'I think you do. You have heard there's a war on?'

'What do you want from me?'

'That's the question, isn't it? But I'd say you might hear some very seditious conversations over the bar in there. You do know what that means?'

'I'm sure I can work it out.'

Stefan had let his irritability get the better of him. He regretted it. As the sergeant spoke, the other detective pushed him, driving him back into the alleyway by the pub. It was only a few feet, but between the walls it was darker.

'He's sure he can work it out, Dan. I like him; I like him a lot.'

The sergeant turned, laughing. Then he spun round abruptly. His fist hit Stefan in the stomach. It was hard and it was unexpected. Stefan dropped to the pavement. The sergeant crouched down beside him, pulling up his face.

'Whoever you are, Eddie, you need to watch yourself. You're a piece of Irish shit, that's all. Let's just call you Paddy, shall we? Paddy, Eddie, what's the fucking difference? As for what I want, if I want you to wipe the shit off my shoes, that's what you'll do. You don't matter here. No Irish bastard matters. There's too many of you, stinking the place up. You should have been more careful about where you got a job. But as you're there, you never know, you might even be useful. As far as I'm concerned, anyone who goes near the Bedford Arms wants watching. I'm watching. This is how we do it in London.'

He stood up. He nodded at the other Special Branch man, who bent down and dragged Stefan up, holding his arms behind him, and pushing them up his back until he cried out in pain. Simpson landed another heavy punch in his stomach. This one was harder. The other detective let go. Stefan crumpled to the ground again, his face scraping against the bricks at the side of the alleyway.

'Another for luck. The luck of the Irish. Sláinte!'

The next morning Stefan Gillespie woke in considerable pain. His stomach was badly bruised; his arms were hard to move; his face was still caked in blood. It had taken him a long time to get to sleep, and the sleep had done little to repair the damage. But nothing was broken. He wasn't sure what it meant. It seemed as if it meant nothing. He was an Irishman, working in an Irish pub. The pub had a reputation, as did its landlord. The Metropolitan Police Special Branch had a reputation too;

they had to keep it up. That seemed to be the extent of it. He could see nothing else. There was no real information the detectives wanted. They knew nothing about him. As for the Bedford Arms, nothing was happening there. Perhaps he should have told them, Special Branch man to Special Branch man. They were wasting their time. But it was a way of wasting time Stefan knew, just as he knew officers in Dublin Castle who worked in the same way. A point was being made, even if no one knew what it was. Territory was being marked too. None of that meant they wouldn't be back, but what for? He had to assume the point had been made. And that once would be enough.

He walked along the corridor to the bathroom and cleaned some of the blood off his face. He had a feeling Willie Mullins would think the whole thing was funny. But as he came down the stairs he could hear something surprising. It was the sound of a piano, playing gently. He stood, listening, smiling at the recognition of something he knew. He walked through from the back hall into the saloon bar. Across the bar, in a corner, there was a battered upright piano. A woman sat at it, playing. He saw only her back and her fair hair. He stopped, listening again. She was unaware of him. He wasn't sure where he knew the piece from. It could have been something his mother had played. Or one of his father's records. Or a concert, in the days when he was first in Dublin with Maeve. He hadn't heard it in a long time; he was startled to find it still in his head.

'That was unexpected,' he said as the woman finished playing.

She turned round on the piano stool.

'A Beethoven piano sonata, I mean.'

She looked at him, clearly embarrassed. Vera Kennedy didn't work every morning as a cleaner at the Bedford Arms. When she did she came in very early. There was no one else up. She knew about the new barman from Anto, but she had not seen him. When the pub was empty, on a couple of mornings, she had sat for ten minutes, playing the piano. This morning she had come in late. But Willie Mullins was rarely up before ten and she had forgotten the new barman. Her embarrassment was no more than awkwardness in the first instant, but then it went deeper. She was revealing too much of herself. It wasn't that it would mean anything to anyone here, but it still wasn't what every cleaner would do in the saloon bar of a pub. It drew attention to her. It was careless. She would shrug it off as if it didn't matter, as if it really was something entirely normal, nothing. But she was surprised the man knew what she was playing.

'It's a bit out of tune. It was number thirty.'

'I wouldn't run to the numbers,' said Stefan.

She looked at him, smiling and registering his face. She saw the blood. Whatever the reason for it, it was a good opportunity to turn the focus on him.

'You're unexpected too. Your face, in particular.'

'Oh, that? It was a brief encounter with a wall.'

'Did you tell the police? It must have been a very aggressive sort of wall.'

'No need. They were there.'

'I see.' She got up and walked closer, looking at Stefan's face.

'You don't,' he said, 'but it is the finest police force in the world.'

'Is that something I'm meant to understand?'

'I won't bother to explain it. I don't understand it myself.'

The woman stretched out her hand.

'You'll be Eddie. Anto told me.'

'Eddie Griffin,' said Stefan, shaking her hand. 'And you?'

'Vera, Vera Kennedy.'

'Do you often play the piano at the Bedford Arms in the mornings?'

'Only when I think there's no one listening. I'm the cleaner.' She pointed at a mop and bucket. 'Those are my real instruments. I'll find you some iodine.'

'It doesn't matter, Vera.'

'No, I'm sure it doesn't, but I'll find some anyway.'

Stefan watched her walk out of the bar towards the kitchen. As she went out, Anto was coming in. He didn't stop as he passed Stefan, heading behind the bar. He took in what he saw and, as he rarely did, felt he should ask a question.

'What happened to you?'

'The long arm of the law.'

'Laurel and Hardy?'

'If that's Detective Sergeant Simpson and friend.'

'That's it. I wouldn't worry. They don't run to much worse than that.'

'That's a comfort.'

'Every cloud...' said Anto, as he started to pull one of the pumps clean. He winked as Vera came back, carrying a bowl, a cloth and a dark brown bottle.

'Sit down,' said Vera. 'The piano stool's fine. Look up.'

'I'm more than happy to.' Stefan looked up at her face, smiling broadly.

Anto snorted.

'Shut your mouth, Eddie, unless you want it full of iodine.' Vera poured the yellow liquid on to the cloth. She grinned back down at him. He knew she was holding back laughter. 'It won't hurt. If it does, remember, it might stop your face going gangrenous and ruining your looks. With luck . . . and a prayer.'

She crossed herself and pushed the cloth down firmly on to his face.

'Ah! Jesus Christ!'

Vera was laughing. Anto joined in behind the bar.

'More iodine! Sure, we'll save your good looks yet, Eddie!'

14

Camden Town

Several days later, as Stefan Gillespie was leaving the Bedford Arms, shortly after the lunchtime session had ended, Willie Mullins was coming in, his face puckered in a frown. It was his normal expression; he was always anxious about something. By now Stefan knew that he was returning from the Southampton Arms where he had been placing a bet or, less likely by the look on his face, collecting some winnings.

'Can you drive?' snapped the landlord.

'I can drive.'

'A lorry?'

'I can drive a tractor, will that do?' Stefan laughed. 'Why?'

'You can make yourself useful, so. Be back by six.'

'You said I could have the evening off.'

'Don't suit. Where you going?'

'The pictures.'

'Oh.' There was nearly a smile. 'Matinee, then. No double feature!'

Willie Mullins walked past Stefan into the pub.

Stefan continued down Arlington Road and into Mornington Crescent. The houses in the terraces here were bigger than those in Arlington Road; there were iron railings and wrought-iron balconies in front of the first-floor windows. Once they had been a few rungs up the ladder of elegance, and gardens stretched along the other side of the crescent. Now the white stone and concrete of the Black Cat cigarette factory had replaced the gardens, and the only thing that distinguished the tenement rooms and flats of Mornington Crescent from those in Arlington Road was that more people were packed into them. It was in a house in Mornington Crescent that Vera Kennedy had a room. Stefan wasn't quite sure which of them had suggested going to the cinema, but several days of early-morning conversation at the Bedford Arms, as she mopped the floors and he bottled up and cleaned out the pumps, had got them there.

A little way along Mornington Crescent there was a group of children, boys and girls, ten, eleven, twelve years old, standing on the pavement around a battered pram and a wooden wheelbarrow. In the pram and the barrow were piled up various pieces of scrap metal: battered saucepans, an old kettle, some brass fire irons, some rusty tin cans. A short time in London had already made Stefan familiar with the gangs of children who trailed around Camden collecting scrap metal. Little of what they collected looked likely to contribute much to the construction of Spitfires, but that was what the children believed. In the pram was a metal beer keg, which nearly filled it. Two of these had been filched from the back yard at the Bedford Arms only days before. Stefan smiled. He could not prove where the keg had come from, and had no inclination to try, but as he stepped out into the road to go round the children, he saw two older boys push another against the railings of a house. He could see a second, dark-haired boy was being held by his arms, struggling to break away. None of the children seemed aware of Stefan. The boy who had been pushed hard against the railings crumpled on to the pavement. He had been hit. A teenage boy stood over him.

'It's our patch. We collect the scrap here.'

'You can piss off.' The boy on the ground glared up.

'You been told.'

'You don't own this street. I live here.'

'Sod off. We'll take what you've got. It belongs to us.'

Several boys and girls moved forward to take the keg from the pram.

'You got no right!'

'What you going to do about it?'

Stefan stepped forward.

'What's going on here?'

The teenage boy turned round.

'What's it to you?'

'I don't much like what you're doing, that's what it is to me,' said Stefan. 'And as that's probably my boss's bloody beer keg, I'll decide who nicks it.'

The children holding the keg let it drop back into the pram. They looked at the older boy, waiting for some sort of direction. The teenage boy wasn't keen to start an argument with an adult. Stefan had a half smile on his face, but it was still clear that he was serious. The boy had to make a gesture at least.

'It's none of your business. We're collecting for the war.'

'Then you can go and collect somewhere else.'

'You going to make us, mate?'

'No, I wouldn't be bothered to make you myself, but if you want me to find a copper to sort you out, I'm happy to. It's up to you, "mate". All right?'

The gang of children was uneasy. The two who held the dark-haired boy had let him go. They all looked as if they felt a retreat was now the best option.

'It's still our patch,' said the gang leader. 'They need to remember that.' He walked away.

The others were drifting away too.

The teenage boy looked back.

'Fucking Paddy!'

Stefan turned round, but it was clear the words were addressed to the boy who had been pushed against the railings. He was pulling himself up again now.

'Gobshite!'

The Irish insult was shouted with an accent that belonged entirely to London.

'You all right?' asked Stefan.

'Course I'm bloody all right.'

The other boy, the dark-haired one, looked more shaken.

'I got to get off, Donal. Dad'll be waiting for me to go home.'

'It's all right. I'll take this down the scrap yard.'

The dark-haired boy looked uncertain for a moment, then he smiled.

'I don't know if I'll be over tomorrow.'

'That's OK.'

He walked away towards Arlington Road.

Donal took a proprietorial hold of the pram.

'I suppose I should ask you where you got that keg, Donal,' said Stefan.

'We found it.' There was a broad grin. 'I know who you are.'

'Do you, now?'

'Vera's friend at the Bedford Arms, Mr Griffin. Over from Ireland.'

'You don't miss much, do you?'

'Not much.' Donal shrugged.

'You don't sound very Irish for a fucking Paddy,' Stefan laughed.

'I was born in Armagh. Mam's from Donegal.' Donal said it proudly.

'Irish enough, then.'

'My dad's English. He's in the Fire Brigade.' He said that proudly too.

'He's got a bit to do, so, Donal.'

Stefan looked up to see Vera coming down some steps several houses along. She saw him and waved. Donal grinned and started to push the pram.

'Pictures?' he said, grinning.

'Walls have ears, eh? What should we see? You'll know what's on.'

'I'd say, *Night Train to Munich*, Mr Griffin. Mam and Dad saw it.'

The boy laughed and wheeled off the pram and the beer keg. He exchanged a greeting with Vera and carried on along Mornington Crescent.

'We'll have to fit in a matinee,' said Stefan. 'Sorry, I thought we'd grab a bite first, but Willie wants me back. I don't know why. Driving somewhere.'

'That's grand. I see you met Donal.'

'I did so. He's told me what we should go and see.'

They turned and walked along the crescent, heading to the main road.

'We're in the same house,' said Vera. 'The Harveys have a flat upstairs from me.'

'He was in a bit of a fight. About scrap metal.'

'It's not the first time,' replied Vera. 'I don't think it's really about scrap.'

'What do you mean?'

'I've only been in the house a week, but Mrs Harvey says he was in a fight on Monday. He won't tell her it's a regular thing.' Vera shrugged. 'I'd say it's mostly because he's Irish. He did tell me a bit . . . that's why he gets it.'

'He doesn't even sound Irish.'

'I've seen the gang that's been picking on him. I'd say they're very careful to make sure there's no one else around when they do it. I think it evens out most of the time – there's plenty of Irish kids. He should get together with them and have it out. I have said that to him. That might put a stop to it all.'

'I see. You're not the nurturing kind then, Vera. Your advice would be for Donal to find a few Irish fellers and beat the shite out of the English lads.'

She laughed. 'I wouldn't put it like that. But we have to hold our own.'

For a moment Stefan felt some words forming in his head, about Tom. It seemed natural to talk about his own child in the middle of a conversation about children, however idle it was. But he stepped back. Going to the cinema with a woman was ordinary enough. It was as much the ordinariness he liked as Vera herself. But ordinary conversations were difficult. The desire to say ordinary things was very strong; ordinary things that belonged to a world that had nothing to do with pretence and deceit. It was not useful that she made him want to say ordinary things. They opened too much up. A false identity, however vague, needed constant attention. It had not occurred to him he would have to work at it with someone he liked. He felt, for a moment, an uneasy fraud. As they walked on together, he found some words that were suitably impersonal.

'You'd wonder why it matters, here,' he said, 'in the middle of all this.'

'What?'

'England, Ireland.'

'Doesn't it matter to you?' she asked.

He glanced round at her, unsure how serious she was. He could see she was more serious than his words seemed to warrant. His reply said nothing.

'I wouldn't look for Kathleen Ni Houlihan in a pram of scrap iron.'

'Well, he'd be better leaving the Spitfire Fund alone altogether. His mother's Irish enough. You'd think she'd find him something better to do.'

Vera spoke lightly, though Stefan could feel a hint of irritation behind her words, or even something stronger. But as ordinary conversation went, irritation with the English was very safe ground. He smiled and put his arm through hers.

'Jesus, you're no easy woman to have an aimless conversation with!'

Early that evening, Stefan was back at the Bedford Arms. *Night Train to Munich* had shown how British wit and ingenuity could beat the Germans with a determination that was somehow effortless and good-humoured. It didn't feel like what was happening in the streets of London every night. But it did come with some entertaining sideswipes at the Nazis, as well as a preoccupation with cricket that amused Stefan as much as most of the audience, though Vera seemed to find it hard to grasp why that was so funny. It gave Stefan the opportunity to tease her on the walk back to Mornington Crescent; there were small things that irritated her that made him laugh and when he teased her they made her laugh too. It was enough to bring them closer. They parted with a kiss.

They both wanted to be brought closer. It was a small victory for ordinary things. Since Stefan had to hurry back to the Bedford Arms, there was little time for conversation. He knew she had only recently arrived in London, as he had, and was making do with casual work, as he was – at least that was the impression he was happy to give. He slid around his own background without noticing that she slid as easily around hers. His own desire not to pursue his identity as Eddie Griffin in depth meant that he had no desire to ask deeper questions. They were passing through. While that was always an element of some Irish life in Camden, it was all the more so because of the war. She remained an unlikely cleaner, but Stefan Gillespie was sure he came across as an unlikely barman. Nobody cared. She told him she cleaned for two families in Highgate, for a doctor who had a surgery in Arlington Road, as well as Willie Mullins at the Bedford Arms. Cleaning was about making do till something came along; there was no more need to know what that might be in her case than in his.

At the Bedford Arms, Willie Mullins was walking in and out of the bar, looking at his watch repeatedly. There was something else for him to be anxious about, though neither Stefan nor Anto knew what it was. Finally the telephone rang in the back room. Willie disappeared and came back in less than a minute, still anxious, but now happy to resume his usual position at one corner of the saloon bar. Without needing to be asked, Anto produced a pint of bitter for him.

'Eddie,' said the landlord, lighting one of his cheroots, 'the driving's tomorrow morning. Too late now. They're bombing over the East End already.'

'OK, let me know, Willie.' Stefan moved away to serve a customer.

The conversation around the saloon bar was about the bombing, picking up on Willie Mullins' words. The East End and the Docks had taken the brunt of the devastation. Some people in the bar had seen it; those who hadn't, had seen some of the photographs. But nothing had yet hit them anything like as hard. The bar was the usual mixture of Camden regulars, English and London-Irish. Stefan recognised many of them. Few of them were names yet, just faces growing more familiar. A lot of people sat at tables round the walls, talking quietly, but as Stefan served, snatches of the talk came over the bar from those who were happy to join a kind of communal, almost anonymous shorthand.

A man in a pin-striped suit; a pock-marked face: 'There's a lot of people homeless. God knows where they'll all go.'

A woman in a camel coat and headscarf; a tight perm: 'They're coming here. Can't get a room all of a sudden. Prices sky high.'

A small, dark man; horn-rimmed glasses: 'You'll know the ones who can afford the best flats?'

No one did.

The horn-rimmed glasses again: 'It's not your East End docker. They have to fend for themselves.'

Nods of concerned agreement, though no one knew what he meant.

Horn-rimmed glasses: 'They got the ackers, right? They always have. They're all over us. If I say the word "Jews",' he whispered and winked, 'I'm a bleeding anti-Semite!'

There was laughter; some of it approving, some uneasy.

The pin-stripe: 'Some might say we're fighting this bloody war for them, eh?'

The conversation faded. There were people still nodding. There were people who had walked away, not comfortable with the direction the chat around the bar was taking. Willie Mullins was deaf to it, his head buried in the *Sporting Life*. Anto was in the public bar. Stefan filtered it out as he worked. He nodded as a small, neat man in a tweed suit approached the bar. He already knew the man as Dr Field, a Highgate GP who had a surgery at the end of the road, close to Mornington Crescent, but he now knew Vera cleaned the surgery there. He had been surprised when she told him she wasn't very happy working for Dr Field. If she found a reason to leave, she would do, but Willie Mullins had got her the job. He had been helpful to her. She didn't like to seem ungrateful. Stefan thought Dr Field appeared amiable enough. Most evenings he stopped at the pub for a drink on his way home to Highgate.

Stefan poured the doctor a bottle of Guinness.

The horn-rimmed glasses, restarting: 'Why don't they send them all up to Golders Green? Let the Chosen Race look after their own. Look at the queues. Half of them are Jews. Always at the front, too. Always got more money or more coupons. You're not meant to say it, but there's a reason people don't like them. They're even in the shelters first!'

A fat, bearded man, hair dyed a startling brown, tapped his

head: 'The reason is we work with our hands. They work up here.'

A woman in a moth-eaten fur; a blue rinse: 'Which means they don't work at all.'

Laughter from the gang at the bar, now thinning out.

An unidentified Irish voice from further back: 'They don't fight either. None of them ever get called up.'

The pin-striped suit: 'Half the Yids are pro-German. They'd change sides tomorrow if the Germans got here. They admire Hitler really. I think they're on the same bloody side. They'll suck up to anyone. And we're fighting for them! For their money.'

An air-raid warden, pushing through to the bar: 'Come on, mate! That's bollocks, isn't it?'

There was some easier, relieved laughter. Then the horn-rimmed glasses: 'Would we be fighting Hitler if it wasn't for the Yids?'

The air-raid warden: 'You're talking out of your arse, mate. Give it a fucking rest!'

There were noises of approval.

Horn-rimmed glasses: 'You ever hear of a Yid who died fighting? I don't think so!'

Dr Field, who had been standing at the bar, drained his Guinness. As he moved to leave, he took a step towards the man in the horn-rimmed glasses. There was silence, almost immediately. The small group still holding the conversation at the bar had not noticed the doctor, but some knew him. The doctor looked hard at the man in the glasses, who was flushed and sweating.

'You should go home, sir. I think even your friends have heard enough.'

'What?'

The doctor turned and walked out. The silence in the pub had spread.

'Who the fuck do you think you are?' roared horn-rimmed glasses.

Willie Mullins had finally put down his *Sporting Life*. 'He's right. Piss off out of my pub.'

Unexpectedly, the man in the horn-rimmed glasses was on his own now. He looked round, expecting a display of support. The space round him grew.

'You can't throw me out of here! Fuck off!'

'Do you want to see me?'

The landlord advanced towards the man. It wasn't often that he looked threatening, but as he passed Anto, the barman reached across the bar with a hurl that he had produced from under the counter. Mullins held it in both hands.

'I don't know you. And you don't know Dr Field, then?'

'That little bastard who just went out?'

'That little Jewish bastard, you mean. Well, that little Jewish bastard had a son. His son died two months ago. He was a Spitfire pilot. What do you do?'

The man with the horn-rimmed glasses looked round again. He could feel the hostility, especially from the people who had echoed his words so lazily before. He sniffed and walked out through two sets of blacked-out doors that kept the lights inside the Bedford Arms from bleeding into the street. Willie Mullins handed the hurl back to Anto and returned to his study of the *Sporting Life*. Anto pulled the landlord another pint of bitter and pushed it across the bar.

Almost immediately, from outside, came the noise of the sirens. There was a low, weary groan that ran through the bar. The same old routine. Glasses were drained. People got up slowly and collected their belongings. A few made their way to the bar for one more drink, just as they would at closing time. The pub would empty out quickly; those last drinks would be down almost in one. But there was no rush. It was an orderly exit, as customers made their way out to shelters at home, to the public shelters along Arlington Road and Camden High Street, and to the Underground stations at Camden Town and Mornington Crescent. As Stefan pulled on his coat and walked towards the door, now with a pillow and blanket, the doors opened and Vera came in. She was unflustered.

'I thought I'd come and scrounge a drink off you.'

'Too late.'

'I know; it started when I was halfway here.'

He stuffed the blanket and pillow into her arms and went back to the bar, where Anto was pulling on his coat. Mullins was still in situ. The *Sporting Life* was folded and in his pocket, but that was it. He was lighting a cheroot. At some point he would go, but like a captain on a ship, he would be the last.

'Good film, Vera?' He spoke as if no one was leaving.

'It was all right. Rex Harrison saved the day and fooled the Germans, who were so stupid you'd have to wonder why they ever won anything at all!'

'But he was batting on a sticky wicket,' said Stefan, returning with two bottles of Worthington. 'And if you don't know your silly mid-off from your third man, you can't expect to stand up to a chap who played for his college, Vera!'

'Apparently I missed the joke.' Vera laughed.

'Come on! I'll explain it to you again!'

'Don't, please. Once is enough. I'd rather stay here and face the bombs.'

Outside, people were walking towards the shelters and the Underground. The sirens were still sounding. Suddenly there was a loud explosion. It shook the street. It was close. All eyes turned back, down towards central London. The usual horizon, but closer tonight. A cloud of smoke rose up. Searchlights pierced the smoke; there was the distant *pop-pop-pop* of anti-aircraft guns. There was the acrid smell, and the heat, carried on a faint breeze. And there was another light spreading up into the pall of smoke; the light of burning buildings.

Another explosion followed, then another.

'It's the stations. King's Cross or St Pancras.' A passing voice.

People were moving faster. There were more blasts behind them. Stefan took Vera's hand. She laughed and shrugged. And now they hurried.

Stefan and Vera were on the escalator at Camden Town, heading down to the platform. The escalator was packed with people performing this near-nightly ritual. It was noisy with the good-humour that still marked the start of these nights; the weariness and tedium, the irritability and discomfort, would set in later. For now the noise was easy enough, loud voices, cheerful cursing, children's laughter. The stone steps between the up and down escalators were full of people who would sit out the raid there rather than push their way through the crowds on the platforms. On one of the steps a man was playing an accordion. People sang along quietly. Children read comics in the dim overhead light. Vera was below Stefan on the escalator. She looked round and up at him.

'I hope it's not going to be a long one tonight.'

As she spoke a roar of noise filled the escalator hall. There was pitch darkness. Smoke swept downwards, over them, full of heat and tiny particles of brick and mortar and wood and glass that cut and scratched. The force of the blast pushed people forward in the blackness, tumbling down the steps and down the escalator as it juddered to a halt. There were cries of pain; there were shouts of people calling out for each other; screams of children. Stefan pulled himself up, He was giddy. The blast rang in his head. The sound around him was somehow distant. Momentarily there was a deep silence. The darkness was pierced by screams that were very different from the noise of panic and collision and hard knocks that filled the escalator and the stairs. The screams came from above, out of the smoke and dust still flowing over the crowd. They were the sounds of people in agony. No one was in any doubt they were the sounds of the dying. Stefan spoke Vera's name and reached out in the darkness. She was not there.

15

Camden Lock

The lights flickered and came back on. They were dimmer than ever through the cloud that hung high in the escalator, but it was enough to see. The noise of shock and the complaints of pain started up again as people began to push down the steps and stationary escalators. Children were crying; people were shouting names; there was coughing and choking; everyone was complaining about the press of people behind them on the stairs. There was no mood of panic now. There were injuries, but mostly they were bruises and cuts. The instinct was to get to the platforms, away from the dust it was impossible not to breathe in, and away from the cries that still came from street level. Some people did try to push up, through the descending crowd, to get out, but most only wanted to get down, down into the deep tunnels and to something that felt like safety.

Stefan Gillespie saw Vera as the lights came back on. She had tumbled only a few steps down the escalator, where those below had halted her fall. She was standing, pushing the hair from her face, coughing out the dust in her lungs. She turned and looked at him. He pointed down. People behind were pushing him forward. She moved the same way. Stefan found himself next to her again and she put her arm through his. Movement down the escalator was steady and controlled, but it wasn't easy for them to keep their feet. She held on to him more tightly. Relief, simply at being alive, was something that hung in the air like the smoke and dust. Everyone felt it. As screams from above echoed, everyone knew that mix of emotions, of joy and guilt. They were all right.

On the platforms and the tunnels between, people were jammed tight. Stefan and Vera stood at the end of a platform. There was room to sit, but no more than that. The force of the crowds pushing down from the stairs had gone. An air-raid warden barged through, but he could get no further along the platform.

'Can we have more men up the top? We need to clear the entrance. There's still people to get out! We need more hands! Can I have some help?'

Several men and some women broke away from the crowd. They said nothing, but wove through the press of people, back the way they had just come.

'Let's have some more of you!' shouted the air-raid warden, and several more people turned and walked towards the escalator. Stefan smiled at Vera.

'No point standing here all night. You keep the blanket.'

He turned to go.

'I'll come with you,' she said quietly.

'You're better off here.'

'I don't know.' She smiled. 'Maybe.'

They walked up the escalator with the others. The escalator was almost empty. The smoke was thinner. The dust that had filled it was everywhere, though, on the treads and the stone steps and the rails. At the top they walked through the tunnels towards the entrance. Here the air was thicker and blacker, and every breath sucked in the choking fumes. When they reached the entrance, the rubble was piled high, blocking the way out to Camden High Street. People were pulling away the stone and the bricks to clear an opening back to the street. A group of men, women and children sat against the walls. They were covered in dust, their clothes and their faces blackened. No one seemed to be tending to them. Whatever injuries they had, there were those with worse. Only feet away, Stefan and Vera walked past the bodies of three people, two women and a child of seven or eight. Another body was being carried to put beside them. A coat was thrown over one of the women, but no one had covered the others. An air-raid warden pointed across the ticket hall and shouted at them.

'Go out the Kentish Road exit and round into the High Street.'

The volunteers turned, following the order.

'They need you working in from the other side.'

Stefan and Vera followed the rest, out into the street. The air was still full of dust; it tasted of burnt brick and stone but it was cold and clean. They walked round into Camden High Street. A large part of the front of the station had collapsed, stretching out across the road. People were working at the rubble, pulling away the debris, throwing it into heaps across the street. There were ambulances. Stretchers were carrying people away from the rubble. Others just sat on the ground, waiting to be seen, some silent, some sobbing. The street was lit by a fire that was burning further along, close to the bridge over the canal. Two fire engines blocked the street and water was pouring on to the flames. Another fire engine stood closer to the station, spraying water on to mounds of rubble that were steaming with heat. Stefan moved forward to start clearing the brick and broken stone. There were picks and shovels, but mostly people worked with their hands. Vera followed; she stopped, hearing her name.

'Vera!'

She saw the slight figure of Dr Field.

'Doctor.'

'Were you down there?'

She nodded.

'You're all right?'

'Some bruises, that's all.'

'I was at the surgery,' he said. 'Didn't you say you'd done some nursing?'

'Not really, just first aid.'

'If you can put a bandage on, that'll do. They've only got a couple of ambulances here. They're all down at Euston and King's Cross. Come with me.'

He walked on. She followed. However quietly said, it was an instruction.

The doctor climbed over a mound of rubble. A man was being pulled out. He was unconscious but he was breathing. The men who carried him put him down without a word and turned back to the heap of brick and stone. Dr Field knelt beside him. He pushed up his eyelids gently. He felt his pulse. His fingers searched the man's limbs. As he pulled open a dark jacket, he saw the stain of blood that soaked the white shirt underneath it. He stood and looked round. He called a dark figure close by, bent over something covered in dust and broken glass. Vera saw that something was the body of an old woman.

'Father Flood!'

'I'm here, Brian.'

Dr Field looked down at the man he had been examining.

'I doubt he'll live to get to a casualty station.'

He turned away abruptly. There was a cry. A child, a girl of four or five, was pulled out from under a stone lintel. As the priest knelt beside the dying man, the doctor climbed towards the child. He looked at her quickly, making a judgement, then turned to Vera. He thrust a canvas bag into her hands.

'Take her to the ambulances. Tidy her up. Bandage her. She doesn't need to go to hospital. Find someone to keep an eye on

175

her. Anyone will do. There'll be someone to take her to a shelter eventually. They're still not here yet.'

The girl looked up.

'I need to wait for my mum.'

'I'm sure she'll be along,' said Dr Field, already walking away.

Vera took the girl's hand.

'All right to walk?'

'Course I am.'

They walked over the debris to where the road was clear.

'She won't know where I am, see, and I've got the tickets.'

The girl held up two Underground tickets.

Vera worked for an hour, following Brian Field from the wounded to the dead, from the dead to the wounded. He made abrupt decisions about who he sent to the scarce ambulances. Bruises and cuts, even broken legs and arms, could wait. She struggled, as she helped him, taking away the less seriously hurt, walking with them or beside the stretchers that carried them, and seeing others into the ambulances. The doctor's decisions seemed arbitrary at times. The priest had been joined by another from the Belgian Church in Arlington Road. The two men followed after the doctor like angels of death, as Field directed them to the people he decided there would be no point sending to the casualty stations. Each time an ambulance left, it was gone for almost half an hour. Until more medical help arrived, only those the doctor felt had a chance were owed that time. He took those decisions rapidly, so rapidly that Vera pulled him back as he walked away from a young man in an RAF uniform whose eyes were wide with fear.

'You can't do that!' she said, pulling him round.

'What?'

'You have to give him a chance.'

'If they get us some more ambulances, Vera—'

'You're deciding whether people live or die. You can't do that.'

'I have to. I didn't ask to, Vera. If I'd left half an hour earlier, I'd be at home. When someone else arrives, they can do it. I'm just the one who's here.'

The doctor walked away and carried on with his work, and Vera carried on too. There was a small gap opening up into the station. The sounds of the people working inside could be heard. There were fewer people being pulled out of the rubble, and there were fewer decisions to be made about who went to hospital and who didn't. Now most people were dead; men, women, children. Vera had been standing for some time, watching as Dr Field stood behind the row of men and women clearing the rubble. There was another body to remove. She saw Stefan working ahead of her. He was never far away. They hardly spoke, but each of them felt the other's presence. Suddenly she saw something under a pile of bricks. She bent down. It was a small hand. She reached out and touched it. It was cold. She knew it would be cold. She had felt a lot of cold flesh that night. Then Dr Field was standing beside her. He bent down too and prised away some of the bricks. The hand was attached to a small, pale arm. But there was nothing else. There was no body. Vera stared. Somehow it was worse than a whole body. And then, as Brian Field pulled away more bricks, she saw the head of a boy. Not a baby, but no more than two.

'Bring me a sack, a bag, Vera. We're close to the worst of it.'
She didn't move.

'There will be more.' He spoke softly. 'It's best to get these things out of the way as quickly as possible. The fewer people who see them, the better.'

Still Vera didn't move.

'I'll stay here. Get something, like I said a sack, a box.'

'I'm sorry, I've had enough.' She looked up.

'I understand. Just bring me something.'

'So you can throw the pieces in a bag?'

'I think that's better than leaving them here, don't you?'

'You know, as a doctor, you'd make a very good butcher. Who lives, who dies, who even cares? All down to you. Now you're going to throw pieces of—'

'I know it's not easy, Vera. We do what we have to.'

'Don't patronise me.'

'I'm not patronising you. I'm telling you to get on with it, woman. If you can't do that, then get out of it. You're no bloody use to the living or the dead!'

Vera was fighting back tears.

'Don't you shout at me!'

They were unaware of people close by watching them. They were both feeling the same things, really, anger and shock, disgust and exhaustion. Stefan Gillespie was one of those watchers nearby, still clawing at the piles of bricks.

'Leave it then, Vera; for God's sake just leave it alone!'

The doctor turned away.

'Can someone get me a sack, a bag, a box? Anything!'

He turned to Vera. 'Get out of here. Go home!'

'You bastard,' she said, furious. 'You fucking Jewish bastard!'

He stared at her, puzzled more than anything else. The words had nothing to do with anything that was going on. He couldn't see where they had come from. He looked at the fury in Vera's face and for a moment he saw some of the uncomprehending anguish that he felt himself. She seemed unaware of what she had said. She was shaking. He shook his head and carried on with his work.

'There you go, Doc!'

A policeman appeared and handed over a heavy sack. The pieces of the child's body were still lying at Dr Field's feet.

'Jesus Christ!' The policeman turned away and crossed himself.

Brian Field knelt down in the dust and glass. He covered the head with the open sack and enveloped it. He cradled the sack in his hand, unmoving.

Stefan approached Vera.

'Should I walk home with you? We're nearly through. I can come back.'

She looked round. She appeared to wonder who he was.

'No,' she said, focusing again, pushing her hair from her face.

She bent down and picked up the small, pale arm. She held it almost tenderly. She moved to where Brian Field was standing. He held the sack open.

'I'll do what I can,' she said. 'I'm sorry.'

'I wouldn't worry,' he replied curtly. 'I've been called worse.'

The work of clearing the debris at Camden Town went on. There were more dead to be found, though there were probably no more living. The flames of burning buildings had died down, but they still lit Camden High Street. Elsewhere over London the bombs had stopped dropping and the Luftwaffe had returned home till tomorrow. More ambulances had arrived, along with doctors and nurses. The night was not over, but Stefan and Vera left the Underground station and walked along Arlington Road. They went into the Bedford Arms for a drink. They said very little. He was exhausted. The shock of what had happened didn't feel close to the front of his mind, but it was there; speaking about it wouldn't help. It was something to get used to. He already knew that. For Vera, speaking wouldn't help either. This was the war she was fighting, in whatever way she could. There was no room for the kind of emotion she had shown that night. She could not allow herself that indulgence. But it had come anyway. It had marked her. She knew there was no difference between London and Berlin. Wherever a bomb dropped on a city, the same things happened. She didn't like her awareness of this. She didn't like reflecting on it. Far from putting her emotion, her confusion, into a box that she could dispose of, it only made her feel angrier. But it was an anger that was directionless. It saw people not enemies. It was not her business to feel or think anything, unless it was about what she had to do. It came into her mind that the man she still believed she loved, Erik Kramer, would have congratulated her on what she had done that night. Not for its humanity, but because it showed how deep her cover went. She had made herself indistinguishable from her enemy, so much so that she could carry their broken bodies out of the wreckage caused by Germany's bombers. He would have applauded her, but for reasons that she knew now would have disgusted her. For the first time since Erik's death, she was glad he wasn't with her.

Willie Mullins emerged from the kitchen as Stefan and Vera sat in the bar. He was unaware of anything that had happened at the Underground station.

'So where were you, Willie?' asked Stefan.

'In the kitchen.'

'All the time?'

Stefan and Vera looked at each other. He must have passed out.

'I fell asleep. I didn't hear the bomb.'

'You're a lucky man, Willie.'

'Jesus, I could have been down there.' He crossed himself. 'Well, if it's not your time, it's not.' He poured himself a whiskey, still not taking in the full extent of what had happened so close, and he went out again, heading for bed.

'You know, I'd love to get away from this,' said Vera quietly.

'Hmm?'

'Get away for a bit. Out of London.'

'I've only had a week of it, so,' said Stefan, 'but tonight was a crash course. So much for singing songs in the Underground.

You can't forget what a few minutes later could have meant. I know what you mean. Some clean air.'

'Maybe we could do something. A couple of days away?'

He was surprised, but he realised he felt the same. He smiled.

'Why not? "Forget six counties overhung with smoke", right?'

'What's that?'

'Something my father used to read me when I was a kid. I can't remember. It was something to do with the Thames. "The clear Thames bordered by its gardens green." It came into my head. He read to me lot.'

'You're lucky. My father was always away working. He was there when I was older.' She laughed. 'But that's when I didn't want him to be so much.'

She stopped. She had spoken more easily about her father than she had in a long time. But the words left her quiet. He had meant more than she realised.

Stefan's mind was in Ireland. For a moment he was at Kilranelagh.

'I don't know when my father stopped reading. I never see him read now.'

Stefan stopped too. He felt the danger. The night had made him want to talk. Not about what had happened but those ordinary things again. But he wasn't Stefan Gillespie. There were no ordinary things, not for Eddie Griffin.

'A trip to the country,' he said brightly. 'Let's sort something out.'

She nodded, smiling. They got up, standing close. He kissed her. Unlike the kiss coming back from the cinema, it wasn't a peck. It lasted a long time.

'You taste of smoke,' she said.

'So do you. I can taste it inside me too. In my lungs, everywhere.'

She nodded. And she had made a decision.

'I don't want to go back to Mornington Crescent, Eddie. Can I stay?'

The next morning Stefan was woken by Willie Mullins – standing over the bed, shaking him. He had fallen into a deep sleep. Only as he woke and sat up, looking round, did he remember that Vera was in the bed with him.

'What do you want, Willie?'

'The job.'

'What job?'

'The lorry.'

'Lorry?

'You said you could drive one.'

'Oh, yes. What now?'

'Yes, it's been dropped off. And I've only got it for the morning!'

The lorry was waiting outside the pub when Stefan Gillespie and Willie Mullins came out. It wasn't much more than a van, with the name of a Covent Garden greengrocer painted on the side. As they drove down Arlington Road the smell of Willie Mullins cheroot was sitting heavily on Stefan's stomach. The smoke of the night before hung about him. Air was what he needed, not smoke.

'You were lucky,' said Mullins. 'They reckon thirty dead.'

'I'm not surprised.'

Stefan said no more and it was all Willie had to say. It was a silence Stefan appreciated. He was part of this now. He assumed nobody said much.

The journey took them east towards the City, but they kept north of it and came down towards the river through Clerkenwell and Whitechapel. Willie Mullins only spoke to give directions. He knew London well, and when they had to turn off the main road to avoid bomb damage he always seemed to know where he was. The debris of bombs and the shells of bombed buildings were everywhere, but as they started out they met these things at intervals. Rubble was being cleared wherever they went; fire engines still flooded the burning remains of the night raids with water. When they came to the river and the docks it got worse. There was still smoke in the air, and the bomb sites spread out around them, wider and wider. Coming out of Shadwell they drove past terraced streets that stood empty, flattened in part, or standing only as broken, gap-toothed cut-outs. Stretching away to the river were the gaunt hulks of burned-out warehouses, lining the Thames. The devastation here was of a different order to anything Stefan had witnessed further north. After last night he knew there must be a body count to match the scale of what had happened to the East End and the Docks, night after night, since the beginning of the Blitz.

They drove through several streets that had fared less badly, past still-standing warehouses. Willie Mullins directed Stefan through the open gates of one of the warehouses. As the lorry pulled in the gates were shut behind them.

'You stay here, Eddie. All you have to do is drive.'

Mullins jumped from the cab, whistling cheerfully.

Stefan took out a cigarette. He watched as the landlord walked across the yard to an office door. A man in a grey suit came, shouting something to the men who had just closed the gates. He clapped Willie on the back and the two men shook hands. Stefan heard the back doors of the lorry opened. Several more workers appeared from the warehouse, carrying boxes, wheeling crates and sacks on sack barrows. The thudding and thumping behind him told him they were loading the van. Across the yard Willie Mullins handed the grey-suited man a wad of notes. Then they turned and walked into the office.

The loading was done within fifteen minutes. The landlord

of the Bedford Arms reappeared and clambered up into the cab. Stefan started the engine.

'Home, James!' Willie grinned, clearly pleased with himself.

Stefan could smell the whiskey on his breath. He had no doubt this was his introduction to the black market. He doubted it was what Terry Gregory and Geróid de Paor had envisaged. It didn't seem it was likely to prove much of a threat to Irish neutrality. But he wasn't so sure it couldn't prove a threat to him.

They drove back to Camden. Willie Mullins took a route further north, and they came down to Camden Lock from Kentish Town. The landlord directed Stefan into the canal basin, past the rows of barges and the warehouses. Across the bridge, in Camden High Street, there was still smoke from the building that had been on fire the previous night. Abruptly they were in darkness. The road into the canal basin sloped down as they turned off it. They were in a wide, high tunnel. Stefan switched on the dim headlights. The arches of the tunnel stretched ahead as far as he could see, and there were turnings off, where more arches pointed away into the darkness. Set in the bays of the arches were high doors.

'What's this?' said Stefan, taking in this underground world.

'It's called the Catacombs.' Willie chuckled. 'But no one's buried here.'

'What's it for?'

'It's mostly storage, warehousing. I rent a bit of space down here. Goes on for bloody miles. You can get all the way to Euston Station through these tunnels. It was something to do with the railway. They used to keep horses down here one time, for pulling wagons. Like pit ponies. It's handy enough.'

Willie Mullins pointed to the left and the headlights picked up a set of doors. There were faded letters on the doors, but Stefan couldn't read them.

Willie Mullins got out and walked to the front of the lorry. He unlocked several padlocks on the double doors and pushed them open. He walked into the cavernous interior under the arch. The lights of the lorry picked out the rows of boxes and sacks already in the store. The landlord switched on a dim overhead light, then beckoned Stefan to drive in. He pulled the doors shut.

That night the air-raid sirens didn't sound. There was bombing to the east and south again, but the centre of London was left alone. It was late when Stefan Gillespie walked from Mornington Crescent to the Bedford Arms. He had been in the bar all evening and Vera had come in with some ideas about what they might do if they took a few days out of London. The events of the day had pushed it out of his mind but she had not forgotten. There was a car outside the pub as he approached it. He recognised it, but he wasn't sure why. The man who got out, as Stefan reached the pub, reminded him. It was the Metropolitan Police Special Branch man he knew only as Simpson. The sergeant grinned.

'Willie at home?'

'He was. The pub's closed.'

'You're a hard man, Eddie. I've a hell of a thirst.'

Stefan ignored him and went into the Bedford Arms. He knew the sergeant would be coming with him. There was nothing he could do to stop that.

Willie Mullins was standing at the bar alone, drinking a whiskey. He smiled as Stefan entered; the smile disappeared as he saw who was with him.

'I'll have one of those, Willie; just the job.'

The landlord looked at Stefan and nodded. Stefan went behind the bar.

'So how's it going, Willie?'

'It's going, Mr Simpson.'

'Bad do last night. The Underground.'

'Bad enough,' said Willie.

Stefan handed the sergeant a whiskey.

'You two have a good drive around today?'

Neither Stefan nor Willie responded. Simpson laughed.

'The thing is, Willie, it hasn't been worth keeping an eye on you lately. Your dancing days are done. That's the view at Scotland Yard, anyway. But I like to keep my tabs on people. You never know. I mean, I never knew you had a store at the Lock. Who'd have thought that would be useful to a fucking piss-artist publican? I wish I'd been in on it, though. God knows what you might have kept up there when the Boys were in and out of here like mustard, eh? But I heard a whisper. The black market's not my beat. That's for the plods. But the whisper said you're the man for that in Camden. And it was worth a look.'

'I don't know what you're talking about, Mr Simpson,' said Mullins.

'No? Do you know what I'm talking about, Eddie?'

'I just pull the pints, Sergeant,' replied Stefan.

'Course you do, you ignorant fucking Paddy.' Simpson grinned. 'And I'm happy to leave you doing that. I'm happy to leave you doing whatever it is you do, Willie, apart from pissing it up. The thing I need is some inducement.'

'Like I said, Mr Simpson, you lost me before you started.'

'My arse, Willie. It's very simple. Mazuma, punts, shekels. I leave you alone with your unpatriotic business venture. You cross my palm with the necessary silver. Fifteen quid a week? I'm not a greedy man, but these are hard times. I'll be back next week to collect. You pay me or you will end up inside.'

The Special Branch man drained his whiskey.

'And you too, Paddy.' He winked at Stefan. 'Feel free to twist his arm.'

He walked out. There was a long silence.

'Jesus, Eddie, there's no cunts like those cunts in Special Branch.'

'There is that,' said Stefan. It was hard to hold back a smile.

He poured the landlord another whiskey. Mullins didn't need to ask.

'Well, this is some place to lie low, Willie, eh?'

'I didn't want you in the first place, Eddie. Why don't you fuck off?'

The landlord of the Bedford Arms took the whiskey and went out to the back hall. Stefan walked upstairs. He could hear Mullins on the phone, shouting. 'How the fuck do I know? He's been watching the place, that's bloody obvious. Well, what the fuck do you think I'm going to fucking do? I don't have a choice!' The words drifted away as Stefan reached the landing that led to his bedroom. He didn't switch on the light. Inside, he lit a cigarette. He pulled back the heavy curtains and opened the window. Somewhere there was still bombing in London. It was a long way out; a series of dull thuds in the distance. He had the feeling that everyone had at times, watching the bombing that had passed over. It hadn't come your way. It was somewhere else. It wasn't here. But he also felt what had struck him several times since the bomb at the Underground. He was a part of this. You didn't get a choice in that. And that made what he was supposed to be doing in London seem more aimless. It was about nothing. It was for nothing. It had turned out to be as pointless as it sounded in Ireland. It would be a lot more pointless if Superintendent Gregory and Commandant de Paor had to extract him from an English jail. It was time to put an end to it. Willie Mullins was not a man noted for his wisdom, but his last words to Stefan that night seemed like excellent advice. It was time to fuck off.

16

The Trout

It was a Saturday when Stefan Gillespie and Vera Kennedy
left the Bedford Arms for Paddington Station and Oxford. It
had been his idea to spend two days walking along the River
Thames, out into the country, but he had done little more than
propose it. Vera had bought the Ordnance Survey maps and
traced the network of footpaths that would let them follow the
river as closely as they could, in places where towns would be
far enough away to be out of sight and out of sound. They had
fixed no particular finishing point, but they had two days, and
the train from Paddington deposited them at Oxford in the
late morning. It was not a busy train. The passengers were
mostly pilots and aircrew heading back to their airfields and
parents and grandparents travelling into Berkshire to visit
evacuated children. Beyond Reading the train stopped at every
station and there were small groups of eager children waiting
at each one.

In Oxford Stefan and Vera turned away from the town
immediately, following the map and the route they had pored
over the previous night. Stefan was conscious that what felt
like the beginning of something was really the end. He had
telephoned his London contact from G2 the previous day to

report that the mostly meaningless events at the Bedford Arms had taken an uneasy turn. He was now involved in Willie Mullins' black market activities, not to mention a Metropolitan Police Special Branch sergeant who knew all about that and was blackmailing Mullins for a cut of the profits. The Irishman he had been told to address simply as Kelly seemed only to be amused by these developments.

'That's a bit of a turn up. Dear old Willie. I suppose it explains why he hasn't been looking for money from us for a while. Interesting stuff, though.'

'I don't know about interesting. I've done enough to be put inside.'

'Doesn't sound like this Special Branch feller's going to tell anyone.'

'I wouldn't want to rely on it.'

The Irish Intelligence officer laughed.

'No, but then that's Special Branch for you, wherever they are.'

'Save the jokes for Gerry de Paor,' said Stefan. 'If it's not dangerous it's still going to be some cock-up if you end up with a Guard in the dock here?'

'It would.' Stefan could almost see the man's grin. 'I'll talk to Dublin.'

There was no more. The phone was dead.

Stefan and Vera reached a footpath below Osney Bridge and walked between the slow, dark river and a long line of poplars. There were still leaves on the trees; every shade of yellow and brown. Although there was no wind, the leaves were falling gently as they walked. There was hardly anyone to see: some children playing by the river; people walking dogs; a lock keeper. It was a clear October day, crisp but not at all cold. The sky was blue. Above all it was quiet.

The walk was undemanding, and to be out of London and

in such a different place was all the conversation they needed. Vera was easy to be with. She had no problem with silence. Stefan could see she took pleasure in it, just as he did. There were no questions. There was only now. It was something they both felt, unaware how much the other felt the same. There was a closeness neither of them had expected. They felt it most when they were saying nothing.

They emerged from the poplars to walk through a boatyard and over a lock. The great open expanse of Port Meadow spread out to their right, all the way back to Oxford; red cattle grazed along the river. They stopped at the ruins of Godstow Abbey and ate sandwiches. Vera produced a sketchbook. She drew the old stones and the ruined walls. Stefan lay on his back, staring at the sky and feeling at ease for the first time since arriving in England. They reached the toll bridge at Swinford and got a room at the Talbot Inn. There were fresh eggs.

The next day the walk was longer, but it followed the Thames as before. They had both worked on the route, but Vera was better at finding the way. Stefan abandoned the map to her with relief, after losing the river and getting them lost for the second time. There were locks again and weirs. There was the town of Newbridge where they stopped at the Rose Revived for a drink. But mostly it was themselves and the river, small and clean, lined with reeds and willows. The only noises came from geese and warblers and from cattle and sheep in the fields. At times it was quiet enough to hear the river flow. It was not an England Stefan knew. It had an order, even in its emptiest stretches, that was unlike the most orderly Irish countryside. It was an easy place to be. It asked very little, but gave a lot, unexpectedly.

Yet the war was still there. It followed them as they walked the Thames. It was the same river Stefan had driven along through the devastation of the London Docks. It led to that. It was the same water. They saw the first concrete gun emplacement as they walked west from Swinford Bridge: a small grey pillbox, set amongst hanging willows, looking out across the river. The concrete box was new. And at regular intervals along the way there were more of them. They formed a line along the river, facing south. Below Newbridge there was a Home Guard platoon, stretched out on the grass around one of the pillboxes; teenagers and middle-aged men took turns squeezing in and out of the gun emplacements, sticking rifles out through the slits at the front and side. There was laughter; no one seemed to be taking it seriously. At Newbridge, at the Rose Revived, a policeman had asked them if they were walking for pleasure, and where they would spend that night. He was mildly interested that they were from Ireland, but only because his mother came from County Carlow. He was satisfied by their identity cards and only really wanted to exchange some grim words about what was happening in London. At the end of that day, before they reached Tadpole Bridge and the Trout Inn, where they would stay for the second night, the last pillbox they saw was still under construction. A concrete mixer rattled noisily by the river, pumping black smoke from its engine. A gang of mostly Irish workmen shovelled the concrete into the wooden formwork. Stefan and Vera stopped for a moment. The gang had been working its way along this stretch of the river for over a month. Their day was nearly over. One more bloody pillbox bloody completed. The Trout Inn was almost in sight.

It had been a long walk and when Stefan and Vera ate at the Trout that evening they were subdued as well as tired. They would be going back to London the next morning. It was something neither of them looked forward to. They didn't say it. They spoke only about the day and the river. Neither of them wanted to think ahead. They went to bed early, and when they lay together in the darkness the silence bound them to each other. But even that came to an end. Falling asleep they could hear the sound of bombs. They were a very long way off. As Stefan heard the first faint thuds, he wondered if it was something else. It kept on. London again. When he did fall asleep, the sound was still in his head.

When Stefan Gillespie woke, perhaps two hours later, Vera wasn't there. He lay in the darkness, aware of a feeling of distance and disassociation, not from her so much, or from where he was, but from himself. There were a number of ways in which, whatever the intimacy between them, he wasn't quite present. For a moment he felt caught between sleep and waking, coming too quickly out of a dream in which he was trapped inside himself, unable to move, unable to speak. The dream had woken him. He sat up and peered into the black room. He had no reason to feel uncomfortable, but he was nevertheless. This woman knew nothing about him. At some points, earlier that day and sitting together that evening, he wondered if he couldn't be more open, if there wasn't room to talk about something true, something small and personal that wouldn't compromise the identity that served him at the Bedford Arms. Did it matter now? Soon he would be gone. So what if there was a farm in Ireland? It only made him like thousands of other Irishmen in London. So what if she knew he had a young son, that he had lost his wife two years after his son's birth? He liked her. He hadn't expected to like her as much as he did. He wasn't looking for reasons to speak about himself; it was about normal life. But he had stepped back from it again. There were dangers in dressing up lies with a few truths. And there was something else; keeping the lies separate stopped them from sullying the truth.

It was too complicated, planting this truth or that into the deception, inserting a few honest words on the blank page that was Eddie Griffin. If there was little to fabricate, there were few mistakes to make. If there was nothing to remember, there was no confusion. It was easy enough at the Bedford Arms. Everything there was effortlessly superficial. There was a kind of decorum among the Irishmen who made up much of the pub's clientele. No personal questions. Young and old, they were all exiles; even the English-born inherited something of that sense of exile from their parents. They might talk about Ireland in expansive terms, with the sentimentality of love and hate, but many of them had left too much of themselves behind to allow for intimacy. The chatter of the bar and the streets was undemanding. Stefan had his role to play. For those with a nose for such things, there were the nods and winks that suggested Eddie Griffin had good reasons not to want many questions asked.

It hadn't been that hard with Vera either. It had moved very suddenly, after the bomb at Camden Town, from casual and easy to something else. Now, lying in the darkness, he felt how abrupt it had been. Not passionate, but just sudden.

The quiet reaches of the Thames could have changed the things they said to each other, but Stefan did not let it happen. He was unaware she had made the same decision for similar reasons. All he knew was that she seemed to prefer it that way too. He didn't ask why. They were together. They made each other comfortable. Why wouldn't that be enough? Yet here, lying in bed, Stefan was less satisfied. Eddie Griffin wasn't a fraud, only a kind of blank. If none of it mattered to her, why should it to him? Wasn't the moment itself honest?

He wondered where she was. She had not disturbed him when she got up. But something told him she had been gone for some time. He got up himself and went to the window. He pulled back the heavy blackout curtains and looked down. A stretch of grass at the side of the Trout led to the river and to

Tadpole Bridge. There was pale moonlight through a scattering of hazy, white cloud and the River Thames sparkled as it flowed under the dark arch of the bridge. He saw her on the riverbank, sitting close to the bridge, smoking and looking out over the stream. He was restless, and he felt the silence and the calm of the night beyond the window. He wanted to take another breath of that still air too.

He pulled on his clothes. He walked down the stairs and through the dark bar, out into the night. He crossed the grass, breathing in the air. The night had a cold scent from the river. The gently rippling Thames was the only sound now.

As he approached Vera he slowed down. He had not thought he might be intruding. But somehow the thin surface of their relationship, even after making love, didn't call for such considerations. She heard him and turned, smiling.

'I didn't mean to wake you, Eddie.'

'I don't know that you did. You were gone when I woke up.'

She drew on her cigarette and looked back at the river.

'It's a fine night,' he said.

'Yes, I like it here.' She turned again. 'I wanted to sit outside.'

Her voice caught. It was hardly anything, but he knew she had been crying. Looking at her face he could see it. She bent to stub out the cigarette.

'I'm glad we came,' said Stefan.

She nodded.

'Are you all right?'

'Of course.' She gave a quiet, dismissive laugh. 'I'm enjoying the night.'

'Maybe we're moving a bit fast . . .'

He said it half-jokingly, but he needed to say something. She was upset. He wanted her to know he wasn't indifferent to that. Maybe it would have been better if he hadn't come out. He was conscious how little they knew each other.

'There's nothing wrong. It's just the way . . . just how life is.'

She looked at the river. She took out another cigarette.

'And how is it?'

It was an attempt to lighten her mood.

'Shit is everywhere, Eddie. Mine isn't very special. Just ordinary shit.'

The words surprised him. He heard a quiet anger in them.

'I feel I've done something wrong, Vera. Look, if you want—'

'It's not about you, Eddie. It's just . . . it was . . . I don't know why I'm saying this . . . you've been the first time, since someone . . . I loved . . . God save us, I sound like a trashy film, don't I? It doesn't matter. I'm being stupid.'

Stefan felt the best response was no response.

'He died. There, that's it. He died. And it was the first time . . . since . . . I suppose such things are worth a moment's reflection, before we all move on.'

Stefan ignored the unconvincing cynicism.

'He was killed in the war?'

'I suppose so, yes.' She said the words slowly, almost to herself.

Stefan took a few steps away from her, towards the river. He looked out at the water. He would say something true, even something that tried to be kind, but he knew instinctively that she wouldn't want his arms round her. She wouldn't want comforting. He knew how that stung when you didn't want it.

'My wife died. She was very young. We were married only two years. It doesn't matter what happened, only that it did. And there was a first time, after that, with someone else. A long time afterwards, I guess, but it still left me feeling . . . I don't know . . . like something else had been taken away from me. It wasn't about guilt. Maybe I thought something had gone that was the last bit of us. That wasn't true, but it felt true . . .' He shrugged. 'I'll leave you to Old Father Thames.'

He turned back, away from the river. As he brushed by her, she took his hand. She held it only for seconds.

'Thank you. I'm glad it was you, Eddie.'

Stefan walked back to the Trout, still hearing the name that wasn't his.

17

Highgate

Stefan had been back in London for three days. He had still not heard from his G2 contact in London. They were taking their time in Dublin. If there was no great reason for him to be there, whether he was there or not didn't seem to feature high on anybody's list of priorities. But he did not want to be pulled any further into Willie Mullins' black market activities, and it was clear that the landlord now regarded him as part of that game. There was another driving job, as soon as the necessary goods had been delivered. Delivery was the word Willie used, but it meant robbery, from whatever ship or warehouse or factory his suppliers could get access to. Stefan had been told it would be that week. Little was said about the encounter with Detective Sergeant Simpson, but it was clearly there among the various anxieties the landlord pondered as he leant on the corner of the saloon bar at the Bedford Arms. He muttered several times, in Stefan's direction, that he would have to pay the fucker, and each time Stefan nodded. He didn't much care what happened between Willie and the English Special Branch man, as long as it happened after his exit. Going, he assumed, would be abrupt. He wasn't sure how abrupt. It only mattered because of Vera. Each time he saw her he was aware that the next day he might be gone. He would have to say something to her, though not much. It would be another lie.

Stefan was opening up when Willie Mullins came back from his morning trip to the Southampton Arms to place the day's bets. He had spent much of the previous night on the platform at Camden Town. The rubble that had been cleared off the street still blocked the High Street entrance, but the tunnels and platforms were busier than ever. Alongside the prayers and superstitions that got people through the nights, once the sirens sounded, there was a strong belief that a bomb would never fall in the same place twice. They had fallen close again that night, on the railway lines into London, but by two o'clock Raiders Passed sounded. Most people stayed where they were, but the trick of sleeping underground still eluded Stefan. He walked back to the pub. There was smoke and dust as usual in the air. There was the ever-present sound of some-one somewhere sweeping broken glass. He slept well. It was only when Willie came in that he heard about a bomb in Mornington Crescent.

'What happened?'

'There's a couple of houses gone. I didn't stop to look.'

The landlord walked out into the kitchen.

Stefan followed him.

'What number?'

'What?' Willie was pouring a cup of tepid, stewed tea.

'Which houses?'

'I don't know.'

Stefan looked at his watch. 'Vera should have been in hours ago.'

Willie frowned and nodded, finally registering why this mattered.

'Shite,' he said quietly.

Stefan had already left.

As soon as he reached Mornington Crescent, Stefan could see the gap in the curved terrace where the roof and front wall of one of the houses had gone, from the first floor up. The house next door had part of its roof missing. Upstairs rooms were open to the morning, hanging over the street. There was rubble all across the road. A fire engine stood nearby, the firemen spraying water into the blasted windows of the ground-floor rooms. There had been little burning, but the walls were still hot and there was broken timber smouldering. He knew immediately that the first house was where Vera had her room. He walked slowly towards it. He didn't want to reach it. He stood looking up at the broken façade. Around him men were shovelling rubble, glass. A policeman was smoking a cigarette, sitting on a pile of bricks, dirty and dusty. He gave a wry smile and shrugged, as everyone did. There was only one question to ask.

'Was anyone in the house?'

'A few.'

'Did they get out?'

'I think so. I wasn't here till this morning. There was an old woman in the top front.' The policeman pointed up at the first house. 'She got it straight off.'

'Have they found—'

'Two in the cellar next door. Floor fell in. That's it so far. They haven't found any more bodies. There's some unaccounted for. Most of them were in the shelters or down the Underground. Not too bad. You looking for someone?'

Stefan nodded.

'Most of them are in the church hall in Delancey Street. Try there.'

The hall was minutes away. Stefan ran. It was full of people who had come up from the shelters to find their homes gone, either in ruins or flattened. Some slept on the floors, others sat at the tables, drinking tea, smoking, reading newspapers. Children played and babies cried. The insistent jollity of *Music While You Work* blared out. There was little conversation. The adults wore weary expressions. For some there was a distant bewilderment. You knew it could happen; you didn't believe it would be you. In the course of the day those expressions would change. That was the only option; the weariness would become resilience, or something like it. You knew it could happen; it had.

Almost immediately Stefan saw two people he knew: Donal, the scrap-metal king, and his mother. They had two rooms above Vera. Mrs Harvey was sitting against a wall, smoking a cigarette, her eyes closed. Donal read *The Beano*.

'Donal!'

The boy looked up. He seemed unfazed by his circumstances.

'Hello, Mr Griffin.'

'You're all right?'

'Yes, we're grand.' He grinned. 'Nowhere to bloody live, though!'

'Donal, that'll do,' said his mother.

'Mrs Harvey,' said Stefan, crouching down, 'I'm looking for Vera.'

'I haven't seen her, Eddie. Did you see her at all, Donal?'

'No.' Donal shook his head. 'She'll be all right. She's bound to be.'

Stefan nodded. It was what he was expected to do.

'We were down in the Tube,' said Mrs Harvey, 'at Mornington Crescent. When we came up it was gone. It took off most of the top floor and the back wall of the house. They only found Mrs Doyle, that I know.' She crossed herself.

'Did you see Vera at all last night . . . before, I mean?'

'No. They don't think there's any more—' Mrs Harvey stopped.

Stefan walked slowly back to the Bedford Arms. He'd got no more information at the church hall. He'd been back to the house but there was nothing from the air-raid wardens or the police or the neighbouring houses. He'd heard the names of several people who had been sent to hospital, but no one knew which hospitals, and the name he wanted wasn't there. He would have to try all the hospitals. It was all he could think of as a place to start looking. He walked slowly into the pub.

'Where have you been?' Mullins shouted across the bar.

'Would you ever fuck off! No one's seen Vera. Since last night.'

'If you didn't spend so much time arsing about—'

'Did you hear what I just said, Willie!'

'She's in Highgate, Eddie.' The landlord grinned. Anto snorted.

'She's all right?'

'I'd say so. She was hurt. But she's out of hospital. At Dr Field's.'

Stefan took a deep breath.

'He phoned for you. There you go.' Willie held up a scrap of paper.

Stefan took the number. He went to the back hall and the telephone.

The doctor answered the call.

'Ah, Mr Griffin, I'm glad I've got you. Brian Field here.'

'Is she hurt?'

'Not much more than concussion. She was unconscious when they found her. They took her to University College Hospital. Nothing wrong as far as we can tell. As she had nowhere to go . . . she's asleep now. She wants to see you.'

'Tell me where you are, Doctor. I'll come straight over.'

'Yes, if you would, Mr Griffin. She seems . . . anxious.'

He heard a slightly odd note in the doctor's voice, as if he was anxious too, but by the time he had taken down the address Stefan had forgotten it.

A few stops on the Northern Line brought Stefan to Highgate. Inner London became outer London; there were green gardens, tree-lined streets and red-brick villas that had space to breathe. In such a red-brick villa, in Jackson Lane, Dr Brian Field was waiting. He opened the door as Stefan opened the gate into the front garden. He spoke easily and cheerfully, but Stefan could tell immediately that there was tension behind his words. It seemed unlike the man he had watched working through the night with the dead and dying at Camden Town Underground station. He introduced Stefan to his wife and his young son as Eddie Griffin; Stefan recognised the boy as the friend of Donal Harvey's who had been involved in the argument over scrap metal the previous week.

'I think we've met.' He smiled at the boy. 'A friend of Donal's.'

'Is he OK?'

'He is. I saw him this morning. He'll be back collecting scrap any day.'

The boy laughed. Mrs Field looked at him disapprovingly.

'You won't be collecting it with him, Simon, not if you can't do it without getting into a fight. I don't know what's the matter with them all!'

'Yes, Ma!' Simon grinned and walked away, whistling tunelessly.

'Will you have a cup of tea, Mr Griffin?'

'I won't thank you, Mrs Field.'

'Well, you can take one up to Vera. I think she's awake now.'

'Do you know what happened, Doctor?' asked Stefan.

'She wasn't in the house when the bomb fell. She was on her

way to the Underground, at Mornington Crescent. She was far enough away. But the shock of the blast knocked her over. Something hit her, but she was lucky. There's a cut to the back of her head, but that's really all. She was unconscious when they found her, as I said. They took her to University College. She had no identity with her – she'd left so quickly. But she had a piece of paper with my number.'

'It was good of you to bring her here.'

'Of course it wasn't,' said Mrs Field, handing him the tea. 'They have to clear the beds for people who need them. She had nowhere to go. It's simple.'

Stefan went upstairs with the doctor. It was a house full of space; a quiet, confident, lived-in space. Vera was lucky to have been brought here. He wondered why she was anxious. Brian Field told him she was again as they walked upstairs, in a quiet tone that seemed out of step with the openness of his wife in the kitchen. He could only assume concussion was still affecting Vera.

On the wall, going up the stairs, Stefan registered several photographs of a young man in his very early twenties. In one picture he wore an RAF uniform. He remembered the conversation in the Bedford Arms: the dead son.

Dr Field opened the door to a small bedroom. He left Stefan to go in and walked back downstairs. Vera was propped up by pillows, still half asleep. Stefan looked at her for a moment. Her face was bruised. Her head was partly bandaged. He put the cup and saucer on a table and sat on the bed. She opened her eyes and blinked. And immediately she did so, she was wide awake.

'Eddie, thank goodness you're here.'

'Well, the luck of the Irish is still holding.' He took her hand.

'I'm fine. It's nothing, nothing at all.'

She was smiling, but he felt the anxiety in her voice.

'It's over. Don't worry, Vera.'

'I need you to help me, Eddie.'

'Course I'll help you. You're all right. That's what matters.'

'I need you to go to Mornington Crescent, to my room.'

'I don't know if there's a lot of it left.'

'You need to do it, Eddie.'

'I don't even know what's standing, Vera. Your room could be in the cellar.' He laughed. 'It's not important. If I can get in at some point, I will.'

'Some point won't do!' She almost hissed the words at him.

'All right, I'll do my best.'

'You don't understand. I need your help. I am asking for your help.'

There was a hardness in her words. He looked at her, puzzled.

'I understand you want your things, but if they're under a pile of rubble—'

'There's a suitcase, Eddie, a small leather suitcase. It's under the bed. I can't let anyone else find it. You have to get it out of there. Will you do that?'

'I see, a matter of life or death?'

She didn't answer him, but her face was tight. Her eyes fixed on him.

'Eddie, I can't explain why this matters. Can't you do it without me explaining? I know enough about you to know you wouldn't want the police looking into who you are or what you're doing in London. I don't either.'

'Is that right?' He spoke more slowly.

'There's no time to argue. I've got eyes. We're not so different.'

Stefan said nothing. He didn't know what she meant. He didn't know if it was about the IRA man on the run he was supposed to be or about the black market goods he was driving round London, or even about the Special Branch man who was blackmailing Willie Mullins. But she knew the Bedford Arms, so she knew some of it, or all of it. As he had thought the first time he saw her, playing Beethoven on Mullin's out-of-tune piano, she was an unlikely cleaner.

'You will do it, Eddie? Straightaway.'

'If it matters that much.' He nodded. 'I'll try.'

She leant forward. She kissed his lips gently.

'I have to get out of here, Eddie.'

'The doctor says you're still concussed. Give it a couple of days.'

'No, I'm not safe here.'

'Jesus,' Stefan laughed, 'I can't think where you'd be much safer.'

'You don't understand.'

'Something else I don't understand?'

'Let me know when you have the case. But don't bring it here.'

The look in her face was harder again.

'You need to go, now. You need to do it, now, Eddie.'

There was a tenderness in her words, a pleading for his help, but that wasn't all. There was a determination in her eyes, far stronger than any anxiety. He left moments later. As he shut the bedroom door he felt Vera had been giving him an order. He walked to the gate with Brian Field. The nervousness the doctor had shown from the beginning showed again. He spoke rapidly.

'Is there somewhere you can take her, Mr Griffin?'

Stefan stopped, surprised. The last words from Mrs Field, only a minute before, had been that Vera could stay in Highgate as long as she wanted, until she was properly better and until she had sorted out somewhere else to live.

'Well, I suppose—'

'She's working at the pub, isn't she? If Willie could find a room for her . . .'

'I'll talk to him, Doctor. I'm sure he could. If she can be moved . . .'

'There's nothing wrong with her, really.'

'You'd know better than I will. It's just that Mrs Field said—'

'She can't stay here. I'm sorry. I don't know how well you know her . . .'

'Hardly at all. We've been thrown together. I don't know what you—'

'I'm sorry, Mr Griffin. I'm sure it sounds odd. I brought Vera from the hospital. It was the right thing. But now . . . I can't explain. She has to leave.'

Walking back to Highgate Station, Stefan was more confused than when he arrived. He didn't know what was behind Vera's anxiety, her almost obsessive determination to recover her suitcase. He wanted to think it was something to do with her injury. He knew it wasn't. He would do what she asked. He owed her that. After all, any day now he would be gone, with barely a goodbye, maybe not even with that. As for Dr Field, there had been something in his face that looked like fear. If he wasn't going to tell Stefan why he no longer wanted Vera in his house, he wasn't going to tell his wife either. None of it made sense.

Stefan did not notice a car parked several houses further down Jackson Lane, on the other side of the road to Dr Field's. There were two men in it, watching him. As he walked towards Archway Road the car pulled out. It drove behind him, picking up speed. He didn't see the interest both men took in him as they passed. The car turned into Hillside Gardens. By the time Stefan reached Highgate Station the car was parked close to the entrance, with a view of him walking towards it. One man was in the car, the other in a telephone box. As Stefan entered the station the second man picked up the phone and dialled.

18

Mornington Crescent

When Stefan Gillespie returned to Camden from Highgate, Mornington Crescent was still full of activity. The Fire Brigade were still working; the rubble was still being searched. Builders were shoring up walls on either side of the bombed houses. There was no chance of trying to get into Vera's house and up to her room. And by the time the activity around the bomb site had died down, it was dark. The sirens were sounding in other parts of London. When Stefan walked past the building one last time that evening, the fire engine was still there, and a flattened van was being towed away from the rubble it had lain under all day. Even if he could get into the house, finding his way through the broken walls and shattered floors in the dark would be impossible. If he used a torch, the light would bring the police and the air-raid wardens. He could do nothing except stand at the bar at the Bedford Arms and wait until tomorrow.

It was not until the next afternoon that Mornington Crescent was quiet again. In front of the bombed houses workmen were clearing a way through the debris that still closed off the road. The fire engine had gone; so had the police. Two air-raid wardens sat on the steps of Vera's house, eating sandwiches. The people who walked past were going about their business again, taking no great notice of what was so familiar in their streets. Stefan walked past the front of the house. It was not unusual for people to go back into bombed houses to retrieve what they could, even if it wasn't safe. But he didn't want to draw attention to himself while people were about. There would be questions. It wasn't unlikely that a policeman might want to go in with him, to see if it was safe, and to see he was after what he said he was looking for. It wouldn't be unreasonable. He didn't live there. But Vera did not want attention drawn to what he was doing either. He had to accept that. He did so without knowing what it was for; he kept his promise.

He moved on into Mornington Place where a wall ran for a short way, closing off the garden of the crescent's corner house. There were piles of bricks and mortar along the pavement, now swept and shovelled into neat heaps. The wall had been damaged in the bomb blast. He looked round and saw no one. He climbed on to one of the piles of rubble leaning against the wall and looked along the back of the terrace. The blast had damaged other houses too. Windows were blown out; the roofs of several back extensions had fallen in; sheds and greenhouses and fences were scattered across gardens. But there was a clear way through to the house where Vera lived. There the rubble lay high and deep: the whole of the roof and most of the back wall of the house. He could see the wallpaper of the room that had been Vera's.

Stefan stepped over the gap in the wall. All the houses here had been evacuated while they were checked for structural damage. They were empty. When he reached the rear of Vera's house, the whole of the ground floor was blocked by rubble. The back wall and the roof sloped towards the open box-like rooms that reached up two more floors, like a smashed, crumbling doll's house.

He climbed up the slope, over the bricks and the stones and the wood and the plaster, and the broken chairs and tables and beds. There was a bath full of bricks, an iron stove, a bookcase still full of books where it had fallen on its back. Everything was wet and sticky from the fire hoses drenching the debris. But there had been no real fires here. And as Stefan scrambled to the top of the hill of rubble he was able to step into the corridor that led from the back of the house to the main staircase. The floors were solid in parts, but there were broken floorboards and beams that had shattered and showed the timbers beneath; there were small gaps to negotiate, where the ceilings had collapsed below. But when he reached the stairs, they were standing. The banisters had gone, but keeping to the wall he made his way up to the next floor. The landing that led to Vera's room was open to the sky, but the walls still stood too, and the door into the room was undamaged. Even the green flock wallpaper that surrounded it was untouched. But when he opened the door he was looking straight across the room at the sky – and the roofs of houses in the next street.

As Stefan stepped forward the floor creaked. He stopped for a moment; holding in a feeling of vertigo. He turned to the bed, in a corner against the room's back wall. It had collapsed under a pile of plaster and wooden laths and slates. He moved carefully to it and bent down. He could see the case, at the top end, under the headboard. He managed to reach the handle. He pulled but it wouldn't come. The broken bed held it. He tried to pull the mattress off the bed, bringing with it the rubble that lay on top. It wouldn't move. And as he pulled he felt the movement in the floor again. He could see that the case was trapped by the bed springs. He pulled the handle of the case again, trying to push the crushed springs that were holding it. Suddenly it gave. He fell back. The floor trembled. The small brown case was bent and squashed. But he had it.

*

Stefan scrambled and slipped down the heap of brick and stone that had been the back of the house only a day before. At the bottom he brushed himself down. He tucked the case under his arm, and as he turned, he saw someone looking at it. Donal Harvey stood beside his pram. It was full of scrap metal.

'Hello, Mr Griffin.'

He looked at Stefan oddly. It wasn't questioning; it was something closer to fear. He didn't want to be caught either. Stefan felt he had to explain why he was there, even to Donal. The boy would be sure to say something to someone.

'I'm getting something for Vera.'

'You seen her then, Mr Griffin?'

'Yes, I have, so. She had a bit of a knock. She's at Dr Field's.'

Donal nodded thoughtfully. He seemed reluctant to move.

'Did you see Simon?'

'His son?'

'He's a good mate.'

Stefan walked forward. He did not want to stay here.

'He's fine. He was asking about you, Donal.'

'You know we're going, Mr Griffin?'

Stefan had to stop; Donal seemed determined to continue talking.

'Right. Where's that, then?'

'I think Bournemouth. Dad's found a flat for us there. He's got to stay here, with the Fire Brigade. It'll be free in a couple of weeks. We'll go then.'

'That's good. You're better off out of this, I'd say.'

Donal nodded. He looked awkward, nervous. Even surrounded by the bomb debris he didn't look as convinced about leaving as he wanted to sound.

'You won't tell I was here, Mr Griffin?'

'I won't. But maybe you shouldn't be. The buildings aren't safe.'

'I don't go in. I just collect up the scrap. Bomb sites are the best place. There's bugger all anywhere else now. I know you're not supposed to do it . . .'

'You could get arrested, you know that.'

'That's for looting. Scrap isn't looting, is it?'

'Even so. It's dangerous.' Stefan looked back at the house. 'I know.'

Donal looked more awkward than ever.

'I've got to go, Donal,' said Stefan, 'and get this to Vera.'

'Will you come here?' said the boy.

'What?'

'Over here.'

He started to walk away, over a flattened fence to the next garden.

'Donal, I have to get on.'

'I can't tell anyone. I'm afraid. I shouldn't be here, you see. Dad'll kill me. I don't want to just leave it. Will you tell them – and not mention me?'

'What is it?'

'He's here, Mr Griffin?'

Stefan heard the urgency in the voice. He followed him into the next garden.

Donal Harvey stood over a pile of debris. There were sheets of corrugated metal lying on top of bricks and timber; the remains of an Anderson shelter.

As Stefan reached him, Donal was pulling away the corrugated iron.

The body of a man lay underneath.

Stefan Gillespie knew who he was immediately: Simpson, the Metropolitan Police Special Branch sergeant, Willie Mullins' blackmailer.

'If Dad finds out I've been on the sites, I'll get the belt.'

Stefan didn't hear Donal.

'They'll find him eventually, I know. But it don't feel right leaving him.'

Stefan looked round. 'What?'

'Leaving him. It don't feel right.'

Stefan crouched beside the policeman's body. He was bruised; there were cuts and grazes; he was covered in the dust that went with the bomb damage. There was nothing that said this wasn't what you'd expect to find. Anderson shelters offered limited protection. The roof of this one had collapsed when the bomb hit the back of the house. But this man didn't live here. The shelter was in someone's back garden. Stefan could have no idea who Simpson knew, who he used for information. Special Branch could have been using a flat. Someone there could have been an informer. Yet none of that rang true. Stefan sensed Simpson was a chancer. Something wasn't right, as Donal Harvey said, but for Stefan that meant something different. He didn't know what. He stood.

'He must have been in the shelter when the bomb fell, Donal.'

'I don't know about that, Mr Griffin.'

There was nervousness in Donal's voice again. He seemed untroubled by the sight of a dead body. It wasn't that. There was something else he had to say.

Stefan looked round. 'What do you mean?'

'I was here yesterday evening. The Fire Brigade was round the house all afternoon. I came back for some scrap after they went. That's the best time.'

Stefan already felt he knew what the boy was going to say.

'I looked under that sheet yesterday. I got some of the corrugated iron out too. And I came today to see if I could get some more. He wasn't there then.'

Stefan sat in his room at the Bedford Arms. On the bed beside him was Vera's battered suitcase. The lock was broken; the lid was twisted and bent. He had decided that he would look at what was inside. There was too much going on to ignore it.

He owed her something, but he didn't owe her so much that he couldn't smell danger. He didn't know why she needed his help, but he needed to protect himself. And now there was Simpson. Stefan's first thoughts about him were not charitable.

If the policeman didn't die in the Anderson shelter, someone had put him there. Stefan had no interest in who that was. Camden really wasn't the Special Branch man's patch; that was clear. He had pushed his way into it to try to get money out of Willie Mullins. How the sergeant died was for someone else to worry about. It had happened within days of his embarking on what must have appeared a certain way to make some cash. Willie Mullins looked like an easy target. Special Branch would have known him because of his connections to the IRA. Fat, lazy, disloyal, timid, always short of money, always chasing off people who wanted paying, he wasn't a man who could offer resistance to the kind of pressure Sergeant Simpson exercised. But Simpson had misjudged. Stefan couldn't know whether he had misjudged Willie, or some of Willie's friends, but there was more at stake now than the embarrassment of an Irish Special Branch man in an English jail; there was an English Special Branch man's murder to tack on. Stefan had already phoned his G2 contact again. He would go the next day. He had an address. There was no time to waste.

He said nothing to Willie Mullins when he got back. There would be no goodbyes. The less anyone knew the better. Willie was still in his position at the corner of the saloon bar. He was at a stage of the day's slow drive towards the inebriation that would eventually send him to sleep that night, when all was well with the world. He was cheerful and jokey, more talkative than usual. A horse had come in at Stratford; that always helped. If Stefan Gillespie looked for signs that anything was wrong, that Willie was troubled by something that day, he saw nothing. It was hard to think Willie knew about a dead Special Branch man under a sheet of corrugated iron almost in the next street. Stefan could not know what would happen when Simpson was found. It was not unlikely that with bodies to be collected and disposed of by the hundred most nights, no one would look very hard at the circumstances. He doubted Donal Harvey would say anything; he had done his duty by telling Stefan. It wasn't the first body the boy had seen. Stefan would say nothing to anybody. There was only Vera left to think about.

He pushed open the lid of the suitcase.

He saw several Ordnance Survey maps. One was folded open. He recognised the River Thames. A line had been drawn along it. It was the walk they had made from Oxford to Tadpole Bridge. Along the route, at regular intervals, rings had been drawn. Where the map went beyond Tadpole Bridge the rings had been replaced by question marks, at the same, regular intervals.

He picked up the sketchbook Vera had brought with her on the walk. He opened it to see a pencil sketch of the ruined abbey at Godstow. Below it was a sketch of his own head and shoulders, as he lay on his back, looking up at the sky. Next was a drawing of one of the concrete pillboxes they encountered on their walk. There were several more, interspersed with sketches of trees and riverbank. The rings were the line of gun emplacements they saw along the upper reaches of the Thames; the question marks were Vera's guess that they stretched along the river, deep across southern England. In the back of the book was an envelope. In it was over a thousand pounds in five-pound notes.

As he closed the case Stefan saw that the lining of the lid had been torn away. There was something there. He took out a small yellow booklet. The cover was plain. Each page was perforated and contained a series of numbers and letters in columns. They appeared to be organised randomly. There were no words. But it was clear what they were. It was a code book. Each page was for a one-off use. At the other end, whatever the means of transmission, whether in writing or by radio, the page used would be matched to its twin. There was no doubt where the book came from. The letters and the numbers were German.

It was getting dark as Stefan Gillespie approached Dr Field's house for the second time. The case was still in his room at the Bedford Arms. If Vera wanted it, that was up to her. He had done what she had asked. He didn't know what he was supposed to do with what he knew now. She was an agent, whatever that meant. It wasn't his war, but it was not information he would keep from anyone in Dublin. What they did with it was for them to decide. As everyone was fond of saying, it wasn't their war either. Except that it was, in one way or another, all the time. There had been a moment, sitting looking at the case in his room, when he had felt a swell of anger. She had used him. But not many seconds passed before the anger was replaced by something like a smile. It didn't feel much like she had. And why not? Why wouldn't she use him anyway? He was meant to be an IRA man on the run. She would assume his interests were the same as hers. Anything that attacked England, however slight, however small. But his next thought was for her safety.

If he owed Vera Kennedy nothing now, he still felt he should warn her. She was right to feel she wasn't safe. He could not tell her who he was. He could not tell her that everything he knew would appear in a report, and the report would find its way from Superintendent Gregory's office to Commandant de Paor in Military Intelligence. He could not tell her that it was highly likely G2 would pass that information on to the British. He could tell her that if there was a way to get out, she should take it now. Just as he was.

*

Stefan Gillespie smiled broadly as Dr Field opened the door, putting on his best and easiest face. However, the doctor was not pleased to see him. He was anxious, still fearful in some inexplicable way. But now it seemed to Stefan it was his presence that was a problem. If fear was part of Brian Field's expression, irritation was there too. He stared at Stefan, then snapped at him.

'What do you want?'

'To see Vera, Dr Field.'

The doctor looked puzzled.

'She's gone.'

'Gone where?'

'I don't know. We left her in the house. When I got back she was gone. That is all I know. There is nothing more to say about it. Please, just go now.'

He pushed at the door, trying to shut it. Stefan put his hand against it.

'I'd like to come in. Better inside, don't you think?'

Stefan shoved the door back, very hard, and walked in.

'I'm sorry, Doctor, that's bollocks. And it's not enough, not at all.'

19

The Catacombs

'I don't know where she went. I don't even know who took her.'

Dr Field sat in his kitchen with Stefan Gillespie.

'But someone did,' said Stefan. 'Don't know, don't care?'

'No, I don't care. Does it matter?'

'I suppose not.' Stefan wasn't sure why he was asking these questions. What he said next was said as much to himself as to Brian Field. 'I suppose she matters. I wanted to make sure she was all right. Don't you know anything?'

'There was a car. My next-door neighbour saw her get in it.'

'She doesn't even know anybody—'

Stefan stopped. He didn't know who she knew or who she was. How could he? He knew she wasn't simply an Irishwoman who cleaned in Camden Town.

'Is that all you want, Mr Griffin?'

'Yes, I guess ... well, I wouldn't mind knowing what happened.'

'What do you mean?'

'You brought her here. She was hurt. You wanted to help her. Your wife told me she could stay as long as she needed. But when I got here yesterday, all you wanted was to get her out.

Now she's gone, all you want is to get me out as well. You want nothing to do with her. I didn't even know her. And neither did you.'

'I gave her a job, that's all. She wasn't much of a cleaner.' For the first time he smiled. 'I'm sorry if she meant something. I doubt you'll see her again.'

'I doubt that too. Why do you say it? She frightened you, didn't she?'

'Look, I'll tell you this. It might make you leave it alone . . . Vera was still concussed when I brought her here, more than we thought at the hospital. She was in a very fitful sleep. I stayed with her for a while. I was a bit concerned. I wondered whether she should have been kept in longer . . . with a head injury, you never quite know . . . Anyway, she started talking in her sleep. It wasn't clear at first. It was only for a few minutes, mostly it was mumbling, nothing more than that. But she was speaking German. I know that. I speak it too.'

'Is that so frightening? You speak German yourself, you just said so.'

'I'm not pretending to be an Irish cleaner, Mr Griffin.'

Stefan laughed. 'No, fair enough, there is that.'

'I didn't even tell my wife. I was afraid.'

'It couldn't have been that frightening. You didn't call the police.'

'No, I didn't. I just wanted her out.'

'All right. Well, I suppose that's it. Is that it?'

'You don't understand, do you?'

'I'm not sure I do, Doctor.'

'My father came here after the First World War, from Germany. I was at university then. I left in the middle of my studies. I finished them here. He saw something . . . I don't know . . . he saw that it was good to get out, that's all. He said it was a better place to be. He said the English aren't perfect, but they'll leave us alone. No one needs to say he wasn't right any more. I have friends, people who came to England through the thirties, who followed us, to escape . . . when it was much clearer what was coming . . . people who were driven out. I could give you a long list of the ones who have been interned now. Locked up because they're Germans and Austrians who got away from the Nazis. But too German to be trusted. You could almost laugh. They're in the Isle of Man now, most of them, behind a barbed-wire fence. They were arrested and taken away, with no charges, no trials. Most of them are Jews, but that doesn't matter . . . The English didn't leave us alone after all. My closest friend is there now, and a cousin, my wife's sister. They've lost their homes some of them, and their businesses. A friend in Hampstead had to sell his practice. He had no money. He got almost nothing for it. He's finished, whether they let him out or not.'

'I have heard something,' said Stefan; it was scarcely anything.

'Something and nothing,' said Field. 'A few of them killed themselves . . . you won't hear that. You won't hear there are Nazis in the internment camps, real Nazis. They took a Jewish boy off a toilet they didn't want him to use and threw him through a window. You don't choose the people they put you with.'

'You had a son, in the RAF. I heard—'

'I don't think a dead son would count for much if they found I was sheltering a German agent in my house. I don't know that's what she is. But she is German, however Irish she sounds. She is pretending not to be German.'

'Maybe life's just easier that way, Doctor, for all the reasons you know.'

'Is that what you think, Mr Griffin?'

It wasn't what Stefan Gillespie thought, but he decided Dr Field would sleep more easily if he could believe something like that. He thought it might be better for Vera, too, if the doctor wasn't left with a nagging doubt about whether he should tell someone or go to the police with his suspicions.

'It's what I'd like to think,' he said. 'She was never going to do much for the Third Reich, not cleaning pubs and doctors' surgeries in Camden Town.'

Brian Field was happier. For the first time he started to think that he had built up something that was as much about his own anxieties as about what had happened. There was sense in what the Irishman said; maybe enough sense. But that wasn't what was in Stefan Gillespie's head walking back to the Underground station in the gathering dusk. Yet he was also glad that Vera Kennedy had gone.

Stefan turned into Arlington Road. Anto from the Bedford Arms almost crashed into him, leaping up from the wall where he was sitting, smoking a cigarette.

'Jesus, there you are, Eddie!'

'I am so. What the fuck are you trying to do?'

'I've been waiting for you. Willie said you're not to be coming back to the pub. There's been some fellers in, looking for you. And they weren't messing.'

'What did they want?'

'I don't know. They came when we were closed. Barged in. Willie thought they were peelers, but he's not so sure. One was up in your room. There was no stopping them. He was after bringing something down. A case, it was.'

Stefan nodded. What else would it be?

'Are they still there?'

'No, but they're around. They were in a car down the road. I don't know where they are now, but Willie's got his spies out. You're to wait in the church.'

Anto gestured across the road. The doors of the Belgian church were open now. A few people were drifting in. Vespers. Stefan Gillespie hesitated.

'You can't stay here, Eddie. Willie will get you out of Camden.'

The barman said it with a certainty that Stefan heard. He nodded. This was the landlord's turf. He knew it inside out. That had to be worth something.

Stefan walked quickly across the road into Our Lady of Hal's. There were only a few people there. As it was Vespers, it wasn't the kind of crowd he might have wished for. But it would do. It was a place to think. He had no idea who the men looking for him were. They could be ordinary detectives, or Special Branch men, or they could be the people who had driven Vera away from Jackson Lane. If they were Germans, in whatever form, and they had the case, then they knew that he knew too much. They would not want him to spread the news. They could be anywhere in the street, anywhere in Camden. He couldn't know how many there were or where they were. He sat back in the pew, into the shadows. The church was dark. There were a few low lights and candles. To the side of the altar, a group of nuns were chanting. 'Deus, in adiutorium meum intende. Domine, ad adiuvandum me festina.' O God, come to my assistance. O Lord, make haste to help me.

Stefan was unsure what to do: whether to bolt for the Underground and try to get out that way or to wait. Willie, at least, knew what these people looked like. He had seen the car. For now, Stefan felt safe. No one would look here. He would wait for Willie Mullins to make haste to help him.

Willie arrived ten minutes later, breathless, sweating, but surprisingly calm. He genuflected and slid into the pew beside Stefan. He said nothing, but he leant forward, bending his head and muttered a prayer. Then he looked up.

'What the feck have you been doing, Eddie?' he whispered.

'Who are they?' Stefan did not attempt to answer Eddie's question.

'I don't know. I thought they'd be some sort of coppers. They weren't any Special Branch I seen before, not in Camden. They didn't talk like coppers.'

'So you just let them in?'

'They weren't asking my permission.'

'What did they say?'

'They wanted to know where you were. Then one of them went upstairs.'

'And he came back with a case?'

'No one told me you were doing anything. Lying low, that was the deal.'

'Where are they now?'

'They're around. I don't know how many there are. There's a car. They made a point of going, but one of the regulars saw the car up by the station.'

Stefan shook his head. He didn't know what to think.

'Maybe I should ask you who they are, Eddie?' said Mullins.

'I don't know either, Willie, not for sure.'

'But you might have an idea, Eddie.'

'Probably not Special Branch.'

'No.' The publican shook his head. 'Jesus, do I even want to know?'

'I don't think you do, Willie. Maybe Germans.'

Willie Mullins said nothing. He closed his eyes. Then he nodded.

'So what now?' asked Stefan.

'Ah, go on.' Willie grinned. 'Now you may piss off, Eddie.'

As the nuns began to sing the Magnificat, the landlord of the Bedford Arms slid back along the pew. He stood up and genuflected again in the aisle, then he walked across the back of the church. Stefan Gillespie followed him.

Willie Mullins opened a door in the wall of the church and walked through. A long corridor ran along the side of the church. Another door opened. An elderly nun came out. She frowned. Willie spoke, unexpectedly, in French.

'Bonsoir, ma soeur.'

'Ah, Monsieur Mullins, cherchez-vous quelqu'un?'

'Pas maintenant, ma soeur, pas maintenant.'

He beamed cheerfully and walked on. Stefan nodded at the nun. She looked only slightly puzzled and carried on towards the church. Willie re-opened a door at the end of the corridor. They stepped into a small, enclosed yard. At one end there was a wrought-iron gate. The landlord pulled it open. They were in a narrow alleyway between the high garden walls of two houses.

'We'll come out in Parkway. I take it you can ride a bike?'

At the end of the alleyway two bicycles leant against the wall.

'Have you got somewhere to go, Eddie?'

'Yes. When I get there.'

'Fucking pity you didn't go there before, you gobshite. What way?'

'Through town. West.'

'They know you went somewhere on the Tube, Eddie. They'll be looking at the station as well as the pub. But they've no reason to think you know that. Where else would you go? I'll take you over the canal. We can get off the street when we get to the end of Arlington Road. Then up to Chalk Farm and across to Swiss Cottage. You'll be on another Tube line then. It'll be grand once we're over the canal and away. I can't see they'll be looking for someone on a bike.'

Stefan nodded. It was dark now, all the darker because of the blackout.

'Just follow me.'

The landlord reached up and pulled Stefan's hat more firmly down on his head. He got on one of the bicycles and rode unsteadily on to Parkway. Stefan followed. They turned towards Arlington Road and rode in the direction of the canal. There were a few cars and bicycles; people were walking home from work. It was busy enough to make their progress along the road unobtrusive.

At the end of the street Willie rode across the junction and stopped. In front of them was a passageway, partly blocked with empty boxes and dustbins. Wheeled market stalls were parked against a wall. Willie took out a cigarette.

'We can cross the canal over the lock. There's a footbridge.'

As he lit the cigarette his eyes followed a car slowly driving towards them from Camden High Street. A van blasted its horn, overtaking the car. Stefan glanced round. Willie touched his arm and then pushed his bicycle towards a gap between the boxes and bins, into the dark passageway.

'Come on, that was the car.'

Stefan pushed his own bicycle forward. 'Did they see us?'

'I don't know.'

'Where now, Willie?'

'You go on in front, Eddie. Just keep going. I'll be behind you.'

Stefan could see the canal ahead of him, and the footbridge over the lock gates. He heard another horn sound. He looked back to see Willie Mullins.

'They copped us. They turned round. They're coming back.'

As they reached the footbridge, the landlord let the bicycle drop.

'Leave it. These are no fucking use now. We'll leg it.'

Mullins ran on to the footbridge. Stefan dropped his bicycle and followed. They ran across the footbridge and on to the cobbles on the other side. Ahead of them were the high walls of the warehouses and sheds and the lanes and alleyways that spread out between them. Willie stopped, listening hard.

'Just follow me. They can't drive over that, can they?'

They turned and hurried on, half walking, half running. Stefan glanced at Willie Mullins, not sure what to make of him. The landlord seemed to have found a new lease of life.

The slovenly inebriation had been pushed aside. He was smiling, even laughing. There was an intensity about him. He was enjoying this now. Stefan wasn't sure how far he could trust that. But it was all he had.

'We'll try something else.' Mullins stopped again, gasping for breath.

He turned a corner. A high black arch stood in front of them. Stefan recognised it. He had driven into it with a lorryload of black-market goods. Willie took a torch from his pocket. He shone it into the entrance. Its beam didn't travel far, but he only needed to check all was clear. He knew this place.

'Listen,' he said, 'I think they sent someone over the bridge.'

They stood still. There were steps. Someone running. Then the footsteps stopped. There was nothing. Then a sound. There were still steps. There was no more running, but the softer steps were following, quietly and more carefully.

'Let's go,' breathed Willie.

The two men walked into the darkness. As Stefan's eyes adjusted he could make out the arches on either side of the high central corridor that was taking them underground. They moved slowly, more concerned with silence than with speed. There was another sound. It was an engine. A car. Willie Mullins pulled Stefan into one of the dark archways. They looked out, around the brick pillar towards the entrance. There were two lights, the narrow beams of two headlights, capped for the blackout. They heard voices. A car door opened. The man who had followed them over the bridge was talking. There was a slight crack, then a ringing of metal as something hit the cobbles. A blaze of light flooded down into the darkness of the Catacombs, then another. They had taken off the headlight caps. The car began to move down the central aisle. On either side two men were walking, keeping pace, looking into each archway.

'Right,' said Mullins quietly. 'Go straight across, next arch down. Keep going. It gets very narrow at the end. There's a wall. We go left, then right. It's like a tunnel. Just walk as fast as you can, but not so fast you trip. You won't be able to see a fucking thing. Keep going, whatever happens. Are you ready, so?'

Stefan was as ready as he could be.

Willie Mullins ran, Stefan followed.

They crossed the cobbles, caught in the headlights of the car. The engine roared. The car accelerated. Men were running. A shot was fired, then another. Stefan felt the bullet hit his shoulder. It passed through his coat and only just caught his skin. The force almost knocked him over. But he was across the central lane now, into the next arch. It was piled high with tyres, but there was a path through it. Willie was still ahead of him. And then there was the wall. There were voices behind, shouting. Mullins paused, panting, pointing to the left.

'Don't call out,' he hissed, 'it sounds for bloody miles.'

In the narrow tunnels, running was impossible, but the landlord kept up a constant pace, pushing in front of Stefan, turning into dark junctions and tunnels, coming out into high-roofed darkness again, back into tunnels. They didn't speak. Willie Mullins walked and Stefan followed. They heard only their own breathing, and the echo of their feet. But now they had heard nothing else for some time; no more running footsteps, no more voices. They walked on.

And then there was fresh air and there was the night. They emerged into a wide, open yard. There were red vans and lorries, and men in uniform working, pulling handcarts piled up with sacks. There was a platform and a goods train.

'Not bad,' said Willie Mullins. He sat down on a low wall.

'Where are we?'

'Euston Station. Not bad.'

Stefan looked round.

'Walk through the yard and you'll see some big gates. Go on through. You'll come out at the bottom end of the station, where the post vans come in.'

Willie Mullins took out a cigarette. The energy had gone. He saw Stefan's arm.

'Jesus, did they hit you?'

'Just about.'

'You'll live. I need to catch my breath. You better go. Take it easy so.'

'You're full of surprises, Willie. I owe you. Thanks.'

The landlord of the Bedford Arms shrugged.

'You're a surprise I could do without now, Eddie. Don't come back!'

Stefan nodded. But he didn't move. There was one more thing.

'Do you know about Sergeant Simpson?'

'Don't fucking remind me! I'll be paying that arsehole as long as this bloody war lasts. And he'll want more. They always want more. The bastards.'

It was clear he had no idea about the Special Branch man's death.

'I don't think you will, Willie.'

'And how do I get out of it?'

'You are out of it.'

'My arse,' laughed the landlord, 'or did you pay him off for me?'

'He's dead.'

Willie Mullins stared.

'In Mornington Crescent. He was in a shelter, in one of the gardens.'

'When the bomb—' Mullins stopped, puzzled. 'What was he doing there?'

'I don't know. I wouldn't want to know. Leave it.'

'What does that mean?'

'It means you may have some friends who didn't like what

the sergeant was doing. And they might have wanted a more reliable solution than coughing up money. I wouldn't search for an answer, Willie. But I'd maybe get out of the game.'

Half an hour later Stefan Gillespie was walking from Notting Hill Gate Underground station along the Bayswater Road. After a short distance he saw what he was looking for and turned into Clanricarde Gardens, a cul-de-sac of high Victorian houses. He rang the bell at the second house. The door was opened by a man around his age, tall, fair-haired. The hall was dark for the blackout. The man did not turn on a light, even after he closed the front door.

'Inspector Gillespie. Gavin Bates, how are you? Do come in.'

'I thought the name was Kelly when I phoned you.'

'What's in a name, old son? You're not Eddie Griffin now, are you?'

'And thank God for that,' said Stefan.

The man led the way into a dingy front room. It was lit by a dim lamp.

'Sit down. You'd want a drink, I'd say?'

'I would so,' said Stefan. He dropped into a leather armchair. He let his hat fall to the floor beside him, but he didn't attempt to take off his coat. The adrenalin that had carried him through the tunnels of the Camden Catacombs had worn off. There was a hard, biting pain that was piercing his shoulder.

Bates stood at a sideboard, pouring two glasses of whiskey.

'There's been no siren so far tonight. If we get one we can take the bottle into the garden. There's an Anderson there. That's the best I can do, I'm afraid.'

Stefan could hear the accent of Cork in the voice, but it lay beneath years of private school and university and England that kept most of it hidden away.

'I need you to have a look at my arm. Not much, but it needs attention.'

He took the glass of whiskey. He winced, indicating his left shoulder.

Gavin Bates peered down at the torn coat. There was dry blood.

'Did you take a knock?'

'No, not a knock; a bullet.'

'Jesus, that's awkward, Gillespie.'

'Yes, it is, damned awkward.'

Stefan Gillespie raised his glass and laughed.

'Do you ever think they've left you in England too long, Gavin?'

PART THREE

THE BURIAL OF THE DEAD

Sir John Maffey asked me if I had ever believed a British reoccupation of this country possible. I said that I felt quite sure it was going to take place and anybody who had as much evidence as I had would have come to the same conclusion. The sustained campaign – in Great Britain and America, and the positive statements made to us by people closely connected with the British Army, made it impossible for my Minister not to entertain serious suspicions about British intentions . . . Maffey said there had been serious and prolonged discussions between the politicians and the Army on the issue of British troops entering our territory. The military pressed very strongly for a decision allowing them to enter our territory, without an invitation from the Irish Government, at the moment of the German attack. The political considerations had prevailed and the Army had to acquiesce.

Letter from Joseph Walshe to Éamon de Valera,
October 1940

20

Sankt-Hedwigs-Kathedrale

Berlin

It was unlikely that anything arriving at the Irish embassy in Berlin had not been looked at by somebody in the Reich Main Security Office. Anyone who had any business with the embassy of a foreign country in Germany, whether that country was an ally or a neutral, large or small, was the business of the Gestapo, whose own stock-in-trade was knowing everyone's business. There was always going to be something suspicious about a German who had a need to speak to people who were not German. However innocent the explanation, such communications should be recorded. At the very least, unless you were engaged on government business, an explanation was certainly needed. And just as anything arriving by post at the Irish embassy at 3 Drakestrasse was subject to scrutiny, telephone calls were also monitored. The details of people who visited the embassy, indeed anyone the Irish ambassador met anywhere, were also recorded. Any German who had dealings with the embassy might expect to be questioned. Meetings between the ambassador, William Warnock, and other foreign diplomats were a particular source of irritation, since they could only be reported by the spies who worked in every embassy. Meetings that involved the American embassy, which still had diplomats in Berlin, were the greatest of all sources of frustration, and the Irish were forever talking to the Americans.

The official German line celebrated Ireland's neutrality as a continuing blow to Britain, but it was not true that the Irish were trusted. Despite their vociferous Celtic credentials, and the enthusiasm of Military Intelligence for Ireland's apparent usefulness against its Old Enemy, it sometimes seemed, at least in the counsels of the Nazi security services, that there was a whiff of the Anglo-Saxon about the Irish. No nation that spoke English could be entirely honest, as America continually demonstrated. English, after all, was a once magisterial Germanic tongue that had been mongrelised until its German roots were barely recognisable. There was something about its shameless pillaging of words from every other language it encountered, indiscriminately, profligately, that reeked of miscegenation. The Irish insisted on speaking it, despite having a language of their own that German scholars had applauded for its ancient purity.

For a number of reasons, Frank Ryan, whether as himself or as Frank Richards, had no business communicating with the Irish legation in Berlin. He was, after all, not even meant to be in Germany. There had been some less than convincing attempts, since his removal from a Spanish jail, to suggest that he had left Europe altogether and had made it to America. It was unclear if anybody believed that. The Irish knew; the British probably knew too. It was also unclear why it mattered very much anyway, except to Frank Ryan himself.

Despite the assurances of his Abwehr supporters, in particular his friend Helmut Clissman, no one knew what Ryan was for. Clissman's aim had been to save his friend's life, and in doing so he successfully exaggerated how useful he might be. But the truth about how ineffectual Ryan would prove as an Intelligence asset surprised even Clissman. Far from showing enthusiasm for uniting the Irish government and the IRA against the British, he spent his time reflecting on an ever-widening gulf between Éamon de Valera and Republicans. In reality the Irish and the British had already taken the guts out of the IRA, leaving only a disorganised rump, racked by internal dissent and disorder. It wasn't what anybody in the Abwehr wanted to hear; especially since it was true.

Nevertheless, the Abwehr protected Ryan as part of its plans for sabotage and rebellion in Ireland. If those never came to anything they were discussed endlessly. The SD and the Gestapo let the Abwehr know they knew, and they let Frank Ryan know too. They had a fat file on him from Spain and a death sentence, if required. But in a country where orders were obeyed irrespective of whether they were rational, and where questioning them was always very unwise, Frank Ryan remained Frank Richards, less an asset than an exotic Abwehr trophy.

Frank Ryan wasn't sure his own government had known his whereabouts. If they hadn't, the Irish policeman he met in Berlin, Gillespie, would have told them. Ryan had made it his business to play the game as straight as he could. He did not go near the embassy. He didn't pass messages home through people he knew in Berlin. He had no reason to trust anyone, even those he considered friends. The circumstances that led Stefan Gillespie to him again, after their first encounter in Spain, had nothing to do with the Abwehr. It was chance. And he took that chance. He sought Gillespie out in Berlin and sent a message home. It expressed little more than his unhappiness with where he was; it said that whatever anyone believed, he was not an enemy. He didn't fully understand that the Irish government was content to leave him where he was. They didn't want him back. But he did know the chance of the Germans landing him in Ireland was fading now. At worst, trust in him was diminishing; at best, he no longer mattered.

He had no intention of playing a more complex game than the one he had been drawn into, but now he had to. Helmut Clissman had given him information he didn't want. It was dangerous information. It was dangerous for Clissman to talk about. Ryan couldn't know whether it came out of his friend's head or whether he was following orders. Either way it left the Irishman with no choice. There were a number of ways the information could reach the Irish government if someone in the Abwehr wanted it to get there. There were probably easier ways than asking Frank Ryan to pass it on. But they might not be ways that would be so readily believed. If he went to the ambassador it was the Irish way too, face to face. It would not get lost. There would be no static.

It was the biggest risk he had taken since arriving in Berlin. If it went wrong it would put him at odds with his handlers in the Abwehr. They would deny all knowledge if they were really behind it. For the Gestapo it would mean there was no one left to protect him. He knew the lines he could not cross. Meeting the Irish ambassador was such a line. The best he could hope for, if things did go wrong, was to make it look as if he had simply bumped into William Warnock. If it wasn't entirely convincing, it still might save him.

He had seen Warnock once, in a restaurant in Kurfürstendamm. If the ambassador had seen him he pretended he hadn't. The two men had met in Dublin, years before, but Frank Ryan kept to the rules. He left the restaurant. When he heard that Warnock ate there a lot, he didn't go back. Now it was a way to contact the ambassador. He phoned the restaurant from call boxes over several days. He usually knew when he was being watched; he knew how to lose anyone following him. The third time he rang, Warnock was there. It was as close to anonymous as a call in Berlin could be. They spoke in Irish. Ryan gave enough information to establish who he was and said he had something to say that mattered. He said he would be at Mass the next Sunday at the cathedral.

There was nothing unusual about Frank Ryan going to Mass, though normally he went to a church close to his apartment. It was less about belief than the comfort of belief. He had known the Latin of the Mass since childhood. It didn't matter that he could barely hear it now. He heard it in his head. It was as much about a memory of home as it was about a relationship with God. And God, he felt, had not played entirely fair with him. Sometimes he went to Mass less to pray than to argue. With few people to talk to, God, at least, was a good listener.

Frank Ryan entered the cathedral of St Hedwig; Mass was underway. It was a great circular space, under a vast dome, lined with pillars. It had an austerity that echoed Ancient Rome more than the eighteenth century in which it had been built. It was somewhere the Irishman had never been before. He had picked it at random, in a part of Berlin he never normally went to, feeling its size would produce the right kind of anonymity. The seats at the back were fairly empty. He stood for a moment, listening to the choir singing the Kyrie. He saw William Warnock sitting close by. He bent and crossed himself and moved along the bench to sit down. Warnock nodded and said nothing. They sat through the Mass and went to the altar together for communion. It was only as the Mass ended and the two men sat, with the crowds around them moving out of the church, that the ambassador finally said something, leaning back slowly.

'I don't think either of us is meant to be doing this.'

'Bhí a fhios agat go raibh mé i mBerlín.' You knew I was in Berlin.

Frank Ryan spoke in Irish.

'I knew. Your Irish will be better than mine, Frank. I'm a bit rusty.'

Warnock spoke in Irish too.

'And Dublin knows I'm here too?'

'Not officially.'

'We shouldn't speak for long,' said Ryan.

'Should we be speaking at all? My impression is that your friends in Berlin would like to keep who you are . . . and what you do . . . to themselves.'

'I don't do anything that could harm Ireland.'

'I'm glad to hear it. That may be a matter of opinion, of course.'

'They know how I got here, in Dublin. They know it wasn't my choice.'

'I don't know anything about that, Frank. It's your business. Whether it's the right business to be in, only you can guess. I'm here because you asked me to come. You said there was something that mattered to Ireland. Is that right?'

'Is that short for "You made your bed"?'

'It's not short for anything. I don't know about you. I don't want to.'

Ryan was silent for a moment. It couldn't be unexpected.

'We should think about a walk, Frank. This isn't the best place for this. I'd say there's a Gestapo man behind a pillar at most Masses. The provost, Father Lichtenberg, has the unfortunate habit of offering up prayers for the Jews. I don't know how long they'll let him do it, but the German Foreign Office has the cathedral on a list of churches the Irish faithful should avoid.'

Frank Ryan laughed. He stood up.

'I can't even find the right church, can I? I need a cigarette, so.'

On Französische Strasse, Ryan and Warnock approached the bridge to the Museum Island. There was a Sunday crowd. This was as busy as they wanted.

'My impression of what happens here . . . is that a lot of people are not unhappy with what's going on in Ireland now.' Frank Ryan lit his cigarette. 'Maybe Dev's neutrality is the best they think they can get. They want to leave it that way. I know a bit, but not much. All I've ever done is talk to people about Ireland. Some Irish history, so. It doesn't amount to much more than that.'

'I told you, Frank, I don't want to know. But you need to know what it looks like from Dublin. I suppose the problem is that some of the people you're talking to might be in the habit of paying visits to Ireland... well, uninvited.'

The two men walked on in silence for a moment.

'What is it you have say, because it's not about all that, is it?'

'There are other people, who think differently about Ireland,' continued Ryan. 'They want more than neutrality. They want Ireland to do something. Not people I know. The Party . . . I don't need to explain all that. You live here too.'

'Let's take that as read. Who they might be. I'm not blind.'

'I think there could be someone in Ireland . . . someone who's been sent . . . maybe not to kill Éamon de Valera, but to see someone else does. There's no point not putting it bluntly. It's information I have. I think you should have it.'

William Warnock took in the words. He didn't seem to respond.

'I think someone wanted me to tell you. Someone here in Berlin.'

'It sounds very complicated, Frank.'

'I wouldn't be saying this if I didn't believe it.'

'Well, I can't know what you believe,' said the ambassador, 'but I'm sure the idea that there are people who might like to see the country without Dev at the head is hardly news in Ireland. Perhaps you've been away too long, Frank. You could take half the IRA men they've shut up in the Curragh Camp and find they wouldn't mind a shot at that. It's why they're in there. I doubt you need to lose sleep over the Taoiseach's safety. Thank you all the same, though.'

'It's not about who's doing it, it's about who's making it happen.'

'And I'm supposed to tell Dublin that Germany wants Dev dead?'

'I'm here because there are people who take it seriously. And they want to do everything they can to stop it happening. I'm just one way, I'm sure. But this isn't the usual game. It's not the usual people. And it's not the usual rules.'

'I don't know what the usual rules are, Frank. I'm a diplomat. But if it's about spies and all that shite, do you think they're short of rumours in Dublin?'

'I'm taking a risk, Mr Warnock. Someone's been sent to Ireland with instructions to work with people in the IRA who want Dev gone. It doesn't come from Military Intelligence. It's a Nazi plan. The SD. I know the agent's a woman. And who she is. Her name's Vera Eriksen. Yes, it's a rumour. A rumour Military Intelligence want you to hear. They believe it. I was asked to tell you, by a man I do trust. Someone who cares about Ireland.'

The two Irishmen stood on the bridge on to the Museum Island. They looked at each other. William Warnock said no more, neither did Frank Ryan. The ambassador nodded. Ryan turned away. Warnock stayed where he was for a long moment, watching the other man disappear into the crowds. He had not smoked during the conversation, though Ryan had chain-smoked. Now he took out a packet of cigarettes. He lit one. Finally he started to walk slowly back.

Frank Ryan sat in a bar round the corner from his flat in Schöneberg. He drank more than he usually drank. It was not what had just happened that took him to the bar and kept him there. It was the feeling of isolation. He assumed William

Warnock had listened. He assumed he would do something, say something, get some kind of message to Dublin that expressed the seriousness of what he had been told. He assumed Warnock recognised that seriousness. He was sure that was true, even if the ambassador would not acknowledge it. But he knew more. He knew the gulf that separated him from his own country. He knew the depths of mistrust there. He had kidded himself about that. And he could do nothing.

When he left the bar it was getting dark. Approaching the apartment block, he saw a car parked outside. He knew who they were. Gestapo. He had no fear they had seen him earlier, or that they had been following him. This was routine, part of the game. It was to let him know that despite his friends in Tirpitzuferstrasse, he was in Berlin on sufferance. And their day would come. It was the same message. Always letting him know they knew. Telling him to be afraid. But he was drunk enough, or stupid enough, not to play the game that evening. He went to the car and tapped on the window. Two men sat in the front. One of them wound down the window. Frank Ryan had a thin roll-up between his lips. He spoke in English, with no suggestion he didn't know them.

'Would one of you lads ever give me a light?'

The Gestapo man looked uncertain. He understood English, but he wasn't sure whether he was supposed to show Ryan that he did. He took out his lighter.

'Thanks, comrade.' Ryan straightened up, drawing deeply on the cigarette. 'You know what, you're never fucking here in the mornings, are you? The times I have to go into the offices in Tirpitzuferstrasse and talk to some half-arsed Abwehr eejit about the state of Ireland. Spies? How do they find them? Because they are eejits mostly. But where are you Gestapo fellers then, eh, when I wouldn't mind a lift instead of the stench of the fecking U-Bahn? Ah, but what can I tell the innocent souls? I can only pass on the information, so acutely observed by another lying Irishman of note, one Captain Jack Boyle, that Ireland like the rest of the fucking world is in a terrible state of chassis. Ein schrecklicker Zustand des Chaos, meine freunde. Of fucking chassis, lads!'

'You need to go home, Herr Richards.' The driver spoke. 'You're pissed.'

'I am so.' Ryan nodded and grinned. 'Just never pissed enough.'

He walked away, into the apartment building and upstairs. He was a lot less drunk than he appeared, just drunk enough to do something absurd. He didn't really know whether it was dangerous. Probably it made no difference to anything. But it would have its effect. The games the Gestapo played were no less games because of the way they often ended. That was part of what it was to live in Nazi Germany. There was no line between what was meaningless and what could cost you your life. Frank Ryan had no reason to believe he had been seen earlier, but there would now be some sort of Gestapo report on his day. It would say that he spent the afternoon getting drunk somewhere. That's all. And that was no bad thing. A reputation for getting drunk was at least a diversion.

He walked into the flat and looked at it with distaste. It was a place he loathed; it had become a cell. He had been in worse cells, but that gave him no pleasure. He went to the window. The Gestapo car was driving away. They had let him know they were there. No point sitting outside while the Irishman slept off a skinful. Frank Ryan sank into the armchair by the window. He liked to sit where light came into the room and touched him. He sat, rolling a cigarette as it got darker. He didn't get round to lighting it. He was already falling asleep. His last thought, as his head dropped for the last time, was one that often filled his mind at night. He would not go home. He would never leave this place. This was where he would die. Sometimes it seemed that was all he had left to wait for.

Deafness – the rushing noise of it in his head – the pulsing of his heart. He had a dream, a recurrent dream, that he was in darkness, climbing a ladder. He could see neither above nor below, except to know there was darkness in both directions. He could feel nothing around him. The darkness closed in, clammy, almost solid. Whether there was space beyond that, or whether he was in some kind of pit, there was nothing to tell him. There was no direction, no height, no depth, only the enfolding blackness. In the dream he kept climbing, slowly, always at the same pace, knowing he had no choice but to climb, and knowing that there was nowhere he was climbing to. It was the kind of dream you want to wake from, that you try to make yourself wake from, and can't.

21

The Glenmalure Inn

Dublin

Since her arrival in Ireland Vera Kennedy, as she still was, had done very little except move from place to place. She made her first contact when she got off the mail boat. She took the tram into Dublin from Dún Laoghaire. She made a telephone call from a box at the GPO in O'Connell Street. It was a number she had kept in her head since leaving Berlin. The phone call produced the right answers to the right questions, and she spent her first night in Ireland at a house in Terenure. For several days she was passed from safe house to safe house; a schoolteacher in Rathmines, a civil servant and his family in Stoneybatter, a priest in Naas. She travelled by tram and train, in and out of Dublin, each day given a new address. She had little conversation with the people she stayed with. It seemed doubtful they knew who she was; if they did, they didn't show it. They made a point of asking no questions. They knew that she was in some way helping the Republican cause, and that was enough. No one looked for a German in her. Her Irishness meant that no one saw more or suspected more.

She was surprised at the pleasure her Irishness brought. She had not been back to Ireland since leaving when her father's job had finished. In Germany she thought of Ireland often, but without realising how much her childhood years had shaped her. She had thrown herself back into being German with a determination and an intensity that belonged to the times. It was what her country and her leader demanded, and there was a sense that she had time to make up. As she walked the streets of Dublin now she felt how deeply this place was a part of her. It meant far more than she had known. She realised too, with some discomfort, how easy she had felt in that strange, short time she had just spent in England. It wasn't simply that she was surrounded by Irish people in Camden. It was like Ireland in too many ways, even as it was unlike it in others. Her feelings about the English had been determined far more by growing up in Ireland than by anything in Germany, where people mostly liked the English, and thought war with Britain was some mistake that good sense would eventually rectify. That was, after all, at least one of the Führer's views. Vera's own feelings, nurtured by an Irish childhood and Republican friends, were a catalogue of what there was to dislike and even hate about the English. Being in London hadn't changed that, yet there were unwelcome contradictions that she carried away with the rest of the debris. But if Vera was uneasy with that, she was not uneasy with Ireland. She was not uneasy with how much she felt at home. She was not at all uneasy with the fact that here, in Ireland, there was no war.

None of the people she met seemed to have any authority to talk to her about why she was in Ireland. The IRA was not mentioned. They were, of course, Republicans. She knew their language, its codes, its shorthand. She was passed round a circle of Republican supporters. People who could be trusted; safe hands. But twice she did have visitors. Two men came, separately, and asked detailed questions, mostly about her journey. They did know she had come from Germany. They were happy enough, eventually, to tell her they were IRA men. They weren't looking for information, but they were gauging her.

For several days she was free to walk around Dublin. There was no reason to suppose anyone was looking for her. She was as invisible as she had been in London, more so. And she was happy to indulge the pleasure of being somewhere again that really was home. But she felt that some of the time at least she was watched. The men who had come to ask her questions were making sure of her. There would be no shortage of double agents. She had to wait, but waiting wasn't difficult. In fact, waiting was increasingly something she wasn't sure she wanted to end quickly. Her very sense of ease in Ireland was troubling. All this doing nothing was giving her time to think. She had another phone call to make. Another number in Dublin. She had to make contact with London Kontrolle, the man she called Adam. He was now in Ireland too.

Leaving London had been difficult and chaotic. Vera had panicked after the air raid, finding herself in the home of a man who was little more than a stranger, apparently helpless. A man who was a Jew. She knew she shouldn't have kept the job when she found that out. It wasn't the feeling she had at first, of demeaning herself, cleaning up after a Jew. She could tolerate that. Adam was right. All that mattered was her cover. No, it was something more visceral, something she wasn't comfortable admitting. It was closer to superstition than her rational mind wanted to accept. London Kontrolle had laughed at her. All that stuff about Jews. He called it mumbo-jumbo. She felt the contempt in his words, though she wasn't sure where it was aimed. Yet she did have a fear of Jews that wasn't rational. She had been taught it. And she had learned it. More than that, she had absorbed it as she had absorbed a fear of darkness and filth and disease, as something that corrupted the very soul. And with the after-effects of concussion still in her head that fear had grown. Dr Field would see. He would know. In some inexplicable, menacing way, he would guess who she was. He would understand she was his enemy. He would simply know and he would hand her over to the British. It was in that panic, in those wild, concussed imaginings, that she had turned to the only person she could. She had asked Eddie Griffin to remove the evidence of who she was from the house in Mornington Crescent. She had no business trusting anyone with that evidence, but she felt it was only a question of time before the Jewish doctor betrayed her. She had to take the risk. She had to cover her tracks. And then she had to get out and get away. But she had underestimated the support she already had. She had panicked when she should simply have waited.

London Kontrolle knew where she was. No fuss was made. No risks were taken. Two of Adam's men came to the house in Highgate when only she was there. They had been watching it. They would have retrieved the suitcase from the bombed house too, without involving anyone. But it was too late. Some fuss did have to be made to recover it. Eddie Griffin had taken it back to the Bedford Arms. The man Vera only knew as Adam was not pleased. Her cover, her invisibility, had been compromised. Her fault, her weakness. It was unlikely an Irish barman would make much of the case's contents, but in conjunction with what Vera had said in the bedroom in Highgate, he might make more of it than he should. It was a relief to Vera when the suitcase reappeared. Everything was retrieved and Eddie had not even been at the pub when London Kontrolle's men took it. She was terrified that her panic might have put Eddie in danger, but Adam had reassured her. Eddie Griffin was, after all, simply an Irish barman. He told her, with the usual lazy smile – as if nothing much mattered – that German Intelligence had no interest in Eddie Griffin. That was a lie, of course. Vera Kennedy's safe, invisible arrival in Ireland mattered a great deal to London Kontrolle. There was work to do. Three days later she was in Dublin.

The waiting ended when a taxi arrived at the house in Clondalkin where Vera Kennedy had just spent the night. The driver did not tell her where he was taking her, but she knew who would be waiting at the other end. She knew the journey too, as the car left Dublin and moved south through Wicklow, close to the coast, past signs for Bray and Greystones. They turned off into the mountains. She had been this way before, on holiday with her mother and father, her sister and brothers. It was a grey, overcast day, with a drizzle that thickened into rain as they drove through Roundwood towards Annamoe and Laragh. The hotel they had stayed at years before was somewhere close. This was where they had walked in the hills, trailing after their father as he explored the ruins of the monastery. But Laragh was quickly left behind and with it Vera's knowledge of where they were. The taxi continued on through the mountains in the rain.

Eventually they came down into a valley, narrow and tight, with a river running through it and the great ruin of an old British army barracks beside it. There was a crossroads. The only building in sight was a pub. A man sat outside in the rain, in a gabardine trench coat and a battered hat. He stood up as the taxi stopped at the pub entrance. The driver grunted. Vera got out. She saw that the man was carrying a revolver.

'Miss Kennedy?'

'It is.'

'You could probably do with a drink.'

She nodded and looked around her. It was an isolated place. She had never been here, but the word meant something. Glenmalure. She thought she remembered a battle, a song. There was always a song. Over three hundred years ago an English army had marched into the dark, steep-sided mountain valley that stretched north of the crossroads. Hardly any of them came out again. There had probably been a cabin there then, where you could get a drink, and a landlord who watched the English soldiers go by. He may have taken their money, if they'd bothered to pay, even as he counted their numbers and passed the information to the rebel runner waiting to carry the news to the Irish army further up the glen. The landlord of the Glenmalure Inn still watched what came and went along the valley, and the men who saw themselves as the inheritors of the old struggle still sat in his back bar from time to time. They did so now.

There were three men. They didn't introduce themselves except by their first names. But they were members of the IRA's Army Council. Vera knew the man called Stephen was Stephen Hayes, the Chief of Staff. He expected her to know. He was pouring whiskey as she came into the room, and he kept pouring and drinking for as long as they talked. She refused the whiskey and drank a glass of beer. She thought Hayes was already drunk. The conversation started with her journey and her movements around Dublin and its outskirts. The preliminaries included the weather and the war in Europe. It was very subdued. The IRA men seemed little more enthusiastic about the war than the weather.

'We asked for another radio set,' said one of the men abruptly.

'We can discuss supplies,' said Vera, 'but it's a question of where they're landed.' She waited for a moment. 'And how they are used. There has been some concern in Berlin that radios have been used for IRA propaganda, not for messages to Germany. They've been picked up and so have the operators.'

There was silence. The man who had spoken scowled. Hayes smiled.

'Are you here to read us the riot act so, Fraulein?'

Vera's awareness of why she was there and what she was meant to be saying was suddenly at the front of her mind

249

again. All the waiting had gone. This was the conversation she was supposed to be having. These were her instructions from Tirpitzuferstrasse. She was also aware, even as she spoke, that these instructions were very different from those other instructions that now came to her via London Kontrolle. Now she was hearing the contradictions.

'What I have been asked to say,' continued Vera quietly, knowing these men would not like what she said, 'is that what is happening in Eire doesn't help anyone. It doesn't help you and it doesn't help Germany. The only people it helps are the English. Your activities have to be directed at the English, in Ulster. That's where your enemy is, where our enemy is. Isn't it that simple?'

'Tell that to the lads locked up in the Curragh,' said one IRA man, laughing.

'We sent you a plan for an invasion,' snapped Hayes. 'We heard nothing. All you've done is send a string of agents. Big on words and not much else. Most of them picked because they don't know what the fuck they're doing.'

'I do know what the fuck I'm doing,' replied Vera. 'I know Ireland.'

'So you know we need arms, explosives, radio equipment, money.'

'Yes. We can talk about arms. As I said, it's a question of getting them in safely. It's also a question of knowing what they are going to be used for. If they're used against the Irish government, that isn't the war any of us should be fighting. Irish neutrality matters to Germany. Because it matters to Britain.'

Vera listened to her own words; all the contradictions again.

'Your bosses think that's Dev's way of fighting for Germany, do they?' One of the other men spoke. The words were said with contempt.

'It denies Britain access to Irish ports,' said Vera. 'You know that.'

'You know Ireland, do you?' said Hayes. 'If it's Dev's way of doing anything, it's his way of holding on to power. And who does that suit? It just suits Dev!'

'It may suit Ireland very well, Mr Hayes, when England's beaten.'

'It doesn't seem to do England much harm in the meantime. She's not beaten yet.'

Vera didn't answer. The contradictions crowded in again. She was being forced to defend the Irish government to men who hated it, and all the time, in the back of her head, was the other plan, the plan that would see the Irish Prime Minister dead and exactly the kind of war these same men seemed to want.

'De Valera's hanging my men, Vera. Did they tell you that in Berlin?'

Vera spoke her contradictions with conviction.

'But if the English invaded, you'd be fighting with him, wouldn't you? With the Irish Army. Together. You're on the same side in the end. We all are. That's why you need to be fighting in Northern Ireland. Attack the English there.'

One of the other Army Council men reached for the whiskey, grinning.

'What are you going to do next, Vera, sing us "Amhrán na bhFiann"?'

'Never mind the shite. Guns, explosives, money!' said Hayes. 'Give us something real!'

'I do have money for that,' said Vera.

'Thank God for small mercies!' said Hayes, more enthusiastically.

She reached down to her bag and took out an envelope of notes.

Stephen Hayes stretched across the table and took it. He opened it and passed it to one of the others, who took out the money and began to count it.

'We're not waiting for the English,' continued the Chief of Staff, 'we're waiting for your lot. An invasion of Ulster. That's the plan we sent. That's what we need. Now. That's how to call Dev's bluff. If Germany's freeing the North, and the IRA's fighting with you, what's he going to do, send his Free State Army to fight alongside the British? If he does, he's finished. If you want us in Ulster, give us a war to fight there. What was all that stuff from Herr Hitler? We heard it too. "They are asking themselves in England, when is he coming? He is coming!" Well, I don't know if they're asking themselves that right now, even if you are bombing the shite out of London. You didn't beat the RAF, so.' Hayes poured another drink and then laughed. 'Or aren't the Paddys meant to notice?'

'It's a thousand pound,' said the man with the money.

'A start, Fraulein,' said Hayes, taking the envelope. 'We need more.'

'If you aim your objectives on the British forces in the North—'

'Let's get something clear, Vera: we're not here to fight for Germany. We're here for Ireland. We know where our enemies are. When the time comes, we'll deal with them. Wherever they are. North or south. Help us, and we'll help you. Give us a war. Arm us and we'll be ready. Tell them that in Berlin.'

Vera looked at the three men in front of her. Hayes downed another whiskey. The bottle was empty. The other two men looked at her and nodded in agreement with the Chief of Staff's words. She stood up. At least the other two were sober, for what that was worth. She doubted it was worth very much.

She remembered the Irishman in Tirpitzuferstrasse, the man who called himself Frank Richards. He was supposed to be an IRA leader. He was very different from these men. She knew he had been a soldier. The rumour was that he had fought in Spain, on the wrong side. She knew very little about him. What he told Abwehr agents about Ireland was nothing they couldn't have picked up by reading a book. She was the only one who knew that. She had only spoken to him a few times, but she saw he told no one what he was really thinking. She knew he didn't like what he was doing. He didn't like Germany. He hid it well. Perhaps she could only see because her eyes were Irish enough to see. But there was enough to read, for her at least, between his spare, cautious words. This was the incompetent, powerless, ineffectual, grandstanding IRA that Frank Richards had hinted at. That was what lay behind his wry smile. And it was in front of her now, capable of holding up a post office in an Irish village, but useless against the British Army all over Northern Ireland. An irritation, no more, to its own government, and more of a threat to its own Volunteers than anybody else. And this was the Chief of Staff, now calling for another bottle of whiskey, while he waited for the German Army to invade and deliver him a United Ireland.

One of the Army Council men drove Vera south from Glenmalure to Rathdrum, a matter of a few miles. She was to stay the night there. The following day she would take the morning train to Dublin, back to a safe house in Stoneybatter. There would be more meetings, when the Army Council was ready. Stephen Hayes expected Vera to contact Berlin now. He expected some movement on arms. It was clear that the more he drank, the more he expected. They had really taken in nothing she had said. As she sat in the car, she wasn't sure where the bigger fantasies lay, in the minds of the IRA, expecting a German invasion at any moment, or in the Abwehr corridors where the Irish experts still claimed these men were a fighting force to be reckoned with. She had been sent to Ireland to tell them to stop fighting each other and fight the English. They would do no such thing. They wouldn't and they couldn't. And she couldn't believe that there weren't people in the Abwehr who didn't know that. There was something pointless at the heart of what she was doing. Except that it wasn't what she was doing now. Everything she had said, peddling the Abwehr line, had not only been pointless, it had been a lie. It was now a game within another game. She wondered how Erik Kramer would have played this game.

The Abwehr had intended Erik to come to Ireland with her to say all the things she had just said. To try to turn the IRA into a force that really could carry out effective sabotage attacks in the North, even in England again. To prepare the IRA, in readiness for supporting German troops in Ulster when that time came. And when it did come, the aim was to build a bridge between de Valera's government and the IRA, against Britain. But Erik was really working for the SD. And they wanted the chaos that would pull Britain into a war in Ireland right now, with the Irish. They would happily sacrifice Dev and his neutrality to that. She had known that in Berlin, but she never had any real idea how Erik Kramer planned to do it. Was that just another fantasy? Another misreading of Ireland? If it had been, it wasn't now. London Kontrolle was an SD plant in the Abwehr too. He had taken up Erik's mission and he was acting on it. And Vera had simply accepted that was what was happening. Hadn't she wanted it too? Hadn't she believed in it, for all the reasons Erik believed in it, because what the Party wanted must be what the Führer wanted?

She felt unsure now. Did she believe it or had she only believed in the man she loved, a man who seemed to know what Germany was more clearly, more passionately, than she did herself. He had helped her feel sure about belonging to Nazi Germany, surer than she had ever done. Now, all the certainty she had was disappearing.

She had a job to do. The job the Abwehr had sent her to do. If it seemed pointless, maybe her judgement was no better than a soldier following orders to go into battle, not knowing where he fitted into the attack. He didn't need to know. Why should she? But she wasn't just following orders, even though the words she delivered to the IRA were the right words. If they were, they were only a ruse in her mouth. In London, Adam had told her to maintain that ruse. When he was ready Ireland would be delivered from its neutrality. De Valera's death was meant to bring war; that was its sole purpose. Vera had not fully absorbed the gulf between her work as an Abwehr agent and Erik Kramer's instructions from the Reich Main Security Office, now so enthusiastically taken up by London Kontrolle. She had believed, that's all; believing without questioning was an expression of faith. But what faith?

Sitting in the car, heading into Rathdrum, she felt with certainty that if the Abwehr could get to her, knowing what she was doing, they would kill her. Something about being in Ireland that had nothing to do with Germany any more made her wonder if they would not be right.

That night, as Vera sat in a room above a grocer's shop in Rathdrum, in another safe house, with another Irish patriot who asked no questions and had little to say except to wish her well, there were two framed pictures on the mantelpiece of the bedroom. One was a picture of the Sacred Heart of Jesus, the other was a picture of Éamon de Valera. She had walked into the town to find a telephone box earlier. She had made her call to the number in Dublin that Adam had given her. She wanted to say something now. She wanted to ask questions. She had let too much happen while she did nothing at all. The voice was not his. It simply asked her where she was and where she would be the next morning. It was time. But for what?

22

The Phoenix Park

It had been raining when Stefan Gillespie returned to Dublin from England, the kind of solid rain that often sits over Ireland, never very heavy but always there. The city was grey and it was very quiet. The first night in the flat on Wellington Quay he couldn't sleep. The sounds of London at night were in his head and their absence was strangely unsettling. Looking out across the Liffey at the lights, the fact that nothing was happening, however welcome, felt unreal.

When he walked to the front door of the house the landlord, Paddy Geary, stood in the doorway of his tobacconist's, as he always did, smoking and talking to passers-by about what was in the papers and about nothing in particular. He greeted Stefan as if he had barely been away. The words were always the same.

'Not much in the way of letters. I've got what there is.'

'I'll come down for them. I'll just sort myself out, Paddy.'

'Bad in London again, did you see in the papers?'

'I saw enough.'

'You ask yourself what the fecking point is, don't you?'

Now Stefan sat in the Commissioner's office at Garda Head-quarters in the Phoenix Park. Gathered round the desk were

Ned Broy, the Commissioner, Superintendent Gregory and Commandant de Paor of Military Intelligence. He had walked into Dublin Castle the day before, to a reception that was as unremarkable as Paddy Geary's. No one asked where he had been; no one questioned why he had been suspended from Special Branch pending investigation only weeks before, or why no one had mentioned it since. Even Sergeant Dessie Mac-Mahon had done little more than grin and shrug his shoulders. It was always clear, to every detective in the Branch, when something that had seemed crucially important to Terry Gregory was no longer a subject for conversation. His unexplained dead ends were the stuff of life.

The men in the Commissioner's office were looking at a pencil sketch. Stefan had spent part of the morning with an artist, describing the woman he had last seen in a bedroom in Highgate. It was an uncomfortably accurate likeness of Vera Kennedy. However necessary, it felt like an act of betrayal.

It was Geróid de Paor who spoke first.

'Is it close enough?'

'It's very good,' said Stefan quietly.

De Paor continued. 'British Intelligence have told us she landed in Scotland a couple of weeks ago with another agent, a man. They arrested him in Edinburgh, but she disappeared. I don't know what information they got out of the man. Either it wasn't much or they're not saying. That would be par for the course. All they've said is that her name, or the name she was using, is probably Vera Eriksen, and that she intended to cross to Ireland at some point.'

'You knew her as Vera Kennedy?' Broy looked at Stefan.

Stefan nodded. De Paor spoke again.

'The problem with what the British tell us is that they're running so many double agents, so many German spies they've turned, who were maybe double-agents all along, that any information that gets back to Berlin is information the British choose to send. They don't want the Germans to know the truth, of course. Every so often they hang an agent to show they mean business, but I'd say they have it under control. I don't think they worry very much about the odd German spy we don't pick up here. They tell us what they want. We do the same. We read the rest between the lines. In the case of the feller who arrived with our friend Vera, either they're keeping what they got to themselves or they gave him the drop prematurely. Whatever happened, they lost her. She went to ground in London. They think she'd lived in Ireland at some point so Camden was a good place to disappear. They reckon she's over here now, but that's all they can say. Or will say. If they're wary about what they say normally, they're even more unforthcoming when they've cocked it up. The only reason we've got this much is because she happened to come Stefan's way in Camden Town.'

Stefan's report about Vera had been the only subject to interest anyone since his return from London. No one had any questions to ask about the reason he went in the first place: Willie Mullins. He had met Vera by chance. What he had found out about her he had discovered partly by chance and partly because she had trusted him. The people she was working with didn't trust him, and he had a bullet wound in his shoulder to show it. He still didn't understand why Vera mattered so much in Dublin. He knew German agents had been arrested in Ireland; he knew some were still at large. None of them were considered very dangerous. They mattered, but Vera clearly mattered more.

The Commissioner turned to Terry Gregory.

'You can confirm that, Terry? You think she's here?'

'Yes, there's definitely a woman agent. I don't know where she is, but she's been through a couple of IRA safe houses. One we know for sure. And she did come in from England. It's unlikely it's not Vera Kennedy.'

'Do you know anything about what she's been doing here?'

'Not much as far as I can tell,' said Gregory,' but that's the way of it. What do any of them do? You look at the German agents we have picked up. The feller Simon, who walked off a beach in Dingle and asked directions to a railway station on a line that closed fourteen years ago. What was the point of sending him? Who was that other one . . .? That's it, your man Willi Preez. The only thing he'd done was send a couple of radio messages back to Germany about the weather. He told the feckers it was raining in Ireland, in code!'

There was some laughter, but when Broy spoke, it was serious.

'You only know what you get, Terry. You don't know what else there is.'

'I know. But it still feels dead out there. I don't know if she's met Hayes and any of the Army Council. But I know what that amounts to. I've heard it from spies we've picked up. And I've heard it . . . well, from elsewhere. It's all bollocks. Getting more arms that never arrive, sabotage in the North no one ever quite pulls off. I still say nothing unusual is happening. Sometimes you know there's a silence that's not right. You know what's coming in isn't true. You know something's going on somewhere else. There's not a sniff of anything.'

'She does feel different, though,' said de Paor. 'She'll pass for Irish, for a start. She didn't walk up the beach from a U-boat asking the way to the nearest IRA man. She can disappear very easily in Dublin. Stefan can vouch for that.'

'I'm sure Inspector Gillespie can vouch for all sorts of things.'

Superintendent Gregory grinned.

'All right, Terry,' said Broy, 'shall we stick to the business in hand?'

'I'm not sure what that business is, sir. I told you. I'm hearing nothing.'

'Do I need to be here, sir,' asked Stefan, glancing at Gregory. 'I've told you what I know. I don't know anything about the rest of it. I can't add anything more.'

'You know her,' said Geróid de Paor. 'You can recognise her anywhere. If she's good at disappearing, we need someone who won't make that so easy.'

'G2 are taking the information from Berlin seriously, Terry,' said Broy.

Superintendent Gregory looked at de Paor. He took out a cigarette.

'You'll know more about that than I will, Gerry.'

He spoke as if he wasn't entirely sure about that.

'You'd better go through it again, Gerry,' said the Commissioner, 'for Stefan's benefit.' He turned to Stefan. 'You need to know why this does matter. And however we handle it, there are good reasons why we don't want a lot of other people to be in this. You are in it. I can see there are reasons why you might not much like it, but that's tough. We're not here to do what we like.'

'Well, one of her pals did shoot you, Stevie,' said Gregory. 'And you an IRA gunman yourself! If nothing else I'd want a word with her about that, so.'

'I'll be sure to take it up with her, sir, if we bump into each other.'

'I think we'd all feel a lot safer if you did bump into her, Stefan.'

The words were Geróid de Paor's, but there was no smile. Ned Broy nodded at him. He opened a file. Every so often he looked down as he spoke.

'We have information that's come from Berlin and it's about Vera Eriksen, Vera Kennedy, whoever she is. Some of it fits with what the British have told us. Some of it helped us twist their arms to give us a bit more. That's why we know she lived in Ireland. We think she spent some of her childhood here. Her father worked here, maybe for Siemens. There was a man called Eriksen, an engineer. She's an Abwehr agent, like the rest of them. We know roughly when she left Germany and we know she landed in Scotland. We know the aim was to get here, via England and Wales. Landings in Ireland have not been successful.'

'If they send us eejits,' muttered Gregory, 'what do they expect?'

'There is that,' continued de Paor. 'But it's the rest of what we've heard that's worrying. We've had all sorts of rumours about German invasions and German parachute landings over the last few months. They're the fag end of what's been going on in England. How much of it was real and how much is bollocks, who knows? It didn't happen, that's all we can say. It doesn't look as if anything's going to happen in England now – not till the spring, anyway.'

'You know that?' asked Stefan.

'Well, it's everybody's guess and it's what British Intelligence believes. That doesn't mean it's all over. It doesn't mean there's not all sorts of damage the Germans want to do to Britain. It doesn't mean we're off the radar either. Stirring things up here, well, it wouldn't be such a mad idea. We know people in German Intelligence want to use Ireland. In the long run it could be for a landing. In the short term it could be about the English using up resources they don't have. But the IRA haven't been any use on that front. There should be chaos in the North. There's nothing. But what if there was a bit of all-Ireland chaos, real chaos. Enough chaos to make England invade. That could be serious. For us and them. Who knows how many British troops that would tie down?'

'There's no sign of that happening, is there?' said Stefan. 'It's a pipe dream.'

'All right,' said de Paor. 'What would it take? What could you do to create real chaos?' He paused. 'What would happen if someone shot Dev?'

'You mean the IRA?' said Stefan.

Gregory shook his head. 'If it was on the horizon, I'd know something.'

'But that's now,' continued de Paor. 'It doesn't mean there's not a few who'd be happy to. They still see Dev as a traitor. I don't think Terry's got them all shut up in the Curragh.' The G2 man looked at Gregory. 'What about the North?'

'There's some up there,' said Superintendent Gregory. 'They don't like what's going on here. Because it's bugger all. They're capable, but they haven't got the support. And the Boys are weak enough without fighting each other.'

'And what if the Germans thought it was a good idea, Terry? If someone in German Intelligence believed Dev was all that stood in the way of Ireland rising up against the British and laying down the red carpet for German arms, a German landing and a holy war in Holy Ireland? Whatever way it turned out, the British would have to invade. They say Churchill's in two minds about that anyway. It's no secret in MI5 and the British Army. And wouldn't they be in the shite then? And so would we. And it would do Germany no harm at all.'

'It's a good story, Gerry,' said Terry Gregory. 'And all down to Vera?' He smiled, shaking his head.

Stefan frowned, struggling to believe any of this related to her.

'What we know is that a plan to kill the Taoiseach was talked about.' Commandant de Paor pointed down at the file in front of him. 'Not just a story. It was a plan, somewhere. Because someone thought that story was better than good. What we've been told is that an agent who landed in Scotland was part of that plan. That someone is the woman, Vera Eriksen. She's the one who disappeared. She's the one the British didn't pick up. She's the one who's here.'

'My question is still how reliable is all this?' asked Gregory.

'It comes from someone who is inside the Abwehr at some level. I'm not saying he'd know too much. I wouldn't say he's even trusted much, but he is there.' De Paor looked at Stefan. 'You know who I'm talking about, Stefan.'

'Do I?'

'You saw him in Berlin. Frank Ryan?'

'I see.'

'We do know he gives German Intelligence advice on Ireland.'

'Not very good advice to judge by their agents.' Gregory grinned.

'I don't think he does anything there by choice,' said Stefan.

'There is another reason to listen,' continued de Paor. 'He didn't come up with this because he sits in an Abwehr office all day. I doubt he does. I shouldn't think anyone tells him anything. But someone told him this. And he was told so that he could pass it on to us. That's how I read it. He's the conduit, but I think the information comes from the Abwehr. Wherever this plan comes from, it's not theirs. But they take this seriously and they don't want it to happen.'

'Surely they can control their own people,' said the Commissioner.

'I don't think that's how Germany works, sir. The military has its Intelligence arms, so does the Nazi Party. They're not all going in the same direction. That's true enough in England.' He smiled at Gregory. 'Even here.'

'I'm shocked, Commandant de Paor! Special Branch is an open book.'

'I stand corrected, Terry. We'll stick to Germany, so. There are Nazis and Nazis, like there are Republicans and Republicans. People go their own way. If it works out you're a hero, if it doesn't, well, retirement might be very abrupt.'

'We are taking this seriously too,' said the Commissioner. 'Terry?'

'No one is going to get to Dev. I'm not at all convinced anyone is trying. That's what I'm getting from the IRA. It doesn't mean there's not eejits out there. There's eejits everywhere. But nothing like that is going to even start without someone knowing and someone talking. We have a wall round him. It would be a big operation. They can't get a bomb at a border post these days.'

'I take that,' said de Paor. 'But there are good reasons why we need to bring this woman in. One of those reasons is that it would do us no harm to show the British that we can clear up a mess they shouldn't have left us with.'

'We'll have her soon enough, Gerry, with Inspector Gillespie's assistance.'

Stefan did not reply. He was still taking in the information.

'I think we have something to thank Stefan for,' said Broy. 'We know what she looks like. We know more about her background than the English do.'

'Ah,' said Gregory, 'there's nothing you won't do for Ireland, Stevie.'

'There are a lot of reasons we need to be on top of this,' continued the Commissioner. 'They're not only about the Taoiseach's safety. I take what you tell me on trust, Terry. But there is no room for mistakes. If the threat of the Germans using us as a back door into Britain has faded, there's still the threat from across the water. And that's what Dev thinks. It wouldn't take much. If someone even got a shot at him, it might be enough. And if Germany was in there somewhere, that would put the lid on it. Irish neutrality is more than just an irritation for Churchill, it's a betrayal. There are calmer voices holding him back on Ireland. For now. But he only needs one excuse to go the other way.'

Stefan Gillespie sat at his desk in the detectives' room at Dublin Castle. The conversation at Garda Headquarters remained a secret, but in a room full of men who all carried elements of Superintendent Gregory's jigsaw empire in various fractured and confused pieces, there was nothing unusual about that. Only Gregory himself had the picture on the top of the box that was Special Branch; only he knew where the pieces went. What was clear was that Stefan was not going to spend much time on the letters and telegrams that had been deposited on his desk from the censorship office at the GPO. They contained material that might be suspicious, supposedly, although the criteria for judging that was so broad and so vague, that almost nothing Special Branch looked at meant anything at all.

Also there were letters and cards to and from men serving in the British Forces. These too contained almost no information that mattered to anybody. They were about family news and trivial events; love letters that almost everyone had come to find it unpleasant to read, once the jokes and the titillation had worn off at the beginning of the Emergency. Although no one was prevented from travelling across the Irish Sea to join the British Forces, it remained an issue of official disapproval on the government's part. At some level these people needed watching, and so did their friends and their families. Lists were kept, though by now nobody took much notice of them. Among the letters and the telegrams were the communications that informed wives and mothers and fathers that a man had died, just now in the desert of North Africa or in a bomber over Germany. Stefan turned over the pieces of paper in front of him, ticking them off one by one to indicate they could go back to the Post Office and resume their journey. His mind was elsewhere. The pile of papers would be dealt with by someone else. He would be doing only one thing now: looking for Vera Kennedy, or Vera Eriksen, or whoever she was, until she was found.

He looked up as Sergeant Dessie MacMahon sat down opposite him.

'Jesus, not more of that shite.'

'It never goes away, however long you go away,' said Stefan.

'And it never means a fucking thing, however many you read.'

'Would you ever notice if it did?'

'Why would I? No one ever told me what we're looking for.'

Dessie took out a Sweet Afton and lit up.

'That reminds me,' said Stefan, glad to think about something else.

'What does?'

'You do. I saw the Commissioner earlier. He mentioned you.'

'And why wouldn't he? Ned and me are always chewing the fat.'

'It was about my father.'

'Ah, Jesus, there's a man would give you work you don't want.'

'Ned sent his regards, and he told me there was something he asked you to do for my old feller. He gathered it all worked out, because he saw the report. That was it. Except he said David was always a pain in the arse. Not that I'd argue.'

Dessie laughed.

'Well?' said Stefan.

'There was some feller killed down your way, a farmer. Coogan, was it?'

'Joe Coogan, yes. What's that got to do with Ned Broy?'

'Didn't you find the body?'

Stefan nodded.

'Your ould feller had it in his head that Mr Coogan didn't top himself as the Guards in Wicklow decided he did. He had murder in mind. And for some reason he kept poking his nose in till the superintendent in Baltinglass told him to fuck himself. Not unreasonable, I'd say. I would have done the same. But Mr Gillespie wasn't having any of that. He got hold of Ned. Apparently Ned owes him an old favour. And Ned told me to do something to shut him up. So I did.'

266

'You did what?'

'I got him the report from the State Pathologist.'

'Just like that?'

'When I heard what he had to say, I thought your ould feller had a point.'

'And what happened?'

'It didn't shut him up. In fact, they arrested a feller for the murder.'

'Who?'

'It was in the paper.'

Dessie started to root about in a drawer, pulling out crumpled newspapers, folded open at different pages. He separated them and passed one to Stefan.

'The son, Joe Coogan's son. David was right. He killed him.'

Stefan read the short paragraph. Paul Coogan, of Rathdangan, County Wicklow, had been arrested for the murder of his father Joseph Coogan. The death had originally been regarded as a suicide, but new evidence had come to light. Paul Coogan was now on remand at Mountjoy Prison, awaiting his trial.

'That'll be a pissed-off superintendent in Baltinglass,' said Dessie.

'Not as pissed off as Paul Coogan.'

Stefan Gillespie looked down at the paper. The events of the day by the Mass Rock above Rathcoyle were in his head again. They were suddenly very clear. He saw Joe Coogan's body. He saw Paul Coogan. Stefan shook his head.

'That's true enough, Stevie, very pissed off.'

'A lot more than that,' said Stefan, 'because I don't believe he did it.'

Later that night, Detective Superintendent Gregory was still in his office. Dublin Castle and the Police Yard were almost empty. In Special Branch there was one other detective in the room beyond the glass partition. Dessie MacMahon was on night duty. He sat in a pool of light in the dark outer office, working on an elaborate accumulator for the next day's racing at Fairyhouse. Terry Gregory was reading too. A book of Yeats's poetry. He read a lot of poetry. He liked Yeats, though he rarely opened a book of his without remembering the file that sat in a cabinet in his office. Few had seen it; Yeats was, after all, a national treasure. Gregory thought it was no bad thing Yeats had died before the war began. The files on too many of the poet's friends were often on Gregory's desk. But no one need see the file on Yeats now. When the time was right he would destroy it. It was the least he could do. But great poetry did not discriminate. It was not particular about where it came from.

The telephone rang. It was a call the superintendent was expecting. He heard the voice and recognised it. There were no preliminaries, just questions.

'Who did she see?'

He listened for a moment.

'And what did she say?'

He listened again.

'That's it? Nothing else?'

He grunted as the speaker continued.

'The usual bollocks. Well, she's no use to you then, is she?'

He took a cigarette from a packet.

'So where is she now?'

He put the unlit cigarette between his lips and lit it.

23

Kilranelagh

The first thing that met Stefan Gillespie that evening, when he took the train to Baltinglass and returned to Kilranelagh, was the new dog. A night at home came with the caveat that if Superintendent Gregory needed him, he would leave immediately. It didn't look as if Gregory was doing anything about Vera yet. No one at Dublin Castle had been told what was happening. There was no search going on. Work in Special Branch continued as if the meeting in the Phoenix Park had never happened, or as if the superintendent had simply put all the urgency that surrounded it on the long finger. Stefan knew his boss had expressed some scepticism about the danger. He seemed to trust his contacts inside the IRA more than anything that came from the Commissioner, or the Department of External Affairs, or Military Intelligence. When Stefan left the Castle for Baltinglass, Terry Gregory was leaving too. He said he was going for a drink, as if he had nothing better to do. But he told Stefan to stay close to the phone.

The dog came out of the barn with the puppy, Jumble, as Stefan walked into the farmyard. It was a black and white sheepdog bitch, quite old, seven or eight. And she did not like the look of him. The puppy ran towards him enthusiastically, but a bark from the older dog stopped him. She moved slowly towards Stefan, her teeth bared. The puppy took his cue and started to bark. He might know this man well enough, but the older dog didn't. Stefan crouched down, smiling, talking in a low, coaxing voice. The bitch's back still arched.

'And who are you? You'll need to get used to me so.'

The door from the kitchen opened and Tom flew out.

'You came, Daddy! I didn't know if you would when you phoned!'

The sheepdog moved forward and stood between Tom and his father, growling. She meant what she said. Stefan stood up. He knew she might bite.

'You need to call off your guard, Tom.'

'Sorry,' Tom laughed. 'She's not a great one for people.'

'Well,' laughed his father, 'there's a bit of good sense. You'd better tell her I'm not people, though, only your old feller, before she takes a piece out of me.'

'Oh, she would,' said Tom, with a certain pride.

'I can see that.'

'She's called Mona. We got her from Rathdangan. Nobody wanted her at all. She belonged to a man who died up there. But she's a grand sheepdog, so.'

Tom walked forward and petted the dog. She wagged her tail. He then ran on again and flung his arms round Stefan. The bitch lay down, still eyeing Stefan warily, but tolerating his presence now, and Jumble, as if receiving permission, joined Tom, and jumped up at Stefan as they walked to the farmhouse. Stefan registered Rathdangan and the man who had died. It wasn't the first thing on his mind, but he had read more about the arrest of Paul Coogan now. He was very uneasy. Something was wrong. He wanted to know what his father had to say.

As usual the conversation at Kilranelagh turned around what was happening at the farm. David and Helena accepted

Stefan's arrival with the knowledge that questions about where he'd been and what he'd been doing would not get real answers. They had long since learned not to bother asking. Tom did the same thing, but he did so unconsciously. He was full of his own world and all he chose to know was that his father was always away in Dublin and couldn't always come home very much. Eating in the kitchen, Stefan was relieved to see that one thing had changed. His father was brighter, stronger somehow, though he had something on his mind. There was a conversation hanging in the air that he seemed almost impatient to have. It wasn't about the farm, Stefan could see that. Things there were better. They were more easily talked about too. David was paying one of his neighbours to do some work, and the new dog had made managing the sheep easier. Some kind of order had been restored at Kilranelagh. The ewes had gone out with the rams the previous week. David seemed in control again. Stefan saw his mother was happier too.

When Tom went to bed, Stefan followed him up a few minutes later.

'What are you reading?'

'I'm reading this.'

He held up a copy of *Kim*. It had been Stefan's once.

'Do you like it?'

'It was hard to start . . . but it's great. It's in India, but he's sort of Irish.'

'Sort of Irish is good,' said Stefan. 'Shall I read some to you?'

'It's all right, Daddy. I'm reading it myself.'

Stefan nodded. He kissed his son and left him reading in the light of a lamp. He laughed quietly as he walked downstairs. A lot had happened in a couple of weeks. And Tom had made a small move in growing up. Stefan knew his son would not even have noticed, but the days of bedtime stories had gone.

*

271

In the kitchen, Helena Gillespie was finishing clearing up. David was helping her, but with only half his mind on what he was doing. His voice had grown quieter when all the obvious things had been said about work and stock and Tom. The war had been there too, but Stefan had no desire to talk about it, and what came from his mother and father was no more than they had been hearing on the radio. Helena put two bottles of beer on the table as Stefan came into the kitchen. She looked at her husband, standing with two plates as if he didn't quite know what they were. She laughed, taking them away from him.

'I'll finish myself, David. Then I'll have an early night. Why don't you two go into the front room and have a drink? You're both in the way here.'

Stefan picked up the bottles and took the hint.

Father and son sat in armchairs on either side of the fireplace in the small, crowded best room. There was never usually a fire unless there was something special going on, but one was burning. It was clear Stefan's mother knew there was a conversation to be had between father and son. He began with the dog.

'Mona was left at Coogan's?'

'Yes. I was up there a few times.' David stopped. 'She was still there, a week after, shut up in a barn. Jimmy Page would go in to feed her. He was feeding the stock till they were sold off. I don't know that he always remembered. No one wanted her. And we needed a sheepdog. She's good.'

'Tom said.'

'Very good,' continued David. He was more serious. 'You've seen they've arrested Paul Coogan. He's in Mountjoy now. That's my doing, Stefan.'

'I did talk to Dessie.'

'I thought I was doing the right thing.'

'So tell me what happened.'

'I thought I had to, Stefan. I told you what Joe Coogan did for me. And I knew you weren't happy about the idea of suicide. You didn't think it was right, did you? And the more I looked at it, the more I saw that. But no one wanted to listen. I wouldn't leave the fecking thing alone. I was . . . I was angry about it . . . maybe I was just angry . . . I'm not even sure what I wanted to prove . . . I wanted to show . . . I don't know how much it was about Coogan . . . how much . . . but I poked my nose in, so. I kept poking. I made my point. They took it in the end.'

Stefan waited, drinking the beer.

'After you'd gone, I went up to Coogan's. There was no one there. It was all open. I just went in. The Guards had finished what they were doing, if they ever started. That pissed me off. There were questions. You had them. No one else did. The man was worth something, wasn't he? That's what I thought.'

'And was he?' Stefan heard the hesitation in his father's voice.

'Maybe not a lot. But that's something else. I saw Jimmy Page there, tending the stock. He didn't want to say much. But it was more than that. He was nervy, very nervy. And when I went into the pub and asked about Coogan, no one had much to say either. No one wanted to say much. I could have understood that, but it wasn't about him killing himself. It was more like out of sight out of mind. No one liked him. That was obvious. He was a drunk. He was a loudmouthed gobshite. And people were frightened of him. Not least his son.'

'The son didn't live there, isn't that right?'

'He moved out a couple of years ago. He stays with a family in the village, didn't have anything to do with his father. They didn't even speak. The daughter had left too. She was older. They think she went to England. The mother walked out years ago, everyone knows that. She got the blame, but a lot of people know better. No one says anything, but you know what they think. I'd say he beat the shit out of the lot of them, fair weather or foul, drunk or sober.'

'Wasn't the son meant to be leaving?'

'Going into the British Army. He wanted out of it, I'd say. Just out, anywhere. That didn't sit well with Joe. They might not have spoken in years but he rediscovered his Republicanism when he heard about Paul. There were rows, even one in the church. And a fight outside the pub. Joe laid him out.'

'That was recent?'

'Yes.'

'It doesn't sound good. For the lad, I mean.'

'No, not now.' David shook his head.

'And what made them change their minds about suicide?'

'I did.'

'I see.'

'I told you, I had the bit between my teeth. If someone killed him, whatever he was, I couldn't leave that. And when I went into the barracks in Baltinglass and Ger Mulvaney told me to fuck off and leave police business to the police . . . I thought, fuck you, Superintendent. But what I did get out of him was the cause of death. The story was he tried to shoot himself, but it didn't kill him. He fell into the river, face down. He wasn't in any state to get out, maybe he couldn't even turn his head. So it wasn't the shotgun that killed him, but it amounted to the same thing. He tried to top himself and ended up drowned.'

'It's messy, but I suppose it makes sense,' said Stefan slowly.

'If he shot himself,' continued David. 'And you weren't at all sure about that. Do you remember? That's what you said. That's what was in my head.'

'Yes, I remember.'

'You weren't sure he fired the gun at all, isn't that right?'

'That was part of it,' said Stefan. 'I'm trying to think back. It was a feeling too. I wished I'd looked harder. None of it looked right. That's all I remember.'

David continued. 'Anyway, I wanted to know more. So I went to see Ned Broy.'

Stefan laughed. 'The Commissioner, just like that.'

'Why not? It was all about old favours. I owed Joe. Ned owed me.'

'And he listened, Pa.'

David smiled. 'Not really. He wanted to get rid of me. He did. By saying if he gave me a look at the State Pathologist's report, on the quiet, would I shut up? So he passed me on to Dessie MacMahon. And Dessie got me the report.'

'And?'

'And he did drown.'

'That doesn't change anything, then. That's what they said. If there's an argument about what happened before, it's too late to have it now. What about the shotgun wounds? Was there any doubt about them being self-inflicted?'

'Well, it was inconclusive in the end. No definite proof they weren't.'

'So how does that get you to murder?'

'Joe had water in his lungs, Stefan. Well, that wasn't so unexpected, was it? He was face down in the River Derreen. And supposedly he'd shot himself. So put it together. Shot himself... fell in ... face in the water. Dead. Once you accept that he pulled the trigger, the rest follows. And everyone accepted it.'

'So there's something else?'

'It wasn't river water in Joe's lungs. There was soap in it.'

'Soap?'

'Yes. Not much. A trace, I suppose you'd call it. Still, however Joe Coogan drowned, it wasn't in the Derreen. But who even read the report? It must have gone to Ger Mulvaney, but why would anyone else bother? There were no detectives on it then. There were no suspects. There was no murder investigation going on. Murder didn't come into it. Mulvaney must have looked at the post-mortem, but how hard? He saw what he needed to see. He'd made his mind up. He just had the paperwork to do. He wasn't looking for a crime.'

'So where did Joe Coogan drown?' said Stefan.

'I don't know. You'd have to say at home somehow. But where does the shotgun come into it? That was fired by the river. How did he get to the river?'

'Someone moved him, as I assume you told Superintendent Mulvaney.'

'With some satisfaction.' David shook his head. 'At the time.'

'And suddenly he had to come up with a killer,' said Stefan. 'He has.'

'Because of me, Stefan. But I don't think Paul Coogan killed his father.'

Stefan didn't think the boy had killed his father either. He had no evidence. He only had his memory of what happened that day by the River Derreen. But he knew about lying. He had watched people lie about everything from shoplifting and poaching to political killings and brutal murders. Nothing about the boy who stood by his father's corpse suggested he was hiding anything. It went deeper than that. The boy wasn't sorry his father was dead. He had looked down at him with a kind of indifference he was not unhappy to show. There were times, as a policeman, you sensed who people were. It was more than just instinct; it was everything you knew, everything you'd learned, everything you'd seen. Sometimes you had to rely on that to make judgements.

'I don't think so either, Pa. I don't know that I've got anything to go on. It's nothing more than . . . well, I just don't see it. I look back at that day, and everything I can remember. There's nothing that would have made me suspect him. But that's not worth a lot to Paul Coogan, is it? Have you got any more?'

'Yes. There was someone else there.'

'What?'

'Someone else hanging around near the farm.'

'Who?'

David Gillespie stared into the fire. He seemed reluctant to speak.

'Who was it?' said Stefan again.

'I spent some time up at Joe Coogan's farm. Just looking around. You know how it is. You don't know what you're looking for. You just keep going. I walked up and down the river. I walked round the fields. Just getting a sense of it. And higher up the river, towards Lugnaquilla, someone had been camping, sleeping out in a bit of wood along the valley. There were some tins, some paper bags, cigarette ends. There'd been a fire. It wasn't far from Rathcoyle. You'd only walk a few fields to Coogan's. Someone slept there for several nights.'

'Do you know any more than that?'

'I did ask some questions in the village. There had been a man around, about that time. Not local. No one knew who he was. He'd been in the shop once and the pub. He hadn't talked to anyone much. There was no connection to Joe. Not then. I went back a week later. And I saw the postman. He'd been ill. I asked him about this stranger. He said he saw him talking to Joe Coogan. He was on his bike. They were some way away and Joe was walking off when he saw them. But he thought they looked like they'd been arguing. He said Joe turned and shouted something back at the feller. Well, fuck off, basically.'

'Is that it?'

'No. There's more. I haven't told anyone yet – I wanted you to—'

David Gillespie stopped. He breathed deeply. He wasn't finding this easy. Stefan waited, absorbed, not sure what it was that his father was struggling with.

'The feller was on holiday, walking the hills. He didn't speak to many people but that's what he said. The descriptions I got could have been better, but they were good enough. Good

277

enough if you've seen the man yourself, if you've seen what he wore, if you know the man well enough anyway. And he smoked Craven A, of course. I've a bag with the cork tips, from his camp. He smoked them when he was here too. He left this house two days before he was seen up in Rathdangan. I don't have any doubt it was your friend Peter Tully.'

Stefan said nothing, looking hard at his father. He wanted to argue, but what David had put in front of him, in every way, placed Peter close to Coogan. He couldn't easily make this man someone else. He could ask what possible connection there could be between Peter Tully and Joseph Coogan. Yet there was one. Someone had seen the two men arguing.

But before he could put any words together, the telephone rang. Stefan didn't move. He was still reaching for the arguments that ought to dismiss an idea that had to be mad. The ringing sounded again. Stefan got up slowly. It could only be Superintendent Gregory.

In the hall, he picked up the phone.

'Stevie?'

Stefan was still full of what his father had said.

'Stevie, are you there?'

'Yes, sir. Yes, I'm here.'

'We have your friend.'

Stefan was somewhere else, trying to push his father's words out of his mind to make way for Gregory's, but for a second it was as if, in the word friend, the superintendent was continuing the conversation he had just left.

'What?'

'Your friend Vera. We know where she is. We pick her up tomorrow.'

24

The Wicklow Gap

It was a little after six the next morning when Detective Superintendent Gregory's car stopped in the farmyard at Kilranelagh. David Gillespie was in the barn, milking. He walked to the door and looked out. He nodded to Gregory as Stefan got into the car then he turned back to his cows. The car pulled away.

'Your father's been making himself unpopular. He's a stubborn man.'

'I gather.'

'But he was right, so.' Gregory laughed. 'I can see where you get it.'

'He was right about something,' said Stefan.

'Well, don't they have the feller who killed the farmer now?'

'I'd say they haven't.'

'That's not what I heard.'

'Being wrong once doesn't stop you being wrong twice.'

'God save us, Stevie, will we be hearing more about dead farmers, so?'

'Not today.' He left the subject alone. 'So where are we going?'

'Your woman is in Rathdrum. She was there last night. She's

been moving around a lot. She's rarely in one place more than a night or so just now.'

Stefan registered the certainty with which Gregory spoke.

'She seems easy enough to find after all, sir. And there's me thinking they'd be scouring the country.'

'Ah, well, there are easier ways. It doesn't pay to let everyone know that.'

The car turned towards Kiltegan.

'She'll be at Rathdrum station at eight.'

'And I thought we had a master spy on our hands.'

'You're not here to like it, Inspector.'

'No. I don't much like it.'

'No one invited her, Stevie. And your wages more than cover a Judas kiss.'

'I wouldn't be the only one giving her that. Someone talked to you.'

The superintendent took out a cigarette and lit it.

'Your friend Vera is trouble – for the IRA, I mean. If something's more trouble than it's worth, the best thing is to get rid of it. If she's just another German agent to get excited about, she'll give them no more than the others. Fuck all. And they'll give her the same. It's a merry-go-round, but not much of a fair. They can move her about from safe house to safe house. If it keeps them happy, who cares? But some of the Boys might be thinking this one's not worth it. I don't know about Gerry de Paor and this plot to bump off Dev. I don't see the IRA doing that. Not at the moment. If there was something to this Dev business, the Boys know all bets would be off. We give them some slack and they don't do anything too stupid. But even so . . . there's something up. Maybe Gerry's right after all. So let's be on the safe side, Stevie. The Boys are easy enough to find. Most of them have the sense to know where the line is. If they cross it, the guns would be back in the game fast. Not their guns, our guns.'

'What will happen to her?'

'Not very much, you know that. She's not in England, is she? There's no rope for her here. We're nice enough fellers in neutral Ireland. We just stick these people inside for a bit and send a stiff note to the German ambassador.'

Stefan lit a cigarette now. That, at least, was true.

'There is a reason we're doing it this way, Stevie,' continued Gregory. 'I've been given Vera on a plate, but I don't want that advertised. We pick her up quietly, just you and me. For now no one needs to know about it at the Castle. I don't want anything leaking out. I have sources who need protecting. Once we have her, we take her to Blessington. We'll meet Gerry de Paor and G2 will take her somewhere to see if there's anything to get out of her. There'll be a trial down the road and not much fuss. They're fidgety in G2 just now. There are things going on that have to be kept out of sight. I'm in it, and you're in it courtesy of Vera. There's a meeting with British Intelligence. They're coming over the border. It's about what we do and what we don't do. When do we cooperate, when do we parade our neutrality? But of course we're not supposed to be doing anything at all, are we? And Dev has to be at this meeting. He'd swear on the rosary nothing of that sort could happen in Holy Ireland, but Intelligence needs him to make an appearance. To show good faith. To show he's behind it. To show the British that if they push too hard they can fuck off.'

'Are you saying Vera knows about this?'

'No. There's no way she could know.'

'But she didn't come at a good time, then.'

'I've told you, if there was some eejit in the IRA planning to take a shot at Dev, I'd smell it. That doesn't mean things can't go wrong. I'm uneasy about something. I don't even know what it is. So let's be safe. What's going on with the British can't get out in any form, to anyone. That is Dev's bottom line.'

The station at Rathdrum stood some way from the town, below the road and out of sight. There was a small station yard and the empty shell of a building that had once called itself the Royal Fitzwilliam Hotel. No one came and no one went as Stefan Gillespie and Terry Gregory sat in the black Ford, waiting for Vera to arrive. No one manned the ticket office or the platform. It was eight o'clock. The next train, to Dublin, was not until nine fourteen. That was the way they assumed she would be leaving Rathdrum. That was the information Superintendent Gregory had. He lit another cigarette. They would wait. But only ten minutes had passed when Stefan saw a bicycle turning into the station approach. A woman was riding it. Gregory put out his cigarette. He reached inside his coat and took out a Webley revolver from its shoulder holster. He registered the look from Stefan. There was always a moment of theatre from Gregory at such times; usually it didn't seem important. He grinned at Stefan.

'I don't know if she can shoot, but she has friends who can.'

'She's on her own.'

'Don't get carried away, Stevie. It's a job not a lovers' meeting.'

They watched as the bicycle continued towards the station.

'Why's she so early?' said Gregory. 'No train for an hour.'

Vera halted at the station entrance. She got off the bicycle and leant it against the wall. She unstrapped a small suitcase from a rack. She didn't go into the station. She stood for a moment, looking across at the car. She seemed uncertain. She was still looking at the car. She stepped forward, then stopped.

'That is her, Stevie?'

'That's her.'

'What's she doing? It's like she's expecting . . .'

'I don't know, sir. Maybe it's not the train. There's still an hour . . .'

'Maybe she's being picked up,' nodded Gregory. 'Let's get it done.'

Superintendent Gregory got out, stuffing the heavy Webley into his coat pocket. Stefan followed. He didn't want this. The sooner it was over the better.

Vera seemed untroubled by their approach. She smiled. But almost immediately the smile changed to a look of bewilderment. She saw Stefan. She said nothing, but she couldn't hide that first look of surprise. The fact that he was there made no sense at all. She only knew that something was very wrong.

'Miss Eriksen?'

It was Terry Gregory who spoke.

'I'm sorry,' she said, 'I think you have the wrong person.'

Vera spoke calmly. She said what she had say, but Eriksen wasn't a name anyone in Ireland could know. There was no mistake. She looked round quickly. It was pointless. There was nowhere to go. There was nothing to do. She had no comprehension of how Eddie Griffin came to be here, but she knew what he was now. She knew that both these men were policemen of some kind.

'You'll know Eddie well enough,' said Gregory. 'Introductions, Stevie.'

The superintendent was smiling. Stefan did as he was told.

'This is Superintendent Gregory, Vera. I am Inspector Gillespie. We are Garda detectives. We know who you are and we would like your cooperation.'

'And we will want to check you for any weapons,' continued the superintendent, taking the revolver from his pocket. 'I'll do any shooting if necessary, Miss Eriksen. I would never ask an old friend to do that to you.'

Gregory nodded at Stefan. Vera stared at him, still bewildered by how he came into this. But it didn't matter. She was where she was. She looked straight ahead as Stefan stepped forward. He took the suitcase and started to frisk her.

Vera said nothing more. There was nothing to say.

The Ford left Rathdrum Station. No one had come and no one had gone. No one had seen anything that had happened in the station forecourt. Pulling across the bridge over the railway line, on to the main road, a motorcycle crossed ahead of them.

Terry Gregory drove. Stefan sat in the back with Vera. He now carried the Webley in his pocket. He said nothing to her; she had said no more to him.

'It's not a bad morning,' said Gregory. 'There'll be a bit of sunshine in the mountains. If you two aren't in the mood to chat, there'll be a grand view over the Wicklow Gap today. You'd pay good money for a coach trip up there.'

Stefan knew there was no point telling his boss to fuck off. There would only be more of it if he did. The best he could hope for was some silence.

It was some time before Vera spoke.

'You knew,' she said quietly. 'Is that it? You knew all that time.'

'I didn't know anything in London, Vera. Until the end.'

She frowned, shaking her head. She didn't believe him.

'Never trust an Irishman in a pub, Miss Eriksen.' Gregory threw the remark over his shoulder with some satisfaction. He was pleased with himself. All the panic in the Taoiseach's office and at Garda HQ and in Military Intelligence, and it simply took knowing where to put the right leverage. That was what he was paid for. That made him indispensable. He knew; they didn't.

Vera looked ahead. Stefan did the same.

The silence hung as heavily in the black Ford as the smoke from Terry Gregory's cigarettes. He chain-smoked all the way through Laragh and up into the mountains. Occasionally he broke the silence to point out something interesting: the road to the monastic ruins and the lake at Glendalough, a mountain here or there. Vera kept her eyes fixed ahead almost all the time, away from Stefan. From time to time she glanced behind her. Stefan registered it only as nervousness or anxiety. Beyond Glendalough, climbing up towards the Wicklow Gap, there was barely any traffic. They passed several tractors; a horse and cart carrying turf; a coach full of tourists heading in the other direction; two or three cars going the same way; a motor cycle that overtook them at high speed and was gone. No one noticed that it was the same motorcycle that had passed them outside the station at Rathdrum. The mountains spread out on either side of the road. The only animals were the mountain sheep, and when they rounded a bend they startled a gang of young Sika stags, drinking from a stream. It was high and desolate, a place of wide skies and great beauty. The purples and reds of the heather stretched from horizon to horizon. Neither Stefan nor Vera had the landscape on their minds, but Gregory had moved from using it as a source of idle amusement to watching it intently now. And most of that watching was through the car's rear-view mirror. There were no more jokes.

'There's a car behind us, Stevie?' Gregory spoke slowly.

He was looking hard in the mirror.

Stefan turned and stared back.

'It's been there for a while, keeping the same distance.'

'Is that so odd?' said Stefan.

'Odd enough. Someone might stay behind you on a road like this. Why not? But nobody drives so carefully that the distance wouldn't change. They'd get close, they'd fall back, they'd be looking out the window, lighting up a fag, having a row with the missus. You'd have to concentrate to keep it just so.'

'How long has it been there?'

'Twenty minutes?'

Stefan glanced round at Vera. For the first time in an hour, she was watching him. As soon as he turned, she looked away. It was quick, but he saw enough to know it wasn't the anger and puzzlement that had been there earlier.

'I'd say Vera's been looking back, on and off, some of the way.' Stefan looked at her. Her face was harder.

'I'd say the same.' Gregory was looking in the mirror again. 'We should have thought more about why she was there so early. Too early. I said it, didn't I? Was she being picked up? I've been cocky, too fucking cocky. You weren't catching the Dublin train at all, were you, Vera? Someone was collecting you.'

Gregory pressed down on the accelerator.

'Now we'll know. And if we're right, they will know we know.'

The black Ford pushed on faster and faster.

Stefan looked back. The car behind them was keeping pace.

'Yes, I'd say they know now, Stevie.'

Stefan took the Webley from his pocket.

He turned back to Vera. He didn't speak. But she knew what he wanted to say. Whoever they are, whatever you think they'll do to help you, do nothing.

The car shuddered. The engine raced. The road was metalled, but it was in no great state of repair. At speed every bump and every hole hit the Ford.

'What is it?' said Gregory.

'What?'

'What's the car?'

Stefan looked back, trying to focus as the Ford swerved and shook.

'I don't know.'

'It looks big enough from here, Stevie.'

'Maybe a Rover. It's got some speed. It's catching us.'

'I can fucking see that!'

Terry Gregory gripped the wheel as the car jumped up and

smashed down over a hump in the road. The suspension screamed and the gears crashed. He swung wildly round a hair-pin bend. As he changed up again and accelerated, the big car was much closer. It was almost on them. They could hear it now.

'Jesus Christ, what the fuck is—'

Coming straight towards them, in the middle of the road, was a motorcycle. As Stefan saw it, he knew now that it was the one they had seen twice already. Terry Gregory spun the steering wheel and braked hard, trying to keep control; as he did so the motorcyclist swerved away, off the road. But a check in speed had been enough. The big Rover was driving beside them.

'Shite, this man can drive!' shouted the superintendent.

He accelerated again, but as he did the other car swerved into the Ford. Gregory gripped the wheel, but he had lost control. The car veered off the road into the heather and peat and rocks. It careered down a slope. It was sliding. The brakes did nothing. It slammed to a halt as it hit a boulder as big as itself.

Terry Gregory was unconscious, sprawling across the steering wheel. In the back of the car, Stefan Gillespie was struggling to get up from the footwell where his leg was wedged. He had hit his head, but the real pain was in his shoulder, where the bullet wound from the Camden Catacombs had barely healed. He still had hold of the Webley. He looked at Vera. There was blood on her forehead, but she was still, composed. She shook her head, glancing down at the revolver. Now it was her turn. Now her eyes told Stefan to do nothing.

He turned as the door was wrenched open. The man who stood there held an automatic pistol. He could see another man walking towards the car. He saw the motorcyclist through the front windscreen, sitting on the bike, gently revving the engine. What Vera had told him without words was true. There would be no point resisting. He lay back against the seat; for a moment he closed his eyes. Vera touched his hand softly. He nodded and threw the Webley out on to the heather.

25

The Mill

The black Ford remained where it was, below the road, with the body of Terry Gregory still spread across the steering wheel. Stefan Gillespie's hands were bound and he was pushed into the back seat of the Rover. Vera was puzzled.

'Just tie him up and leave him here. What are we taking him for?'

'Shut up,' said one of the men.

He grabbed Vera's hands and took more rope from his pocket.

'What are you doing?'

The man ignored her. She said the same thing again, in German.

'Was machen Sie gerade!'

'A real German bitch, eh?'

The man laughed.

Vera stared; this was absurd.

'What?'

'Shutten zie up, sweetheart! I can gag you if that's what it takes.'

'You know who I am. You don't need to tie me up!'

The man pulled open the car door and pushed her in beside Stefan.

'What about the other one?' It was the driver who spoke.

'He's unconscious. He doesn't look good. Even so—'

'It'll do. It could be hours before anyone finds him up here. We'll be long gone. You can't see the car from the road, can you? Nobody killed if possible, that's what the boss said. A missing spy's one thing. It's not such a big deal over here. But a dead copper would have every Guard in Ireland looking for us.'

The motorcycle pulled away. The Rover followed. The man in the front passenger seat turned round. He held the automatic. He laughed cheerfully.

'All right in the back?'

'Will you tell me what's going on?' said Vera.

'Keep quiet, keep still. I won't shoot you, but I'd be very happy to crack this over your heads.' The man looked from Vera to Stefan. 'Either or both.'

Vera sat back, bewildered. Now this didn't make sense.

The driver reached to the dashboard and turned on the radio. The sound of Glenn Miller's band crackled out from the speaker: 'Pennsylvania 6-5000'.

Stefan leant back in the seat. He spoke quietly, in German.

'Not the rescue you were expecting, Vera?'

She turned to him, surprised. He had not spoken German before.

'If they're the fellers you were waiting for in Rathdrum, they don't seem the friendly sort. They don't seem very Irish. They're certainly not German.'

She nodded. The same thought was in her head too.

Stefan continued in German.

'That'll be because they're English, I'd say. Whatever that means. Too posh for policemen. That's more or less what

Willie Mullins said when some fellers turned up at the Bedford Arms, looking for Eddie Griffin and that suitcase I rescued for you. Did you know one of them took a shot at me?'

'No, I didn't.' She felt she needed to say it again. 'I really didn't.'

'Well, it's worth bearing in mind.'

The man in the front passenger seat turned round, looking at Stefan.

'I thought you were Irish?'

'I am.'

'Well, cut out the German. You can both keep your mouths shut.'

The driver turned up the music.

Vera spoke again, almost in a whisper, leaning closer to Stefan.

'So who are they?'

Stefan shrugged and shook his head.

'If you don't know and I don't know, I think that puts us on the same side, or something like it.'

The big Rover left the mountains and drove towards the outskirts of Dublin. Somewhere beyond Tallaght they pulled off the main road and followed a narrow road back into the country for several miles. The car turned into a disused farmyard. There was the shell of a roofless house and a rusty, red Dutch barn, half full of rotting hay. An unmarked van was waiting there, the engine idling; a man sat in the cab. Stefan and Vera, still bound, were pulled out of the Rover and pushed and prodded into the back of the van. It was partly packed with boxes. The man with the gun told them to sit on the floor. He climbed in after them along with the man who had driven the Rover. Then he pulled the doors shut. The two men sat on some of the boxes. There was a little light through the dirty glass panels in the van's back door. The man with the automatic pushed it into his shoulder holster, but the other one now held a Thompson machine gun. It lay across his lap.

The van moved off and they were soon back on the road. They travelled for a long time. Part of that time they were in Dublin; there was traffic and noise. And then they knew they were out in the country again. That was as much as Stefan could tell. They passed through towns, but he had no idea where they were. He lost all sense of direction. They could be anywhere.

It was almost three hours later that the van slowed down quite abruptly and started to bump along what was clearly an unmade track. When it stopped the two men in the back pushed open the doors. They beckoned Stefan and Vera out. They were in the courtyard of a big stone building. It was old and sprawling, two storeys high, three in one place. Neat red brick framed door and window openings; it was strong and well built. It was largely overgrown with dark ivy. It looked like some kind of mill, but it had been long out of use. Around it were trees. There was the sound of a river, quite loud. Stefan thought there must be a weir. There was nothing else to tell them where they were.

There was a car outside the building; next to it the motor-cycle.

The two men who had watched them since the Wicklow Gap ushered them through a wide, heavy wooden door. The room inside was large. There was a flagged stone floor and a large wooden table. There was old, dusty furniture stacked along one side of the room: chairs, sofas, chests of drawers. There were old farm implements too, rotting crates and boxes, part of a broken cart, a rusting tractor engine. The atmosphere was dry and cloying; there was woodworm everywhere. It was a place where unused and unwanted goods of every kind had found their way. Maybe once there had been a purpose in storing all this junk, but that must have been long forgotten.

A small, elegantly dressed man stood by a big open fireplace at one end of the room. It was almost as high as he was. It was colder in the mill than outside. A smokeless fire of worm-ridden wood burned brightly. The man was warming his hands. He turned.

'Vera,' he said cheerfully, 'a bit of a cock-up on the travel front.'

She recognised the bald head and the thick-lensed glasses and the lazy smile. It was London Kontrolle, the Abwehr handler she knew as Adam, the man she had met in King Street and at the Open Air Theatre. She had seen him again, too, before she left for Ireland. This was all his work. But why?

'Are you going to explain this, Adam?'

Vera spoke coldly. Her first thought was anger. She held up her wrists.

'Yes, I'm sorry. No need for that now. Better safe, though. Jack—'

Adam glanced at the man who had driven the Rover. Jack took a penknife from his pocket. He walked across the room to Vera and cut her hands free.

'What do you mean better safe?'

'Just what I say, Vera. We weren't expecting the Guards. We weren't expecting anyone, except you. It seems you weren't as invisible as I'd hoped.'

'What about him?' Vera pointed at Stefan. 'Does he need to be tied up?'

'I don't suppose so. It doesn't matter now.'

Adam nodded. The man with the penknife cut Stefan loose. London Kontrolle peered at Stefan.

'One of my men did get a good look at you in Camden, Mr Griffin. And obviously Vera now knows who you are. Who you really are, I mean. I assume you're responsible for Garda Special Branch knowing where Vera was. I'm at a loss to understand how you got to her in London. We had no idea. I'm not often at a loss. How?'

'Serendipity. That's how my superintendent would put it.'

'I'm not with you, Mr Griffin, or whatever your name is. Vera is ahead of the game, but won't you enlighten us as to who you've come to the party as today?'

'I'm a Garda detective. I assume you've worked that out.'

'Do you have a name?'

'Detective Inspector Stefan Gillespie.'

'Stefan, no need to stand on formalities. Adam will do for me.'

One of Adam's men perched on the edge of the table, smoking a cigarette and holding an automatic idly in his hand. It wasn't pointed at Stefan or Vera, but there was nothing idle in the man's eyes. The man who called himself Adam did all the talking. His men said very little. Now they were bringing in boxes and equipment from the van and piling them on the table. Stefan noted more clearly things he had already glimpsed on the journey. The boxes contained guns and ammunition; all the markings were in German. On the table, next to a folded Ordnance Survey map, was an open leather case, no bigger than a briefcase. It was a radio. That was German too. Stefan had seen one before; it had been recovered from where a German agent had buried it. He also recognised the small book sitting next to the radio. It was Vera's code book.

Stefan and Vera still stood close to the fire with Adam. Vera had said only a few words. She was waiting for an explanation for all this, and it hadn't come. The man in front of her was supposed to be a German agent, like her. He had called himself London Kontrolle. He had known all about her. He had known her secrets. He had known about Erik Kramer, the man who died in Berlin, the man she had loved, the man who was an SD plant in an Abwehr operation. He had taken over the mission Erik Kramer had told her about, the plan to involve the IRA in assassinating the Irish Prime Minister and give Britain a war to fight in Ireland. He had issued her instructions. He had sent her here. But something had already been eating away at her trust. Why had his instructions meant her doing nothing? Why had he been using her simply to lay a false trail?

Already Vera had started to question where her loyalties really lay. She had been ready to betray her Abwehr mission and turn it into something else, something she knew the Abwehr opposed. She had betrayed her colleague, Karl Drücke, because of that, because of a faith that somehow, now, she no longer quite believed in. Simply being in Ireland had changed how she looked at herself. And now, today, men who worked for Adam had treated her as a prisoner, even as they rescued her. And it wasn't over. Despite the fact that the ropes tying her hands had been cut, despite the easy words of the man she had known as London Kontrolle, Vera still felt she was a prisoner. All her senses told her that. She turned on him, quite suddenly, in voluble, angry German.

'What the hell do you think you're doing? I've been tied up. I've been threatened. Thrown into the back of a van. Why am I a prisoner? I am. I know.'

Adam answered in English.

'I don't think we need to keep up the German, Fraulein.'

'No, perhaps not,' said Vera quietly. 'Your men certainly don't make very convincing German agents. Or IRA men. So I don't know who you are. I know you did a good job as London Kontrolle. I had no reason to doubt you.'

'I shall take that as a compliment, Vera. Perhaps you can still think of me as London Control. Simply spell it differently. I'm afraid you've been in the hands of British Intelligence since you walked into the house in Covent Garden. In fact, since you picked up the telephone at Waverley Station. That's not true over here, of course. Until today you've been entertained by a variety of IRA men and Republican hangers-on. You had your own contacts and I was happy to leave you to it. Just long enough to show who your friends are, but not long enough for you to fall into the hands of Mr Gregory's Garda Special Branch. They were sharper than I anticipated. Since I assumed they had no idea you were here, I wasn't expecting them. And there they were, picking you up before I could use you properly. Just when I was reeling you in. That would have complicated things. But we've extricated you.'

'I don't understand. I've done nothing except hide in London and get shunted around to half a dozen safe houses here. What was the point of it?'

'The point is the little project your dear friend Major Kramer had in mind in Berlin. The one the Abwehr wouldn't much like. A dead de Valera, chaos in Ireland, British invasion, war. Not a daft idea at all. I thought you were keen on it. After all, it was one of the reasons you shopped your travelling companion, dear old Drücke. Because he might have got in the way. Because he wouldn't have done anything to contradict his orders from Tirpitzuferstrasse. I got the chance to interrogate Karl. He told me all about that. And you were right: he did have instructions to make sure it didn't happen. He paid some price, Vera.'

She was silent. She had not forgotten Karl Drücke.

'Karl was extremely cooperative. Normally cooperation like that would have saved him from hanging. But like you, I didn't want him buggering things up by letting anyone else know what was going on. Anyone else in British Intelligence. After I got what I needed from the interrogation it seemed wise to draw a line under any further chitchat from Karl. You were too useful.'

'Karl was a mistake,' she said. 'The whole thing was a mistake. I should have left him alone. He was only doing his job. I was the one who was wrong.'

'I'm sorry if you've changed your mind. Doubtless you've sensed your friends in the IRA weren't as receptive to knocking off Mr de Valera as the Reich Main Security Office anticipated.

On balance, as far as Germany's interests are concerned, I think the Abwehr have a more realistic view. Leave well enough alone. And perhaps you see that too. I don't know who you met from the Army Council but the idea would have frightened the life out of them.'

'You might be right. I'm not sure why I'm here at all.'

'Yes, it's all a bit of a fiasco; but then it is Ireland, isn't it?'

'And I still don't understand why you're here?' Vera looked harder at Adam. 'What's the point of this? You've tricked me, yes. You've had me running round Ireland, knowing what I was doing. But none of that's useful to you.'

Stefan simply listened to this conversation, looking into the fire, understanding most of it in the light of what he had been told at Garda HQ. What he didn't understand, any more than Vera did, was what this British Intelligence officer was doing with all this. But he knew there was danger. Vera did too.

Adam took out a cigarette case. He opened it and offered cigarettes to Vera and then to Stefan. Stefan took one. There was a box of matches on the kitchen table. He picked it up and lit the cigarette. The Englishman watched.

'You're still a puzzle, Inspector. We almost crossed paths in Camden. But that was Mr Griffin, of course. Now you're a Garda Special Branch officer.'

'What do you care? Why are we here? I see no point in this either.'

'Why were you in London, Inspector?'

'It was nothing to do with Vera. I didn't know who she was, not till the end. You hid her too well. But Ireland is a small place, even in County Camden.'

'That's a useful observation, Inspector. Too clever perhaps.'

'I can't see what you want from this,' said Stefan.

'Why would you? I didn't really want you at all. That's to say, you're an unexpected bonus. Cake and icing. You'll be helpful, Inspector Gillespie. You'll add local colour.'

'We do know about the assassination plan . . . whatever it is . . . or was,' continued Stefan. 'That didn't come from me, though.' He looked at Vera, then back to Adam. 'In fact, I think it came from Germany in some shape or form. If British Intelligence wanted to stop it, this is an elaborate way to do it.' He stubbed out the cigarette. 'Not to say fucking reckless. Why let her come to Ireland at all?'

Stefan's words were testing Adam. He couldn't grasp any of this, but he wanted to know more. He wanted to know where the danger he felt actually lay.

'I suppose reckless is one word. But you have the wrong end of the stick, old man. British Intelligence doesn't know. That's to say, British Intelligence apart from a few of us in MI6 who found this an opportunity too good to pass on.'

'You've lost me,' said Stefan.

'The point is not to stop it but to make it happen. Then provide all the proof that the Germans were responsible. Obviously in that our Miss Eriksen is the proverbial prima facie evidence. Her travels round the Emerald Isle with assorted Republicans give a whole caravan of conspirators. Unfortunately, the IRA men who are going to help her dispose of your prime minister will disappear without trace. Because they're not IRA men, as you can tell. They work for me. It's what you might call a private enterprise operation. I suppose a little bit like the original one Major Kramer brought out of the Sicherheitdienst. My bosses don't know about it. And they'll all think the Germans were responsible. If they don't, they won't care. Britain will occupy Ireland, and there's no shortage of people in Whitehall and the Army who'll applaud that.'

'What?' Vera shook. 'Why on earth would you—'

'Extraordinary, Fraulein.' The Englishman laughed. 'In Berlin, you were party to a plan to kill dear old Dev and you were happy to discuss it with me while you thought I was a German agent, but now you're here, you're shocked that somebody else is going to do the same thing, positively appalled. Really? You should be pleased. I'll even be sending a message to the Abwehr to say mission accomplished. Or rather you will be, Vera. I'll use your code book and a radio from Berlin, which it will appear you left here when the job was done. It will be on a frequency British and Irish Intelligence can pick up. It will come as rather an unpleasant surprise to Admiral Canaris. But then I do sometimes wonder if Major Kramer and his chums in the Sicherheitdienst don't have a point about the Abwehr's ineptitude. Are they playing for a win or draw?'

'Why would you want to do it at all?' Vera asked.

'The same reason someone in Berlin thought it might be a good idea. Self-interest. Not the same self-interest, naturally, but the same principle. The very fact that Germany can contemplate using Ireland against Britain, in any way at all, makes it essential that we take the initiative. Because some of us believe Ireland is a clear and present danger to Britain in too many ways. No access to Irish ports is costing convoys thousands of lives. The country's a soft target if a German invasion comes to the mainland. It's harbouring German spies, a German embassy, would-be saboteurs, however incompetent. The sensible course would be to invade and make Ireland safe. But the powers that be are too timid. I'm taking the opportunity to force their hand. This is the kick Mr Churchill needs to shout down the naysayers. It's not hard to understand.'

'You won't get near Dev,' said Stefan. 'This is mad. You know that.'

'Oh, we'll get near enough. And today is the day we do.'

The Englishman's smile exuded confidence. He looked at his watch.

'Which means there's work to do, old man. Lock them up, boys.'

*

Stefan and Vera were taken to a storeroom along a short, arched corridor. The door was heavy and old, but a new bracket had been screwed into it to hold a new padlock. It was a smaller space with a low wooden ceiling. Like the entrance hall, the room was stacked with debris: brass bedsteads, packing cases, a heap of long-abandoned turf; wicker chairs, a huge horsehair sofa with the stuffing hanging out, tables, cupboards. There was another open fireplace, high and deep; it was almost entirely taken up by an ancient cast-iron range. In front of it were piles of paper and hessian sacks. The room smelled of rats and warm, earthy dry rot. There were three small windows along one wall and at one end there were double doors.

As the door from the corridor closed, Stefan examined the room. The windows, high up, looked out to the front of the mill; he could see the car, the van, the motorbike. They would just have been big enough to climb through but there were two iron bars set into the stonework of each one. The double doors at the end of the room had been nailed and boarded up a long time ago. Furniture and wood had been piled up against them, as against the walls. Some of it could have been moved, but the doors were oak, metal-studded. Nothing would open them.

Stefan walked across the room. He sat on the big sofa. Vera was standing by the door. She hadn't moved. She was taking in what had just been said. She was struggling to accept that she had been played, from the moment she got to London. But the question now was what to do next. Stefan turned towards her.

'You can look yourself, but I don't think we'll find a way out.'

'No, I don't think we will. Any ideas, Eddie – what do I call you?'

'Stefan.'

'So you are German?'

'My grandmother was German. That would be another sort of Germany altogether, though. The one you were playing on the piano at the Bedford Arms.'

'I'm glad you've got time to talk politics, Stefan. Perhaps another day.'

She walked towards him and sat at the other end of the sofa.

'Did you see what they were bringing in?' said Stefan.

'Yes.' Vera nodded. 'Guns, ammunition and dynamite.'

'And a couple of Thompson machine guns. You'll know the song, surely, Vera? "Where the bayonets flash and the rifles crash, To the echo of the Thompson gun." You'd think every German agent would have it handy, so. One chorus of that in the pub, they'd take you straight to the IRA Army Council.'

'Is that more politics or are you telling jokes now, Stefan?'

'Nothing says the IRA like a Thompson. Sure any eejit would know.'

'I think I preferred you as Eddie Griffin.'

'It's evidence, like your man Adam says. The boxes are German. The guns, the ammo, the dynamite, all German. It has to be, doesn't it? That's the point. They're not bringing it in to take it out again. They don't need an armoury for an assassination, however they do it. It's here to be found. If your friend Adam has some way to get to Dev, it's here to prove the IRA did it, in conjunction with a German agent, instructed by a German agent. That's you.'

'Yes, I'm sure you're right, Stefan. But you know the truth. And so do I. That means two things; well, one thing, the same thing. I have to die, because I'm evidence too. He doesn't want evidence that talks. The same goes for you.'

'Yes,' said Stefan, standing up. 'You put it very succinctly.'

He took out a packet of cigarettes. He took one and offered her one.

'Still, it's not all bad news.'

Vera bent nearer, holding the cigarette to her lips as he struck a match.

'No?' replied Vera. 'What's the good news? I could do with some.'

'Well,' said Stefan, holding the matches, 'at least they left us a light.'

26

The White River

In the mill storeroom Vera Eriksen stood on a low cupboard, looking out of one of the high windows. Stefan Gillespie was pulling the stuffing from a sofa; he had ripped the cracked leather from it. In front of him there was more horsehair, more cloth stuffing and dank mildewed kapok. There was a heap of it now. He looked up. He could hear the engine of the car outside; the doors slammed.

'What's happening?'

'Adam and two of the others are going.'

'Then there are two left.'

Stefan picked up armfuls of the horsehair and stuffing. He heaped it by the furniture and packing cases and the furniture that was stacked, higgledy-piggledy, against the big doors at the end of the room, and he pushed it into gaps. He had already torn paper grain sacks into strips. He had strewn these along the floor, laying them on to the debris and screwing them up into the same gaps.

'Just pick up any bits of wood for kindling, anything that's small. Put them along the bottom; shove them into the paper and the stuffing, little piles.'

Stefan carried on heaping up the soft material while Vera

picked about in the debris for everything that was small and dry and broken. They worked as quickly and as silently as they could. There was a sloping pile of paper and stuffing and kindling stretching the width of the double doors. Stefan went to the fireplace as Vera continued working. He brought back hessian sacks and draped them over some of the furniture, higher up on the pile. Then he stopped.

'I don't know, the stuff's as dry as a bone but there's rot too.'

'Once it takes . . .' replied Vera. She seemed surer than him now.

'If it takes,' said Stefan.

'Come on!' She shrugged. 'Isn't it smoke we need most?'

Stefan nodded and bent down. He looked at her.

'You go, Vera. Just get into the corner, behind the cupboard. Hide.'

She smiled. 'I know.'

'Do you think you can take one of them long enough for me—'

'I'm sure I can, Stefan.'

'One of them will have to come in. I'm hoping both. The smoke won't take long to seep out. They'll smell it. If the fire takes hold, they'll hear it. We need to rely on some good old-fashioned panic. Whatever else they expect—'

'Let's do it, Stefan. It's a chance. It's not a bad one.'

Stefan turned to the fire they had laid. He struck several matches that went out as soon as they touched the paper. But then the paper caught. It burned slowly. It was barely more than a glow. He worked his way along the stack of furniture and wood. Soon there were islands of red smoking paper. Then there was more, flames here and there as the scraps of kindling caught. The flames were small, only flickering, but there was more and more smoke. Wood was burning deeper. A bigger flame licked up from the floor.

Vera was still looking.

'Go on,' said Stefan. 'Get yourself hidden.'

She walked across the room, below the windows. She squeezed behind a cupboard and a pile of wooden crates. Stefan stayed where he was, watching the fire. It was taking well. Some of the bigger pieces of wood were starting to burn and smoke was rising from the horsehair and the sacking. He turned to the fireplace and pushed his way in, crouching at one side of the range. He pulled a pile of filthy sacks over him. They had discussed several visions of what might happen; each could as easily end with them dead as overcoming their captors. They both had another vision, in which the two men simply let the storeroom burn. But they did not discuss it. If Adam didn't really need Stefan, he needed Vera.

Stefan could feel the heat now. He could hear the fire, burning harder and faster than he expected. He knew the room was filling with smoke. It was round him in the fireplace. It was already getting difficult to breathe. They needed smoke, enough smoke, but not so much it would choke them. Smoke would hide them, protect them, for just long enough. Surely smoke would be seeping out from the door to the mill. The two men must smell it, see it. If they were outside, it would be pouring from the window openings. By now, wouldn't they hear it?

Stefan heard the men outside the door. Their voices were indistinct but there was confusion, surprise; only a step to panic. He heard the door pulled open.

'Fucking hell! The place is going up!'

Both men were coughing. One was more clear-headed than the other.

'Where are they?'

'I can't see!'

'You can see enough. Shoot him, right, and get the woman out?'

'And where do I shoot, Chris, anywhere in particular?'

305

'Get in there and do it!'

Stefan didn't move. He could feel rather than hear one of the men walking into the room, coughing. He would have a gun. He would be looking round, ahead. He must be walking towards the double doors and the flames.

'The fucking heat. The ceiling's burning!'

'They're there. They have to be somewhere. Get them!'

'Nothing's going to stop this, Chris!'

'They can't get out, can they? Shoot the man and get her out!'

'I can't see them anywhere,' said the man in the storeroom. 'I can't see a thing!'

'Move some of the bloody furniture!'

'Like hell!' The man in the room coughed again. 'Come in and cover me!'

Stefan's senses told him the other man was in the room now.

'Find them, quick,' said the man called Chris. 'We need to get out.'

Stefan heard something heavy fall to the ground. A piece of furniture had been moved, some crates. One of the men was close to the fireplace, at the end of the room where the fire had not yet spread. But the smoke had; the smoke was everywhere. It would have to be now. Stefan gripped the heavy chair leg he had with him. He had to go now. He had to take the chance. There was no time.

Another heavy object fell as it was pulled to the floor.

There was a prolonged fit of coughing. Then a cry of pain.

'For fuck's sake! Ah! I've bloody – one of them's—'

Stefan pushed away another sack. He could see the room. But he did not move. There was a haze of smoke hanging high at this end of the store. At the other end there was much more smoke; behind it a wall of flame reached to the ceiling. One man had his back to the fireplace, facing away from Stefan. He held a gun, pointing at the second man, across the room. The second man was struggling. Vera was behind him, holding him. She had one arm round his neck. The other arm was at his back, twisting his arm up hard. He cried out in pain again. He waved the other hand, trying to reach round to hit her. There was an automatic still in his fist, but suddenly it flew across the room. Vera held him harder than ever, with a combination of strength and skill. Stefan could see she knew how to do this; she was strong. The man's body stood between her and the gun that pointed across the room at her. Any bullet would pass through him.

Stefan stood up slowly, inching forward.

'Shoot her! Shoot the bitch, Chris!'

'Get out of the way then. Get away from her!'

'I can't! I can't, I—' He flailed his free arm wildly.

There was a small, crisp snap. It wasn't loud, but Stefan heard it. So did the man pointing the gun. The head of the man Vera was holding flopped down. She still held him, like a shield. But he was dead now. She had broken his neck.

She let him drop.

The other man had been too startled to shoot instantly. Now he raised the gun, furious, panicking wildly. And Stefan smashed the chair leg into the back of his skull.

Outside the mill Vera held a gun on the man called Chis. Smoke rose from one end of the building, through the windows and the roof. The stone walls and the heavy slate roof were resisting for now. The fire was contained, but it had burned through to the next floor already. It would not be long before it reached the roof timbers. Chris was tied, hands and feet, by a belt and a rope. He sat on the floor, his back against the van that had brought Vera and Stefan from Dublin.

Stefan came out of the mill. He had the Ordnance Survey map with him. He knew where they were now, south of Dundalk, a few miles from the coast and the border with Northern Ireland. He stood over the MI6 man.

'You need to tell me what's happening, Chris.'

The man said nothing.

'I know where we are. I can see what's marked on the map. The mill here, the White River down that way, running behind the mill. And a bridge.'

He pointed at the map.

'So what does that mean?'

'I don't know,' said the MI6 man.

'You don't know?'

'I'm doing a job. I don't give the orders. You'll have to ask Adam—'

He stopped before the surname. Stefan shook his head and shrugged.

'Let's not worry about the names. I don't care. I don't think etiquette should feature too much in your calculations. Let's just stick to Adam, so.'

The man was more nervous. Stefan's voice was quiet but he could hear the menace.

'Come on. I don't suppose there's a lot of time, is there, Chris?'

The MI6 man wanted to sound more confident than he was.

'Not for you, Gillespie. They'll be back when they see the smoke.'

'Will they? What about the job? What about disposing of Dev? That's what's going on, isn't it? That's what your boss was so keen to tell us about.'

Chris did not respond.

'Tell me about it. Where is it? How's it going to work?'

The MI6 man laughed. It wasn't entirely convincing, but he was trying.

'I don't think you have the right security clearance, Inspector.'

Stefan took out a small automatic and aimed it at the MI6 man.

'I don't know. I could shoot you.'

'You won't find out much if I'm dead.'

Vera had said nothing, but her eyes were fixed on Chris, unmoving. Every so often he glanced up at her. She didn't register the glances, but her eyes stayed on him. She had killed one man. She unsettled him more than Stefan.

'That's true, Stefan,' said Vera. 'So I'd be careful where you aim.'

'That's the thing, Chris.' Stefan lowered the gun. 'Why would I kill you?'

He pulled the trigger. A bullet smashed through one of Chris's knees.

He screamed in pain. 'For fuck's – my God – you bastard—'

Stefan crouched down by the MI6 man, who was groaning with pain.

'There are three boxes of dynamite in the mill. Overkill, I'd say. But you took them in yourself. I don't know how long before the fire reaches them, but if you can't tell me anything, we'll have to go and find your boss and ask him. I assume he's somewhere along the river. X marks the spot? It's on the map. I could shoot you again. But I'm worried about the time. And the dynamite. Or should we be happy for the mill to go up? Whatever's going on by the river that would show all's not well. Far and wide. And what if we went off in search of Adam and left you trussed up by the dynamite. I don't mind you going up too. You are on a patriotic mission, Chris. How is that for a bit of *pro patria mori*?'

The MI6 man looked from Stefan to Vera. He pushed aside the pain that was still cutting into his leg. He was frightened now. Vera moved closer to him.

'Do you really want to call our bluff, Chris? Do you think we care?'

The Englishman stared up at Vera. She was smiling quietly.

'It's your choice,' said Stefan. 'Time isn't on your side.'

309

A stab of pain slammed though the MI6 man again.

'All right.'

'All right what?' Stefan looked at his watch. 'You have five minutes.'

'There is . . . there's a meeting today, your Intelligence and ours, MI5.'

Stefan nodded. He knew something about that meeting. He remembered now. Terry Gregory had told him. It was near here, close to the border. He knew how few people had any information about it, even in the Irish government. It was a degree of collaboration between Britain and Ireland that could destroy de Valera's credibility at home and make room for a resurgent IRA. Germany would see it as a repudiation of Irish neutrality. That would mean a lot more than hard words if Germany won the war. That was why it had to be done secretly, even in the Taoiseach's office and the corridors of government. But British Intelligence knew. They had details too. And one way or another those details must have found their way to the man called Adam and his rogue operation.

'Where is this meeting? Do you know the details?'

'There's a house at Castlethomas, some sort of estate. It's been taken over by your Intelligence people, G2. It's no great secret. It's their border base.'

'But you're not invited to this meeting obviously, you and your boss?'

'This is as near as we get. There's only one road in and out of the estate. It's been closed since this morning. But it's only a couple of miles from here.'

'And how did you get in here?'

'There's a dirt track, across from the east, from another road. That's the way we came in with you. It runs along the White River. Not easy to follow.'

'And not easy to find.'

'Some of us know Ireland better than you think, Inspector.'

'So what happens? What's the plan?'

The man hesitated.

'I wouldn't rethink it, Chris. What do you reckon, Vera?'

'I think time is probably quite short. You gave him five minutes, Stefan.'

'All right,' continued the Englishman, 'there's a bridge over the White River. The track to the mill doesn't go all the way to the road. It's blocked off by fields and ditches. But you can get there. We got there. The bridge is mined now. They can blow it from . . . show me the map . . . that's where Adam . . . here—'

Stefan had put the map in front of the MI6 man. He jabbed his finger.

'They'll be there now. It's about a quarter of a mile from the bridge.'

'And that's the way Dev will be coming in to Castlethomas?'

'That's the information we—' Chris closed his eyes in pain.

Stefan frowned. It was still hard to see any of this working.

'You're never going to get away, though. They'll close the border.'

'We only have to get to the coast. Ten minutes from here. There's a motorboat.'

Stefan nodded, looking down at the map. Now it made sense.

'And that'll take you into Carlingford Lough? Northern Ireland.'

The MI6 man nodded.

'What about the rest of it? What about Vera?'

The Englishman shrugged.

'Do you shoot me here or somewhere else?' said Vera.

'I'd shoot you anywhere, you fucking German cow.'

Vera laughed. Then she looked at Stefan hard.

'So?' he asked.

'So,' she answered.

'I have to try to stop it. Are we still on the same side?'

Vera smiled. 'I've lost track. I don't know if that means we are or not. Still, it'll have to do.'

The motorcycle pulled away from the front of the mill. The MI6 man lay by the van, still trussed up. Stefan drove. Vera was on pillion. They moved slowly for several minutes, negotiating the bumps and pitfalls of the yard until they reached the grassy track. Stefan stopped as the way became clearer. He looked ahead through the trees, along the green track. He looked round at Vera who was holding the map. She held it up and pointed towards some pen markings.

'It should be straight along there. That's what Adam's marked.'

Stefan glanced back towards the smoke from the mill.

'How long till the fire reaches the dynamite?'

'The boxes are by the door. I don't think it'll be long.'

'Adam and his lads have to get away, Vera. At all costs. The whole thing depends on a German agent and IRA gunmen. We know that's what you were for all along, that's what all the evidence is for. If they're caught, it's a fecking disaster. British Intelligence officers trying to kill Dev. So when the mill goes up, what are they going to do? It'll be heard for miles. They have to get out!'

'So they'll run?'

'I can't see they've got any choice.'

'But the bridge is still mined. It could still go up,' said Vera. Stefan nodded. He kicked the bike into gear.

They followed the track through the trees for almost a mile.

'They'll hear us,' he shouted back.

'Probably,' replied Vera. She took an automatic from her pocket.

As they rounded a bend, the trees were thicker. The White River had been on their right and now they were moving away from it. The track climbed towards a wooded knoll that looked down on a road and a bridge further along the river. In front of them was the car that had been outside the mill. Out of the trees came one of Adam's men, pulling a gun from a shoulder holster. Stefan turned the throttle. The motorbike raced towards the car. Vera reached out and fired, sending the man sprawling for cover. At that moment there was a huge explosion behind them. Adam ran from the trees too, taking out his gun. But he stopped, staring not at the motorbike, but past it, to the mill, and the pall of black smoke rising up behind the trees.

Then there was a second explosion.

Stefan Gillespie swerved to the side of the track, leaving it for a moment, weaving through the trees that lined it on one side. But no more shots were fired now. The man called Adam and the other two Secret Intelligence Service men stood by the car, still staring at the smoke. And Stefan and Vera were past them, back on the track, heading to the river and the road. The MI6 men simply let them pass, and as the motorcycle disappeared, they were already running to the car.

It was not much further until the track ended. There was a ditch ahead, a field gate, a stretch of barbed-wire fencing. Stefan stopped, looking back at the map.

'Can you open the gate?'

Vera got off and tried to open the gate. It was wired shut and she took several minutes to undo it. Then they were in a field. The river was on their right again. They crossed the field and another gate brought them on to the road. The little stone bridge, arching over the White River, was behind them.

Vera shouted.

'What do we do now?'

Stefan pointed down the road. The drove on, slowly, for several minutes, seeing no one. Then there were two motorcycles in front of them, driving towards them. They were army outriders. Behind them was a black limousine. There was another car, an army vehicle, further back. They were stationary. Several men from the last car were walking forward. One of them carried a machine gun; the others held revolvers. They stopped on either side of the black limousine, looking ahead, where the great pall of smoke from the mill hung in the air.

Stefan halted the bike. He got off and so did Vera. Now the attention of the convoy was on them. He held up a gun and threw it behind him. Vera did the same. They put their hands in the air and walked forward. They reached the two army motorcyclists. One of them held a revolver. Stefan and Vera stopped.

The men from the military car approached.

Stefan knew them before they knew him. One was Dessie MacMahon.

'Stay completely still and keep your hands up!'

It was the man with the machine gun giving the orders.

'Ah, come on with you, you know me, for God's sake!' Stefan grinned.

'Jesus, Mary and Joseph!' said Dessie.

But Stefan and Vera stood very still, their hands raised.

The door of the limousine opened. The man who got out wore the dark hat that was Éamon de Valera's hallmark and the long black coat, too long and too tight. It was not Dev. The man leant on a stick and limped. It was Terry Gregory.

27

Oxford Town

There are lies, damned lies, and there are things that it seems wise to pretend never happened. The rogue action to create enough chaos in Ireland to make a British invasion inevitable came into the last category. G2 had identified the man called Adam as Adam Lambert, a senior Secret Intelligence Service officer with a reputation for cavalier operations. Irish Military Intelligence had some help from MI5, who didn't mind embarrassing MI6 if it was useful and it didn't go too far. There were politicians and military leaders in Britain who, had the plan worked, and had German fingerprints been found all over it, along with the grubbier ones of the IRA, would not have enquired too deeply into how it happened. Under those circumstances it wouldn't have been necessary for Éamon de Valera to die, as long as it came pretty close and it was obvious that Ireland could not secure its own Prime Minister, let alone its borders. British feelings of anger about Dev's intransigent neutrality went deep, even among those who knew how one-sided that neutrality really was. They went deep in the British Army and they went as high as Winston Churchill in Whitehall. Churchill had been in two minds about sending British troops into Ireland for months. In the mornings he listened to those who thought it was a bad idea. In the afternoons, after a bottle of champagne, he lent his ear more readily to those who disagreed. The mornings usually had the best of it, but Adam Lambert's rogue project would have put an end to the bad-thing argument.

However, the plan had failed. Not only had it failed, it had now never existed. Beyond a few people inside MI6, and a select few elsewhere, no one knew anything. Half a dozen people in the Irish government knew, and a few others, like Terry Gregory and Geróid de Paor and his superiors in G2. It was in nobody's interests to pursue it further. For a time it gave Dev unspoken and unacknowledged favours to call in from the British. That was never a bad thing.

For all practical purposes there was no evidence; there were no statements or records. Adam Lambert had retrieved his remaining operative and reached the boat that took him across the border. An unidentified dead man was discovered at a ruined mill on the White River after a fire. The MI6 men who worked with Lambert would find themselves in out-of-the-way foreign fields across the globe, but that was it. Lambert himself was hauled over the coals, but he was too valuable to lose.

Detective Inspector Stefan Gillespie would say nothing, neither would Vera Kennedy-Eriksen. The evidence that had been so carefully planted had gone up with the mill; what was left was collected by Geróid de Paor and disposed of. In the end, Éamon de Valera did not make the journey to the Intelligence meeting at Castlethomas. The Taoiseach's authority could be stamped on secret dealings with Britain in other ways. And Dev, who had a considerable belief in destiny, decided that even the threat of an assassination attempt was a sign not to be ignored. He should always steer clear of personal involvement in anything that compromised his Republican credentials. It was, after all, something he had been conscious of when negotiating the Anglo-Irish Treaty almost twenty years earlier.

When getting your hands dirty became unavoidable, especially with the English, it was always better to send someone else.

Superintendent Gregory took the route de Valera would have taken to the Intelligence meeting on the border. He was unsure if anything at all would happen, but he was taking no chances. In reality, Adam Lambert's plan was scuppered before he knew it. He was too English not to underestimate what the Irish knew. Gregory also had a missing German spy to find, not to mention a missing detective inspector. His contacts in the IRA could offer him nothing in the way of information. When he took the Castlethomas road, it was as much because he had nowhere else to look for Stefan Gillespie as it was for Éamon de Valera and Ireland.

It was a week after the events beside the White River that Stefan Gillespie was called into Superintendent Gregory's office. He had returned to his usual duties. The detectives' room was quiet. It was reflective of the way Gregory ran the Special Branch that spurts of unexpected activity were quickly forgotten and replaced by the usual routine of chaperoning government ministers, following people who, for the most part, knew they were being followed, questioning informers who had no new information, and reading the letters and telegrams that someone, somewhere, thought needed reading – and almost never did. There was always the prospect of taking over a murder investigation that the Commissioner felt was too serious for his ordinary CID men to handle, but murders seemed few on the ground. Dublin was quiet too and, as everyone said, when you looked across the water that was something to be very grateful for.

'You've done it again, Stevie.'

'What's that, sir?'

'Not to mention your fecking old feller.'

'Oh, yes?'

'Oh, yes, is it?' Gregory pushed a report at Stefan across the desk.

'This feller in Baltinglass, Superintendent Mulvaney, has got every other superintendent in the south-east complaining about Special Branch interference. And I haven't lifted a finger.' Terry Gregory grinned. 'Well, apart from letting Dessie MacMahon lift his finger. Now Ned Broy's got CID in Wicklow Town on to him. They took over the investigation into this dead farmer up in the middle of fuck-knows-where. They arrested your man Coogan's son. Now you've written a letter telling them they don't know what they're fucking doing and someone should be talking to a feller who lives in Oxford who stayed with you the night before he walked up to Rathdangan to maybe top a farmer he'd never seen before. So tell me, have I got that about right?'

'I wouldn't say altogether, sir. You're heading in the right direction.'

'I'm glad you think so, Inspector.'

'I have had time to think about what my father found out—'

'Has he got no cows to milk or sheep to bloody lamb?'

'It's early for lambing, sir.'

'All right, Stevie, let's be serious. This is a mess. And there's no question that your old feller put together more evidence than the rest of them combined. But you're saying there is a link between this friend of yours, Tully, and the dead man. You're saying Joe's Coogan's wife – Brenda, is it – had some connection to Peter Tully?' Gregory looked down at the report. 'She was the woman he wanted to marry. I don't know why he'd wait half a lifetime to get his own back. This report says she walked out on Coogan fucking years ago. If Peter Tully had waited much longer, the man would have died of old age!'

'I don't know the details,' said Stefan. 'I don't know if they were really going to be married. Her family got in the way of it. I know it left a scar on Peter. She was a woman called Brenda, and it has to be the same one. I asked my father to find out who she was. I don't see there can be any doubt she's the woman Peter knew when he was younger. She came from Aughrim, he told me that much, and so did Brenda Coogan. I'm not looking to involve my friend, sir. I don't want to involve anyone. But he was there, camping by the farm, close to where Coogan was found. Someone killed Joe Coogan. That's for sure. The body was moved. It's hard to see it any other way. He certainly didn't die by the River Derreen.'

'It's still a bit of a stretch, isn't it? How long ago was all this?'

'Long enough.'

'Right, well, it can't be left there, can it? Between Baltinglass and Wicklow Town, they didn't even know this feller Tully existed. So with all that, the Commissioner has handed it over to me. It's a Special Branch job. We'll leave the culchies to fume.'

'I see.' Stefan was quiet. The reality of what this meant was something he had stepped away from as best he could, but Terry Gregory's banter was palling. He'd had enough. Peter Tully had been a good friend. He didn't know what had happened. He didn't know what the truth was. He wanted to believe there was an explanation that didn't mean Peter was a murderer. Yet he knew two things. He was sure. Paul Coogan did not kill his father. And Peter Tully had been there.

'There is one other thing, Stevie. The son tried to kill himself.'

'Jesus, I didn't know that.'

'He's in Mountjoy. He tried to cut his wrists. It almost worked. It seems likely he'd do it again if he got the chance. Never mind that we look like we're a bunch of eejits, if we're about to find out he's innocent, and then he dies . . .'

'You do need to talk to Peter Tully, sir.'

'No, I don't, you do, Inspector.'

'Oh, no.' Stefan shook his head.

'Oh, yes. You're the only one who knows what the fuck is going on.'

'He's a friend. I think I've done enough. More than enough.'

'The arrangements have been made, Inspector. The English are prepared to let us send someone to interview him. Whatever that throws up, we take it from there. I've spoken to Scotland Yard. There'll be someone to hold your hand in Oxford. You go tomorrow. If you don't like it, don't blame me, blame your dad. Old policemen should take a tip from old soldiers and fade away.'

As Stefan Gillespie walked out of the Castle yard that evening, he saw Geróid de Paor walking in. The two men stopped to speak. The attempt on de Valera's life had been consigned to the back of both their minds. But there was one thing that wasn't easily put away. Stefan had last seen Vera by the burning mill as she was driven away in the back of de Paor's car. He did not know where she was.

'You're avoiding me, Geróid,' said Stefan cheerfully.

'Would I ever do that?'

'I did phone.'

'Ah, well, you know how it is.'

Stefan knew the G2 man was uncomfortable.

'Is Vera in jail now?'

'I don't know.'

'Well, who does? I'd like to visit her. Is that a problem?'

'It wouldn't exactly be the usual thing, would it, Stefan?'

It was there again; de Paor was avoiding the question.

'She'll be in court at some point, won't she?'

'You know it backwards. On this one nobody wants her in court.'

'Then what's going to happen to her? Don't we owe her something?'

'Stefan, the thing is . . .' Commandant de Paor lowered his voice. 'There was nothing we could gain from keeping her here. In fact, it was better not to.'

'What does that mean?'

'As far as I know she's in England.'

Stefan stared at him in disbelief.

'She was driven up to Belfast. I'd guess they took her to London.'

'You gave her to British Intelligence?'

'This is not a conversation I can have, Stefan. Forget it, please.'

'She's a spy. They could hang her. You know that, don't you?'

'She'll be useful to them, I'm sure. I doubt they will.'

'That's all you've got to say? You doubt they will!'

Geróid de Paor's features hardened.

'Yes, Inspector, it's all I have to say. And all you have to say. Clear?'

Stefan watched de Paor walk away. It was clear. That was the end of it.

Stefan Gillespie arrived in Oxford from Birmingham. It had been a long journey from Holyhead, disrupted by train cancellations and the traffic of war. He left the station and turned towards the town, looking down towards Osney Bridge and the Thames footpath he had taken with the woman he knew as Vera Kennedy. It was not even three weeks ago. It felt unreal. And it had been. He had been someone else. She had been noting invasion defences that were being built along the river as they walked to rid themselves of the Blitz that was in their lungs. She had almost cost him his life in London. But without her help he might not have survived at the White River Mill. There was little point thinking about it. Yet all that seemed more straightforward than what he was doing now. He was there to question a man he had once been close to. He was even there to trap him in some way, if that's what it took to find the truth about Joe Coogan. He wished he could turn the other way and take the slow walk to Tadpole Bridge.

At Oxford police station he was shown to the superintendent's office. He recognised the curt hostility at the same time he recognised the Ulster accent. Superintendent Vance was probably from Antrim. He had left it a long time ago but he carried his own Ireland with him in his opinion of the Garda Síochána. And as the stilted conversation proceeded Stefan saw, on a shelf of family photographs, a picture of a young man in the uniform of a Royal Irish Constabulary sergeant; it could only be the superintendent. Vance told Stefan that Scotland Yard had agreed to him interviewing Mr Tully. He didn't need to add that he felt they were wrong. He told Stefan that Mr Tully would permit this as a private citizen, no more. He reminded Stefan several times that he had no authority whatsoever as a police officer here. He also told him more than once that Mr Tully was a fellow of an Oxford college. That required proper deference.

He dispatched Stefan with one of his men and one more caution about deference. Inspector Jack Rossiter was an Oxford Town man through and through. He didn't much care what Stefan was doing or where he came from. He was just another policeman. He walked him through the town, along the High Street and past the Radcliffe Camera to the Bodleian Library. Mostly he talked about the weather and about rationing. He said nothing about the buildings they passed. They walked under the Venetian arch over New College Lane and turned down a narrow, twisting alleyway to a rambling collection of low, scruffy buildings that made up the Turf Tavern, built into the back of what remained of Oxford's city walls. Stefan had a room there for the night. Jack Rossiter stayed long enough for a pint of beer and then left. If he liked his city, the best thing he had to say about it was only that Stefan would get a good night's sleep at least.

'No bombs, that's the thing. We ain't been bombed at all.'

'You're lucky then.'

'They do say Adolf has his eye on the old place as his capital when he invades. That's why he looks after us.' The inspector grinned broadly. 'Invasion? Aren't likely!'

As a grey day turned to greyer dusk, Stefan Gillespie sat in the stalls of New College Chapel. He had walked only yards between the high stone walls that penned in New College Lane to the college's porters' lodge. The porter told him Mr Tully would be in the chapel for evensong. Stefan had turned into the wide, neat, square quadrangle. The high medieval walls of the chapel, full of stained glass, filled one side of it.

He had seen Peter Tully straightaway, as he slid into one of the chapel stalls. Peter had seen him and nodded. This was a place Stefan knew in a way. He knew the smell of ancient stone and old wood. He knew the high arched roof and the reredos behind the altar, packed with rows of apostles and saints. He knew the stained glass that now came alive with the last light of the day. Above all he knew the music. It was a smaller space than St Patrick's Cathedral in Dublin, where he had sung as a boy chorister before his father left the DMP and moved to Baltinglass. It was smaller, but it bore the same long centuries of singing. And he could feel that. It wasn't that he believed in anything that represented the God the prayers were spoken to, but he knew there was something else here, somehow, that he did believe. He didn't have a name for it. But it was nonetheless real. There was a place in him that this place touched. It mattered. It had not left him. He looked at the boy choristers, remembering Dublin, when he sang every day in the cathedral and barely knew that people were fighting and dying in the streets beyond. He knew about death now. He knew a lot about it. Death had brought him here. He recognised Purcell's slow notes; an anthem for the funeral of Queen Mary.

'Thou knowest, Lord, the secrets of our hearts.'

*

Evensong was over. Stefan Gillespie and Peter Tully walked in the cloisters that lay behind the chapel. It was almost dark but the moon was up, a round moon that lit the grass and the great holm-oak at its heart and shone into the dark arches of the walkways. They were alone. They walked slowly, passing walls filled with plaques and monuments and engravings to the dead of centuries.

'Do we dive straight in?' said Peter Tully wryly.

'You tell me.'

'I've never been questioned before, Stefan. I don't know the routine.'

'I guess it depends what you're going to tell me. I don't know whether I'm here to find some way to force you to tell me what happened or you're just going to say it. I do have questions. I can't make you answer them.'

Peter took out a Craven A cigarette and lit it.

'We could start with those,' said Stefan.

'What do you mean?'

'My father collected a lot of them in the woods above Joe Coogan's farm. I know you were there. I could ask you if you were, and you could lie.'

'I could. But I won't. I lie a lot. I don't much like it.'

Stefan looked, not understanding. Peter Tully laughed.

'We all do our bit. The war. My bit is getting together every week with a group of people who . . . make things up. We're given all sorts of information. It might be about a German general and his mistresses, on a good day his boyfriends. It might be about some civil servant in a little German town who's fiddling the books. People taking bribes is always good. There might be a scientist working on some new engine or explosive, anything you like. He's been sounding off about the Nazis, saying uncomplimentary things. That could make him a feller you'd have sympathy with, but if he ends up in a concentration camp, well, whatever he is developing stops, or slows down at least. There are thousands of snippets of information that come out of Germany, in all sorts of ways. From agents, from refugees, prisoners of war. Idle stuff. Gossip, not much more. And that's only what's true or might be. Often we make things up. Rumours, scandals, things to panic about, things to make you distrust your neighbours, your leaders. A long runner is the idea that if you joined the Nazi Party early on, your sons won't be sent to the front. Always a winner. It's the Valley of the Squinting Windows, eating away at the littlest areas of life. And evidence suggests the Gestapo are the boys for picking up anonymous accusations. We work from the bottom up. These things get fed back to Germany. Into the papers, on to the radio, to barracks, offices, factories, universities. I don't know how well they work. But our masters approve. Sometimes the right rumour even gets people killed. That's *our* finest hour.'

'We've both ended up in the shadows, Peter. You'll be good at lying. I'm not bad myself now.'

'Good enough,' said Tully, 'if I wanted to lie.'

They walked on in silence. Peter Tully stopped, pointing at a small plaque on the cloister wall. It wasn't very old. There was enough moonlight to read it.

'I often look at this. I come back to it over and over again.'

Stefan bent closer and read the words aloud.

'In memory of the men of this college who coming from a foreign land entered into the inheritance of this place and returning fought and died for their country in the war 1914–19.'

There followed three German names in red.

Peter Tully smiled.

'No one will be putting up a plaque like that at the end of this war.'

'No, I don't think so,' said Stefan.

'You want to know if I killed Joe Coogan. That's why you're here.'

'Yes, it is. You do know his son's been charged with his murder?'

'I didn't, not until yesterday.'

'So are you going to tell me what happened, Peter?'

'I didn't kill him, Stefan. But I did watch him die. I let him die.'

28

The Turf Tavern

At one end of a passage at the side of the Turf Tavern, running past the kitchen, there was a small garden. Some benches and tables sat between the pub and the remains of the city wall. No one was in the garden on a late October night that had become quite cold, except Stefan Gillespie and Peter Tully. There was cloud across the moon. The only light came from the windows of the pub. It was a private place that night, and Peter found the darkness an easier place to speak in, sitting on a bench hard up against the turn in the wall that once marked the boundary of the city of Oxford. New College lay on the other side of the wall. He sat facing Stefan. The pint of beer in front of him was still untouched.

'It started a long time ago. You know that. I talked to you about Brenda. But only because she'd returned, in an unexpected way. She'd been in the backwoods of my life for a long time. It wasn't that I'd forgotten. She had been put away, where she was supposed to be. Then something happened, just over a year ago. A friend of mine, Robert, is a doctor in Swindon. He told me about a young woman at the TB sanatorium. She was Irish, from Wicklow, and he knew my associations. She was dying. That was all there was to it. She wouldn't speak to anyone, barely to him. He wanted me to see her. I don't know what made him say it. Hospital visiting isn't my strong point. But he pushed me. I think he wanted me to do some good, maybe because he couldn't. Something like that. He showed me some drawings she'd made one day. It was all she ever did. She'd sit in the hospital conservatory, drawing. And drawing very well.'

Peter Tully lit a Craven A.

'I recognised some of the drawings. Mountains. The same ones over and over. You'd know them too. Keadeen and Lugnaquilla. That's what made me get involved. Oxford is a place you don't do that much. You don't get involved. I could see these places mattered to her. And I realised they still did to me. I'd half forgotten that. So one Sunday I went. She was very young, early twenties. She was drawing when I got there, in the conservatory. They wheel the beds out there, but she was in an armchair, with a table in front of her. It felt like a barrier as well as place to draw. She didn't want much to do with people. She didn't want me there. But I started to talk about the mountains. I said all sorts of things that were about me, not about her at all. It was when I heard myself describing the "bi-vallate" hillfort on Spynans that I decided to leave. I was almost about to stumble into my standard undergraduate lecture on the Iron Age! But as I left, she looked up for the first time. She smiled for the first time. She tore a piece of paper from her notebook and gave it to me. A little pencil sketch of Keadeen.

'I went almost every Sunday for two months. I'm not sure what we talked about a lot of the time. But she drew less and spoke more. I knew her as Eimear. I knew she'd lived on a farm somewhere off the Military Road. She didn't talk about that. I didn't know why she'd left her home. I knew she'd run away, that was all. And it was painful. I think she liked the fact that I never asked. I only knew why she'd left near the end, when I found out who she was.'

Peter Tully stopped. He took a long drink from his glass.

'And who was she?'

'Brenda's daughter. The Brenda I talked about. That's the connection.'

'I see. She did marry Joe Coogan, then?'

'Yes. You know that. It's why you're here.'

Stefan nodded.

'I only said part of it before. But it happened when I was at Trinity, not much older than Eimear was. I spent a summer down your way. I was mapping hillforts. Or maybe I was just doing anything that kept me away from everything else. I didn't want anybody's War of Independence. A war of anything. I'd lost friends in the mud of Flanders. Now people I knew, friends as well, wanted to kill each other in Ireland. I met Brenda in Aughrim. She worked at the pub I stayed in. It doesn't matter how these things happen, except that they do. And a week in Wicklow turned into a month. When the summer ended we saw less of each other, but we had plans. We'd be together. Or maybe I just thought we would. Maybe I did all the talking and she always knew. I don't know. She didn't ever tell anyone about me. Just one friend. That should have told me something, shouldn't it? As soon as her family found out, it ended. Strong Republicans, stronger Catholics. There'd be no Protestant marrying their daughter. They sent her away. I didn't know where. When I went to Aughrim to ask, no one would speak to me. There was a cousin in Kilkenny who'd just been killed by the Black and Tans. They were unimpressed by me saying I didn't take sides. Her brothers followed me out of the village. They did what you might expect. This time fists, they said. If I came back they'd be happy to use a gun.'

'And that was it?'

'More or less. I heard she'd married a farmer, that's all. A man called Coogan, outside Rathdangan. Well, you know about that now. There was nothing I could do. I got on with what I was, who I was. I wanted to be out of Ireland. I didn't belong. If anything came out of what had happened with Brenda that was it. I wanted to be here, that's what I decided. She wasn't the only reason, but it pushed me all the harder. I saw her once more. Not long before you married Maeve. I came down to Baltinglass and stayed with you. I took your bike and went up the Military Road. I decided to climb Lugnaquilla one more time. I saw Brenda on the way back, in Rathdangan. She was coming out of the post office. She recognised me immediately. But she'd changed so much. If she hadn't stopped me I'd have walked past. She looked old. That's the only way to put it. She wasn't, but her face was. It hurt me to look. She knew it. We exchanged the pleasantries you'd expect. Then there was nothing to say.'

For a moment the two men sat in silence in the darkness.

'And in Swindon, you found out Eimear was her daughter?'

'Yes. I hadn't been to see her for a while. She wasn't in the conservatory any more. She hadn't got long to live. You could see it. I think she'd only mentioned her mother a couple of times before. Then she'd just said, "But she went away." But she spoke more now. She showed me her notebooks. All her drawings. They were nearly all landscapes, mostly mountains, but there were two faces. A woman and a boy, over and over again. Always the same. I knew the woman. I knew from the first drawing I saw. Brenda. As I remembered her, older, but not like the woman I'd seen in Rathdangan. Brenda was her mother.

'I sat by that bed a lot. Often Eimear was asleep. Nothing was going to stop her dying. I didn't want her to die alone. They'd found her drunk and unconscious by the Thames, in Reading. The police knew her as a prostitute, but she mattered so little they couldn't be bothered to lock her up. She was Irish and had TB. That's all anybody knew. They sent her to hospital. I suppose that was something. Anyway, I got to know more in her last days, more than I wanted to. She was delirious sometimes. I heard about her mother and her brother. Her father was never mentioned. But he was there. She'd watched her mother being broken. That's the only way I can put it. A woman who was always hurting in some way, in every way. I think Brenda didn't only take her own beatings, she took them for her daughter and her son. There must have been happier times in their lives, maybe that's why Eimear drew the mountains, but I never heard her talk about them. All the rest was fear, and all that fear was her father, Joe Coogan.'

Peter drained his glass and lit another cigarette.

'She died peacefully enough, I think. I wasn't there when she did.'

'So when was this?' asked Stefan.

'Three months ago, a bit more.'

'And that's what brought you to Ireland again?'

'Yes. I knew it wasn't a good idea. But I came anyway.'

'To do what?'

'I thought Mr Coogan should know his daughter was dead.'

'Did you think he'd care?'

'No.'

'Perhaps you thought he should pay for it.'

'I won't deny it. I'm sure that was in my head, Stefan, yes.'

'It's hard to think it wasn't.'

'I also thought he might know where Brenda was. I wanted to find her. I wanted to do something. I wanted to help her.' He laughed. 'I can see you looking at me, Stefan. Jesus, you're thinking. No, it wasn't remotely rational after all this time. But I'd known that's the thing. I'd known when I looked into her face that day in Rathdangan, I saw how broken she was. Not the way Eimear must have done. But enough. I saw she was suffering. What did I do then? I smiled and went away.'

'What else could you do?'

'I owed her more than that. And it wasn't only about Brenda.

It was the children too. Eimear and her brother, Paul. I don't know how Brenda walked away from her children. I saw enough desperation in Eimear not to make judgements about her mother. Perhaps she thought it was about her. If she went it would stop. Perhaps she thought she could get them away one day. I don't know. But when she left, nothing did stop. I think Eimear did what her mother did. She took the beatings that were hers and then her brother's too. Brenda went to Scotland. That was the last they heard of her. It seems there were some letters but only for a while. Not for long. I don't know how old Eimear was when Coogan started raping her. But that's what I heard in her words. She didn't tell me it happened, but when she was delirious, I could put enough together. So Eimear ran away too. I don't know that story, what happened between then and the TB ward. I could fill in some of it. I'm sure you could as well. And when I think about it, I wish I couldn't, I really do.'

Stefan waited before he spoke.

'None of that's going to get Paul Coogan out of a murder charge, is it?'

'I hope this will.' Peter Tully took an envelope from his jacket. 'I wanted you to understand. I suppose that doesn't matter very much. Or there's no one for it to matter to. But this is what happened when I went back to Rathdangan.'

Stefan took the envelope. He put it in his pocket.

'Tell me now. I want to know what I'm taking back, Peter.'

'You can read it. I'm tired thinking about it.'

'I need to know if I believe you,' replied Stefan. 'You have to say it.'

'You must have finished those bloody pints by now, gents!' The landlord of the Turf appeared out of the darkness. He carried two pints of beer for them. 'I won't get rich the rate you're drinking.' He put the drinks down and went away.

Peter drank slowly. He nodded and spoke again.

'I went up to Rathdangan after I left you. And I found him. I wasn't sure what I wanted to do, why I was there. I slept up behind the farm. I spent some time in the village. Eventually I spoke to him. He couldn't understand what I was saying. I think he was puzzled more than anything. I told him his daughter had died. I don't know what he thought. It felt like . . . nothing. He didn't ask where, he didn't ask how. He didn't ask where she was buried. That was in Rathdangan. A row. But I couldn't leave it. I went to the house. He'd know I knew what he was. That was what I kept telling myself. Words, bloody words. I don't know what made me think they counted for anything. He denied nothing. When I asked him if he knew where Brenda was, it was as if he'd found some great joke he'd forgotten about. He laughed. "You're the fucking Prod who wanted to marry her. Jesus, the circus is in town!" He said he had no idea where she was. He hated her still, you could see it. She walked out on her children, he kept saying. If she was dead, it was better than she deserved. He meant all that self-righteousness too. Then he took a shotgun. He said if I came back, I'd get that.'

'But you did go back?'

'I went to the pub. Then I took a bottle of whiskey back to where I was sleeping. I thought about going to the Guards. But with what? I had his daughter's dying words about what he'd done to her. Surely that was worth something? Course it wasn't. Mad! But I still wasn't convinced he didn't know where Brenda was. I wanted to get something out of him. He could tell me that, if nothing else. Couldn't he do one fucking decent thing? I wasn't thinking straight. Why would I be? And I won't say there wasn't part of me thinking about that gun and turning it on him. I think I wanted to see him frightened.

'So I went to the farm again. It was almost dark. He didn't come to the door. I went in. I heard him, cursing, complaining, then singing, for God's sake. He was bloody singing. I walked through the kitchen and there was a bathroom, at the back of the house. I remembered Eimear laughing about it. It was almost the only thing she said about the farm. Her mother's bathroom, her wedding present. Her pride and joy. He was there in a great bath full of water, still singing. When he looked round, he didn't seem bothered I was there. I think he said, "I reckoned you might just have the balls to come back." He leant out of the bath, and he had the shotgun again. He stood up, stark naked, holding the gun. There was a chair, in front of me. I picked it up and threw it. It hit him full on. He fell back into the bath. His head hit the taps. He must have knocked himself out. His head was under the water. He came up, gasping and spitting out water, and he slipped down again. It was a big, deep bath. His head was bleeding. Maybe he was concussed. Maybe it was drink. He couldn't pull himself out. It didn't take very long. I can't say I was too shocked to help. I didn't. I simply let him drown.'

'I see,' said Stefan quietly. 'Then what? Why didn't you just leave him?'

'It was panic. It didn't make me run, but it made me feel I had to hide the truth. I didn't know if anyone had seen me near the farm. I had been in the pub. I'd asked questions about him. If there was an investigation, the Guards might look for me. And I'd been in the house. My fingerprints were all over the place. They were on the chair I threw. I needed time to get away. All I could think was, if they don't find him for a while, if they don't know it happened in the house . . . and there was the shotgun. If it looked like he killed himself, wouldn't that do? I'd make sure there were no fingerprints on the gun. If it happened somewhere else, no one would think about the house. So I tidied the bathroom. I pulled clothes on him as best I could. I found a wheelbarrow to get him down to the river. And I blasted his face. It would look like he'd done it. I had picked up a few things around Rathdangan. He owed money.

There was talk he'd be thrown off the farm. I thought it might be enough. It didn't have to all fit. Nobody liked the man. Would anyone even care? It didn't occur to me there'd be any suspects.'

'You were almost right,' said Stefan. 'No one did care. No one did want to know. I saw something was wrong, but I wasn't going to chase it. There was only my father. He owed the man a favour. He thought he owed Joe Coogan his life. It might even be true.'

29

The Royal Parks

London, Regent's Park

Commandant Geróid de Paor sat on a bench on the Broad Walk of Regent's Park, by the Readymoney Fountain. It was mid-morning. There were few people in the park. He had several of the day's newspapers beside him. He was reading the *Daily Telegraph*, looking out over the top of the broadsheet every so often and checking his watch. He saw a round, red-faced figure walking across the grass, through the trees. He folded up the paper and put it with the others.

'So how's it going, Willie?'

The landlord of the Bedford Arms sat down. He sniffed.

'It's been a while,' continued de Paor.

'I'd say not long enough,' replied Mullins.

'You've been very quiet. We haven't heard a peep from you.'

'I'm out of all that. I made it clear to your man Bates last year.'

'You're not telling me you don't keep your ear to the ground?'

'I'm hard of hearing these days, Mr de Paor.'

'That'll be the bombing, eh? We miss you, Willie, we do so.'

'You can feck off. That's all I've got to say to you. I'm done.'

'You're not as busy as you were, I know that. But you could be busier.'

'And I don't need your money.'

'Ah, it was never about money, Willie. And you're not telling me there aren't a few of the IRA Boys passing through the Bedford Arms when they're in London. You're still well thought of in Dublin. And if a feller was looking for someone to maybe hide him away for a bit, well, I still reckon you'd be the man. You'd know where the peelers are looking and where they're not. You know everyone, you always did. It's a hard time with the IRA here. They need all their old friends. The English are on them, like we're on them back home. And the Germans never come, do they? But they're out there, waiting for the right time. You know who's around. You know who's coming and going. You see them all. I hear there's a lot of coming and going from Belfast now. Hard fellers. We don't get much from up there. Jesus, they're a tight-lipped bunch.'

'You should maybe ask your mates in the Ulster Constabulary.'

'We'd get more from the Boys, I'd say. The Ulster Prods trust the English less than we do. They don't even give much to Scotland Yard, from what I hear.'

'Is that it, Mr de Paor? I've heard it all before. You're wasting your time.'

'No, I don't think so. We want you back, Willie.'

'Not even for real money.' The landlord of the Bedford Arms stood up. 'You asked me to come, I came. That's the end of it. You can fuck yourself.'

'You're making enough on the black market then?' said De Paor.

'Is that the best threat you can come up with, Commandant?'

'Not at all, Willie. A birdie tells me you had a problem with your black market business. A detective at Scotland Yard wanted a cut. That's the Met for you. The best police force in the world. DS Simpson, would that be the name?'

Willie Mullins had been sweating after his walk; now he sweated more.

'Died in an air raid, handily enough. He's dead and buried now, but I don't know what Special Branch over here would make of it, if they found out there was more to it. If they knew some of your pals topped Sergeant Simpson.'

'I don't know what—'

'Don't give me your bollocks. Remember Eddie Griffin?'

The landlord took a slow breath.

'I see.'

'I'm glad you see. He found the body, didn't he?'

'Whatever happened, it was nothing to do with me.'

'I'm sure, but we're not talking about a court of law. It's a gang of English Special Branch men finding out a London-Irish arsehole they know and despise had his hand in an old pal's demise. We'll make sure they get enough. It's only a story, I know. But it's a good one, so. And unhappily, it's also true.'

Willie Mullins nodded. 'What do you want?'

Commandant de Paor gathered his newspapers and stood.

'I had a walk through the zoo on the way. Do you know what they did when the war started? Killed all the snakes. The lot. You see, one bomb in the wrong place and they could have been out, poisonous bastards, all over the park, all over London. Of course, we don't have any snakes in Ireland, but we do have things that bite. And we need to know where they are, just in case they get loose. We want you back in the old routine. We want you giving the Boys a home from home. We want to know everything you see, everything you hear.'

'How did you get to Eddie Griffin, Mr de Paor?'

'It's my job. Walls have ears, don't they? We'll be in touch, Willie.'

Geróid de Paor turned. Willie Mullins was still frowning. No one had known Eddie Griffin, no IRA man in London anyway. That wasn't impossible, but it was unusual at least. When he was sober, Willie's mind worked. It did now.

'He was one of yours. Eddie fucking Griffin! He was no gunman at all.'

The G2 man glanced back and smiled, walking away.

'Maybe the shadow of a gunman . . .'

Green Park

Two men walked down St James's after a good lunch in one of the clubs. The conversation over the meal had been the familiar combination of idle gossip and war shop; the perennial speculation on the progress of the conflict. The real conversation began when they reached Green Park and no one could hear them. One of the men was Adam Lambert, the man Vera knew, for a time, as London Kontrolle. They walked lazily past St James's Palace and up towards Piccadilly.

'The Irish don't want to pursue it,' said the other man. 'We have such a blanket of denial that there's not a lot they can say. You were never there. No one was there. No one tried to kill anyone. The Irish only have their policeman. MI5 have the German woman, but she'll play the game. I imagine the threat of a rope guarantees she'll do what they want. Of course, it doesn't mean MI5 won't be watching us. It's not about you, Adam. If they can put the knife into MI6 they won't miss a chance. Mistakes have consequences, especially stupid ones.'

'Vera seemed to offer an opportunity. I thought it was worth a go.'

'I think your days of initiating jaunts without bothering to tell anyone are over, Adam. I've put a lid on this, but only because nobody wants to know what happened. We also lost a man. Doesn't go down well when it's for bugger all.'

'You quite fancied a bit of disarray in the Free State in the summer. When it looked like Adolf was about to cross the Channel. You thought it might be worth a try. Stoking the fires. But you didn't know how. I stumbled on how.'

'Perhaps the wind is changing in that department,' said the other man.

'Is it? Pity you didn't tell me. I thought what Moscow wanted was Britain and Germany at each other's throats, wearing each other out while the Comrades build up their strength for the future and take whatever pickings they can in Eastern Europe. And they're not doing too badly on that front. I thought giving Britain a bit more to worry about in Ireland was no bad thing at this end. After all, aren't we supposed to think that the British imperialists are the worst of the worst? Hitler can be managed until the time comes to deal with him properly, that's what Joe Stalin believes. Don't forget the Party line, old man.'

'Don't try to be too clever, Adam. I'll always be cleverer than you, and I'll always be better informed. No more foolish risks. Is that understood?'

'Is that a reprimand from Moscow?'

'Only from me. I'm sure Moscow will reprimand you in due course.'

'Well, it has made me some new friends,' said Lambert, laughing. 'I've a bit of a reputation for being a hard-line patriot now. Pass that on to Moscow!'

'One thing matters to Moscow above everything else.' The other man lowered his voice; he spoke more sharply. 'Whatever the outcome of the war between Britain and Germany, it's crucial that we come out of it with our roles in British Intelligence not just intact but enhanced. It's taken a lot to get here. Nothing that draws the wrong kind of attention to any of us . . . can be tolerated.'

'I take the point. But sometimes I feel I'm doing nothing.'

'Nothing is enough, for now.'

340

'Isn't all that a little over-cautious, Comrade?'

They were approaching Piccadilly. There were more people.

'I'm always over-cautious. That's why I am where I am in MI6. It's even why you're where you are. Don't forget that.'

Then, quite suddenly, the other man laughed, and clapped Lambert on the back. 'Anyway, it's done. You've made yourself persona non grata for the time being, Adam, and I've had to stretch myself to cover for you. And stretch like buggery! But a spell abroad will sort it out. War makes for short memories. Out of sight, et cetera. Have a break and take a couple of weeks off, then we'll send you to Tehran maybe.'

'You couldn't find me somewhere worse?'

'There are those who'd like to. You'll cope. A break first.'

'Yes, I thought I'd go up to the Lakes, Ullswater.'

'Great stuff, old man. "I climbed the dark brow of the mighty Helvellyn . . . On the right Striden Edge round the Red Tarn was bending." If that doesn't clear your head, Adam, nothing will! You really must climb Helvellyn!'

It was ten days later that Adam Lambert's body was discovered on the slopes of Helvellyn, below Striding Edge, the sharp ridge that snakes up to the summit of the mountain from the east. The search found him quickly. He had been walking alone; only one other walker saw him on the way up from Glenridding. He wasn't seen alive again. It had been a warm day for the beginning of November. The weather was clear. It was high walking and the slopes were steep on either side, especially running down to the Red Tarn, but it was not difficult. There was no real climbing, only a bit of scrambling. And Lambert had been a climber as a student. The path was narrow, yet no one could miss it in good light. But somehow he had missed his footing. It wasn't easy to fall, but he did. He fell over a thousand feet before his body finally broke on the rocks below.

30

Lugnaquilla

Wicklow

It was November before the body of Joseph Coogan was buried, in the small cemetery at Cranerin, where there was no village and no church, just the mountains looking down; Keadeen, Slievemaan, Lugnaquilla. Only a handful of neighbours came, and it was a silent, unexpressive funeral. There was no family there to mourn. There were very few who knew everything that had happened at the farm by the River Derreen over so many years, but people had heard enough to be uneasy with reciting the prayers that would send Joe Coogan to God. In particular, they didn't much want to reflect on what they all knew and ignored in the past.

Paul Coogan had been released from Mountjoy. The charges against him had been dropped. He had already left Ireland to join the British Army. There had been an exchange of letters between the Justice Department in Dublin and the Home Office in London about the possibility of charges against Peter Tully. But inertia set in. The Home Office was not interested. It wasn't their business unless the Irish made an issue of it. A crime had been committed, though it was unclear what it would be if it ever went to prosecution, and in Dublin no one seemed in any hurry to clarify that. Even if Peter Tully appeared in an Irish Court, the outcome of the trial would be doubtful. Worse, it would inevitably attract attention in the British press. It occurred to someone in the Justice Department that the English newspapers, deeply hostile to Irish neutrality, would be more interested in fifteen years of abuse, violence and incestuous rape in the Wicklow Mountains than in whether Peter Tully should have saved the life of the man responsible. It was a long way from dancing at the crossroads.

Standing a little way back from the group around the open grave at Cranerin were Detective Inspector Stefan Gillespie and Superintendent Ger Mulvaney from Baltinglass. It was common enough for policemen involved in investigating deaths, especially murders, to attend the funerals. It could be a mark of respect for the victim's families. It could be because the investigators had come to feel a closeness to the victim that made the relationship personal. Sometimes it was simply a duty that marked the end of a case. However an investigation ended, the police had their own lines to draw. A funeral didn't only give the dead absolution. But it was duty that took Superintendent Mulvaney to Rathdangan, and a desire to see an end to the whole business. When he found that Stefan was at home, he suggested they drive up together. It was also a way to build a bridge again between the Gillespies and the Gardaí in Baltinglass. Stefan came, unsure why. Perhaps to draw his own line, or to draw it for his friend, Peter Tully. He knew the full story, as Peter had told it. Perhaps he was there because of the real victims: a mother who lost her children, a dead daughter, a son who had lost his family and now even the place he grew up in.

The priest seemed anxious to dispatch Joe Coogan as quickly as possible. He fumbled the words. Stefan was conscious that as the coffin was being lowered into the grave, the priest was looking at him and Mulvaney, uneasy, even nervous. And when it was done, he left the graveside abruptly and walked across to the two policemen. Other people left without lingering. No one had a reason to stay, apart from the two gravediggers, waiting to fill in the grave.

Only one man stood over the grave. Jimmy Page, the man who had worked for Joseph Coogan. He was clutching a rosary, muttering prayers that he had been repeating over and over again since the early hours of that morning.

The priest nodded to the two policemen. It was clear he wanted to say something, but for a moment none of them spoke. The usual remarks, about the service or about a good send-off, were out of place. The priest broke the silence.

'Jimmy Page was with me last night in confession.'

Stefan and Mulvaney were surprised. It wasn't a thing a priest would say.

'I told him he had to speak to someone. He should speak to you.'

They turned towards the grave. Jimmy Page was still there, but he was facing away from it now, staring at them. His mouth hung open, as it always did. He clutched his rosary tighter. Stefan saw he was shaking with fear.

It was a little later that a group of men left the empty, deserted farm that had belonged to the Coogans. Stefan Gillespie walked with Superintendent Mulvaney and Jimmy Page; the priest followed with the two gravediggers, who carried pickaxes and shovels. They walked through the fields at the back of the farm, then out on to the rough grazing that led to the slopes of Lugnaquilla. They walked for half an hour, along the course of the Derreen, with the mountain rising ahead of them. They stopped close to the river, by a twisted clump of ancient blackthorn. Jimmy Page showed them where to dig. The gravediggers cleared the matted grass and the heather. It took some time, but when they reached peaty soil, the going was easier. The first bones appeared quickly afterwards; humerus, scapula, part of the ribcage. Then the skull.

Brenda Coogan never did leave the farm beside the River Derreen all those years ago, though she found a way to leave a life she could no longer bear to live. It was Jimmy Page who found her, in the barn where she'd hanged herself. And Jimmy Page had brought her body here with Joe Coogan, under a heap of straw in the tractor's link box, to be buried and forgotten. In those days Joe Coogan had a reputation that he felt counted for something in the area. There were things that mattered to him. One of them was the deep shame of a suicide.

When Superintendent Mulvaney drove Stefan back from Rathdangan, he dropped him by the school at Talbotstown, so that he could wait for Tom. It was Tom's voice Stefan wanted to hear. And when school finished, the two of them walked slowly back to Kilranelagh, talking. Stefan said little, but Tom's head was overflowing with all the ordinary business of his busy life. He clutched a hurl along with his school bag. They had been playing at school that afternoon and he had scored a goal, his first ever goal. There would be a lot to say about hurling now, for at least a week, until some new enthusiasm pushed it out of his head.

The arguments and alliances of the playground at Talbotstown were rehearsed in all their complexity; but the familiar names washed cheerfully over Stefan. There would be a party, too, Tom continued, at the weekend, at his friend Conor's at Woodfield Glen. Conor's uncle was coming from Athy with his projector and the three Mickey Mouse reels they had been watching at Conor's parties since they were small. Tomorrow afternoon there would be a real film, when Stefan took Tom to see *The Mark of Zorro* in Carlow. And there was the book he was reading, *Kim*, the source of endless secret games Tom played with his friends just now or on his own with Jumble and the new dog, Mona, in the fields and woods of Kilranelagh, playing the Great Game with Kimball O'Hara, all over India. Tom was still talking as they reached the farmyard, but then he was gone, thrusting the school bag and the hurl into his father's hands and disappearing into the fields at a run with the barking, leaping, joyful dogs.

Stefan's mother was in the kitchen. There was the smell of the evening meal. She was pouring a cup of tea. She put it down and pointed to the table.

'There's a postcard for you, Stefan.'

He picked up the card. He recognised the picture. It was a black-and-white photograph of the Trout at Tadpole Bridge. He knew it was from Vera, if that was what she was really called. He realised suddenly that he didn't know. He laughed. She had found him . . . wherever she was. He read the message.

'Sweet Thames, run softly, till I end my song . . . it seems I will get to.'

It was unsigned. He couldn't read the postmark properly, but he thought it was Faringdon, close to Tadpole Bridge. And the only place she could have got the postcard was surely at the Trout itself. He had seen them for sale in the bar. She must have posted it herself. She must have been back. That meant she was free, at least free enough to do that. She was safe. That's what she was telling him. He smiled. It wasn't much. Barely anything. He knew that what mattered was often very small. It could be almost nothing. Yet it was always something.

346

Notes & Acknowledgements

Germany

In September 1940, three German spies landed near Port
Gordon in Scotland, a woman, Vera Erikson (supposedly
Danish), and two men. The group's original leader had died in
a car accident after a send-off party in Berlin. Vera was picked
up with one of the men at Port Gordon. The other man was
arrested at Edinburgh, after depositing his case in the left luggage office. The men were tried and executed. Vera disappeared.
It is assumed she was useful to British Intelligence. There is
evidence she was on the Isle of Wight at the war's end. The real
Vera was Russian rather than German and may have been a
double, even triple, agent; she may have worked as a Soviet
spy. German Intelligence was divided into two distinct
branches: Military Intelligence, the Abwehr, run by Admiral
Canaris, and the Nazi Intelligence arms of Himmler's Reich
Main Security Office, in particular the Sicherheitdienst or SD.
There was considerable rivalry between the two organisations. The Abwehr was remarkably free of Nazi ideology and
there were questions about its loyalty, not to Germany but to
Hitler. It has been said that Canaris did not want Germany to
lose the war, but he did not want Hitler to win it. Abwehr

officers were implicated in the 1944 plot to assassinate the Führer. Canaris was executed. The Abwehr was disbanded; the SD finally replaced it.

Frank Ryan, ex-IRA leader and International Brigade officer in the Spanish Civil War, features in several Stefan Gillespie novels. His role in Berlin, after the Germans engineered his release from one of Franco's gaols, despite his anti-fascism and despite the fact that he was on a Gestapo death list, remains ambiguous. The Abwehr agent Helmut Clissman knew Ryan in Ireland in the 1930s. He played a role in persuading the Abwehr that Ryan could be useful, partly, perhaps mostly, to save his friend's life. I don't believe Ryan ever ceased to be an anti-fascist; there is reason to view his survival in Germany in that light.

Ireland

Irish Intelligence operations were split between the Garda Special Branch, which dealt with internal threats to the state, primarily the IRA, and Military Intelligence, G2, which observed external threats and the military consequences of the war beyond Ireland. German spies were pursued by the Special Branch, but G2 was an important channel of information, given its close relationship with British Intelligence. Cooperation between G2 and British Intelligence is well documented, though much evidence has been destroyed. As in any Intelligence war, what was said and what wasn't, on either side, was part of a Great Game in which political expediency ruled. It was essential for Éamon de Valera that his policy of neutrality appeared unsullied by such cooperation, both to Ireland and the world.

The Abwehr's Irish spies were remarkably incompetent. Few were not captured immediately. Their aims were unclear, because of naivety about the real strength of the IRA, and because German belief in the Irish government and IRA uniting to fight Britain was unrealistic. Ireland's neutrality was not anti-British nor, in the context of the war, was de Valera. There were plans to land German troops in Ireland (not just Northern Ireland) to trigger an anti-British uprising. These did not quite fade with the postponement of Operation Sea Lion (the invasion of Britain) in 1940, but they were fantasies after the invasion of Russia in 1941.

Britain

Britain's main Intelligence services in the Second World War were MI5 and MI6 (the Secret Intelligence Service). MI5 was concerned with internal threats, MI6 with operations outside Britain. Scotland Yard's Special Branch also handled internal threats, especially political dissidents; the IRA was their remit. British Intelligence, MI6 in particular, had already been infiltrated by Russian agents at a high level. In 1940 the Soviet Union's policy was determined by the Non-Aggression Pact between Stalin and Hitler. The Communist Party line, worldwide, was that the war was down to aggressive capitalism and imperialism; the real enemy of socialism was Britain and its allies (and America). Whatever Stalin thought about facing Hitler eventually, he was buying time. He was happy enough to see Germany on the verge of destroying what was left of democracy in Europe. In the story I have let an MI6 Soviet mole take the chance to stir that pot.

In 1940 there were many voices angry about Ireland's neutrality. They saw it as a danger to Britain. Winston Churchill certainly felt that, especially over the closure of Irish ports to Atlantic convoy traffic. Ireland's position in the event of German invasion was also seen as a threat. The opposite view was that neutrality was saving military resources that would otherwise be needed to protect Ireland, and that war in Ireland would follow attempts to take over the country. What would be the response of tens of thousands of Irishmen in the British forces? Invading Ireland seemed a real possibility, but in the end calmer voices prevailed.

A number of books were particularly useful. As always, the Irish Department of Foreign Affairs' *Documents on Irish Foreign Policy* was invaluable. John Bryden's *Fighting to Lose* presents compelling evidence that German Military Intelligence operations reflected the anti-Nazi agenda of Abwehr leaders, Canaris especially, at a deeper level than is generally recognised. Sean O'Callaghan's *The Jackboot in Ireland* and Enno Stephan's *Spies in Ireland* are still the fullest accounts of Germany's Irish espionage. I owe the kind of conversation about Jews you might have heard in a 1940 London pub to George Orwell's essay, 'Anti-Semitism in Britain'. It is a sad fact about modern Britain that Orwell would no longer have to scour saloon bars for such sentiments. The chapter in Regent's Park's Open Air Theatre is a nod to one of the greatest novels of London (and Ireland) during the Second World War, Elizabeth Bowen's *The Heat of the Day*. Lastly, I owe elements of this story to my grandmother, whose tales of Ireland during the War of Independence and London during the Blitz, in particular Mornington Crescent, filled my childhood. For those interested, the Bedford Arms did once stand in Arlington Road. It is long gone; a plaque marks its demise. In Baltinglass the tip of the musket Sam McAllister's statue holds is still missing.